OPHIUCHUS FLINCHED

TALES OF CIEL
BOOK 2

Z. BENNETT LORIMER

HIGH TRESTLE
PRESS

This is a work of fiction. All of the characters, events, and organizations portrayed in this novel are either products of the author's imagination or are used fictitiously.

OPHIUCHUS FLINCHED

Copyright (c) 2025 assigned to High Trestle Press LLC

Library of Congress Control Number: 2026902175

All rights reserved.

Cover design by Zefanya Maega

A High Trestle Press Book
Address
Ames, IA 50010

ISBN 978-1-968122-04-1 (Ebook) | ISBN 978-1-96822-05-8 (Trade Paperback)

First Printing, February 2026
Printed in the U.S.A.

For Liz

PROLOGUE: MULDOON

"I turn the false Governor Muldoon over to you and our host for judgment. You all can figure out what to do with him."

Muldoon felt a tug on his bound wrists, then a spark of pain as the ropes fell away and blood rushed back to his extremities. The sudden return of control over his arms unbalanced him, and he nearly toppled face-first into the dirt. His shoulders screamed as he caught himself.

He felt that sanctimonious dragoon retreating with a blast of unnatural wind.

Muldoon reached up with one aching hand and removed the greasy sweep of unwashed hair from his eyes, only to find Ansel's square head looming over him. He'd had limited interactions with the man, but those few occasions were enough to leave the impression of a stubborn midwit swollen on his upjumped status and authority.

The Governor of Volturnus shook his head in silence as two liveried footmen materialized to flank Muldoon. Those stoney eyes of his performed outrage with admirable commitment, but it was obvious to Muldoon that Ansel was enjoying this.

"Can you stand?" Ansel asked.

In answer, Muldoon stood.

Ansel sniffed the air, lips curling back from a wide row of burnished teeth. He snapped at his footmen. "Escort the Lord Governor inside the manse, and see to his bodily needs. Once he's presentable, bring him to my office."

Muldoon batted away the staff's attempt to place hands on his person and marched himself inside.

A silent valet helped him extricate himself from the soiled garments of his captivity, while maids shuttled steaming buckets of water to a claw-foot tub. Muldoon refused to acknowledge their ministrations, guarding the depths of his humiliation. When they were finished, he lowered himself into the tub with a prurient sigh and dismissed the lingering valet with a limp-wristed wave.

The water scalded his sensitive skin, searing the infected boils accumulated during his harsh term of incarceration. Reveling in the bathwater's cleansing report, Muldoon closed his eyes and sank beneath the ablutions.

He stewed in his resentment and his filth, all the while picturing the Volturnian Draft Lieutenant responsible for his arrest. Vanna Strait—a name he'd not soon forget. She would pay for her insolence. Of all the indignities visited upon his noble person by these provincials, her indictment cut the deepest. If it hadn't already been obvious to Muldoon, this latest episode certainly confirmed the weakness of Kelestina's position. Admiral Siprichor sent him here to help Her Lightness bring this wild land under control, and he'd done a fine job on Aeolus. His success would have continued, if not for the Bluethorn's arrival and the credulity of the Aeolians who were only too willing to drink from his forked tongue.

Muldoon's predecessor, Dama Anyela, had retired too late. She'd stayed in the position of governor well into her dotage, and the duplicitous Aeolians took advantage of her senility. It didn't take Muldoon long to discover all the cunning ways the local craftsmen had been cooking their books, clipping their tithes at the port and undercounting the shipyards' production. The lazy shipwrights were working at less than two-thirds capacity, and the longshoreman paying less than *half* of their annual dues. It was all a lawless mess, but he could hardly fault doddering Anyela for the oversight. The true fault rested with Kelestina, who seemed content to let these infractions slide.

A knock at the washroom door announced the arrival of a young maid who offered her services to help Muldoon clean himself. He accepted with a nod and extended his arms over the rim of the tub. The maid soaked a cloth in a bucket of fresh water and began applying perfumed lye to Muldoon's skin, scrubbing until his arms and shoulders became red and raw. She moved on to his greasy hair, each pass of her sodden cloth returning a speck of strength to Muldoon.

When the maid was finished, she handed Muldoon a monogrammed towel embroidered with Ansel's heraldic crest. She turned her back respectfully, offering the Patrician guest a modicum of privacy.

Muldoon rose from the bath and affixed the towel around his waist. At his grunting signal, the maid returned to pat his shoulders dry and comb out his auburn hair. She left him with a modest plate of food, a fresh Patrician uniform in Ansel's gray and brass, and a single black band for his hair.

Muldoon declined the services of a waiting valet. He dressed himself, but had little stomach for the food. He took two bites of a seasoned dinner roll, then turned to inspect himself in a full-length mirror. The warm bath had restored some of his color, but the mark of his struggles lingered in the fine lines around the corners of his eyes and the dark circles beneath them. He prodded at these imperfections with the pads of his fingers.

Jokai fend—he'd aged a decade in a week. Cursing under his breath, he proceeded out of the washroom and into the hall where one of Ansel's armed sentinels waited at stiff attention, ready to escort him to the Lord Governor.

Muldoon found Ansel at his hardwood desk, performing his importance by inspecting a stack of papers that might as well have been blank. He scanned the chamber's spare decorations as he waited for governor to acknowledge his arrival. The single portrait of a galloping white mare looked as expensive as it was kitsch, though he did admire the set of craftsman armchairs opposite the desk. In the corner of the office, a standing timepiece taunted him, *tick-tick-ticking* as its brass pendulum swung back and forth.

Ansel scrawled a flamboyant signature across one of his papers and finally looked up from his labors. "Ah. That's better. Feeling restored, I hope?"

Muldoon returned an acid smile that never reached his eyes. "Yes, your conscripts are very dutiful."

"They are," Ansel agreed. "We value decorum here on Volturnus."

Eyes tightening, Muldoon absorbed the jab. He gestured at one of the craftsman armchairs opposite Ansel's desk. "May I?"

Ansel nodded. "As you will."

Muldoon took the offered seat and crossed his legs, drumming one set of fingers across his knee.

Ansel holstered his fountain pen in a golden desktop mount and met Muldoon's gaze. The governor's square jaw worked back and forth as he studied the dispossessed Patrician before him. "What am I to do with you?" he finally asked.

"With me?" Muldoon's fingers stopped tapping. "I assume you'll conscript a unit of armsmen and restore me to my rightful seat on Aeolus."

Ansel's thick, black eyebrows crept together across his brow like caterpillars joining to mate. "That's quite the assumption."

"What do you intend to do about your renegade dragoon?" Muldoon continued. "Lieutenant Vanna Strait. I assume she'll be called to account?"

Ansel shook his head in disbelief, salt-and-pepper hair frozen in its lacquered coif. "I warned Kelestina that you weren't ready for this charge, did you know that? No matter your pedigree, youth and inexperience lend themselves poorly to the task of governing the plebiscite."

"You must be joking." The condescension struck Muldoon like a pistol shot from pointblank range.

"I'm not known for my sense of humor," Ansel said.

"You know little and less of what you speak." Muldoon felt his self-control wearing thin as Ansel's stationary.

"Is that right?" Ansel's smirk finally pushed him over the edge.

"Aeolus was a mess when I arrived!" Muldoon raised his voice. "Kelestina's court has done her a grave disservice in this land. The plebiscite lives in excess. Over a decade of colonization, and still you've turned but a fraction of this land's yield to the Throne's devices. The plebeians take advantage of our host's forbearance, and *none* of you possess the managerial skill to herd them back in line. It's no wonder the Bluethorn worked his way under this land's skin with such ease. None of you are paying any damned attention!"

Ansel waited calmly, permitting time for Muldoon to burn himself out. "Are you quite finished?"

Muldoon pressed his lips shut. If he spent any more time glowering, the lines around his eyes were sure to become permanent.

"I'll take that as an affirmative." Ansel leaned back in his chair and threaded his fingers together, perching them atop his uniformed gut. "Her Lightness Kelestina *prefers* that we take a gentle hand with the plebiscite in this land. We aren't expected to *wring* them for every last drop of blood. She prizes stability over production."

"How benevolent!"

Ansel's ample eyebrows turned down. "Sarcasm is unbecoming of a Patrician."

"So is incompetence," Muldoon sneered.

"Damnit, man!" Ansel slammed one meaty palm atop his desk. "We aren't here for kite-ships and libras of grain."

"I'm sure the Armada will thank you for keeping them well-provisioned with plebeian good will."

"The plebiscite *is* the provision, you childish fool."

The two Patricians stared across the desk at each other, locked into a silent battle of wills. Muldoon realized he might have overestimated this man. "Midwit" was far too generous. The Governor of Volturnus recited his litany with the zeal of an imbecile.

Muldoon had dealt with plenty of imbeciles before. He knew the type. Shouting wasn't likely to pierce his thick skull, so Muldoon left his outrage to simmer and attempted a different tack.

"How long has it been since you last visited Toran?"

The unexpected question struck a chip of hesitation into Ansel. "I really couldn't say. Decades."

Muldoon suspected as much. "Then allow me to fill you in on the latest developments: the war isn't going well. The Agnar have broken from their leash and now raid freely across the veldt and deeper into Rydia. Admiral Siprichor had to abandon our positions around the inland sky, and now the Akkadians are playing footsie with the Jokai-damned Hellicon League. Umar is our last Toranese stronghold, and it's practically under siege."

"That sounds awfully histrionic," Ansel said. "We have consulates on every outlying island for leagues around the eastern coast. Hellicon is surrounded—penned in."

Muldoon almost envied the man's ignorance. How simple it must be presiding over these tame Elementalists a thousand leagues from the nearest conflict.

"It's the damned Gullivari, Ansel. The Bluethorn and his saboteurs are fighting an asymmetric war—and they're winning. The Ring has operatives threaded throughout the Doric Sky. They're on Brundis and Takomar— even Vangulmark has been infiltrated. They're throttling our supply lines.

The Bluethorn and his ilk—they'll diminish the Armada by a thousand cuts and leave the Hellicon League to deliver the killing blow."

An uncomfortable silence passed between them, with only the ticking of Ansel's gaudy clock to season it.

"That's all very troubling," Ansel allowed. "But what does it have to do with the Zephyr Isles?"

"Everything!" *You brainless hayseed.* "The Admiral sent me to Kelestina to ensure that these islands start to *produce*."

Muldoon could almost see the wheels turning inside the governor's thick head as he tried to square this new information. Failing, he simply gave up.

"None of this matters," Ansel said. "Siprichor may have shipped you across the sky with a wish list, but you're a member of Kelestina's court now. Her Lightness isn't as enamored with the Crystal Throne's adventurism in the west. Her interests tend to the esoteric. I admit, serving Her Lightness can be an adjustment, but her goals in the archipelago have always been steadfast. We Patrician servants are charged only with prosecuting them, never questioning. We have been tasked with cultivating the plebiscite—a task you failed on Aeolus. Catastrophically."

Muldoon blinked, dumbfounded by the dullard's sanctimony but hardly surprised. His voice became very low. "You'd have me—what, then, Ansel? Apologize to the plebiscite for all the trouble I caused? Grant them tacit permission to return to their foot-dragging and their fraud?"

"Oh, I think the kite-ship has long-since sailed on disingenuous apologies."

"Surely my position is to be reinstated—"

"Surely *not*." Ansel reveled in his return to stable ground in the discussion. "I've already exchanged messages with Aquilon. You're to report to the palace and receive judgment from Her Lightness, and don't expect a warm reception. If I'm reading the subtext of Kelestina's missive, she's more likely to have you staked to a geode than restored as a magistrate of her court."

Muldoon scowled. "Now who's being histrionic?"

Ansel propped his hands back atop his stomach and leaned back in his chair. "As soon as you're fit and able, I'm to ship you off to Aquilon without delay."

"And what of the dragoons who violated my person? Will they be called to meet the same justice?"

"They will not." Ansel snorted, the curling set of his lips too smug by half. "The dragoons are too popular among the plebiscite, and our host would not see their ample Gifts squandered."

Bereft of counterarguments, Muldoon shut his mouth and closed his eyes. His humiliation was finally complete. He fastened one of the brass buttons on his uniform and stood up, offering Ansel a stiff, shallow bow. "Then I will prepare for departure this evening. You'll make the arrangements?"

Ansel nodded. "Kelestina will send a coach."

"Very well." Muldoon affected Patrician composure as he took his leave, turning his back to Ansel to conceal a decidedly un-Patrician expression turned hideous with rage.

Staked to a geode... She wouldn't dare. Muldoon was a *born* Patrician. A Gifted servant of the Great Admiral Sprichor and a decorated war veteran, to boot. He had too many friends in high positions across the sky—too many powerful patrons waiting in Toran.

But the skies were vast, and Toran was far away.

1

EFFIE

Effie sat rigid at the edge of her padded seat inside Kelestina's carriage. She could feel the effects of the Nectar beginning to ebb, but her heightened senses remained. Kelestina sat across from her, long fingers folded across her lap, studying her with those liquid-green eyes. The smoky tint applied to her face in the shape of wings seemed to gleam on her polished skin.

Effie watched her host's Celestial body sway with the motion of six hippocampi pulling their carriage into flight. Only moments ago, she'd been sailing on the back of a wild dauphine, and already the experience felt like a distant memory.

Those fleeting moments returned to Effie in montage. Kelestina met her on the shore of the Moonflow Lagoon. She approached with open arms and shocked Effie with a covetous embrace. Effie nestled stiffly in those porcelain arms, surprised by the unexpected heat burning within a body that felt hard as glass.

You marvelous child, Kelestina whispered in Effie's ear. *You precious, precious gift.*

Those were the first and only words that passed between them. Effie had violated a sacred ceremony to prove her worth. She wasn't sure what to expect in response to her insolence, but she was increasingly certain she would not have to endure any punishment for crashing the Ascension.

Through their brief flight to the top of the cliffs, Kelestina continued to watch her, unblinking. The intensity of her gaze made Effie want to look away, but she feared any flinch might be taken as an insult. She forced herself to match Kelestina's gaze, even though the cold beauty of the Celestial form threatened to blind her.

The carriage glided to a stop, and Kelestina unfolded her hands. "If you'll excuse me for a moment."

"Of course—" Effie stuttered. Her host bent her crystalline head to exit the carriage.

Effie heard a few sounds of muffled conversation, then Kelestina returned, with Sire Ansel behind her.

Ansel's broad shoulders and barrel chest crowded the coach. He crammed his thick body onto the bench next to Kelestina, obviously struggling to keep his girth from imposing upon the Celestial's space. He still looked unbalanced as the hippocampi pulled the carriage back to flight.

Her Patrician governor's discomfort broke some of the tension in Effie. She bent her head, performing a seated bow. "Sire."

The sound of her voice sent a jolt through the governor. He attempted to cover it up by adjusting his position on the bench. "Miss Strait."

His adjustment jostled Kelestina, earning him a vicious side-eye that only Effie saw.

"Tell us your name, child," Kelestina said.

Ansel supplied it before Effie could gather enough words to speak, "This is Effie Strait of Volturnus."

Kelestina's blue lips turned down. "I assume Miss Strait can speak for herself."

"She can," Effie confirmed, watching Ansel wince at the implied rebuke. Her ears popped as the carriage climbed higher, sailing across the canopy of the Volturnian jungle.

"I don't recall an Effie Strait on your Ascension List." Kelestina's Celestial poise drew stark contrast with the discomfited Patrician beside her.

This time, it was Ansel who struggled to find his words, so Effie returned the favor by cutting in. "I wasn't on the list, Lightness."

Kelestina glanced between Ansel and Effie. "That seems a grave oversight on our part."

"The girl isn't Gifted, Lightness." Ansel's voice returned to him stran-

gled, every accented syllable tight and clipped. "She didn't meet the qualifications—"

"*Miss Strait*," Kelestina corrected, "certainly appears to meet the qualifications. Wouldn't you agree?" Ansel melted back into his seat, but
Kelestina pursued. "That was a question, Ansel."

"There are so *many* Giftless plebeians in my care..." He fidgeted with
his hands as he began to dissemble. "I-I had no way of *knowing*—"

"But you did," Effie cut in again. "I *told* you as much at your stable. I
practically *pleaded* with you to add my name to the Ascension, and my
sister presented the same case only days before you made your list."

The emerald glow in Kelestina's eyes dimmed as she turned her body to
face her imperiled courtier. "Is this true, Ansel?"

The governor's face turned the color of an overripe plum. His voice
failed him for the second time. Effie felt a smirk twitching in the corners of
her lips as she watched him squirm. If she could bronze this moment, she'd
wear it on a chain around her neck for the rest of time, but she knew it was
unbecoming to gloat.

"It isn't the Lord Governor's fault," she offered instead. "He suffers
from a failure of imagination."

Kelestina continued to stare at Ansel. "That's a generous sentiment,
Miss Strait. Perhaps we need to revisit these so-called *qualifications*." Her
dun gaze regained its luster as she returned to Effie. "Let us thank the Jokai
the Lord Governor's *lack of imagination* didn't prevent you from taking
matters into your own Gifted hands."

Thank the Jokai, indeed...

"With all due respect to your customs," Effie said. "No man—Patrician
or otherwise—was going to keep me from mounting that dauphine."

The remainder of their brief flight passed in silence, with Effie and
Kelestina at relative peace and Ansel writhing inside his skin. The carriage
came to a stop once more, as the hippocampi floated onto the platform of
the trolley connecting the northern landing of Volturnus to Aquilon's
southernmost tip. Their motion resumed with a jerk as the ferryman
cranked them across the cables adjoining the neighboring isles.

The trolley teetered as it processed over empty sky, and Volturnus
receded behind them—for what Effie realized might be the final time. She'd
been so focused on the Ascension—on her moment of triumph over the
dauphine—that she'd hardly spared a thought for whatever came next. Her

future had seemed so small these last few years, her destiny shrinking around her as she entered her majority and the Ascension Day approached. No more. In one act of impetuous bravery, she blasted every locked door lining the hallways of her life off its hinges. Once again, her destiny seemed as wide as the skies of Ciel.

Kelestina's carriage floated to its final landing, and one of her Patrician attendants opened the door to escort them out. Ansel nearly stumbled down the ladder in his harried attempt to escape the confines of the carriage. Kelestina extended one hand, inviting Effie to proceed behind him.

For the first time in Effie's life, her feet touched the surface of an island that was not her own.

First of many, she was now assured.

Ansel joined the other Patricians awaiting Kelestina in a line. Aside from Ansel, Effie only recognized Sire Aeryon, the stick-thin Governor of Avernus and Dama Lilyn, the squat magistrate tasked with governing the Spurs. She assumed one of the unfamiliar faces belonged to the Governor of Nimbion, but the other two proved more difficult to place.

The first looked almost too young to be a Patrician—of an age with Vanna, at least thirty years younger than his nearest Patrician peer. He bound his auburn hair back in a high ponytail, his smooth face clean-shaven, but for a manicured strip of goatee. The second stranger hid his face behind a dark blue hood. Effie assumed his advanced age from his arching posture and the fine lines on his blister chin. Notably, he was the only one of Kelestina's retainers not dressed in a gray and brass suit.

Kelestina called Effie to her side and linked arms with her. Celestial glass twined around rough plebeian skin, eliciting a tiny gasp. The two paced several steps behind the line of Patricians as they walked the marble path to Aquilon Palace.

On a clear day, the palace's jagged outline was visible to the naked eye from Volturnus' northern promontories. Effie had seen its silhouette many times from the top of Widow's Peak and from the landing camp near the trolley, but even those distant impressions of crenelated walls and twisting spires did nothing to prepare her for the palace's proximate majesty. The palace jutted from the crust of Aquilon like a natural crystal, its substance a seamless spread of cerulean blue, frosted to opacity and remote as a sculpture made of ice. Its outer wall rose 100 feet above the surface, capped by swirling crenelations and fortified drum towers armed with catapults and ballistae. That wall seemed to stretch the length of Effie's entire village, covering the full expanse of Aquilon's elevated plateau.

Still clinging to Kelestina's arm, Effie processed up a twisting gallery of marble stairs and passed under an arched barbican that welcomed them with open jaws. Beyond the outer wall, they entered a vast foreyard planted with flowering topiaries and an unfamiliar purple vine that crept up the interior walls, grasping the cerulean glass with talon-like thorns.

Kelestina's extensive staff paused from their work in the gardens to bow before leading line of Patricians. The palace servants wore dark blue embroidered suits with a single buttoned seam running from the collar to the knee. The uniform's high collar and thick cuffs featured black piping and brocade accents patterned to match their silk pants. Effie marked a blue circlet adorning the heads of a few different servants—some indication of rank among the staff. Each kneeling servant pressed their forehead against the manicured lawn as Kelestina and Effie passed.

Effie knew the bows were intended for Kelestina, but it still felt odd to stand on the receiving end of such deference. Not *bad*, exactly—just...*odd*.

The twelve twisting spires of the interior palace climbed even higher than the outer wall. The tallest of the two vanished inside a low line of cumulus clouds drifting lazily across the Aquilonian sky. As Effie gawked at the imposing towers, she noticed small figures winging between them, flitting back and forth, occasionally landing on a domed rotunda or inside the nook of an open window cut into the palace glass. At first, Effie mistook them for dragoons, but as one glided to a landing atop the palace entrance, she realized it was flying on *wings*. She stared so hard at the feathered sentinel, that her feet caught on the last set of marble stairs leading up the palace, and she nearly stumbled flat on her face. Kelestina caught her, pausing to let her find her footing and finish admiring the unusual sight.

"They're Avians," Effie said, still watching the white-feathered specimen perched on two taloned feet. It flexed its muscular arms beneath its wings and began picking at its feathers with three-fingered hands. The Avian attendant tilted its head to watch their approach with a red-ringed eye.

"They are." Kelestina's smile seemed more indulgent than kind, but that face of molded glass gave every expression a frozen edge. "The Dove Clan has served Solaris for centuries. I'm fortunate to have a flock of twelve in my service, scouting the skies of Aquilon, carrying messages, and tending to tasks in all those hard-to-reach places."

Effie shook her head, still watching the Avian preen atop the palace wall. "I had no idea there were Avians in the archipelago."

"I think you'll find the skies of Ciel full of strange and wonderful surprises." Kelestina gestured at the waiting entrance, sunlight catching on the sharp tips of her teardrop nails. "Come. We have many sights to show you—more wondrous than domesticated Doves."

Effie watched the Avian snap its beak and bend its white head as they passed beneath its perch. For the briefest second, she could have sworn its red-rimmed eye watched her with equal interest.

Aquilon Palace opened to a marble-tiled foyer split by two staircases of transparent glass. The stairs spiraled up to a frosted balcony and arched hallways leading to the second floor. A wide, black runner followed a third passage between the two sets of stairs. It unfurled to the threshold of a tall blue door set with rubies, emeralds and jet.

The six Patricians awaited Kelestina and Effie in a receiving line along the edges of the runner. At their head, a dark-skinned servant wearing one of the blue circlets around a coiled bun of ropey braids bowed to Her Lightness and then to Effie.

Kelestina at last released Effie's arm to acknowledge her servant with an extended hand. Effie wasn't sure if she was expected to do the same, so she offered a tight smile and remained still at Kelestina's side.

The servant stepped through the receiving line of Patrician lords and clasped hands with Kelestina. She kissed their host's knuckles, then turned to Effie, lips quirking as she scanned her up and down.

The woman's probing made Effie suddenly self-conscious. She'd spent half a day perched on a cliff, waded through the moonflow, and tilted with a wild dauphine. Dry mud still clung to her boots, and she noticed a bloody tear in one leg of her canvas pants. She was a wreck.

"This is the Pilot?" the servant asked. Her voice dripped with a foreign accent that Effie couldn't place.

Kelestina nodded. "Yes, Dagda. This is Miss Effie Strait, and she is the most Gifted Pilot I've encountered in a century of searching."

The servant—Dagda—scanned Effie again with newfound reverence. "She is small."

"She has room to grow." Kelestina's blue lips bent into a thin smile.

"Find her a chamber in the Twin Spire and see that the maids have it properly provisioned."

Dagda's eyebrows lifted as she turned back to Kelestina. "The Twin Spire? Surely she'd be more comfortable in the Crab—"

"Perhaps," Kelestina allowed. "But Miss Strait is going to be a woman of import to the Crystal Throne. She'll need to acclimate to a certain degree of pampering."

"Very well." Dagda gestured for Effie to follow. "Come, child. Up the second stair..."

Effie moved to follow Dagda as she had been instructed, but before she mounted the first step, she turned back to Kelestina.

"Lightness..." she ventured. She had so many questions. Settling on none of them, she blurted them all. "What will become of me? My friends on Volturnus—my sister—will I be able to see them before I depart? And where am I going? What happens *next*?"

Kelestina raised one hand to halt the barrage. A white flash burned across her emerald eyes. "I know you have many questions about your future. I would answer them for you—and I will in time—but first I must discuss a few open matters with my court. Go with Dagda, now. You will be sent for."

"Yes, Lightness." Effie bowed again, then turned to follow an increasingly impatient Dagda up a sweeping spiral staircase made of gold and glass.

2

EFFIE

Dagda led Effie down a long hall margined by tiled walls. Beams of sunlight entered through a series of lancet windows along their path. Effie kept falling behind as she paused to take stock of her surroundings.

"This way," Dagda prodded her along. "Please try to keep up."

The palace's strange geometry disoriented Effie—not a right angle or straight line in sight. Each hallway flowed into the next, banking and curving through inclines and descents. Every ceiling spiraled to a distant point or a domed rotunda, and the uniform blue of the palace glass continued in a single unbroken pane. After only a few minutes of walking, Effie doubted she would ever be able to find her way back to the entrance without a guide.

Dagda received deferential nods from every servant they passed. A group of young maids caught idling squeaked at the sight of her and scurried back about their tasks.

"What is your position here?" Effie asked.

Dagda spared a glance over her shoulder without slowing. "I am honored to serve as Her Lightness' majordomo."

"Is that like a butler?" Effie drew comparison with the conscript who managed Sire Ansel's staff.

"It is not."

They passed through another banked hallway in silence, until Effie ventured a second attempt at conversation. "I don't recognize your accent. Are you from the Zephyrs?"

"The palace staff came over with Her Lightness from Solaris. We are none of us Zephyri."

"Then where *are* you from?" Effie scowled at the braided back of Dagda's head. The lack of straight answers on Aquilon was beginning to frustrate her.

"It is a distant island in another sky."

"Does it have a *name*?"

Dagda made a hissing sound with her tongue pressed between her teeth. "You ask many questions."

"I ask fewer when I get better answers."

Dagda hissed again, and that was the end of their discourse until they reached the entrance to the Twin Spire. Dagda turned to her then, barring the entrance with an outstretched arm. "We house many honored guests in this tower. I'll ask that you avoid disturbing their privacy and resist the urge to wander."

Effie propped her hands on her hips. "What if I need something?"

"The staff will see to your needs."

"And what if I get bored?"

"You will be provided with amusements, as well."

Effie threw up her hands in surrender. "I guess you've got it all figured out, then!"

Dagda tilted her braided head. "As you say. Please follow me."

Another spiral staircase greeted them inside the Twin Spire. Effie followed two steps behind Dagda, gawking at an eclectic sequence of stained glass murals depicting steamships and zeppelins, exotic cities, pitched battles, and sundry Leviathan in flight. They must have climbed half the tower before Dagda stopped again, indicating a door next to a mural of an emerald tortoise cutting through the sky on six winged flippers.

"Your chamber," Dagda said.

Effie's gaze lingered on the tortoise, while Dagda tapped her foot impatiently until she gave up and preceded the majordomo into a bedroom fit for a queen.

Soft, incandescent light poured from the ceiling, haloing a fine area rug, a vanity, a narrow glass desk, standing bookshelves, a wooden armoire, and a bathing suite set off to the side in a tiled alcove. The canopy bed looked wide enough to accommodate at least five girls the size of Effie. Instantly, its plush quilt called to her. With the effects of the Nectar now good and vanished from her system, the physical exhaustion of the day's events had returned to claim its toll.

Effie caught the scent of rich food wafting from a covered silver tray on the desktop. Forgetting Dagda, she paced across the chamber to inspect. Kelestina's cooks had provisioned her with a fresh plate of whipped turnips and roast pheasant covered in some kind of succulent glaze. *Gooseberry,* Effie concluded, after venturing a juicy bite. A small, unopened bottle of cherry liqueur stood next to the tray. Beside it, a flask of clear water and a set of frosted crystal glassware.

Still chewing her pheasant, Effie left the food to inspect the bathing suite. She tested one of the gilded knobs on the tub, and running water burst forth from a swan-necked spout. She ran her fingers through the water and nearly choked on her tongue. Not only did the water arrive by sorcery, but it was already piping hot!

Dagda's voice reached her from the doorway. "I trust you find the accommodations suitable?"

"Um, yes," Effie stammered. "This will do just fine."

Nodding, Dagda marched to the lancet window over the bed and indicated a purple banner hanging from the sill. "If you need anything from the staff, simply drape this call skirt outside your window. One of our Doves will come by to receive your request."

"That's a handy system."

"Yes."

Effie caught a glimpse of herself in the vanity looking glass and quickly adjusted her windswept hair. She looked just as plain and disheveled as she feared.

"If there's nothing else," Dagda said, "I'll leave you to your convalescence."

Effie's eyes settled again on the canopy bed with its fluffy white pillows and downy quilt. "How long will I be staying here?" she asked.

"As long as Her Lightness requires."

Effie rolled her eyes. *Why do I even bother?*

"Will that be all?" Dagda made no effort to hide her eagerness to leave, and Effie saw no reason to continue enduring her frosty company.

"That will be all," she said.

With another curt nod, Kelestina's majordomo left, and Effie was finally alone.

The sudden silence paired eerily with the luxurious confines of her glass cage. Unsure where to start, she paced the chamber several times before catching another haggard glimpse of herself in the vanity. Groaning, Effie returned to the tub and set it to fill while she went to work on the platter of food. Once she reduced the plate to a pile of bones and a buttery smear of turnip, she uncorked the cherry liqueur, poured herself a snifter, and undressed before lowering herself into the tub.

The hot bath kneaded life back into her weary bones while the tart spirit sanded all the edges off her tension, threatening to lull her to sleep. The suite came provisioned with a wide array of ointments and tinctures in assorted vials of colored glass. Effie experimented with each one until her bathwater boiled over with effervescent foam. She massaged a lilac-scented scrub into her tattered hair. It took her forever to finish rinsing the ointment away and by the time she was done, her fingers and toes had shriveled to prunes. She pulled a porcelain plug to let the bathwater drain and stepped dripping onto the tiles to pat herself dry with a set of ivory towels. With her hair bound up in one of them, she glanced down at the tarnished outfit she'd discarded in a heap at the foot of her bed. It hardly made sense to undo all her fastidious cleansing by returning to a sweaty tunic and a bloodied pair of canvas pants, so she checked the contents of the armoire for better options.

Kelestina's staff were certainly thorough. They'd provided a full complement of outfits, including a set of the Celestial's blue livery, a gray and brass Patrician suit, a nightgown, a silk slip, a diamond-encrusted formal gown, and several casual dresses dyed in expensive hues. Effie pulled out one of the dresses in an eye-catching robin's egg blue. She inspected the garment's lace bodice and extended its wide, gauzy silhouette. Too casual, perhaps, but the diamond gown seemed overwrought in the extreme. She laid the dress out on her bed next to two other outfits for comparison. In Kelestina's livery, she'd look like a servant, and that wouldn't do, but the Patrician suit seemed presumptuous. She eventually settled on the dress, which fit her dimensions so perfectly it left her a little unnerved. So attired, she sat at the vanity to brush out her hair.

She smiled at her revived appearance in the looking glass. The scrub had imbued her hair with a healthy violet sheen, and the hot soak restored much of her natural color. She pinned up her hair, and the visage staring back at her reminded her suddenly of Vanna.

For her entire life, she'd been subjected to unsolicited commentary about their resemblance. Effie always bristled at the comparison, but she could no longer deny its truth. She was still softer than her sister—possessed of a rounder face with a less prominent chin and a plumpness to her cheeks that Vanna's training had ground away. Effie's nose was smaller and her eyes a slightly lighter shade of green, but in adulthood, the two had grown more similar than not. She imagined Vanna's snaggletoothed smile onto the reflection in the vanity, and the image uncorked a well of longing that surprised her with its depth.

Effie knew she might never see her sister again. All she had left were memories, and the reminder of their common features suddenly seemed a priceless gift. She mourned the loss of all that time she wasted on resentment these last few months. It all seemed so trivial, now. At least they had reconciled before the Ascension. Effie was thankful for that. Enduring bitterness might have numbed the sense of loss, but that would be cold comfort in the years of estrangement to come.

Seeking distraction, she opened the vanity drawer and pulled out a set of cosmetics. She lined up jars of contour, foundation, and unguent—uncapped a complete prism of polish and paints. She discovered glass cylinders of eye make-up in every shade of the open sky. Smiling again, Effie went about constructing a mask to match her environs.

She passed hours testing every bottle. By the end, she'd applied so many layers of clashing accents that she looked more like a mummer than a sophisticated Dama of a Celestial court. She cleared the canvas with a damp, gray washcloth and began anew, limiting herself to a thin foundation that matched her natural tone and a dash of blush along her cheekbones topped with a light dusting of powdered gilt. At last, she applied a dark purple accent to her eyelashes with an absurdly tiny brush before packing the rest of the ointments away.

The first warm colors of the approaching sunset crept into the chamber through her lancet window. Effie contemplated dangling the call skirt just for a chance to speak with one of the Avian servants, but she wasn't sure how a Dove might react to having its time wasted to satisfy her peasant curiosity.

She could always sleep. The canopy bed didn't look any *less* inviting than it had upon arrival. If she allowed herself to recline across that downy quilt, she suspected she'd not be long for this world, but with so many new things to experience, unconsciousness seemed like a terrible waste. She drummed her clean nails atop the vanity, and her eyes finally settled on the door.

She saw her own mischievous smirk in the looking glass.

Effie stepped into a pair of soft white slippers and crept across the room. She half-expected to find the entrance locked, confirming her chamber for a prison in truth, but the crystal doorknob turned easily in her palm, and the door swung silently open on its oiled hinge.

Resist the urge to wander, Dagda had said.

If she meant it, perhaps she should have been more forthcoming. Insolence had served Effie well enough to this point. In fact, her oppositional temperament seemed to be among her most virtuous traits.

She stepped out of the chamber and began to climb the Twin Spire.

Dagda mentioned other important guests in the tower, but Effie saw no one as she circled the spiral steps. She passed more closed doors—even pressed her ear to a few—but heard nothing to indicate the presence of another resident. She'd nearly reached the top of the spire when she came upon another door left slightly ajar. She pushed the door a few more inches. With no protests forthcoming, she let herself inside.

The chamber was set up much like her own, with a wide canopy bed and a tiled bathing suite, but this one showed more signs of prolonged habitation—a pile of discarded laundry at the foot of the bed and a line of open tinctures next to the sink. She pushed deeper into the chamber and gawked at its bizarre decor.

Wide sheets of canvas defaced with charcoal scrawl covered every inch of the walls and much of the marble floor. A canted drafting table occupied the space where Effie's vanity stood. In its open drawers, Effie spied a set of complex measuring tools and charcoal pencils of varied widths. A fresh canvas lay unfurled across the desktop with the first tentative scribbles already adorning its edge. Effie picked up a metal compass and pressed its sharp tip against the pad of her finger, just on the verge of drawing blood.

Based on the furnishings, she might have assumed the chamber belonged to some court portraitist, or else a visiting artist of royal renown, but the charcoal drawings plastering the room looked nothing like court portraits nor works of expensive art. The wild scribblings seemed almost directionless—overlapping clusters of chaotic lines, simultaneously precise and illegible, as if the artist layered several designs on top of one another, obscuring any clear impression a viewer might hope to glean. Effie had seen abstract paintings before, but even those esoteric works at least possessed some semblance of internal consistency. There was no beauty in these drawings—no subtle craft to appreciate nor suggestions of interpretative form. On the contrary, the artist responsible for these drawings seemed almost at war with his creations. With so many scribblings haphazardly pinned to the walls, the chamber looked less like the den of some brilliant aesthetician and more like how she imagined the lunatic colony on Lonely Spur.

The works fascinated Effie as much as they appalled her. She drifted around the room, tracking this disturbed individual's descent into madness through each charcoal stroke. So taken with morbid curiosity, she nearly forgot she was trespassing until a yelp from the doorway reminded her.

"I—I'm sorry." Effie whipped around with one hand clutching her lace bodice.

She expected to find a disheveled madman standing in the door, but instead her eyes landed on a boy in a Patrician uniform with brass buttons undone. The open jacket hung from narrow shoulders incapable of filling its bust. He looked just as shocked as she felt and twice as terrified.

"Who are you?" The boy's tenor voice quailed with an adolescent crackle. "What are you doing in my room?"

"I didn't mean to intrude," Effie said. "I got a little lost on the way back to my chamber—and I found the door ajar."

He held his guarded expression, still skeptical. Effie extended her hands in peace, hoping to calm him, but when she took a step toward him, the boy shrunk away.

"I'm not going to bite." Effie tried to affect an innocuous smile. "I'm Effie Strait. From Volturnus."

The boy's brown eyes narrowed as he watched her from his defensible position in the doorway. "You shouldn't be in here," he said.

"No, I shouldn't," Effie agreed, holding her smile firmly in place. She let her eyes wander the room again. "I didn't mean to snoop, but I was intrigued by your artwork. You made these yourself?"

His posture softened at the compliment. He took his first tentative steps inside the room. "They aren't *art*," he corrected, though he didn't sound like he took any offense. "And you don't have to pretend you like them. I know what they look like."

Effie nodded. "If not artwork, then what are they?"

The boy stepped around Effie, moving toward a small crate next to his bedside table that held another set of canvas sheets furled up and bound with twine. He counted the bound canvases twice and rearranged them before turning back to her.

"They're maps," he said, and Effie recognized the glint in his eye for boyish pride. "I'm a cartographer."

Effie fought the urge to giggle. She didn't want him to think she was mocking him. Instead, she walked up to one of the largest and most frenetic drawings tacked to the wall and scanned it, tapping one finger across her lips. The boy didn't seem like a lunatic, but she had a hard time imagining any sane sailor mistaking this madness for a map. She turned to the boy and folded her arms across the bodice of her dress. "You seem a little young for a cartographer."

He blushed. "And *you* seem a little overdressed for a trespasser."

Effie did laugh then. She batted her painted eyelashes, introducing even more color to the boy's smooth cheeks. She found herself quickly warming to the boy, and realized it was because he reminded her of Kai. Not the confident, hard-bodied flier he'd become, but the gangly sidekick he'd once been—back when she could still look down her nose and see the top of his sandy head. This self-styled cartographer couldn't have been more than thirteen or fourteen, but then again, boys always seemed younger than they were.

"What's your name?" Effie asked.

"Imerigo Vinson," he said. "From the Isle of Myin."

"Well, Imerigo Vinson from the Isle of Myin—it looks like we'll be sharing the Twin Spire for a time, though no one will tell me how much. I'm just six floors down if you're ever looking for company."

His eyes brightened at the suggestion, but the moment was fleeting. His face quickly turned down to the floor. "I'm not supposed to bother any of the other guests..."

Effie laughed again, and the pleasant sound drew his attention back from the floor. She winked at him. "Neither am I."

"*Ah-hem.*"

Both Effie and Imerigo jumped at the sound of a third voice creeping in from the doorway. One of Kelestina's liveried servants hovered there, looking pointedly displeased.

"I didn't invite her!" Imerigo sputtered. "She was here when I came back from the yard!"

The footman glowered at Effie. "This way please, Miss Strait." It sounded more like a command than a request. "I'll show you back to your room."

Effie flashed the footman an unapologetic smile before turning back to Imerigo and curtsying with the wide silhouette of her light blue dress. "It was a pleasure meeting you, Master Vinson."

He smiled weakly as she turned back to the waiting servant at the door. The footman's stern gaze lingered on Imerigo as she strode out of the room. He followed Effie in silent reprimand all the way back to her chamber door.

"We do ask that you refrain from disturbing Master Vinson," the footman said as Effie flopped onto her bed. "His work is very important to our host."

Effie pulled off her slippers and tapped a mock salute across her bodice lace. "Message received."

The footman performed a stiff bow and left, closing the door behind him.

3

VANNA

Vanna struggled to extricate herself from the gathering after the Ascension. The rest of the islanders began sorting into social circles for the valedictory feast, but Vanna swam against their current. She needed to be somewhere else. It didn't matter where, as long as it was elsewhere. Away. Her bruised ribs complained with every breath, but she continued to fight the crowd until she finally broke free.

Bael had vanished just as surreptitiously as he appeared. The mere fact that he was somewhere on Volturnus made Vanna feel terribly exposed, but even that vulnerability seemed secondary to this fevered urge to escape. She slipped through the line of covered wagons clustered around the jungle's edge and entered a torrid sprint.

With the sounds of the feast receding behind her, Vanna began to cry. She tried to outrun the tears, but the agony outpaced her. She burst through the tree line at the other end of the jungle and collapsed to her knees on the open road, sobbing uncontrollably.

If only Effie had *warned* her. If only she'd confided her plans. Vanna could have *steeled* herself against this moment. She would have been better prepared!

Effie didn't confide in her. Her sister knew better than to betray her wild intentions. Vanna would only have tried to stop her, and Effie never let anyone stand in her way.

Vanna turned her head to the sky and screamed.

She felt robbed.

She didn't begrudge Effie her secrets or her triumph, but she resented how abruptly her sister had taken herself away. It wasn't fair—not to either one of them. Circumstance had robbed them of the chance to say goodbye, and now Vanna had to face the rest of her life on Volturnus alone.

Concerned her cries might draw unwanted attention from the cliffs, Vanna collected herself and drove a hard pace to cover the lonely miles back to her empty home.

She slammed the cottage door behind her and drifted toward Effie's room.

The bedroom was just as she'd left it—the covers turned down and the curtains drawn. Vanna felt her eyes burning again as she scanned her sister's abandoned effects—an empty bowl; the small stack of books piled atop her nightstand; the foggy looking glass mounted to her wall. She fingered a dark cosmetic pencil beneath the looking glass, then walked over to inspect the short row of linen shirts and knee-length dresses clustered beyond Effie's closet door. The Avernian gown she'd bought for her sister hung untouched from a wire clip, a dozen seamstress pins still holding its shape for display.

Vanna shut the closet and fell back on her sister's well-kept bed. As she sunk into the pillows, she smelled floral remnants of the lilac crush Effie used to fragrance her hair. How long would it linger? Days, perhaps—but not weeks. Her sister's ghost still haunted this space, but it was a thin presence, all too easily exorcized by no ritual more ardent than the passage of time.

It had been the same with their parents so many years ago, but their parents were dead in truth and Effie was only gone. Somehow, that made the longing more fervid.

At least Effie would be happy—or so Vanna hoped. She'd proven her doubters wrong. She'd be a Pilot now. She'd bond a Leviathan and fly the Eight Skies of Ciel. It was everything she'd ever wanted.

A chill prickled on Vanna's skin as the setting sun slipped beneath her sister's windowsill. She wondered dreamily if Effie watched that same sunset in the distant Aquilonian sky. Emotionally drained and still exhausted by her injuries, Vanna felt her eyelids flutter as she drifted toward a shallow sleep.

In that liminal space between waking and dream, she saw Effie standing in cruciform atop a floating dauphine. The triumphant image melted into Bael's mustachioed face, and Vanna moaned softly. His foreign voice cloyed at her unconscious mind.

That's not going to be good for her...

A warning, perhaps. Or else, a poisonous lie...

Vanna wasn't sure how long she slept before the sound of heavy fists pounding against the cottage door woke her with a start. She jerked upright, heart thumping. She crept out of Effie's room, alert from the shock. The knocking continued.

"Open up, Vanna. It's Kendy. Let me in. We need to speak."

Jokai fend... Now agitated, Vanna ripped open the door. "*Balls of the deep,*" she cursed. "What time is it?"

Kendy walked past her without invitation. Jaffe, Seulin, and Kai followed behind, looking sober. Kai, at least, had the humility to flash a weak smile and an apologetic nod as he passed.

"Did you know?" Kendy asked, his blue eyes frigid as he glowered back from inside her own home.

"Excuse me?" Vanna felt her hands twitching into fists.

"Did you know what your sister was planning?" he clarified.

"Of course, I didn't know!"

Jaffe and Seulin joined their commander at his side. Kai lingered a step behind, red with embarrassment. "She could have been killed," Kendy admonished.

"You think I don't know that?" Vanna's temper flared. Who was he to storm into her cottage spouting accusations and demanding confessions? "Effie keeps her own counsel—you know that! She kept me in the dark just like the rest of you."

"You can't expect me to believe—"

"You need to stop talking now." Vanna's tone stole the words from Kendy's lips. "I had to watch my sister *jump off the edge of the island* only to rise from the dead on the back of a wild dauphine! *Then,* I had to lose her all over again when she disappeared into Kelestina's carriage. No, I didn't *know* anything. And you'll have to excuse me if I don't have the appetite for your insinuations."

Jaffe and Seulin both averted their eyes, and Kai seemed to shrink a head-and-a-half in his shame.

Kendy's jaw worked back and forth. He folded his arms across his chest, biceps flexing. "It was reckless. Ansel isn't going to be pleased. Effie violated the ceremony."

"Oh, I doubt we'll hear a peep from Ansel." Vanna stared pointedly at each of the dragoons who invaded her home—forced them to meet her eyes. "Effie proved herself right in the end. She *Ascended*. That's more than any of us can claim. You all saw the way Kelestina embraced her on the bank of the lagoon. I don't expect my sister will meet with any repercussions for her insolence."

Kendy tapped one finger against his elbow. "Maybe so..." He shook his head, sighing, and with it much of the heat bled from his voice. "I'm sorry for the intrusion, Vanna. I just didn't expect... We all knew Effie was special—"

"We didn't, though..." Kai looked more surprised than anyone to hear himself speak. Vanna and Kendy both stared at him. "We all just...*disregarded* her after she failed to manifest. None of us believed in her—not as much as she believed in herself."

Kendy grunted, but Vanna knew Kai was right. She loved Effie with all her heart, but she didn't believe in her—not truly. She petitioned Ansel to add Effie's name to the Ascension List, but she never imagined her sister might actually succeed in piloting a wild dauphine.

"It's been a difficult day for us all," Kendy finally said, turning back from Kai to Vanna. "I know you must be processing your sister's Ascension, but we still have the matter of the missing Aeolians to address."

Still irritated by her commander's behavior, Vanna returned a stiff nod. "I take it their zeppelin is still unaccounted for?"

"We spoke with the Ascendants from Avernus," Jaffe cut in. "The Aeolians sent word when they left the island, but they never crossed Avernian airspace."

"I've asked the Avernian Wing Commander to remain on Volturnus for an extra day with a draft of his strongest fliers," Kendy said. "We're going to assemble at the windward landing tomorrow to figure out a plan."

A missing zeppelin and a pirate at large on Volturnus. Hard to imagine it was all one fell coincidence.

"There's something else..." Vanna ventured. She glanced at the younger fliers. "Perhaps we'd better discuss it in private."

Kendy's eyebrows crept toward his scalp. He nodded and dismissed the other three. "Go get some rest. We've got an early day tomorrow."

The failed Ascendants didn't argue as they slinked past Vanna. On his way out, Kai looked like he wanted to say something, but Vanna's grim expression was enough to keep him quiet as he slipped out the door.

Once they were alone, Kendy took a seat at the kitchen table. With the younger fliers gone, he collapsed into his open hands, shaking his head and groaning. "I'm sorry... I shouldn't have stormed in here with them. It's been a day."

Feeling a trickle of sympathy for her commander, Vanna lowered her hackles and joined him at the table. "I understand. And I'm sorry for what I'm about to tell you."

Kendy looked up from his hands, blue eyes hooded with exhaustion.

"Bael is on the island," Vanna said.

"*What?*" He shot up on the edge of his seat.

"He approached me at the Ascension Ceremony—threatened me."

"Why didn't you say something?"

Vanna shook her head. "No time."

"We have to inform the governor."

"No!" Vanna's vehemence took him aback. "What I mean to say is, I don't think it's a good idea to involve Kelestina's magistrates. Not yet at least."

"Are you mad? We have a pirate on Volturnus! Sire Ansel needs to know. He can help—"

"If Sire Ansel finds out about Bael, he'll turn this island upside down. The Patricians won't risk another situation like that one we untangled on Aeolus."

"*I* don't want to risk a situation like Aeolus," Kendy countered.

"Neither do I," Vanna said. "But I don't think it's in the best interests of the island to provoke an open war. We don't even know what Bael wants yet."

"I've got a few good guesses."

Vanna grabbed his hands across the table. "Please, Kendy. I'm just asking for time to investigate myself. I don't want Bael on Volturnus any more than you do, but if we can handle the situation without stirring the Patricians to frenzy, that's what we should do."

Kendy stared at her for an uncomfortably long time. Finally, he squeezed her hands. "I won't have his serpent tongue slithering in the ears of any of our fliers..."

"Nor will I," Vanna insisted, squeezing back.

Kendy still eyed her with skepticism, but he released her hands in surrender. "Fine. It's against my better judgment, but *fine*. I'll give you one week to handle things quietly, but proceed with caution, Lieutenant. We both know what he's capable of."

"Thank you."

Shaking his head, Kendy stood up from the table and moved for the door. He paused with his hand on the wrought-iron handle and turned back to her. "She did look amazing, didn't she? I never imagined..." his voice trailed off.

The ache of Effie's loss tightened in Vanna's chest, but she would not let her commander see her cry. "I know," she said.

Kendy nodded solemnly, then took his leave.

Once he was gone, Vanna walked to the supply closet and dug out a heavy hemlock beam caked in cobwebs and dust. Her bruises screamed at her as she hoisted the beam and dragged it across the floor.

For the first time since returning to her family cottage, Vanna barred her door.

4

MULDOON

Muldoon adjusted his position in an uncomfortable glass chair as he waited on Kelestina with the rest of her expectant court. Six Patricians sat around the dining table of Aquilon Hall with a heavy crystal chandelier looming over them. The fixture's sprawling trellis of bangles refracted the day's dying light, speckling the conference with droplets of auburn and gold.

Muldoon stared blankly at Governor Aeryon of Avernus, sitting rigid as a saber, thick gray hair spiked back with oil in some gross imitation of the Celestial crown. To one side, Governor Lilyn of the Spurs worked her way through a tray of walnuts, popping each morsel in her plump mouth one at a time. On the other side, Governor Ansel glowered dyspeptically into a snifter of orange brandy.

Beside Muldoon, Governor Maribel of Nimbion sighed dramatically, drawing a cruel stare from the only face at the table that he couldn't place. This final courtier had already been waiting in the hall when the retinue returned from the Ascension. She declined to introduce herself and now sat casually with one ankle crossed over the opposite knee as she needled her gum line with a crass, silver pick. She had the look of Vangulmark about her: sienna skin and hair so blonde it looked almost white—unkempt but for the halo of a single, circlet braid.

She stopped picking when she caught Muldoon staring. Her slit nostrils flared, and Muldoon jerked his eyes away, engaging with his folded hands atop the table.

The tension only broke when Kelestina swept into the room from the keep. Caelig, her robed Skald, followed at her heel like a dutiful pet. The Patricians stood to receive them, with the newcomer slowest to rise. As she did, Muldoon noticed the crossbar hilt of a seax sticking up from her belt.

"Please be seated," Kelestina said, drawing up to her jagged throne at the head of the table. The Skald took the lower seat beside her. "We have much to discuss."

Dama Lilyn quickly swallowed the half-chewed walnut in her mouth and produced a weathered parchment. "It's been a while since the last successful Ascension," she prefaced, "but I did find the precis from that time." She began to read from the scroll. "We are to send word to Solaris by engine courier announcing the Pilot's discovery. The girl is granted three days and two nights at the palace to recover before her cleansing and the transit to Bol Haram. Your staff should use that time to discern the girl's academic deficits so the Collegium can begin preparing her course of study—"

Kelestina cleared her throat, halting the governor mid-sentence. "While I appreciate the thoroughness of your research, Lilyn, I'm uncertain past precedent applies to our current circumstance."

Inquisitive eyes perked up around the table. Only Muldoon seemed to read Kelestina's seditious subtext, but he kept his suspicions to himself.

Caelig's tongue made an obscene clicking sound as the Skald moistened his withered mouth to speak. "Miss Strait demonstrates *significant* potential. It is the judgment of Her Lightness that the girl presents an opportunity for our sect that ought not be squandered in the traditional manner."

Aeryon's wild eyebrows crept up his narrow head. "Is that not the purpose of her course of study at the Collegium? I know what passes for schooling on these back-sky isles, and it's hardly sufficient to prepare her for service on a Leviathan warship."

There's an understatement.

Armada Pilots needed to read technical sky charts and to navigate their Leviathan by instruments alone. They needed training in logistics and mathematics and aeronautic engineering—not to mention the historical and cultural context that was a prerequisite for integration with the upper echelons of Celestial society. Gifted though she may be, this Volturnian was a formless lump of provincial clay without the Collegium to mold her. He'd be shocked if she could even read.

Clicking filled the silence as Kelestina drummed the razor points of her nails against the glass tabletop. She nodded to Aeryon before assessing each of her courtiers in turn. "As you say, Miss Strait will need to be educated, but the Collegium is not the only academic kiln in which a capable Pilot might be forged. I've discussed this matter at length with Skald Caelig, and he agrees that it would be unwise to ship Miss Strait off to Bol Haram to become fodder in an interminable war of attrition. We prefer to keep the young prospect close at hand, in the hope that her abilities might be turned to more productive ends. The efficacy of this plan, of course, depends on the discretion of our court." Her eyes settled on Muldoon, catching his bald look of dismay. "Something to add, Sire?"

Muldoon girded himself, straightening his lapels. "I...am uncertain how freely to speak, Lightness."

"Try us, Sire." Invitation notwithstanding, Kelestina's glass stare urged caution.

Hardly a permission structure. Muldoon shook his head, attempting diplomacy. "I believe I am the most recently returned from Toran among this court. If I may advise, Admiral Siprichor needs every able Pilot we can muster. If Miss Strait is as Gifted as we all believe, then it's even more imperative we see her trained, bonded, and shipped off to bolster our forces along the front line."

Kelestina's eyes narrowed to emerald slits, and Muldoon swallowed hard.

Great was his fear of Celestial punishment, but even greater was the need to persuade Her Lightness off this duplicitous course. It sounded like she planned to withhold the girl from the Armada, and that would be a grave crime indeed.

He looked around the table for support. Ansel and Aeryon offered only blank stares, one petrified, the other seemingly confused. He tried to catch Maribel's eyes, but she averted them. Lilyn slowly shook her head.

"Muldoon."

"Yes, Lightness?" When had his name become a curse?

"Tell me, Sire—whom do you serve?"

A loaded question if he'd ever heard one. "I—I have always been loyal..."

"*Whom*, Sire."

"I—I serve the Crystal Throne."

Kelestina's nails screeched across the glass as her long fingers bent into a crooked claw. Her voice filled the Great Hall like a resonant bell. "The Crystal Throne is an *empty seat*. Its will lives only within the Hundred Frozen Souls, of which I am one. I understand you spent substantial time as one of Siprichor's trusted retainers, but the admiral transferred your commission to *me*. You gave me your oath."

Muldoon felt heat rising beneath his collar. He bent his head to hide the sweat beading on his brow. "As you say, Lightness."

"Is this going to be a problem for you, Sire?"

"No, Lightness. I spoke out of turn."

Kelestina continued to watch him as her Skald's harsh voice again entered the fray. "His Lightness Admiral Siprichor invited misfortune upon his Armada when he cast every Skald from his court. He offends the Jokai of the land and sky, and our soldiers pay the blood price for his heresy."

Wrong. Muldoon tried to hide his acid glower. Siprichor banished the Skalds because they were nattering gadflies, brimming with sanctimony and divine frivolity. They interfered with his prosecution of the war at every turn and spied for his enemies within the Celestial Court.

Muldoon silently stewed as Caelig droned on. "We who watch the skies have read the auguries, and their message is clear. It can be no coincidence that the Jokai saw fit to furnish us with this girl just when we are on the cusp of revealing the Titan's lair. The cartographer's work continues apace. Our path has proven righteous, and we are so clearly blessed. It would be an insult to toss this girl away on a blind warrior's folly—"

Kelestina raised her hand. "You go too far, Skald. However recreant our brother may be, he remains one of the Hundred Frozen Souls and thus deserving of your deference."

The Skald bowed his hooded head. "I beg your forgiveness, Lightness."

"You needn't beg." Kelestina flipped her hand as if to cast the apology away, then turned back to her table of Patricians. "Let us return to the practical matter of the girl's education. I plan to keep her existence a secret of this court and will therefore require a member of the court to serve as her guardian and tutor. She cannot remain at Aquilon. We entertain too many emissaries who might take notice and discover her nature."

Muldoon heard Ansel shifting on his chair as he girded himself to speak. "If I may interject, Lightness—Miss Strait and I have already established something of a rapport. I humbly submit myself for the task of her guardianship and education."

Muldoon rolled his eyes at the table.

"The girl's a Pilot," Lilyn said, voicing Muldoon's objections for him. "And a future Patrician. She's not a scullery maid for you to defile, Ansel."

Ansel nearly choked on a mouthful of brandy. "That's slanderous!" he sputtered.

Lilyn snorted, casually chewing another walnut. "It isn't slander if it's true."

They carried on exchanging jabs. Muldoon found Aeryon's eyes across the table, and the two shared a private smirk.

Kelestina raised her hand again, commanding silence. Her glowing eyes drifted to Lilyn. "That was unbecoming, Dama. We'll not have any discord in this hall."

Lilyn muttered her false apologies.

"The point is well taken, however," Kelestina continued, deflating Ansel's brief triumph. "You've proven a fine administrator, Ansel, but you lack the formal schooling necessary to prepare Miss Strait. Moreover, you are beset by your duties managing the plebiscite on our most populous island."

Ansel began to protest, but a harsh stare from Kelestina silenced him. "We have another guardian in mind," she said. "A thoroughly schooled Patrician with fewer obligations to the court."

Muldoon froze as the eyes of Kelestina's court simultaneously turned his way.

"Sire Muldoon," Kelestina supplied. "You were born to your status and raised in the Celestial schools of Umar. Moreover, you've been wanting for a service to perform since your plebiscite revolted against your governance."

Aeryon cocked one curious eyebrow, and Muldoon felt a pit yawning open in his gut.

"I—I couldn't possibly..." Muldoon gawked at several smug faces around the table. Again, he found no allies flocking eagerly to his cause. "I expected—that is to say, I was *hoping*—I'd see my governate restored. Now that tempers have cooled on Aeolus—."

"That ship has sailed," Kelestina stated flatly. She indicated the Vangish woman seated at the opposite end of the table. "Allow me to formally intro-

duce Dama Sigyn, newly consigned to our court after a long term prosecuting the Throne's business out west. Sigyn will be serving as the new
Governor of Aeolus, and I have every confidence she will restore the island
to complacency and productivity."

Muldoon gaped at the Vangishwoman as she removed the silver tooth-
pick from her mouth and performed a seated bow. "It is an honor to serve,
Your Lightness." Her rasping voice slithered from her throat like a lurking
adder. "The plebiscite will be well taken care of."

Muldoon scowled at the usurper before turning his gaze back up the
table to his host. "Please, Lightness—I beg you to reconsider. I haven't the
temperament to serve as this girl's tutor."

"The proper temperament can be learned," Kelestina countered. "Or
else faithfully *performed*."

"I have a poor history with her sister," he sputtered. "She will be
improperly predisposed to my counsel."

Kelestina turned to Ansel, rousing him from his sulking heap. "Is it
your experience that Miss Strait and her sister share a common
complexion?"

"It is not," Ansel grumbled. "I've found the younger sister to be the
more agreeable of the pair. She possesses a certain capacity for...*circumspec-
tion* that the elder decidedly lacks."

Kelestina rewarded him with a satisfied nod. "Then it's settled. Sire
Muldoon is hereby assigned as the girl's Patrician guardian and personal
tutor. You will both be returned to Volturnus Island and provided quarters
at the governor's manse."

"*What?*" Ansel and Muldoon raised their voices in unison.

"It is our judgment that the girl will be most comfortable among her
kin," Kelestina said. "Though, she will be too busy with her course of study
to assist with any plebeian concerns. We grant her the night to recover at the
palace. *Muldoon*," she spoke his name sharply, warning against any further
argument, "you will go to her at breakfast to deliver the news. A coach has
been tasked with facilitating your transit back to Volturnus."

Still seething, Muldoon pressed his lips back together and bowed his
head. "As you command, Lightness."

Kelestina lingered on him a moment longer, perhaps wondering if he
could be trusted with such a delicate task. Without hinting at her assessment, she finally broke her gaze and addressed the table. "I must turn my

attention now to the matter of Aeolus. Sigyn. Aeryon. Please remain. The rest of you are dismissed."

Lilyn and Maribel rose quickly from their seats with a pair of stiff bows. Still stunned by his assignment, Muldoon was slow to follow.

It was an outrage—a humiliation. To be reduced to a mere tutor—a *guardian* for a naive, provincial girl. It was an insult. Siprichor sent him to this land to help cultivate its bounty, but that argument carried water like a sieve in this court. Kelestina and her aged Skald made it quite clear what they thought of the war effort.

As he passed Sigyn, her hand shot out from under the table and seized his arm. She squeezed it with threatening strength.

"Fear not," she rasped. "I'll take good care of your plebeians."

Muldoon jerked his arm free, scowling as he took his leave.

Best of luck, you snake-faced bitch.

He exited the Great Hall, planning to spend the rest of his evening stewing in his guest suite over a solitary meal, but he encountered Dama Lilyn lingering in the antechamber. Her eyes tracked him, hands clasped in front of her squat body.

"Poor Muldoon," she lamented. "Too blinded by self-pity to see the gilded path laid out before him."

"You too, Dama?" Muldoon bristled, turning to countenance this latest indignity. "I expect better from you, though I'm growing accustomed to disappointment." The Governor of the Spurs had been the only member of Kelestina's court to receive him warmly upon his arrival in the archipelago. Among Kelestina's magistrates, they were the only two born of Toranese stock—he from Umar and she from Odenta-of-the-Inland Sky. For that kinship, her jibe cut him deeper than it should have.

A knowing smile danced across Lilyn's lips. "I'm not here to offer insult, Sire, but rather advice."

"*Unsolicited* advice," Muldoon grumbled.

"The best kind always is." Lilyn's fluttering laughter further raised his hackles. "Her Lightness has furnished you with a prime opportunity, though I'm not sure she even realizes it."

"Of course!" Muldoon's voice dripped with sarcasm. "I've always dreamed of a demotion to scholiast. Do you think the Skalds will pen a history of my academic reign?"

Lilyn parried his unworthy response with a flat stare. "You would agree that this girl's Gift is exceptional?" she asked.

"It certainly appears that way," he said.

"And an *exceptional* Pilot is likely to enjoy an *exceptional* career in service of the Crystal Throne..."

Muldoon sighed.

"Your position places you closest to Her Lightness' most coveted asset," Lilyn continued. "You'll work with this girl for years—day and night. If you avoid turning her against you with your acerbic disposition, you'll be her closest confidante by the time she's ready to accept her first commission."

Muldoon edged closer. She finally had his attention. "Go on."

"Who do you think will be in the best position to follow her up the ladder as she ascends the Celestial kyriarchy, hmm?"

Oh. *Oh.* Muldoon thumbed the strip of manicured goatee across his chin. "You're suggesting I treat my term of indenture as...an investment?"

Lilyn's face sprouted another tight-lipped grin. "I knew you weren't half the fool you've been playing at. Don't cut off your foot just because a goat pissed on your boot. Take this commission seriously. Earn the girl's admiration—her trust. Patience yields the greatest rewards." Lilyn watched his expression to ensure her words were sinking in. "I think I'll take my leave now. Have a pleasant evening, Sire."

Lilyn left Muldoon standing in the antechamber with much to think on.

5

EFFIE

One of Kelestina's young maids brought breakfast to Effie's room. She'd fallen asleep atop the bedspread in her make-up and clothes, which saved her the trouble of changing. She ate at the vanity, repairing her smudged make-up between bites of scallion omelet and black currant toast.

The pink juice provided with her meal tasted so bitter she nearly spat it out. She crossed the room in pursuit of her fresh flask of water, when a curt knock came at her chamber door.

She answered through a mouthful of half-chewed food. "Come in!"

Effie expected to see Dagda's charmless face, or else another nameless member of Kelestina's seemingly endless staff, but when the door swung open her eyes landed on the young Patrician from Kelestina's retinue.

Effie squeaked, quickly covering her stuffed mouth.

The man was sharply dressed in a fresh-pressed uniform, smooth cheeks gleaming from a recent shave. With one arm folded behind his back, he performed a courtly bow. "Miss Strait."

She remembered to swallow her food, then quickly straightened, returning the gallant gesture with a quick curtsy.

He cocked one thin eyebrow as he straightened from his bow. "Expecting someone else?"

"No—" Effie stammered, now blushing. "I mean—no one in particular."

A querulous expression worked its way onto the Patrician's face.

"What?" Effie demanded.

"If you don't mind my saying so, you clean up much better than I expected."

Rude. Effie scowled to hide the color rising in her cheeks. "If that's supposed to be a compliment, you're doing it wrong."

He squinted at her, eyes moving up and down her figure. She had seen plenty of lascivious faces pointed in her direction, and this wasn't quite that. He seemed more piqued than titillated. "I barely recognize you from the Ascension. If not for the hair..." his voice drifted. "The hair is memorable. Is it a common color on the islands?"

Effie shrugged. "Common enough, I guess."

He seemed to shake away an errant thought, returning to the matter at hand. "My name is Sire Muldoon of Umar. I've come to provide an escort."

The name rang a distant bell in Effie's mind. She studied this young Patrician anew but still couldn't place the face. With so many unanswered questions burning in her mind, she didn't let herself linger on the mystery.

An escort. This was it then. She was leaving the archipelago—possibly for good. She should have been ecstatic, but it all seemed to be happening very fast.

"Will I be able to see my sister?" Effie asked.

"I'm sorry?"

"Before we leave the Zephyr Isles, I'd like a chance to see my sister on Volturnus—to say goodbye."

Muldoon began to shake his head. "I don't think you understand—"

"Please!" Effie ran to him and grasped his hands. "She's the only family I have left, and I'm not sure if I'll ever see her again. Wherever we're going, I need to speak with her and let her know I'm okay."

A sly smirk spread across Muldoon's expression.

"You mock me?" Effie tossed away the man's hands. "You're cruel. I'm only asking for a small allowance—a brief trip to Volturnus and a few minutes to say our goodbyes. Surely, our host would understand. I demand to speak with Her Lightness!"

Smiling now with all his teeth, Muldoon shook his head, raising both palms in surrender. "Please, Miss Strait. You misunderstand. Your request is no trouble. You'll have all the time you require to see your sister—and anyone else on Volturnus, for that matter."

"Oh." Effie took a step back. She pointed her toes together, blushing. "Why didn't you just say that?"

"You hardly gave me time to speak."

"That's fair."

"Come." Muldoon offered his arm. "There is a carriage waiting at the trolley port to deliver us to Volturnus. The maids will collect your effects and have them delivered to your new quarters."

Effie hesitated before accepting the lead. "My new quarters?"

"I'll explain as we walk."

Effie silently processed Muldoon's explanation, hardly uttering a word the whole way through the winding labyrinth of Kelestina's palace and the long descent of marble stairs that led to the trolley.

She wasn't leaving the archipelago, after all. She wasn't even leaving Volturnus. She'd be quartered at Sire Ansel's manse—not half a league from her family cottage—where she'd begin a course of study at the direction of this young Patrician, Sire Muldoon.

"The training will be rigorous," he insisted. "Our host expects you to achieve the same level of proficiency they'd require at the Collegium."

"Okay..."

Effie couldn't decide if this unexpected turn offered relief or bitter disappointment. Either way, the whiplash was proving difficult to absorb.

"Why?" Effie finally asked as they sighted the horse-drawn coach awaiting them at the landing. "Why won't I attend this Collegium? Is there something wrong with me? With my Gift?"

"Hardly..." Muldoon's placid expression tightened around the eyes. "Our host's reasons are her own. It's not for us to speculate."

He looked like he was fighting the urge to say more, but Effie chose not to pry.

He opened the carriage door for her. When she stepped inside, she found Sire Ansel waiting on the bench. They acknowledged each other awkwardly as she took the opposite seat.

"Governor."

"Miss Strait."

Muldoon squeezed onto the bench beside Ansel, and the coach jerked into motion.

Neither man spoke as they crossed the trolley cable and trundled down the north road toward the village. Ansel stared out the window the entire time, pointedly avoiding eye contact. Muldoon, at least, looked in her direction, but only to study her like a confusing new toy. Neither one looked particularly happy about their present situation.

"You're both riveting company," Effie finally said. "Is this the level of conversation I should expect from my future housemates?"

Ansel's jaw tightened, but he kept his gaze pointed out the coach window.

Muldoon looked at her quizzically. "You don't look particularly interested in conversation, either. I thought you'd be happy about this decision."

"I'm not unhappy..." Effie started. She hadn't sorted out how she felt just yet. "I'm pleased I'll be able to see my sister. It all just seems a bit anticlimactic, I guess." She shook her head. "I think I'm just surprised."

"Plenty of surprise to go around," Ansel muttered.

Muldoon's side-eye suggested he felt the same.

The overland transit took much longer than travel by hippocampi. It was nearing dusk by the time Kelestina's blue-suited driver pulled up to Sire Ansel's manse and deposited them on the flagstone walkway along with two black trunks.

"Leave the boxes for my footmen," Ansel said. He preceded them inside without another word.

Effie and Muldoon shared a private glance.

"The governor doesn't seem too excited about his new boarders," Effie observed.

That drew a small smile from Muldoon. He extended one hand down the flagstone walk. "After you, Miss Strait."

"Glad to see Patrician etiquette isn't entirely dead on this island." Effie stuck her chin in the air as she proceeded up to the manse.

Ansel's butler, a slim Volturnian named Granger, greeted them in the vestibule. He assigned them each a house maid, and Effie followed hers to her new room. The accommodations paled in comparison to the Twin Spire. If anything, the space was a bit smaller than Effie's room at her family cottage. But the bed was already made with a down comforter and multiple pillows, and the chamber did come furnished: a hardwood dresser, an empty closet, a standing mirror, and a small corner desk with a glowing oil lamp. It all made the room feel a bit cramped, but at least she'd be comfortable.

Just as Effie's stomach was beginning to rumble, two footmen arrived with her trunk, followed by a maid with a steaming dinner plate. The footmen placed the trunk at the foot of her bed and opened the latches lest she risk any damage to her Gifted hands. Its contents included all the ointments and tinctures from her bathing suite in the Twin Spire, in addition to the cosmetic set she'd tested and the full wardrobe from her armoire—minus Kelestina's livery.

The young maid avoided eye contact as she set the dinner plate on the desk. Effie realized she knew the girl, though she barely recognized her in Ansel's gray and brass, with her long, chestnut hair bound up in a functional bun. The knitter's daughter, Ina Laurens.

"Ina!" Effie blurted out.

Ina tensed at the sound of her name, then turned to offer Effie a deferential bow. "I just came to deliver your dinner, Miss Strait."

"Stop that!" Effie waved away the formality, but Ina's face only tightened. "You don't have to bow to me. I'm not a Patrician. And you can still call me Effie."

Ina was only a year older than Effie. She'd been one of the flouncing spectators who made a point of watching the dragoon cadets at drills. She and Effie had never been close, but they certainly knew each other well enough to forego all this deferential nonsense.

"Will that be all, Miss Strai—*err*—Effie?" Ina kept her head turned down, still avoiding Effie's eyes.

Her behavior left Effie speechless. Ina had always seemed so vibrant at the landing. She thrived on all the attention she drew, and boys certainly seemed to like providing it. Who was this mousey imposter?

"That will be all," Muldoon provided, breaking the tense stand-off. At some point, he'd slithered up to her open doorway, where he now stood with one hand perched on the frame as Ina hurried past him. "I take it you're already acquainted with some of the governor's staff?" he asked.

"I know most of them—their faces at least," Effie said, still chewing over Ina's unusual behavior.

Muldoon nodded. "I'm not sure they all know quite what to make of your new status."

"I don't have any new status," Effie countered. "It's not like I'm suddenly Patrician. I'm just...Effie Strait."

Muldoon stepped into the room without invitation, inspecting her empty desk and the contents of the trunk as he did. "That's not exactly true," he finally said. "You're a Pilot and an honored guest of their Patrician governor. They've been instructed to see to your needs as they would with a visiting emissary."

"See to my *needs*?"

Muldoon nodded again. "And you are empowered to command them as you see fit. You may not wear the brand, but our host has afforded you the privileges of a Patrician while you're a guest in this house."

Effie needed to sit down. She pulled out her desk chair and flopped onto it. "That will take some getting used to—on both ends."

"I imagine it will," Muldoon agreed. "But remember that the workings of a Patrician household depend on this hierarchy. You can no longer simply trot down to the kitchens to procure yourself a snack, nor can you interfere with the cleaning protocols—the groundskeeping, the laundry and the like. Any attempt to do so would only disrupt the house's natural order. You'd make the staff's job harder, and they'd be left with little recourse to point it out."

Effie turned to her plate of food. She hoisted a turkey leg and took a morose bite. It seemed ridiculous to complain about such doting service, but the thought of ordering around these people she grew up with made her queasy.

Muldoon peered into her trunk again. "I see our host has provisioned you for your new life. A bit sparse, but it's certainly a start. You'll be permitted to collect any personal effects from your former home at your convenience."

My former home. That would be a comfort, at least. Effie took another bite of her turkey leg. She thought she caught another smirk percolating in the corners of Muldoon's face as he watched her dab the grease from her lips with a cloth napkin.

She quickly swallowed and asked, "Will I be *permitted* to visit my sister?"

Muldoon nodded. "Naturally. You're not a prisoner, Miss Strait. In fact, you're freer than most. When you're not at your studies, your time is your own. I'm informed that the governor hosts a formal dinner every Moonday. As members of his household, we'll be expected to attend, but beyond that you may take your leisure as you see fit."

"That's something, I suppose." *No more chores. No more assignments from the censors.* Awkward though it may be, her newfound status certainly had its perks.

"I think I'll let you settle in." Muldoon drifted back toward the door. "I'm in the west wing—down the hall past the dining room." He paused at the entrance, leaning back toward her. "But if you *need* anything, you should send a servant."

Effie rolled her eyes to the manse's wooden rafters. "Message received."

"If you do decide to wander into town, don't stay out too late," Muldoon continued. "Your studies begin promptly at Second Bell. I'd hoped we'd have a proper library at our disposal, but the governor's study will have to suffice. It's just down the hall at the end of the wing."

"I look forward to it," Effie said, only half sarcastic.

That strange querulous look flashed across Muldoon's expression again —as if something just occurred to him, but he thought better of speaking it out loud. "As do I," he said. "Good evening, Miss Strait."

6

VANNA

Vanna overslept for the first time in her life. By the time she reached the windward landing, the dragoons were already assembled, including a handful of her cadets. Feeling irritable, she waved off the chorus of cautious greetings as the wing parted to clear a path for their lieutenant.

Kendy stood with Commander Taros of the Avernian Dragoons and a small draft of four suited fliers wearing the inverted fleur of their island's South Wind banner. Neither paused from their tense discussion as Vanna stepped up to join them.

"...not much to go on," Taros said. "There's a lot of open sky between Aeolus and Avernus. I recommend we fly for Avernus—see if we can't gather information to refine the search."

Kendy scratched a line of black stubble along his chin. Vanna couldn't remember the last time she'd seen her commander without a clean shave. "Time is working against us. We risk losing any evidence of the zeppelin to the elements, and if there are survivors, they won't remain among the living for long."

Commander Taros was a decade older than Kendy, with light brown hair and a matching beard. His cheekbones carved deep lines in his face as he stroked that beard, considering. After a meaningful pause, he shook his head. "Even with my draft, we don't have enough fliers to cover the territory. We're better served looking for a lead."

Kendy nodded gravely, and Vanna seized on the silence, attempting to catch his eye.

He ignored her. "Let me speak to my fliers," Kendy said to Taros. "Just a moment."

Vanna followed as he peeled away. "He's right," she said. "You can't canvass the entire sky."

"Nice of you to join us." Kendy said it without breaking his gait.

Vanna absorbed the jab and jogged to his side. "How many fliers are we taking?"

Kendy stopped a few paces short of the waiting wing. "*We're* not taking anybody anywhere. I spoke with the medics this morning. You aren't fit to fly."

Vanna gaped at him. "I think it's *my* decision when I'm ready to fly."

"Actually, it's mine." She began to protest, but he cut her off. "You know as well as anyone how thin the line is between life and death over open sky. I won't risk it if you're not ready."

Vanna shut her mouth. She wasn't accustomed to hearing anyone tell her she wasn't capable, and the sound of it chafed—moreso because it was true. She'd struggled just to pull on her flight suit this morning. She wasn't ready to fly.

"Then who *are* you taking?" she asked.

"Everyone who can windshape," Kendy said. "Including Seulin and Kai." Before she could argue, he turned away and continued walking toward the wing.

Vanna chased him. "You can't do that, Kendy! They're still cadets!"

"Not anymore," Kendy said.

As they pulled up on the wing, Vanna spotted East Wind patches freshly pressed to the breasts of Kai and Seulin's flight suits. She grabbed Kendy by the arm, forcing him to face her. "I'm supposed to decide when the cadets are ready for active duty."

Rage flashed across his expression, but he choked it back, restoring his brittle facade of command. "They're ready," he said matter-of-factly. "We can't hold them back any longer. You baby them, Vanna. Seulin's been ready for months, and Kai's as dedicated a flier as we've had in years."

"It takes time—"

"We don't have time!" Kendy closed his eyes and breathed, rubbing a gloved palm over the strip of black hair that ran down the middle of his head. "The skies are changing, Lieutenant. The rebellion, the missing zeppelin...*Bael*." He spoke this last one very low. "I need every able flier we can muster."

Vanna ran through a dozen counterarguments in her head, but none of them held water. Her shoulders slumped. "You really expect me to twiddle my thumbs on the ground while you lead my cadets into danger?"

"You have another task," he said. "Or did you already forget?" *One week*, he mouthed.

Vanna fell back on her heels as she watched her commander return to assemble his wing. She stood alone while the dragoons sorted themselves. Twenty-six windshapers in the corps. Twenty-five minus Prestor, who was missing with the Aeolian zeppelin. *Twenty-seven* plus Seulin and Kai. Vanna couldn't remember a time when they'd sent such a large contingent off-island. Her heart ached to fly with them, but her head knew that Kendy was right. In her current condition, she'd only be a hindrance, and if her strength failed her over open sky...

The Long Drop went all the way down.

Kendy delivered curt instructions to the wing, and the windshapers began to peel away, following him up the landing to regroup with Commander Taros and the Avernian fliers. Kai lingered at the back of the pack, eyes questing for Vanna's attention as he drifted toward her.

"I'm sorry you won't be flying with us..." he muttered.

"So am I—" Vanna bit back any bitter commentary.

Kai drew closer to her, and she placed a palm against his chest. She fingered the East Wind patch newly sewn to the breast of his flight suit. His soft brown eyes looked so eager, but eagerness and readiness were not the same. She could only pray to the Jokai that Kendy did not conflate them.

"Remember your fundamentals out there," she told him. "It's always harder to go up than down. The wind is your ally, but it usually needs some convincing. Work with it. Don't try to boss it around." She realized she was still touching his chest and patted him awkwardly. He closed one big hand over her palm.

"That's good advice," he said.

"Go on." Vanna nodded up the landing. "Don't keep the commander waiting."

Reluctantly, he released her, then tapped out a salute across his patches before gusting to rejoin the wing.

Vanna lingered just long enough to watch the dragoons glide into formation across the western sky. For the first time, she was the one left behind. There was no worse feeling in the world. She felt the urge to race home and wallow behind closed doors, but knew that would only sharpen the sting of exclusion. Better to let a distraction occupy her mind, so she turned to the task of locating Bael.

Without a lead to follow, she worked her way around the village, interviewing the likeliest candidates who might have bumped into someone who didn't belong—starting with the merchants and longshoreman who worked at the ports.

The need for discretion complicated her task. How was she supposed to ask if anyone had seen any blue-haired pirates without letting on that she was searching for a blue-haired pirate?

After ten meandering conversations, half the port workers thought she'd lost her marbles, and she was still nowhere close to finding a lead. Bolo caught her slinking away from the port and interrupted the forecast he was providing to intercept her.

"You look like someone pissed in your tea, if you don't mind my saying."

Vanna did mind. "It's been a frustrating day," she grumbled.

Bolo pumped his plump hands placatingly. "Couldn't help but over-hear your chat with Shamus and Helga. What is it—exactly—you're looking for?"

I can't tell you exactly. Vanna sighed, too exhausted for another elliptical conversation. "Someone who isn't supposed to be here," she answered when Bolo didn't take the hint.

Bolo rubbed the back of his round head. "That's not much to go on." He chuckled good-humoredly.

Vanna stared at him. "I'm aware."

"I won't pretend to know exactly what it is you're after—but if you're looking for smugglers and ne'er-do-wells, it isn't likely they slipped in through a regular port of entry."

"Do I hear an alternate suggestion?" She was in no mood.

"You're too young to remember this, but back before our host arrived, the island used to see more black traffic. Wasn't usually the port workers who sounded the alarms back then. There are a couple abandoned landings in the southern lees. Good spots for smugglers and pirates to put down.

The farmers working the outlying fields used to spot 'em. Plenty of false alarms, of course—you know how farmers can be. Eyes play tricks when they spend too much time staring into the open sky at night. But if you're looking for someone on Volturnus who's not supposed to be here, couldn't hurt to ask around the homesteads."

It wasn't bad advice. Vanna offered Bolo her grudging thanks and trudged back to the village. She considered stopping by the tavern for a nightcap, but the convivial atmosphere around Janus' hearth was a poor match for her mood. Committed to a day casing the homesteads, she decided to turn in early.

Vanna couldn't remember the last time she'd returned home in such a dark mood. She pushed open the door to the cottage, looking forward to nothing besides a bowl of thin stew and a cup of tea.

She found Effie, instead.

7

EFFIE

Vanna slumped inside the cottage looking beaten and exhausted. Effie almost didn't recognize her. The two locked gazes, and Vanna became even paler.

"Effie."

"*Jokai fend*, Vanna. You look like you've seen a haint."

Vanna paused in the doorway and rubbed her eyes.

"Still here," Effie said, performing a graceful twirl. "Not a mirage."

Vanna ran to her then, and the sisters embraced. Remembering Vanna's injury, Effie held her sister gingerly, but Vanna's strong hands didn't reciprocate, bunching the fabric of Effie's fine Celestial dress.

"I—I didn't—" Vanna's voice matched her complexion, white and drawn.

"I know," Effie said, affectionately combing her fingers through her sister's short hair.

"I thought I lost you."

"No such luck."

Vanna's laughter was half a sob. When she finally withdrew, she pressed her hands to Effie's face, seeking further assurance it wasn't all some fevered illusion. "How is this possible?" Vanna asked.

"It shouldn't be," Effie said. "I'm as surprised as you are."

"How long do I get?"

Effie shrugged. "Indefinitely."

Vanna's expression turned curious.

"I can explain." Effie turned to the wood-burning stove and began to fill the kettle. "But it'll take a minute. Might as well set the tea…"

Vanna provided a rapt audience as Effie recounted everything that transpired since she crashed the Ascension. Effie explained how she waited inside the cliffs until the other Ascendants failed out, and how her mind touched the waiting dauphine. Vanna's eyes went wide at the description of Aquilon Palace and the Avian attendants soaring between its spires.

"What's a majordomo?" Vanna asked.

Effie shrugged. "It's like a rude butler, I guess."

Effie's story finally arrived at the Twin Spire. A small smirk worked its way onto Vanna's chapped lips as Effie cataloged all the lavish furnishings.

"You are looking unusually pampered," her sister chided.

"I think you mean *properly* pampered."

They shared another laugh, and Effie felt herself begin to relax. She skipped over her chance encounter with Imerigo Vinson and his unsettling charcoal drawings. She still didn't know what to make of the boy and his maps, but she was quite sure she wanted to work out that puzzle on her own.

Her story finally caught up to the present day. Effie described the disorienting feeling of awakening at Aquilon Palace, assuming she'd be shipped off somewhere far across the sky only to learn she'd be returned to Volturnus and quartered at Sire Ansel's manse. When she mentioned Sire Muldoon, the rest of the blood drained from Vanna's face.

"What?" Effie prompted, pausing from her tale.

Vanna shook her head. "Muldoon is the former Governor of Aeolus. He's the Patrician I arrested for abusing the plebiscite."

A new connection blazed across Effie's mind, joining the distant memory of Vanna depositing a soiled prisoner on Sire Ansel's lawn with the more recent impression of a courtly Patrician lord.

"He's dangerous, Effie," Vanna said. "Some of the things he said to me… I don't want you anywhere near him."

Effie began to shake her head. Her body felt suddenly cold. "I don't know if I can avoid it. He's been assigned as my tutor. He's going to be staying with me at the governor's manse."

"He's on Volturnus?" Vanna suddenly stood up from her seat, breath quickening.

Effie eyed her sister warily. "Oh, sit back down. What're you going to do? Sail up to the manse and hogtie him again? He's a Patrician, Vanna. You're lucky you got away with it the first time."

Still seething, Vanna slowly lowered herself back into her seat. "He's a bastard."

Effie tried to square her sister's vitriol with her own first impressions of the man. He'd been arrogant, certainly—perhaps a bit dismissive—but he'd yet to show her any face resembling the monstrous impression he'd given Vanna.

"Look at me," Effie said. "I promise I'll be careful—but I can't avoid the man. We'll be working together daily."

Vanna crossed her arms. "I don't like it."

A familiar irritation prickled inside Effie. How quickly Vanna fell back on her patronizing routine. *You don't have to like it*, she wanted to say. *This is my life.* But Vanna's state-of-mind seemed more fragile than usual, and Effie didn't see the point of provoking her. Instead, she stood up from the table, bussed her teacup, and made for her room.

"I'm allowed to bring some things with me up to the manse," she said. "You want to help me pack?"

Vanna helped her fold up her clothes and collect toiletries and ornaments from around the room. As she unearthed their mother's old opal necklace, Effie sensed her sister's mood darkening again. Vanna paused from her task to linger over the heirloom.

"What's got under your skin?" Effie finally asked as she deposited a pile of small-clothes in the nearest pack and tested the duffel's weight.

"It's nothing."

Effie dropped her bags and perched her hands on her hips, blocking the door. "Are you really this unhappy that I'll be sticking around?"

Vanna jerked out of her trance. "Of course not," she said.

"Then what is it? I told you I'll be mindful of Muldoon—"

"It isn't that, either—at least, not entirely. I've just got a lot on my mind."

That seemed like an understatement. Whatever Vanna carried, it went beyond the fear that she might lose Effie for good. Something else was weighing her sister down, and not even the news that Effie would be living up the road seemed to lighten it. When Vanna didn't elaborate, Effie picked up her bags. "Well, if you decide you want to unburden yourself, you know where to find me. I won't be a stranger."

Vanna saw her out the door, but throughout their brief goodbye, Effie couldn't shake the sense that some new barrier had grown up between them—so different from the gaping chasm that crashed through their relationship in the months leading up to the Ascension. This felt more like a wall of frosted, Celestial glass. Effie could still see through it to the distorted images on the other side, but it muffled any attempt to communicate across its icy expanse. It wasn't like Vanna to keep things from her. Even dragoon business, she typically shared to the extent that Effie showed any interest.

She heard Vanna bar the door behind her and stopped to stare at the locked cottage. Only two days had passed since she last woke up in the ashwood bed her father built, but how long ago that fateful morning felt. From this familiar vantage in the heart of Volturnus Village, she saw her old life receding on the horizon, already a thousand leagues away.

Effie might have been back, but she wasn't home.

8

KAI

Kai soared.

The open sky filled him up, transformed him by the alchemy of friction and lift. His body ignited. He became a shooting star, cutting its blazing path across the firmament. He'd drilled over open sky more times than he could count, but never out of sight of the Volturnian shore. Out here, the wind lived wild, untamed by the stifling ground. These feral winds whispered their erratic intentions through his Gift, and he whispered back, coaxing them to fall in line, drawing them cautiously beneath the ruffles of his flight suit. Every gentle tailwind, he accepted with grace. Every turbulent eddy, he cast sternly aside. He made an ally of the air, just as Vanna had instructed, though he discovered more mischief than reluctance in its character.

The crossing to Avernus took a little over two hours. As their formation approached the leeward shore, Kendy passed back the air-sign to reduce altitude, followed by the signal to disperse. Kai banked into a flying chevron with his draft, led by Dray at its forward point.

With aquiline grace, the combined wing broke into three drafts, with the bulk of the fliers destined for the New Village in the lees. Another team dove south to interview the stevedores and longshoremen who worked the southern port, while Kai's team sailed north to contact the miners at the quarry.

The team at the village had the largest field to plow, but they were likely to find more rumor than fact. If anyone had seen anything unusual in the skies around the archipelago, it would have been the haulers who shuttled raw ore to Grenport—or else the merchants entering the archipelago from points unknown across the skies. Kai selfishly hoped his team would be the first to pick up the Aeolian zeppelin's scent. It was his first mission as a fully-fledged dragoon, and he lusted after any opportunity to prove his worth.

The winds weakened as they crossed over the shoreline. A ring of mountains loomed on the horizon, its highest peaks reaching well beyond the altitude of their crossing. At Dray's signal, Kai slowly released his grasp on the winds and drifted over the jungle canopy, toward the boiling quarry beyond.

Avernus was a much smaller island than Volturnus and dominated by forbidding terrain. The Lumite Mountains cut across the island like the teeth of some titanic saw—a hundred times as high as the steepest cliffs on Volturnus. The early Volturnian settlers had tamed much of the island's jungle to make way for agriculture, but Avernus left theirs to wild—splitting the New Village in the south from the quarry in the north. As a result, temporary shelters had cropped up along the foothills where miners and quarrymen spent long weeks away from their families as they pursued their backbreaking work.

The quarry pit's milky eye marked their descent, its rocky sclera veined by ladders and scaffolding. Mine shafts flanked the chasm, and rings of yurts speckled the savannah for miles around.

The draft put down just outside an adjacent mining camp where three laborers sat around an open fire, prodding at a dented pot of stew while it cooked. Kai eyed the workers warily as Dray checked in with Raji, Maya, Lya, and Seulin before making his way over.

"Strong flying, kid," he said as he checked Kai's flight suit for holes. "We might just make a dragoon out of you, yet." An affectionate punch to the arm sent Kai stumbling back a step.

"Barely broke a sweat," Kai said. His eyes lingered on the crosshilt of Dray's bastard sword protruding over his shoulder. Incredible, that the burly flier could keep himself aloft with its weight strapped to his back.

"Wait here with the draft," Dray said. "These Avernian miners can be prickly. Let's let Kendahl loosen the soil before we start digging."

Kendahl was the Avernian flier assigned to their draft. She'd already approached the miners waiting on their pot of stew. From a distance, Kai watched the dark braid on the back of her head bobbing up and down as she nodded along with some unheard conversation. The Avernian dragoon reminded him of Vanna—though not as graceful in the air nor half as pretty.

He had to swallow his disappointment when he heard about Vanna's grounding from Kendy. He always envisioned joining the corps on her wing, and he wanted her to see him in flight almost as much as he wanted to fly in the first place.

She won't be grounded forever, he reminded himself.

They'd have years together in the corps. Sooner or later, her memories of him as a raw cadet would fade. He'd spend every day replacing them with new impressions of a capable dragoon—a dauntless flier she could count on to watch her wing.

Kai drifted over to join the rest of the draft as Dray walked up to speak with Kendahl. Seulin had just finished retying her windswept hair. She flipped back her braid and looked up at him with a starry-eyed expression that matched his own mood to a tee.

"Incredible, isn't it?" she said. "Open sky."

Kai shook his head in wonderment. "No other feeling like it."

"Seems a waste to spend any time at all on solid ground." Seulin rocked back and forth on her heels.

Raji crashed through the moment, wagging his finger in mock admonishment. "Easy now, fledglings. Even a condor needs to find its perch now and again."

"Leave 'em alone, Raji," Lya chided. "You remember your first time."

Raji rounded on her. "Actually, I don't. Too much of old Janus' ale. I can hardly remember what I had for breakfast."

Maya stepped in, hand perched on the pommel of her rapier. "I can refresh you, if you like." She was the eldest in the draft and only subordinate to Dray by Kendy's preference. "The first time Raji made the crossing, he got so carried away, he broke formation on a wild gust. Claimed so much altitude, he lost his breath and fainted. Nearly gave himself the Long Drop."

Kai gaped from Maya to Raji. "No!"

"Oh, yes," Maya said. "Flynn caught him in her arms and carried him to the ground like a newborn babe." She cradled her arms mockingly.

"Forgot about that..." Raji grumbled.

Lya socked him in the arm. "No, you didn't."

Kai laughed along with the good-natured ribbing. Even Raji joined in. The comradery filled him up almost as much as the open sky. It was exactly how he always imagined it would feel to finally be part of the corps. He was hardly the only Volturnian orphaned by the Butcher's attack. He had his uncle, but no siblings to share in his lot. At least Vanna and Effie had each other. He always envied them, and though they treated him like a surrogate brother, it just wasn't the same. This feeling in the corps was much closer to the fraternity he longed for.

Dray and Kendahl returned from the mining camp, and Kai thought the muscle-bound leader looked unusually thoughtful.

"What's the good word, Lieutenant?" Maya asked.

Dray scowled at her. "You see a bronze wing on this suit? Only lieutenant we've got is Vanna Strait. I'm just filling in."

Maya tapped out a sarcastic salute. "Whatever you say, boss."

Kendahl brought them all back to business. "These quarrymen and the miners will talk to us. Just stay away from the other camps."

Kai glanced around at all those other camps; they stretched out beyond each horizon. The foothills were more camp than quarry. There must be a hundred different yurts set up in two-dozen circles.

"What if someone in the camps has the information we need?" he asked.

Dray raised a cautioning hand and nodded back at the miners. "We have it from our new friends over yonder that the men off-duty won't take kindly to a bunch of dragoons interrupting their leisure time."

Kai felt his temper prickling. "Who cares about their leisure time? Surely this is more important—" Kendahl's glower shut him up. Kai glanced at the rest of the draft, but no one seemed eager to offer support.

"Not to them," Kendahl said. "Mining lumite is a hard life that makes harder men. Won't sit right with most of these folks, getting worked over by some beardless Volturnian cadet."

"I'm not a cadet—" Kai stepped forward and felt Seulin's hand on his sleeve holding him back.

"Did I sound like I was finished?" Kendahl's stare made Kai feel about three feet tall. She held him with her silence until she was content he wouldn't start up again. "You're not gonna get any answers from a miner who doesn't want to give 'em, and if you try to force the issue, I can guarantee you'll get something far less useful for your trouble, besides."

Kai hung his head and shrank back beside Seulin.

"The quarrymen never leave the island anyway," Dray added. "It's the foreman and the haulers we want to meet. If anyone's got a whiff of our missing zeppelin, it'll be one of them."

After agreeing to the terms, they followed Kendahl up the winding path to the fenced quarry. A guardsman waved them inside, and Dray pointed out the packing center—a two-story building as big as a Patrician manse, but far more utilitarian with its barred windows and boxy design. Empty oxcarts lined up outside two vaulted freight entrances, waiting to be filled with the day's haul.

"Kendahl and I are going to speak with the foreman on duty," Dray said. "The rest of you split up and question every hauler you can find."

"They'll be the only ones who don't look busy," Kendahl added.

Kai tapped out a salute across his fresh Volturnian patch and turned up the road with the rest of the draft.

"Not too friendly here," he observed.

Seulin offered noises of agreement.

"Avernus is a hard island," Maya said. "Never had enough land to farm, and mining lumite's the only proper source of coin—except for the ports. They depend on trade with Volturnus and Nimbion just to feed themselves, and I suppose they've always had a bit of a chip about it."

A small band of filthy quarrymen fresh from the pit passed them on the road. Each man and woman eyed them like a cadre of liveried tax collectors. One spat in their path, pausing briefly to leer.

"That's some chip..." Kai grumbled, but only once the quarrymen were well out of earshot.

"It is what it is." Raji shrugged. "The Avernians—and the Aeolians, to some extent—they have a certain impression of us. Think we're living fat and easy on the eastern isles, planting orchards and mashing berries into jam."

"Farming's hard work, too," Kai countered.

Raji shifted his head, considering. "Different kind of hard. You just have to tread lightly. Don't give these miners any reason to think you're looking down on 'em. They're still Zephyri, and Zephyri pull together when there's a need. Just look at Kendy and Taros—two boulders cut from the same cliff."

That counted for something, Kai supposed. He wasn't so sure about Kendy and Taros, though. He caught the Avernian commander glowering at the back of Kendy's head a couple of times back at the landing, and he suspected the older flier resented the Volturnian commander's greater force.

As they closed on the packing center, the scent of the quarry became overpowering—a foul alchemical blend of sulfuric brimstone and something sickly sweet like burning hair. Kai coughed to peel the odor off the back of his throat, but he never quite dislodged it. They split up once they reached the freight doors, and Kai found himself awkwardly navigating his way around the unfamiliar environment, trying to parse the quarrymen from the haulers. Despite Kendahl's sarcastic advice, everyone looked plenty busy. Shirtless laborers bent their slick backs cranking pulleys and winches, while runners received each container and transferred the haul to wheeled carts. The carts followed a short span of track inside the center, where still more laborers waited to pack the stone for weighting and transport. All the while, quarrymen cycled in and out of the pit. Soiled bodies crusted in rock dust and spent powder emerged from the abyss as quickly as the clean ones in canvas overalls arrived to replace them.

"Fire in the hole," a distant voice echoed from somewhere deep within the abyss. A moment later, an explosion sent Kai tumbling to the ground with his arms bracing his head.

Cruel laughter reached his ears as he regained his feet. Kai spotted a crew of quarrymen resting against an empty oxcart with a broken axle. An older woman with short, gray hair passed a drum of tobacco to another worker and tucked her head in her hands, mocking Kai's reaction. Another round of laughter from her friends sent Kai stalking off in the other direction, feeling hot under the collar.

The workers crowding the nearest freight door looked more approachable. One set barked orders at the packing team, directing carts of ore onto floor scales. Another set paced the waiting line of oxcarts, making notes on slate tablets with wedges of chalk. Kai straightened his suit collar, mustering his best dragoon decorum to make his approach.

"Ahoy!" He waved at one of the haulers inspecting an overfilled cart.

When the man didn't look up from his slate, Kai gritted his teeth and pursued him. "I'm Kai Bowker, a dragoon of Volturnus—"

"I can see that," the hauler grunted, still eyeing his tablet as he continued around the cart.

"I need to ask you a few questions…"

The man still refused to acknowledge him, so Kai lurched forward and grabbed him by the arm. The hauler stiffened in his grasp before lowering his slate. Eyebrows turned inward as he looked up at Kai.

"We're investigating a missing zeppelin from Aeolus," Kai said.

"What would I know about that?"

The man pulled against his grip, and Kai remembered Raji's warning. He released the man's arm, holding his palms up deferentially. "I just need to ask a few questions. You work with the freighters, no?"

The hauler nodded stiffly.

"We just want to know if anyone's seen anything—any unusual ships in the western skies? Distress signals? Signs of piracy?"

The hauler tapped his foot impatiently. "I really don't have the time for this—" He shook his head, attempting to return to his tablet.

"Please, sir. I know your work is important, but so is mine. We're talking about 100 missing Zephyri. If it was your family on that zeppelin, I'm sure you'd expect the dragoons to be thorough."

That finally seemed to strike a chord. The hauler sighed and, again, let his tablet drop. "I haven't heard anything like what you're describing from our freight crews. We're all working doubles to prep a week of overload shipments to make up for the delays."

"What kind of delays?"

"Ground delays in Grenport. We're working with half a fleet, and we're running the risk of missing our monthly quotas." He peeked down at his slate, shaking his head. "It's gonna be close."

"Any idea why?" Kai asked.

The hauler shrugged. "Port Authority closed two of the shipping lanes out of an abundance of caution."

Kai's temper prickled again, but he quickly stamped it out. "You didn't think that was relevant?"

The hauler shrugged again, dismissive. "Don't see how it could be. The lanes run between Grenport and Aeolus. Nothing to do with any transit routes inside the archipelago. Now, if you don't mind, I really need to get back to work."

Kai let the man carry on.

He spoke to two more haulers chalking shipping containers and a third overseeing the laborers as they weighed each container of ore. None of them offered any additional insight, though they did confirm the shipping disruptions out beyond the archipelago.

With his allotted time running short, Kai searched the freight area for another clean body to interview. Out of curiosity, he reached into an untended oxcart and picked up a fist-sized chunk of lumite ore. The white rock was surprisingly light. He juggled it in his hand a few times before drawing upon his Gift to balance it on a spiraling gust. Something in the rock's character reminded him of the Moonflow Lagoon—as if time and the crushing weight of the mountain range had compressed the island's ether into stone. With a puff of wind, he sent the ore arcing back into the cart.

"Neat trick, flyboy." A voice as white and gritty as the ore itself reached his ears. "You do parties?"

He turned around to find the squat laborer with the spiky gray hair he'd seen mocking him next to the broken cart. Bristling, he began to walk away, but the woman's voice pursued him.

"Thought you were looking for answers?"

Jokai fend...

"Couldn't help but overhear..." she teased. "I spend a lot of time drinking with the freight crews who overnight at camp. Sailors like to talk."

Kai stopped walking. He assumed this laborer was only screwing with him, but he accepted the dangle anyway and stalked back over. She barely stood as high as his chest, but there was a sturdiness about her that didn't seem easily challenged. "What's your name, um, miss?"

"Gar," she said, moving her wad of tobacco from one side of her mouth to the other with her swollen tongue.

"Just *Gar*?"

"Yep." She perched her fists on her hips and spat a black wad onto the ground. Repulsively, her lip held the distended shape impressed by her chaw.

"What have you heard?" Kai no longer had the patience to dance.

"Oh, just that the ground delays at Grenport aren't really about an *abundance* of caution."

"Is that right?"

She nodded once. "To hear the freighters tell it, the caution is pretty damn justified."

It was starting to seem like quarrymen had the same penchant for drama as sailors. "Can we skip the suspense, please?"

"I'm talking about piracy, kid." Gar's lips peeled back, revealing two incomplete rows of black-stained teeth sticking out from bleeding gums. "And not some petty crew with flintlock pistols and kite-ships. There's a *Leviathan* lurking out west."

Kai froze. The isles hadn't seen a Leviathan pirate in ages—not since their host arrived. Not since the Butcher. Excitement and terror bound together to form a complicated knot in Kai's stomach. Grenport was far away—100 leagues west of Aeolus—but a Leviathan could cover more sky than any man-made craft. One-hundred leagues was still too close for comfort.

"To hear it told, the beast sunk a Toranese airship on its way into port," Gar continued. "Those long-haul ships sail heavy. She wouldn't have been easy pickings. Port Authority's keeping it quiet so they don't spook the other merchants."

If there was any truth to Gar's tale, it didn't bode well for the archipelago. He had to ask... "Did any of these freighters say what the Leviathan looked like?"

Gar stuck her tongue in her distended lip as she chewed the question over. "It's all word of mouth. None of them got eyes on the beast."

"I understand." Stories had a way of shifting as they passed from lips to ears, and that went double for sailors' lips and ears. "I'd still hear it."

Gar checked over both her shoulders before leaning in conspiratorially. "They say it's a *snake*—a golden-plumed serpent with a bone-white head." She leaned back. "Imagine that? Makes me happy to spend most of my days underground."

A plumed serpent. It didn't sound like Devil Ray, but the image chilled Kai all the same.

He'd lost track of the time, so he thanked Gar for her help and gusted off to reconnect with Dray and the rest of the dragoons.

They reconvened outside the camps. Nobody else had found much to share. The ground delays at Grenport were the talk of the quarry, and Maya picked up similar rumors of piracy, but with none of the detail Gar had provided. It was enough to make Kai question the veracity of the laborer's tale.

"I can't believe not a single freighter saw the zeppelin—not so much as a glimpse." Raji shook his head. "Those are busy transit routes between Aeolus and Avernus."

"Unless something knocked the zeppelin off course..." Kendahl mused.

Kai caught Dray watching him with squinting eyes. "You look like you want to say something," he prompted.

Kai realized that the eyes of every dragoon in the draft were suddenly pointing his way. He worried he'd sound like a credulous fool, but he couldn't keep Gar's story from the others. "I did hear something from one of the quarrymen," he ventured. "Not a first-hand account, so I don't know how much to believe..."

"The laborers aren't prone to tall tales like the sailors," Kendahl said.

Kai nodded. "She said there was a Leviathan attack on a Toranese airship out of Grenport."

Silence, then. Kai became acutely aware of the quarry's percussion echoing from the distant pit. Each dragoon face reflected back a different mixture of curiosity and fear, and Kai shared in each and every blend.

"What kind of Leviathan?" Dray asked the question on everyone's mind.

Kai's throat felt suddenly dry. "A golden-plumed serpent with a bone-white head."

9

EFFIE

Effie slept fitfully on that first night in Ansel's manse. She tossed and turned in the new environment, tormented by the ambient sounds of the household and its unfamiliar scent. The morning seemed to arrive the same moment she finally found sleep. A maid awakened her, delivering breakfast and drawing the curtains to let in the sun.

Effie shielded herself from the oppressive light. Once her eyes adjusted, she realized Ina had been replaced by a stout woman approaching middle age.

"Good morning, Miss Strait." The maid clasped her hands in front of her apron and bowed, revealing a bonnet cinched to the top of her head. "You'll have to eat quickly. Sire Muldoon is expecting you in the governor's study at the top of the hour."

Effie groaned as she sat up in a pile of twisted sheets. One of the shoulder straps on her cotton nightgown had slipped from her arm in the night. She bashfully restored it and realized the maid was still standing at attention, likely waiting to be dismissed.

"What happened to Ina?" Effie asked.

"I'm sorry, Miss Strait?" The maid furrowed her brow. "Is there a problem with my service?"

"No." Effie shook her groggy head. "Of course, not. And it's just Effie

—no more of this 'Miss Strait.' I'm just curious. It was nice to see a familiar face."

The maid anxiously shuffled her hands. "Ina asked me to see to your needs. She...wasn't feeling well."

"I'm sorry to hear that." Effie carefully swung her legs over the bed. Her toes recoiled from the cold wood floor. The maid read her discomfort and quickly fetched a pair of slippers from the closet. "Thanks," Effie muttered as her feet entered two fur-lined cocoons. "Please tell Ina that I hope she feels better."

"I will, of course, Miss Strait." The maid's eyes shifted from side to side. "...Will that be all?"

"Yes, yes." Effie waved her away. "You are, um, *dismissed.*"

The maid performed another quick bow before scurrying away.

How do Patricians live like this? She'd never get used to all the tedious formality—no matter how long she was stuck in Ansel's manse. Effie sighed as she began to sift through her trunk for an outfit to wear.

All the dresses from Kelestina's palace felt too formal for a daily lesson with Muldoon, so she turned to her duffels from home and pulled out a white cotton top and checkered skirt hemmed modestly below the knee. With only minutes to spare, Effie quickly brushed out her hair, took two bites of morning sausage and grabbed a slice of buttered toast to eat on the way.

She crammed the last crust of toast in her mouth as she entered the study. Muldoon was already waiting for her, sitting perched against a desktop as he thumbed through a thick tome bound in dark red leather. He'd foregone his Patrician suit in favor of tight-fitting beige pants and a white silk shirt with ruffled sleeves. The seashell folds of a beige cravat spread out from the collar of his jerkin, but it was the golden buckle on his black boot that caught her eye, twinkling as he tapped his foot along with his reading.

Effie felt the sudden urge to cover up. Her checkered skirt seemed dull against the rich burgundy of his jerkin, and the smooth silk of his undershirt only highlighted every unpressed wrinkle her own clothes sustained in transit. If this was what passed for casual in Kelestina's court, she would need to recalibrate.

Adding insult to injury, Effie realized she'd neglected to change out of her slippers. She contemplated darting back to her room, but before she could escape, Muldoon looked up from his book.

"Ah! Miss Strait." The smile he offered was warm enough, but the tight set of his almond eyes reminded Effie of her sister's warning. He checked the timepiece on his desk with a contented nod. "Right on time. A fine start, though I daresay punctuality will be the least of your trials in this room."

Muldoon stood up from his perch against the desk and walked over to another table set with reading lamps and an intimidating tower of leather-bound books. A slate board propped against an easel loomed over the study space. Muldoon drummed his fingers against the back of a chair and scanned the adjacent bookshelves before extending his arm and inviting her to sit.

"I hope you slept well," Muldoon said. "We have quite a bit of ground to cover."

Effie took a seat at the table and tucked her slippered feet beneath her chair. She eyed the stack of books warily, thick spines of crimson, brown, and gold lined up in a perfect row.

Muldoon's upper lip twitched as he clocked her trepidation. "Before we begin, I'll need to assess your deficits. Are you literate?"

The insinuation banished all lingering embarrassment from Effie's mind. Offense, as it turned out, made a potent balm. Muldoon's eyebrows drifted up his brow as he awaited an answer to the perfunctory question.

"You mean *word* reading?" Effie crossed her eyes and dangled her tongue from the side of her mouth. "Goodness! I only know how to spell my name and count as high as my fingers and toes." She stared at her open hands, feigning confusion.

Muldoon bent his head to her. "It's a reasonable question. I'm only trying to determine where to begin."

Effie dropped the dopey performance. "And I know the difference between *what is said* and *what is meant*."

A wry smile quirked the Patrician's lips. "Fair enough." Muldoon raised his hands in surrender, then indicated the tower of books. "If you can read, we'll start right in with the course of study."

Effie's eyes drifted back to the tower. "That's quite the course you've charted."

"Our host expects you to demonstrate proficiency in the Six Academic

Graces—the same disciplines taught at the Collegium, and at every Celestial school in the sky, for that matter. Civics, history, geography, physics, literature, and mathematics."

"We can skip the last one," Effie said. "I can already do sums by hand and keep books with an abacus and a table."

"Is that right?"

Effie nodded with increasing confidence. "Since I was ten."

"How's your facility with polynomial algebra?" Muldoon asked.

"Poly-what, now?"

"What about your trigonometry and your polyadic logic? Can you perform transformations in three dimensions or complete a geometric construction using only a protractor and a compass?"

Effie shook her head from side to side. "You're saying a lot of words..."

Muldoon leaned over the table. "Mathematics encompasses a whole world beyond those sums you're so proud of. And those multiplication tables you've been using as a crutch? They won't be permitted in this study. You're to memorize them, or else master a method for performing them by hand." Muldoon ran one finger along the tower of books and drew out a dun gold text. He tossed the book in front of Effie with a *thud.*

Principles of Higher Maths, Effie read, *by Nichomedes.* She flipped through, scanning page after page adorned with long strings of numbers, letters, and other symbols stranger still. When she looked up at Muldoon, he was standing over her with arms crossed, looking smug.

"This entire book's about math?"

He nodded gravely. "I'll order the second volume down from Aquilon once you're done."

Muldoon proceeded to walk her through each text one by one. She'd have reading assignments to complete ahead of each lecture, with every day of the week dedicated to a particular subject. Oral examinations would be conducted at regular intervals to ascertain her progress. By the time he worked his way to the bottom of the tower, Effie's head was so full of new terminology and names that she thought she might faint.

Muldoon was excitedly describing a volume of Toranese history when a firm knock at the study door interrupted him. She saw the irritation plain on his expression as they both turned to discover Sire Ansel in his leather riding clothes.

"Can we help you, Governor?" Muldoon asked, sounding not-at-all-willing to help.

Ansel snorted derisively. "*Jokai fend*, man—you've been cloistered away in here for half the day."

"That's how studying works," Muldoon said, impatiently tapping his foot.

Ansel dismissed him with a wave of his meaty hand. "I came here to speak with Miss Strait." Effie perked up at the sound of her name, and Ansel looked pleased to draw her attention. "I wanted to invite you to join me on my afternoon ride. Surely some time with the mares will be a welcome respite from all this sophistry." He scanned the room, wrinkling his nose as if he smelled something foul.

Effie looked from Ansel to Muldoon, who was now standing rigid with his jaw working back and forth. She got the unsettling sense she'd become enmeshed in some kind of tug-of-war between the two Patrician lords, and unfortunately it seemed like she was the rope.

Turning back to Ansel, she bowed her head respectfully. "It is a kind offer, but as you can see, I'm beset by my studies. I can't imagine I'll have the time to tend to your mares. Not now or ever."

Ansel clearly hadn't come prepared for rejection. His posture deflated as if he'd been poked with a rapier. His face began to redden as he looked from Effie, seated at his study table, to Muldoon standing over her.

"You heard Miss Strait, Governor." Muldoon sounded positively gleeful. "Her Lightness wouldn't look kindly upon any interruption to her studies."

Ansel bared his teeth at Muldoon as a shiver of rage passed over him. He glowered down at Effie. "This is your wish, then?"

Effie affected a perfect guileless smile. "It is, Sire."

A short vein throbbed in the governor's forehead. He huffed once, then turned on his heels to exit the study.

"And Ansel—" Muldoon called after him. The governor paused in the doorway to glance back over his broad shoulder. "Do close the door on your way out."

Grumbling, Ansel slammed the door so hard that dust shook from the tops of his bookshelves.

Effie felt a brief kindling of petty pride, but when she turned back to Muldoon, the wild expression on the Patrician's face made her instantly numb. Her curt dismissal of the governor's invitation clearly amused him, but his cold smile dripped with more cruelty than mirth.

She'd been quick to dismiss her sister's warning, but every line of that grinning face begged a second judgment. Suddenly, Effie wished she *had* accepted Ansel's invitation. It seemed safer than remaining trapped with his man.

Muldoon must have noticed her unease, because he quickly restored his teacherly mask. "What's wrong?" he asked.

Effie looked down at her hands, felt herself shrinking into her seat. "It's nothing..."

Muldoon tapped his small strip of goatee. He pulled out the chair opposite Effie and took a seat so that they shared a level. "It is a sacred relationship between a pupil and her tutor," he said. "If this is going to work out, we need to be honest with one another."

Honest? The irony of that word restored Effie's faculties as well as her temper. She slowly lifted her chin. Muldoon met her judgment placidly.

"My sister warned me about you," Effie said.

Muldoon blinked. "Did she now?"

Effie nodded slowly. "I believe you two met on Aeolus? She didn't come away with a very high impression of you."

If the accusation bothered Muldoon, he didn't show it. He rather seemed introspective, drumming his fingers atop the leather spine of a history book. At last, he sighed. "I was wondering when this would come up."

His response momentarily disarmed her. Effie had expected a denial— or at least some dissembling rationalization. This reaction seemed more like a tacit admission of guilt.

"I'm afraid your sister and I met under tender circumstances," Muldoon prefaced.

"You were imprisoned."

He dipped his chin in confirmation. "My manse had been ransacked by pirates. I'd been locked away for a fortnight when your sister arrived with the Volturnian dragoons. It pains me to recount the circumstances of my capture. The pirates did not handle me gently. I was beaten. Starved. Forced to live in squalor without a bath or a latrine."

Effie cringed.

"Yes." Muldoon acknowledged her disgust. "It was all quite unsavory.

As you can likely imagine, your sister found me in a state of considerable distress. Even so, the way I spoke to her was unworthy, a poor representation of my character and class. Your sister could have handled the situation better, but that doesn't forgive my behavior. I regret it, and I am sorry."

The description of Muldoon's tribulations horrified Effie, but it was the apology that truly stunned her. She'd never heard the like forthcoming from any Patrician lord—certainly not from Sire Ansel. Effie searched his bearing for any overt signs of deception.

It wasn't hard to imagine such a difficult time might put a man out of his right mind—especially one so accustomed to gentility like a Patrician lord.

"Vanna can be rigid..." Effie allowed.

Muldoon's almond eyes softened, questing to draw her back. "Will you permit me the opportunity to demonstrate my true character, Miss Strait? A clean slate."

Stunned a second time by the request, Effie could only stammer, "Of course, Sire." She was surprised to find how much she meant it. Everything would be so much easier if Muldoon wasn't the monster Vanna feared. She'd be stuck with this man for better or worse, and she desperately needed to believe that he was good.

He had already shown a capacity for humility uncommon among his peers. Effie would show him her character in turn. A clean slate. She, at least, had the grace to grant such an anodyne request.

"It's Effie," she finally said. "No more of this 'Miss Strait' nonsense. The servants are already driving me insane."

"As you wish—Effie." Muldoon straightened in his chair, adjusting his jerkin as he did so. "In the spirit of your tutelage, you may drop the honorific in this study. No more 'Sire.' Muldoon will suffice. And *please* extend my apologies to your sister."

"That's a noble gesture," Effie said.

"One long overdue. I've heard things, as well..."

Effie perked up and found Muldoon's practiced smile awaiting her.

He winked. "I wouldn't want to make an enemy of Vanna Strait."

10

KAI

The dragoons regrouped back at the Avernian barracks. The combined wing packed inside Taros' command center at the back of the bunkhouse, leaving barely enough standing room for Kai to breathe. He shuffled awkwardly, attempting to carve out space to match his size, but as soon as a vacuum opened, Seulin glided in to fill it. Giving up, he leaned back against the fresh timbers of the bunkhouse wall.

Everything in Avernus glowed with the flush of youth. It made the village seem bright by comparison to ancient Volturnus, but Kai knew the Avernians had paid for its fresh sheen in blood. Years ago, Maug the Butcher's relentless bombardment reduced the Old Village to ash and ember. The Avernians picked a new site to rebuild, and now the freshness of every timber offered fell reminder of those dark days.

Every islander in the archipelago had reason to dread the return of a Leviathan pirate—the Avernians, perhaps, most of all.

The pommel of Dray's sword clipped Kai in the chin as the ranking flier pushed his way to the front to join the command table at Kendy's right hand. Seulin caught Kai scowling and rubbing his face.

Chuckling, she poked him in the ribs with her elbow. "Not his fault you're built like a hemlock."

Kai took the insult in stride. She could mock him all she wanted; his height had its advantages. Among the junior fliers pushed to the edges of the summit, he was the only one with an unobstructed view.

Kendy and Taros appeared to be arguing as they pored over a sky chart that one of them had tacked to the table. Kendy pointed emphatically at two regions of open sky between the isles, circling each one over and over as they talked. Dray forced his way into the discussion, looking eager to catch himself up. When Taros turned to speak with his lieutenant, Dray leaned over to Kendy and whispered something in his ear.

Kendy nodded and began to rise, but Taros stopped him with a hand on his shoulder. Kendy seemed momentarily dismayed, but he ultimately yielded the floor. They were guests here, after all.

Taros stood up and scanned the assembled dragoons. When he spoke, he projected his voice so the fliers in the back like Kai could hear him clearly. "Our investigation has borne fruit. Two teams of fliers at the port collected corroborating accounts of wreckage in the vicinity of the leeward skerries. The region doesn't intersect the Aeolian zeppelin's planned path of approach, but we must operate under the assumption that some unknown influence pushed them off course. Moreover, a merchant sailor testifies that a Gifted scout among his crew spotted a burning vessel around the time the Aeolian zeppelin disappeared."

At that report, anxious murmuring rippled around the room. Some dragoons still clung to hope that the zeppelin would turn up intact with its passengers unmolested. Kai wasn't so naive.

"Why didn't they attempt a rescue?" The question piped out of a young Avernian flier standing across the room.

Taros acknowledged him. "The merchant crew claims they thought it was a wraith. They took it for an ill omen and adjusted their course to avoid the apparition."

The grumbling from the dragoons turned sour.

"Superstitious bastards," Seulin muttered.

"More like cowards," Kai whispered back.

Kendy leaned over to receive another message from Dray, and with Commander Taros' permission, he granted his acting lieutenant the floor.

Dray was built like a golden yak. He had to clip the sleeves of his flight suit just to accommodate his muscular arms. At the head of the gathering, he cut a more powerful image than either Kendy or Taros, but he wasn't half as practiced at projecting his voice. Kai strained to hear him. "My team at the quarry picked up another rumor that might be relevant. The haulers claim a Leviathan pirate's been preying on ships out of Grenport."

"He could have mentioned that I collected the report," Kai grumbled.

Seulin rolled her eyes as the murmurs grew to a crescendo. Kai only caught bits and pieces, but one name bubbled up from multiple tongues.

"From their description—" Dray raised his voice, fighting the chatter, "—it doesn't sound like Devil Ray. That doesn't mean we can be any less vigilant. The Butcher is hardly the only Leviathan pirate who poses a danger to the archipelago."

Kendy tapped him on the arm and motioned for him to take his seat. He untacked his sky chart from the table and stood up next to Taros.

"We'll divide into drafts and canvass the area surrounding the skerries. It will be a hard day of flying, with few places to put down along the way. Anyone who doesn't feel up to it may elect to remain on Avernus, no questions asked."

He unfurled the map again and held it high for the whole room to see. Kai squinted at the sky chart, leaning as far forward as the crowd permitted. He barely made out a red wax line encircling a vast expanse of sky south-south-west of Avernus.

"What is it?" Seulin whispered. "Can't see a damn thing over all these ogres."

"It's a whole lotta sky," Kai answered.

"Real helpful."

Commander Taros dismissed the corps but remained behind with leadership to iron out the details of their plan. The rest of the dragoons dispersed to spend the night quartered in the New Village.

Kai woke up early and arrived at the leeward landing before dawn. The mission drew even more fliers than left Volturnus. All twenty-seven of the Volturnian dragoons answered the call, as did an additional fifteen from Avernus. With so many bodies, they'd be able to cover the entire expanse in a day.

Kai and Seulin were reassigned to Dray's command with responsibility for forty square leagues of open sky.

"Conserve your strength," Dray cautioned. "This won't be like the crossing to Avernus. No telling how long we'll be airborne—or what we'll encounter while we're up there."

He armed each flier in his draft with an alchemical flare gun. "Strap these to your flight suits. You see anything—wreckage, survivors, unusual debris—you fire three flares straight overhead for maximum loft. Check your trajectory first to make sure you don't hit anyone."

Kai stared at the alchemical gun in his palm. He'd never used one before, but the tool looked simple enough. Only button was the trigger. He felt Dray's hand return to the barrel of his gun and press it forcefully against his chest. "Don't point it at anyone," he chastised.

Kai felt color rising in his cheeks. He nodded and quickly clipped the flare gun to his belt as Dray moved on down the line.

They took off with their backs to the rising sun. About an hour out from the Avernian shore, their draft picked up an unfriendly headwind. Kai leaned heavily on his Gift to maintain velocity, and the resulting turbulence shook him out of formation more than once. Dray eventually flashed the air-sign for ascent and drew them upward until they found a smoother altitude.

Exhaustion had already begun to creep inside Kai's bones by the time they reached the search area. After another hour of fruitless flight, they sighted a small barren skerry a few degrees off their formation's starboard side, and Dray flashed the sign to put down. Kai was so winded by the time his feet touched the ground that he went down to one knee, bent over and gasping. The other fliers looked just as expended. Raji collapsed flat on his back, and Seulin biffed her landing, leaden legs unable to hold her weight. Only Dray and Maya looked like they had any steam left in their valves.

Dray walked immediately up to the edge of the island and scanned the horizon. By the time he was finished, Kai had nearly regained his breath. He forced himself to stand tall, even though his muscles screamed for mercy. The rest of the draft remained collapsed on the ground.

"Weather's not doing us any favors," Dray said. "Anybody see anything?"

The exhausted dragoons all shook their heads.

"*Balls of the deep*," Dray cursed. "Still got a lot of sky to cover." He looked around at his sorry draft, a scowl twisting his craggy face. "You're all pushing too hard!" he shouted. "Didn't I warn you? How the hell do you plan to get back to Avernus if you're already tapped out? *Jokai-damned fledglings*." He spat on the ground.

Maya walked over and put a calming hand on his shoulder. "That isn't helpful."

Dray shrugged her off.

He wasn't wrong. Kai didn't know how much longer he could keep going at this pace. In the battle of wills between his Gift and the wild winds, the winds were gaining ground.

Shaking his head, Dray reached into his satchel and drew out a small glass vial stoppered with a wedge of cork. He held the flask to the light, revealing its purple contents.

Kai stared reverently at the glowing dram. Any Volturnian would have reacted the same. The apothecary's Nectar was the most valuable commodity the archipelago produced—almost sacred by reputation.

"I've only got the one dose," Dray said. "You'll have to share it—one swig a piece."

He uncorked the vial with his teeth and held it up to Maya, but she declined.

"Save it for the fledglings," she said.

Dray nodded and handed the vial down to Raji. The winded fliers passed the morsel of Nectar around, each taking their sacrament in turn. When Seulin finally pressed the vial into Kai's hand, there was barely a drop left clinging to the bottom.

Kai tipped the vial into his mouth and chased the last remnants with his tongue. The effect was instantaneous. The rumbling in his stomach stilled, and the canteen strapped to his hip seemed suddenly beside the point. Trembling muscles hardened with newfound strength, and he sensed a burning abundance returning to his overtaxed Gift. The colors of the wind swelled around him, profoundly vibrant.

The draft gathered themselves up from the ground, fresher than before they took off. Dray looked satisfied by the returns, but only grudgingly so.

"It won't last," he cautioned. "But it should be enough to finish the job and get us all back to Avernus."

Dray broke the draft down into pairs and assigned each team an altitude to scan along the geodesic. He sketched out the search plan on a sky chart, but with so few points of reference in the open sky, Kai lacked the navigation ability to make much sense of it. He followed Maya, who at least seemed to know where she was going.

They zigzagged for hours at a level 300 feet below the meridian. The skerries surfaced at unusual altitudes, so they had to conduct their search in three dimensions. Throughout it all, Kai felt the Nectar burning in his veins. So bolstered, not even the stiffest headwind could deter him.

He felt the first signs of the Nectar's ebb in the tendons of his legs. He relied increasingly on the natural currents to hold him aloft, reducing the pressure on his Gift so that he might conserve his strength for the journey back. Just as he arrived at a new equilibrium, he saw Maya pull up on a gust and visor her hand, staring westward into the sun. He tapped his Gift to perform a matching maneuver and tracked her line of sight.

Three twinkling flares climbed the horizon, burning brilliantly at the apex of their arch.

Kai glided toward Maya until they were close enough to speak over the howling winds.

"They've got something," she said.

"How far out?" he asked. Kai lacked the experience to accurately judge distances in the open sky. He still had so much to learn.

Maya bracketed a hand over the sun's white orb, then slowly shifted it down to the nearest shoreline. "Five leagues, give or take. Hard to say what altitude. Let's track it from the meridian."

Kai tapped out a salute and followed Maya into her climb.

11

KAI

The rest of the draft caught the same signal from their respective vantages. They all fell into formation along the way. Dray's team was among the last of the dragoons to converge around a canted skerry thick with low brush. Kai first sighted the signal fire burning on the island's surface, then the barrage of dragoons dropping from the sky.

They'd found something, all right. The surface swarmed with bedraggled Zephyri.

Shambolic bodies encircled the dragoons as they landed. Kai put down just outside a writhing mass of clutching limbs. He shared a grave look with Seulin as they both followed Dray into the mix.

Kai attempted to track the survivors he passed, but quickly lost count. He saw burn scars and puncture wounds—traumatic injury of every shape. He caught a glimpse of an amputated limb and quickly averted his eyes. So many injured—a few too grievously to stand. Those who still had the strength clustered around the dragoons, voices raised in desperate chorus. Kai passed a young woman with a missing ear clutching two young children against her sides.

Kai broke away from the group and knelt to offer his canteen. She tearfully accepted and dribbled the first sips into each child's mouth before drinking herself.

He spoke softly only after they had been fortified. "It's all right. We're here to help."

The young woman sobbed with wordless gratitude.

"You're from Aeolus?" he asked.

She sniffed and nodded.

"Were you aboard the zeppelin bound for the Ascension?"

Another stuttering nod. Her green eyes looked so hollow and distant. Kai almost couldn't bear the sight of them. She tried to return his canteen, but he pressed it back into her hands.

"Keep it," he told her. "I'll be back soon."

He left to find Kendy, who was standing beside Taros and Dray, deep in discussion with a group of dragoons that emerged from the band of survivors. Kai recognized the West Wind patch of Aeolus on a few battered flight suits—and the face of one man wearing an East Wind patch, the perfect twin to his own.

Prestor.

Prestor and Hal had been aboard the zeppelin. The two veteran fliers had been part of an earlier mission to Aeolus. Kai didn't know the details other than the fact that Hal had been injured, and the two had stayed behind to keep the peace.

"...thank the Jokai you found us." Prestor's voice sounded brittle, on the verge of crumbling to dust. His flight suit was torn in three places, and a blue-green welt mottled one side of an exposed arm. "Three days we've been living off what little forage this skerry provides. There's a freshwater pond on the other side of the briar, but we've nearly drunk it dry."

"What happened here?" Taros demanded. Kai didn't care for the harshness in his tone.

Prestor's eyes jumped like a frightened rabbit. "Pirates," he said. "Scouts spotted a hostile craft as soon as we left Aeolian airspace. The zeppelin's captain adjusted our course to avoid confrontation, but the pirates pursued. It's like they were *looking* for us." Prestor's eyes drifted a thousand leagues away, and his lower lip began to tremble.

"Look at me, Prestor. What manner of craft were these pirates flying?" Kendy spoke soft and steady, and Kai privately hoped the contrast might shame Taros into improving his temperament, though the Avernian commander looked unmoved.

Prestor's focus tunneled around his commander's eyes. He struggled to find his voice again.

Kendy rested a bracing hand on Prestor's shoulder. "What you've been through—it must have been awful. I can only imagine. But we need to know."

"It was a Leviathan," Prestor said. "*Jokai fend*, I can still see those pitiless red eyes—"

"What *breed* of Leviathan," Taros demanded.

Prestor flinched, then shook his head from side to side in a daze as if he'd been struck in truth. His voice returned to him in a panicked surge. "A demonic serpent with a head like a bleached skull! It *struck* the zeppelin, Kendy. Its jaws tore through the envelope, and pirates flooded the breach. We were boarded before anyone could reach the lifeboats."

Taros muttered something under his breath that Kai couldn't hear.

"The dragoons," Prestor continued. "W-we tried to save as many civilians as we could carry, but it all happened so fast. Blades flashing everywhere. Pistols firing. I could feel the zeppelin losing altitude. I-I grabbed two twin girls in my arms and flew them to the skerry..." His haunted eyes lost focus, began to drift over Kendy's shoulder. "They had a brother with them—an older brother. He was standing right there. But I couldn't carry them all. I couldn't carry him..."

It was all too much. Kai wanted to weep for what Prestor had endured. Instead, he hoped his stoicism might burnish this broken man—his brother, now—against the horror that had been thrust upon him.

"These people are all starving—dehydrated." Taros' voice carried the cadence of accusation. "Why didn't you fly for help?"

It took every ounce of Kai's restraint not to cuff the Avernian commander in the face.

"No one left is in any condition to make the crossing," Prestor said. "And we couldn't just abandon these people—we couldn't abandon anyone *else*."

"What do you mean, 'no one left'?" Kendy asked.

"Commander Halle took a small draft back to Aeolus," Prestor said. "They went to gather a fleet of kite-ships to rescue us, but they've been gone for days."

Kendy nodded. "Then help should be on the way. We can count on Halle." He turned to Dray. "Send the dragoons out among the survivors.

Find anyone with injuries requiring immediate attention. Tell the corps to distribute their rations and canteens—starting with the children."

"Aye." Dray tapped out a salute, but his eyes lingered on Prestor, even as he turned to carry out Kendy's order.

Kendy surveyed the survivors, already clustering around the scattered dragoons. His expression slowly darkened as he turned back to Prestor. "Where's Hal?"

Kai didn't think that Prestor's gaze could become any more distant, but the question pushed him even farther away.

"Prestor..." Kendy prompted.

"I-I saw him," Prestor said. "I saw him as I carried the twins through the breach. He was fighting off three pirates at once—and he was *winning*. Hal was always so good with a sword...but he couldn't windshape. He wasn't strong enough in the Gift. He wouldn't have been able to escape the wreck."

Kai watched his commander deflate before his eyes. He understood the feeling, for Prestor's words shook him to his very core. He knew dragoon work could be dangerous, but the Volturnian corps hadn't lost a man in action since the Butcher's terrible reign. Fourteen years of peace wiped away in an instant.

Death had returned to the archipelago—once again carried on Leviathan wings.

Dray clipped Kai with his shoulder as he passed, shaking him from his trance. "Come on," he said. "You heard the commander. Let's see these people watered and fed as best we can."

The Avernian and Volturnian dragoons tended the survivors to the best of their limited abilities. Nayla and Kendahl carried trauma kits on behalf of each corps, but their spare furnishings offered little comfort to the more grievously injured. Once all the rations had been distributed and the canteens drunk dry, Kai spotted Prestor sitting by the signal fire next to two young girls—no older than five or six. The twins stared blankly into the fire as Prestor coaxed them to eat the last remnants of a jerky stick.

It was difficult to tell if Prestor wanted company, but Kai went to him anyway. He sat beside him and quietly stared into the crackling flame.

After a long time, one of the twins' eyes became heavy. She curled up against Prestor's thigh and drifted off to sleep. Prestor gently stroked her thin, red hair, still watching the fire blankly.

"Sun's going down," he said.

Kai perked up, surprised to hear the man's voice after so much despondent silence.

"You should all head back to Avernus," Prestor continued.

"No one's going anywhere," Kai said. "We'll wait for Halle's kite-ships with the rest of you."

Prestor swallowed, still staring into the fire. He didn't speak again until the western horizon drank up the last sip of dying sun. "Everything changes now..." he murmured. Both girls were now sleeping against his leg.

Kai didn't know what to say. No words he could offer seemed likely to meet the moment. Companionship was all he had to give, and so he stayed, staring into the fire next to Prestor as the rest of the dragoons moved about the skerry, discussing plans to attack the coming day.

The last lingering effects of the Nectar vanished from Kai's system, and exhaustion returned with bitter interest. Kai didn't realize he had fallen asleep until a thrumming sound awakened him with a sudden jab. The choppy noise blanketed the skerry, battering his eardrums and vibrating his chest.

Another day had dawned over the archipelago. Prestor and the twins were gone, off to join the gathering at the edge of the skerry where the carvel hull of a massive airship approached from the western sky.

The ship's propellers filled the air with their white churn, drowning out the sounds of all the desperate survivors flooding the shore. Kai had never seen such a vessel—twice the size of the largest zeppelin, powered by steam and six square sails billowing from three masts, each thicker than the trunks of the oldest Volturnian trees. Two banners hung from the mainmast: an ax and sword over a dark red field and the curling West Wind of Aeolus.

Kai dusted the signal fire's dying ash from his flight suit and jogged out to the western shoreline to join the others. He spotted Seulin standing amid a small group of Volturnian fliers, looking up at the approaching craft in shared awe.

"What is it?" Kai asked.

Seulin shook her head. "Never seen it's like."

"That's an Armada ship," Maya said as she slipped in between them. "A Celestial galleon. Kelestina's called in the aero-marines."

Kai's eyes widened with renewed awe as he glanced back at the galleon's approach.

The airship's wide hull descended through the open sky, growing by inches and feet, threatening to crush the brittle skerry beneath its girth. Before the vessel impacted the shore, it cut its propellers and dropped its sails, restoring the skerry to relative silence.

Ropes and ladders launched over bulkheads, catching ground with grappling spikes. With a gaseous hiss, a gangplank separated from the hull on steam-powered valves. Soldiers in Armada-blue uniforms streamed onto the island from the ladders and ropes.

"Look!" Seulin grabbed Kai's arm and pointed at the crow's nest atop the mizzenmast. Four dragoons leapt from that perch, gliding down to the skerry just ahead of the first soldiers to make ground. Kai saw a middle-aged flier with short pink hair soaring along a narrow arc. She landed with a powerful gust and made a beeline for Kendy and Taros. He felt Seulin and Maya peeling away and followed them to join the rest of the gathering wing.

The pink-haired flier was apparently the Wing Commander of the Aeolian Dragoons. Kai overheard bits and pieces of her exchange with the officers from the other islands.

"...just sorry it took so long," Halle said.

"You're here now," Kendy clapped a hand on her shoulder. "That's what matters."

"And you brought the Armada," Taros added.

"About that..." Halle's voice got lost in the renewed commotion as a formation of soldiers marched down the gangplank, leading a brown-skinned woman with stark blonde hair tied up in a circlet braid. Kai saw flashes of a Patrician suit beneath her long, gray peacoat. He thought he knew all the archipelago's Patricians at a glance, but he didn't recognize this one.

The woman's honor guard cut a swathe through the huddled mass of survivors and dragoons. She stopped suddenly, halting the soldiers, and scanned the faces crowding around. Her soldiers kept everyone at a distance with long bayonets capping the ends of their flintlock rifles.

The Patrician spread her arms, parting the open lapels of her peacoat. Kai noted the hilt of a short sword strapped to her belt. It was even more unusual to see a Patrician carrying open arms, but Kai supposed these strange circumstances called for caution.

All eyes turned inward as the Patrician spoke. "Don't be afraid of the aero-marines. They're here for your protection." Her toneless rasp made Kai's hair stand on end. "My name is Dama Sigyn of Jarvik—Governor Sigyn to many of you. I've only recently arrived to accept my commission."

A new Governor of Aeolus. The appointment was well timed and long overdue.

"Commander Halle informed me of the trials you all faced. You must be very brave to have survived such an encounter. You're safe now." Sigyn's slit nostrils flared as she scanned the haggard faces hovering beyond her soldiers' bayonets. "I understand my predecessor lost your trust. That's regrettable. Know that it is my intention to serve faithfully as your lord and protector. I make each of you this promise: no man, woman, or child of the Aeolian plebiscite will ever need to fear such brazen acts of piracy—not while I occupy the governor's seat. I only regret that I was not called to this position sooner. If it had been so, this tragedy might well have been avoided."

Kai heard whispers of prayerful gratitude bubbling up from the crowd. *About time* and *Jokai bless.* A few of the survivors began to weep.

"The wounded will be cared for aboard my flagship—the *Jormung-hast*," Sigyn said. "We've got food and water waiting below deck. I will see you returned to Aeolus by day's end. As for this Leviathan raider..." Her golden eyes hardened as she gripped the hilt of her sword. "I vow to you that I will see him destroyed or else driven from our skies for good."

The grateful outpouring turned to cheers of acclimation.

It was quite the speech, Kai had to admit. Exactly what these trauma-tized people needed to hear.

So, why was he so unsettled?

12

EFFIE

The first days of Effie's course of study challenged and overwhelmed her, but in the best possible way.

They began with a geographic survey of the Doric Sky, followed by an introduction to early Toranese history and her first frustrating foray into the world of symbolic algebra. Muldoon moved quickly through his lectures. He assigned hundreds of pages of text each night, which he expected her to retain and synthesize with his lessons. Most nights, she fell asleep over her desk with a leather-bound book as her pillow.

It all seemed very disjointed at the outset—the way Muldoon lurched from one subject to the next—but by the end of her first week, Effie was beginning to see the dim outlines of a higher order. The Six Academic Graces seemed so disparate at first, but they complemented each other in surprising ways.

Geography was destiny in the Doric Sky. The pre-Celestial history of the Toranese city-states had been shaped by their positions on the continent—their access and exposure to the open skies, as well as to each other. The physical laws she'd only begun to digest determined how easily far-flung isles could gain access to the wider world, and the algebraic formulas she was still struggling to decode unlocked a greater understanding of their relative economies and needs.

The enormity of the task consumed her mind as well as her time.

Effie had hoped to see Vanna more often than she did. Despite her alleged freedom, her studies kept her functionally confined to Ansel's manse. She made a point to roam the grounds every evening just to get some fresh air, but she hadn't ventured beyond the hilltop since her first trip to the cottage to pack. She caught Ansel's eye once during her daily constitutional. Even from a distance, she felt him tracking her from his perch atop Cloudcutter. Beyond that uncomfortable close encounter, the governor seemed determined to avoid her entirely, which was just as well.

Effie almost felt guilty for her earlier efforts to manipulate him. She'd spent so much time fawning over his stuck-up mares—feigning admiration, perhaps too convincingly. Her sudden change of heart likely revealed the ruse, and that must burn for a man like Ansel. Each time she felt herself creeping toward the edge of true remorse, however, Effie remembered that the governor *hadn't* included her on his list. She'd had to take matters into her own hands. If Ansel now had to live with the knowledge that he'd been played, that was all to the good. He deserved to be taken down a peg or two.

With the first week of her studies drawing to a close, Effie arrived at the study to find Muldoon unloading a wooden crate of heavy frames and parchment scrolls. One of those scrolls was already unfurled across the table, its edges pinned down with glass weights. She saw genuine excitement alight in Muldoon's eyes as he waved for her to join him, his boyish grin so unlike his typical smile, which always seemed half a smirk.

The scroll turned out to be an intricate sky chart that stretched the entire width of the table. Effie squinted as she studied the complex navigation symbols painted across the lined map in various colored inks. She'd been through several sky charts in her geography text—had already started to learn the expansive alphabet of navigation symbols utilized by the Crystal Throne—but this chart was an order of magnitude more complex than anything she'd encountered yet.

She quickly recognized the shape of the Doric Sky, bounded on its eastern edge by the Caliban Range and on its western edge by the continent of Toran. A continent, she'd learned, was much like an island, only larger. So large, in fact, that its proportions boggled the mind. Her eyes quickly found the Zephyr Archipelago in the northeast quadrant of the map, an insignificant collection of dust set against the grandeur of the open sky. You would need to gather 100 archipelagos in one contiguous blob just to cover but a fraction of Toran's landmass. Effie's mind struggled to conceive of what life would be like on such a massive world—to journey 1,000 leagues without ever finding open sky.

Beyond the identifiable features, the map was a challenge to read. None of the islands were labeled, their shorelines highlighted in a variety of tints. A grid of intersecting lines overlaid the chart, every section of open sky inundated with crosses and arrows of blue and red that swirled in erratic patterns.

Effie looked up at Muldoon. "Not a very useful map, is it?"

His brow furrowed quizzically. "Why would you say that?"

"It's all blank." Effie ran one palm over the map's face. "It's pretty enough, but a sky chart's only as good as it's key."

"It has a key." Muldoon pointed at a small box in the corner, crowded with rows of navigation symbols.

Effie shook her head. "What use is a map without any names?"

"Little use, if you're sitting in your cottage daydreaming about faraway lands. Plenty, if you're piloting a Leviathan in the Celestial Armada."

Effie crossed her arms in front of her chest. "I'm pretty sure Leviathan Pilots still need to know where they're going."

Muldoon matched her pose, tapping one finger against the pleated elbow of his linen shirt. "An experienced pilot already knows where they're going. It's the *how* that more often presents a problem." He uncrossed his arms, opening both palms to the sky chart below. "This is a Navigator's Matrix—it's a specialized chart describing the character of the skies and the altitude of the islands, to the best of any flat diagram's ability."

Effie's brow furrowed as she studied the chart anew. From her readings, she recognized about half the symbols in the key. Bold lines represented altitude, color-coded to indicate inclination and declination within a small range. The arrows looked like wind vectors, but she didn't understand why some ended in standard carrots, while others drew toward X's and O's.

Muldoon retreated into his teacherly poise. "The land sets the boundaries of the navigator's task, but the winds set the terms of every decision in between. A navigator on the open sky would use a chart much like this one to plot the safest and most efficient passage between the isles."

That seemed intuitive to Effie on its face, but nonsensical upon further inspection. "But the winds are always changing..." she ventured.

"You're thinking of the weather—and yes, the weather has many changeable moods to which a Pilot must remain responsive—but the higher altitudes accessed by airships and Leviathan are dominated by prevailing currents generated by stellar procession and the rotation of Ciel itself. These winds do shift seasonally, but predictably." Muldoon tapped a golden diamond at the top of the map's key. "This notation tells us we're looking at an Autumnal Variation—the prevailing currents between the Harvest Ides and Wolf's Calends."

Prevailing currents... Vanna used to speak of this phenomenon in the context of dragoon operations. Certain seasons brought better conditions for transit east and west between the isles of the archipelago. This sky chart told Effie how much more complex these considerations became on the grand scale of the Doric Sky.

"If you're keeping up with the geography text," Muldoon said, "you should be able to identify the Bolkan Isles at a glance."

Effie's eyes crawled the map until she found a large archipelago bounded by two long barrier islands on its southern edge—a few hundred leagues north-north-east of Toran. She pointed confidently, and Muldoon rewarded her with an approving nod.

"Very good," he said. "You see how the longer vectors converge and twist toward the barrier islands in the south. Then these, originating in the Gulf of Hellicon, run counter to the prevailing winds. What are these notations telling us?"

"That it's easier to approach the Bolkans from the south and east than the north and west?"

"Yes." Muldoon pointed at a row of black lines ending in X's. "But these vectors here warn that cyclones organizing in the Brundisian lees are likely to be drawn up toward the barrier islands. Another factor for any pilot to consider."

They spent several hours poring over the sky chart together, breaking down the map's symbology and applying various conditions to hypothetical scenarios. By the end, Effie saw the sky chart in a new light. What once had been an inscrutable drawing now seemed crammed with invaluable insight.

"What about the highlighting around the islands," she asked as they were nearing their break for lunch. "I think those are altitude lines." Now that she looked more closely at the blank landmasses, she realized the chart looked much more crowded than the ones she'd encountered in her text.

"It's a keen observation," Muldoon said. "The topic's a bit far afield of our lesson today, but since you're curious: there's a fatal flaw at the heart of modern cartography. Our world exists in three spatial dimensions, and any effort to transform a three-dimensional object onto a two-dimensional scroll requires some deformation."

Effie thought she could see where this was leading. According to her text, the vast majority of Ciel's landmass surfaced at a common altitude—the Prime Meridian, in navigator's parlance. That accounted for most of the major islands—the Zephyr Archipelago, Grenport, Vangulmark—even Toran. It didn't account for everything, though.

"How do cartographers handle islands that surface at an unusual altitude?" Effie asked.

"Therein lies the conundrum," Muldoon said. "Most sky charts simply display the meridian altitude, but that only gives us a very specific slice of Ciel. A good Navigation Matrix attempts to account for the missing islands with altitude highlights. You see this island here?" He pointed at a small island shaped like a crescent outlined in dark green. "The colored border tells us that it surfaces 1,000 to 3,000 feet above the meridian. But even a well-made matrix like this one has its limitations." He pointed back to the key. "Here the cartographer tells us that he's only captured the islands that surface within 5,000 feet of the meridian, on either side."

"There are islands more than 5,000 feet off the meridian?" It seemed inconceivable. Effie already knew from her first physics lessons the incredible challenges posed by operating at such great heights or crushing depths.

Muldoon's smile regained that smirking quality she'd come to loathe. "My dear girl—there are stranger things in the skies of Ciel than you could even dream of."

They concluded half-past the lunch bell, and Muldoon began to pack up his crate.

"What else you got in the box?" Effie asked, curious eyes creeping over its rim to count the many furled scrolls within.

"My personal collection," he said, clutching the crate protectively from two thin handles. "Finally returned from Aquilon. Rare maps are an interest of mine. I...collect them. As a hobby." He seemed ashamed of the admission and quickly changed the subject. "I'll see you at the Moonday feast this evening?"

Effie had almost forgotten. Governor Ansel hosted a weekly feast that

Muldoon and Effie were expected to attend. "What happens if I decline?" she asked.

Muldoon looked jestingly aghast. "You wouldn't dare leave me alone with these people. Don't forget, I'm the one who controls your syllabus. I'd find a way to make you pay."

He winked over his box of maps.

Effie decided not to incur the wrath of her tutor. She donned one of the silk dresses from Kelestina's armoire and allowed a matronly handmaid to curl a wave into her hair and apply her make-up. The feast began promptly at Seventh Bell in Ansel's formal dining room.

Effie was seated beside Sire Muldoon, who looked especially dashing in a long-tailed coat and satin cravat. She did wonder how he planned to keep the flamboyant ruffles at the ends of his sleeve from dragging through the gravy, however. A visiting merchant from Grenport sat opposite them, beady eyes surveying the profligate platters of food with eager interest. Ansel occupied a high-backed chair at the head of the table, still pointedly avoiding any eye contact with Effie.

Six different servants tended the feast, Ina among them. The familiar face was a welcome addition to the stiff meal. Effie hadn't seen her around the manse since her arrival, and she was starting to grow concerned. She tried to catch her eye as Ina moved through the dining room, replacing the appetizer course with trays of meat, roasted potatoes, and fine cheese.

"I hope you're feeling better," Effie said.

Ina hadn't expected the direct address. She nearly dropped the empty platter she was carrying. "Yes, Miss—err—Effie. Much better."

Muldoon watched Effie curiously as she leaned back in her chair to hold Ina's attention. "Not that I've been unhappy with the other staff, but I would like to see you around my chamber again—if that's possible? Feels more like home." She hoped the warmth of her smile might thaw Ina's stiff composure, but the girl only seemed to grow more rigid at the request.

"I understand," Ina said. "I'll see what I can do."

Effie watched her scurry from the dining room as fast as she could respectfully escape. When she turned back to the table, she found Ansel glowering at her over a forkful of pork loin dripping with gravy and mash.

He slowly lowered his fork, slate-gray eyes fastened on Effie. "How are you finding your accommodations, Miss Strait?"

"Um, fine," she said. The governor's eyes darkened. "Good, I mean. I am comfortable. Thank you, Sire."

Ansel turned to address his merchant guest. "Miss Strait has just begun a course of study in the Celestial method. Her tutor keeps her quite busy—and entirely to himself."

"That's a high honor." The merchant's jowls quivered as he bent his head to acknowledge Effie.

"It is," Ansel agreed. He pointed his fork at Effie. "I hadn't pegged you for such an unrelenting book worm. It would be a shame to see such a vibrant spirit *strangled* for lack of sunlight."

Muldoon dabbed at the corners of his mouth with a cloth handkerchief and interjected on her behalf. "Miss Strait is quite studious. She performs in the manner expected of a Celestial collegiate, and I am pleased to report that she exceeds my expectations at every turn." Effie beamed as Muldoon lifted his own fork to his mouth and delivered a small potato. "Not that you'd know anything about that," he added.

Ansel slammed down his elbow, shaking the table. He glared at Muldoon, who continued placidly chewing his potato without interruption. The merchant's eyes flickered nervously between the two Patricians. Effie shared in his discomfort, but hers was at least seasoned with a dash of amusement. She returned tentatively to a pile of gravied mash.

The dessert course arrived much later. Behind bowls of yellow custard, Master Granger interrupted the dinner to deliver a folded message to the head of the table. He bent to whisper something in Sire Ansel's ear as the governor scanned the missive. Ansel dismissed his butler, wiped his mouth and stood up from the table.

"You'll have to excuse me—pressing business down from Aquilon."

This drew a serious glance from Muldoon. "What's the nature?" he asked.

Ansel looked from Muldoon to his merchant guest attacking his bowl of custard like he feared it might be taken away. "Piracy in Aeolian airspace," Ansel grunted. The merchant nearly choked on his spoon. "Our newest courtier appears to be dealing with it. More, I'm afraid I cannot say."

Effie was quite certain there was plenty more that Ansel could say. Whether he *would* say it was another matter. She watched the governor scan the missive once again. "Muldoon," Ansel said. "You'll attend me in my office." It wasn't a request.

Muldoon's eyebrows crept up with interest. He slowly nodded. "Of course, Sire."

"Ina," Ansel grunted. Effie heard a squeak from the corner of the dining room. She hadn't even realized that Ina had returned, but there she stood, trying desperately to blend with the furnishings. "I'll take my dessert in my chambers after we're through." He glanced up from his missive. "Do deliver it in person."

"Yes, Sire." The tremor in Ina's voice unsettled Effie even more than the odd specificity of the request.

Nobody else in the dining room seemed to think anything of it. Muldoon excused himself and followed Ansel out. Once they were gone, Effie watched the merchant reach across the table to claim Muldoon's untouched dessert. He pumped his eyebrows at her. "More for us, eh?"

She had to sit and watch him slop down a second bowl of custard before mustering the gumption to take her leave.

As she made her way back to her chamber, Effie thought she heard someone crying down the hall. She went to investigate but only caught the backs of two livery skirts swishing quickly out of sight.

13

VANNA

"Ow."

"Quiet." Rindra, the village's senior medic, prodded Vanna's bruised ribs with two stiff fingers. It seemed a strange method of healing, but Rindra wasn't known for her bedside manner. "Swelling's come down considerably," Rindra said. "Still ugly as all nine hells, but I think we can dispense with the bandages. How's your range of motion?"

Vanna flexed her arm, rotating her shoulder in its socket. Her chest still burned as she reached maximum extension, but she nodded. "Feels better. I don't notice it as much when I sleep." Not that her sleep had improved, but there were other factors contributing to her restlessness.

"Should be good as new in another week or so," Rindra concluded, turning to make a note in her treatment journal.

"Does that mean you'll clear me for duty with Kendy?"

"I won't hold you back anymore, if that's what you're asking. When you get back to flying is up to you now. Just don't push it. Listen to your body."

Some good news, for once. Vanna leapt off the medic's table and pulled on her shirt.

"I mean it," Rindra cautioned. "You crash out, and you'll only find yourself back on my table."

Vanna already had one foot out the door. "I'll take that under advisement."

A week had passed since the dragoons flew for Avernus. They still hadn't returned, and Vanna's sour grapes over her grounding had turned to concern. If anything happened out there that she could have prevented...

She couldn't let herself think that way. She'd only spiral. Moreover, she had her own problems to deal with. She wasn't any closer to finding Bael, and her time was already up. As soon as Kendy set foot in the village, she would be forced to confess her failure. Then Kendy would go running to the governor, and Sire Ansel would turn this island upside-down. It was small comfort that Rindra deemed her back to flying form. Vanna had never felt so powerless.

She'd taken Bolo's advice and interviewed more than half the farmers living on the homesteads beyond the village walls. Unlike the port workers, the homesteaders *loved* to talk. They chewed her ear off for hours, rambling around in circles until she nearly forgot what she'd come for in the first place. The farmers thought they saw all kinds of things from their open fields. The night sky played tricks on the eyes. One man claimed he'd seen a trail of Lantern Wisps climbing the road to Widow's Peak. Another swore he'd met a flock of Avian warriors passing through on their way to join some distant siege. He even showed Vanna a long gray feather that could have come from any mangy skygull as "proof."

One story did catch Vanna's attention, if only because she heard parts of it corroborated by multiple sources. The laborers living on the orchards south of the village testified to strange lights and sounds coming out of the Green Maw. They attributed the happenings to fae creatures congregating around the forbidden jungle, preparing their infernal rites. The island's Jokai grew restless, or so the farm workers claimed.

"Saw a Witchhawk, clear as day," one of the orchard keepers insisted. "Shot a straight line east across the Maw. Long as a kite-ship, it was—hellfire tail burned brighter than the midday sun. It's a bad augury, that's what it is. You know the rhyme: Hawkwing west, hope for the best; Hawkwing east, better fetch your priest."

Vanna didn't have a priest. She didn't believe in Witchhawks or Lantern Wisps, either. She was just superstitious enough to abide the taboo around the Green Maw, but she knew of one woman on Volturnus willing to risk the Jokai's wrath by trespassing.

Bells jingled as Vanna entered the apothecary through the storefront door. She waved to Nadia, one of Ava's two long-suffering apprentices, who stood behind the counter, meticulously filling tiny vials of tincture from a larger flask. Nadia glanced up, but didn't return the wave.

After a second glance, Nadia cocked one eyebrow and carefully set aside her supplies. "Are you...looking for a tincture?"

"Would that be so strange?" Vanna propped her fists on her hips.

Nadia studied her in that penetrating way all the apothecaries had mastered. The whole lot of them made Vanna uncomfortable. A few of the villagers swore the apothecaries could read a mind as easily as a sky chart. As she sat there under Nadia's judging eyes, she almost believed it.

"Mostly repeat customers in this shop," Nadia finally said. "By your age, most folk have already formed an opinion about what we're selling and decided whether or not they're buying it."

That was true enough. There were a few fliers in the corps who swore by the arcane tonics and remedies peddled at the shop. Vanna wasn't one of them. Even the Nectar turned her off. She didn't trust anything she couldn't understand, and any alchemical augmentation to her Jokai-given Gifts seemed like a dangerous crutch.

"I'm not here to buy anything," she admitted.

"You don't say."

"I need a word with Ava."

Nadia folded her arms across her chest and studied Vanna again with that same penetrating gaze. Without another word, she disappeared into the back of the shop, and Ava soon emerged to replace her.

The half-blind apothecary held her arched back with one hand as she shuffled around the counter. Long ago, the two might have stood eye-to-eye, but age had compressed Ava so that she had to crane her neck to meet Vanna's gaze. She strained her back, wrinkled mouth working back and forth like she was chewing over a cherry pit.

"You're the other one," Ava said.

Vanna furrowed her brow. "I'm sorry—the other 'what'?"

Ava fanned one gnarled hand dismissively. "My credulous apprentice thinks you've got important business for me. Out with it, then."

Straight to the point. Vanna couldn't believe Effie actually considered a lifetime indenture with this prickly crone. "I understand that your work takes you into the Green Maw on occasion—"

"*Do* you understand it?" Ava interrupted. "Or have you just *heard*?" Her milky eye gleamed like one of the frosted bottles of tincture lining the walls.

Vanna propped her hands on her hips and straightened her posture so that the height differential became even more pronounced. "I'm here on official business in my capacity as an officer of the Dragoon Corps. I'm looking for information about a potential threat to the island. The homesteaders south of the village report suspicious activity around the Green Maw. I need to know if you've seen anything strange on any of your trips into the jungle."

"Bah!" Not one to be intimidated, Ava's wrinkled lips bent into a gap-toothed scowl. "It's only strange things in that jungle, girl. You're going to have to be more specific."

"It's *Lieutenant*, actually."

Ava shook her head. She studied Vanna anew, and a curious notch formed on her thin brow. "So different..." she muttered, seemingly to herself.

Half the village already thought Ava belonged in the lunatic colony on Lonely Spur. Vanna hadn't previously counted herself among them, but she was starting to come around to their way of thinking.

"I'm not sure I'm following," Vanna said.

"Oh, I'm quite sure you're not." The notch disappeared as Ava broke into a quick fit of maniacal cackling. "You want to learn about the Maw, ask that sister of yours. She's been there more recently than anyone else."

Effie? In the Green Maw? Vanna shook her head, trying and failing to make sense of the woman's ramblings. "You're mistaken. Effie's barely been outside the governor's manse since her Ascension."

"Is that right? What about *before* the Ascension?" At Vanna's obvious confusion, Ava's cackling returned with even greater force. "Your sister speaks honest falsehoods like she's got a Jokai's tongue sewn inside her pretty mouth. Such a shame. She'd have made a fine apothecary." Ava cackled again as she turned her back to Vanna and hobbled toward the counter. "When you're ready to tell me *exactly* what you're looking for, you're welcome to take another crack. Until then, don't waste my precious time with stupid questions." With that, she vanished back into the stockroom.

It wasn't just Ava's time that was wasting.

With nothing to show for her efforts yet again, Vanna made her way to Janus' pub and took a seat at an empty table close to the hearth. She wasn't hungry, but she definitely needed a drink.

A young server with sandy blonde hair deposited a tankard of ale in front of her with a solicitous wink. His features reminded her of Kai, but an earlier version—Kai before he gained confidence in his Gift and started filling out from his training. Kai had been hanging around her more and more since becoming a cadet. The shadow irritated her at first, but now that he was gone, she found that she missed his steady presence. If Kendy let anything happen to him on this mission, she'd kill him.

She nursed her ale as the tavern slowly filled around her. Farm workers and craftsmen filed in as their workdays cascaded to a close. A small group of dragoons who'd also been left behind tried to summon Vanna over to their table, but she waved them off, turning back to the fire crackling in the hearth.

Alone with her drink, her thoughts drifted to Effie. Her sister's sudden reappearance on Volturnus came as a shock, if a welcome one. She hadn't returned to visit the cottage since that first night, and Vanna could only hope there wasn't any nefarious explanation for her absence. Effie had landed in a hawkwasp's nest—even if she refused to see it. Between that vile bastard Muldoon and Ansel's lecherous intent, she faced as much danger as any dragoon over the open sky. All the servants and comforts in the world wouldn't change that fact. Vanna only hoped her sister had the good sense not to let down her guard.

Out of the corner of her eye, Vanna saw the plump barkeep, Janus, leaning conspiratorially over a table of craftsmen as she delivered a tray of drinks.

"...and now she's back in the village," Janus said. "I'm telling you— Kelestina doesn't want her. She tossed her back in the lake like a two-headed pike."

Vanna's ears perked up as a few of the craftsmen made sounds of agreement. Only Kai's uncle Kellen, who ran the village bakery, looked skeptical.

"I was standing at the cliff's edge during the ceremony," one of the craftsmen said. "I had a clear view of the whole thing. Wasn't nothing like Royon's Ascension—or Gareth's before that. Those dauphine looked bewitched."

Effie. They were gossiping about Effie!

"I'm telling you," Janus continued, "the Strait girl was hanging around the apothecaries just before the Ascension. I saw her myself—roaming around the village at unnatural hours, consorting with spirits. Something's off there—I'm telling you."

The craftsmen all muttered curses. A few made warding gestures across their chests.

That was enough for Vanna. She slammed her empty tankard on the table, drawing the attention of the gossiping cohort. When the craftsmen realized who she was, they became suddenly interested in the contents of their drinks. Only Janus failed to muster any shame. The barkeep left her tray on the table and folded her arms beneath her heavy breasts, daring Vanna to say something. Vanna met her challenge with an acid stare. She threw a pair of coppers on the table and stormed out of the pub, leaving a trail of whispers in her wake.

Bewitched? Consorting with spirits? Give me a Jokai-damned break.

As soon as Vanna stepped out into the naked night, a gloved hand clamped down across her mouth. She began to flail, but another arm wrapped around her, holding her arms against her body, squeezing until her healing ribs cried out. Her kicking feet left the ground as the unseen assailant dragged her into a lightless alley behind the pub. She tried to scream, but the effort only filled her mouth with the taste of leather and grit.

"Quiet now." Hot breath tickled in her ear, carrying with it an accented voice.

Recognition renewed her struggle. She flailed her legs impotently, attempting to land a kick. The assailant jerked her still.

That voice returned in her ear. "I didn't come here to hurt you, but I can't have you making a scene."

Vanna felt another painful twinge in her ribs as the arm around her tightened. Her breath quickened. She felt her heart beating in her neck and in her ears as she gave up the struggle and let her body go limp.

"That's better." Out of the corner of her eye, Vanna saw the end of a thin mustache perched over her shoulder. "If I let you go, can I trust that you'll keep your composure? If I have to fight my way out of here, it isn't going to end well for your kin."

Reluctantly, Vanna nodded. Bael kept her mouth covered for another second before she finally felt the pressure entangling her abate. She exploded out of his arms and whipped around, seizing her Gift.

Beneath the dark green hood of his cloak, the ends of Bael's blue mustache quirked with amusement as he clocked the currents of wind twisting at Vanna's feet. "Easy, Lieutenant..." He raised his hands, exposing empty palms, free of threat. "A great, big bird said you were looking for me. Well, here I am."

"How dare you lay your hands on me!" Vanna tugged the reins of her Gift, holding the winds at the ready.

Bael pressed one finger over his lips, hushing. "I couldn't keep waiting around for you to track my scent. I have a warning to deliver—a threat to Volturnus."

"*You're* a threat to Volturnus," Vanna shot back.

Bael shrugged nonchalantly. "Depends who you're asking."

Vanna kept up her guard. Bael pumped his hands at her, urging caution, then slowly reached up and folded down his hood. Even within the alley's utter dark, she picked out the man's almond eyes and the straight rows of tight blue braids that ran the length of his head.

"It's not just Volturnus I'm worried about. Your whole archipelago's in danger," he said. "You've got a pirate in the area—real grim bastard. Goes by Captain Whitefang of the Leviathan Bone Adder."

Vanna let her Gift slip, and the winds retreated.

Bael noticed and tipped his braided head to her. "Whitefang's ranging pretty far afield of his usual haunts. Bone Adder usually stalks the shipping lanes out of Kensha. Not sure what drew him out to your corner of the sky, but I have my suspicions."

A Leviathan pirate and a missing zeppelin. As a rule, Vanna didn't believe in coincidences. That wasn't how the Jokai liked to play their games. Not since Maug the Butcher arrived on his black-winged skate had the Zephyrs faced such a deadly threat—if Bael could be believed, that is.

This supposed Leviathan wasn't the only snake flashing its fangs at Volturnus.

"Why should I listen to a word that comes out of your mouth?" Vanna asked.

"I already told you why. Remember? Back at the governor's manse on Aeolus. We're allies fighting the same war, you and me. You just haven't realized it yet."

He let that reminder sink in.

"We lost a zeppelin in the skies east of Aeolus..." The words bubbled from Vanna's lips of their own accord. "A little over a week ago. The other dragoons are out conducting a search."

Bael stroked the point of his blue goatee, nodding thoughtfully. "That *is* interesting..."

"You said you had *suspicions*."

"It's just a theory."

Vanna sensed Bael drawing her in. It was all very artfully done—the intimations, the subtle dangle. She shook her head to dispel his serpent-tongue glamor. "If there *is* a dangerous pirate in the archipelago, Kelestina will deal with it. We can't fight a Leviathan with pitchforks and Elemental-ists." *We tried it once before...*

"I wouldn't put too much faith in the Celestial Armada," Bael countered.

"I'm not listening to this—"

"Ask yourself—" he pressed, "—why would a Leviathan pirate fly 3,000 leagues across the Doric Sky just to attack a civilian transport? They weren't hauling gold or goods. *Jokai fend,* they weren't even hauling *weapons.* They were hauling Aeolians."

And just like that, he drew her back. "What are you hinting at?" Vanna hated that she asked it.

"Don't play dense, Lieutenant. If there's one thing I know, it's people, and I pegged you the moment we met. You're clear-eyed. A free thinker. That's why I pulled you into this alley instead of your boot-licking commander. *Think.* Who on this quaint archipelago has cause to punish the Aeolians, hmm?"

Vanna *was* clear-eyed. Clear-eyed enough to see Bael questing for a place to plant his seditious seeds—a mind already tilled by doubt. "No," she said. "You're a conman—a Jokai-damned incendiary device. I should turn you into Governor Ansel."

"Then why haven't you screamed?"

Vanna found she didn't have an answer—at least not one she was ready to admit to herself.

Bael's lips tightened as he restored his green hood. "When you're ready to accept the truth and save your people, I think you know where to find me." His cloaked body melted into the shadows as he withdrew, but his voice lingered. "You were getting warmer."

14

EFFIE

Effie took to certain subjects quicker than others. Geography was fast becoming her favorite—and her first engineering lessons seemed to be the most practical of the lot. Toranese history, on the other hand, amounted to memorizing long lists of dead kings who all seemed to share the same five names.

Civics was by far the worst.

Effie thought she pretty well understood the rigid kyriarchy of the Celestial class system. How naive she'd been. She'd spent the night grinding through a dry treatise authored by some long-dead Skald on the petty minutiae of the Crystal Throne's social order.

Muldoon scratched at his slate board as he recapped the reading. "Even the Hundred Frozen Souls of the Celestial Court must abide by an evolving order—defined by fiefdom, sect, religious privilege, and military rank. An Admiral of the Fleet may exercise authority over a Feudal Host, depending on the size and productivity of her fiefdom and the influence of her vassalage. Even the meanest Feudal Host, however, outranks a landless commodore or imperator. In the event that two honors overlap, the calculation becomes more complicated..."

More complicated? Effie propped her arm on the study table and slumped against her hand. She felt her eyelids sinking. She watched

Muldoon's high ponytail bobbing as he droned through his lecture and continued sketching out a growing flowchart on the mounted slate.

"...As you likely read, the Skaldic priesthood outranks the Patrician class by the letter of the law. In practice, however, a Patrician may elevate himself above the clerical strata through his attachment to a court of notable authority and by serving as a vested magistrate in said court. When I served as a vested retainer in the court of Admiral Siprichor, for example..."

Effie's mind drifted. Muldoon's voice disappeared into a vast skyscape streaked by gauzy clouds and endless leagues of open blue. She fell from the study and landed atop the alpha dauphine, arms extended in cruciform.

"Effie..."

The rest of the pod swirled around her, summoning winds stronger than any Elementalist could dream of harnessing...

"Effie... *Miss Strait!*"

Effie's head popped up from the table to find Muldoon looking down at her, brandishing a wedge of chalk. "I'm sorry—am I boring you?"

"Eh..." Effie rubbed her eyes. "Kinda."

Muldoon's nostrils flared. He'd asked her for honesty, but right now he didn't appear to appreciate her candor. "If you aren't prepared to pay attention, then you might as well scamper back to your room and take a nap. I'm not performing this lecture for my benefit."

"I'm sorry," Effie said. "I just don't really see the point of all this..." she gestured at the complicated diagram sketched on the slate, "...*this*. Who cares if a Gifted conscript outranks an Armada aero-marine, or which Skald can tell which Patrician how to tie his shoes? How does any of this make me a better *Pilot*?"

Muldoon sighed, tapping his wedge of chalk against his folded arms. "When you graduate from my guardianship, you will be stepping into a sophisticated, complex society on a scale you can't even begin to comprehend. No matter how well you prepare, the transition will be dizzying. You'll have a much easier time finding your way, if you understand where you fit into all of *this*." He opened his stance to indicate the diagram scrawled across the slate.

Effie met the chart with the blankest of stares.

"Effie." Muldoon scratched the back of his head and adjusted his folded ponytail. He took a seat at the table. "Your Gift with the Leviathan confers *status*, and status is the only currency worth a damn in the service of the Crystal Throne. Unlike so many of your peers—even the Patricians—you will have options before you. Which Celestial you choose to serve—and in what capacity—will determine the course of your life."

Effie's eyes drifted back to the diagram. So many interlocking tiers of relationships, fealty, and privilege. It all seemed so contrived. "I don't like it," she said.

"You don't like options?"

"I don't like the idea that my birthright determines the *scope* of my options."

Muldoon shook his head. "You misunderstand. Your birthright opens up a world of possibilities, but it will be your *choices* that elevate you. Or diminish you." He reached back and tapped the slate board with his chalk. "That's why you need to master the system before you begin making them."

A question surfaced that had been gnawing at Effie for some time. She finally felt well enough acquainted with her Patrician tutor to give it voice. "Only the Gifted may be elevated to the Patrician class—isn't that right?"

"It is." Muldoon hesitated, stroking the wedge of chalk between his fingers. "A Gift is one predicate condition. As is a formal education and service to the Crystal Throne."

"So, what's *your* Gift?" Effie asked.

Muldoon stopped thumbing the chalk. He set it down and folded his arms across his chest. "Let's see if you can work it out. You're well into your survey of pre-colonial Toranese history—or you should be, if you're keeping up with your reading."

"I am," Effie insisted.

"Good. Then you tell me. What calling is most common among the peoples of the Umar Steppe?"

Effie recalled an unusual map from her history text. Just as the Zephyr Isles produced primarily wind Elementalists, each region of Toran had its own native proclivity. Her history book laid these affinities out in a handy regional map, but there were so many. She had a hard time placing them all from memory.

"The steppe's in the south...west of Rydia and the Inland Sky..." As she spoke through her thought process, she searched Muldoon's body language for some hint, but he wasn't budging. "There are Elementalists in the south —fire aspected?"

Muldoon bent his head. "Is that a question?"

"Are you a pyromancer?" she guessed.

Muldoon sat back in his chair and shook his head. "You're thinking of the plains people from the Agnar Rift."

Balls of the deep. That did sound familiar. Effie chewed her lip. What did she remember about Umar? Its list of dead kings was a short one. Before the Celestials arrived, the city-state was ruled by a despot—a God-King who reigned for 1,000 years. The Umafex—Gifted with an unnaturally long life.

"You're a Vitalist!" Effie nearly shouted it.

A tight smile worked its way onto Muldoon's lips.

"So, what's your Gift? Are you a true healer?"

"Not as such," Muldoon said. "My mother had that Gift. She was one of the most sought-after healers in Toran. My Vitalist Gift has a different character."

"Care to elaborate?"

Muldoon's tight smile became playful. "I'm afraid it would be too uncomfortable to demonstrate. Let's just say I'm a very difficult man to kill."

That would have to be enough to satisfy Effie's curiosity. Muldoon was clearly finished entertaining this line of interrogation. "That reminds me." He stood up from the table and walked to his satchel propped atop the study desk. Effie watched him pull a small parchment scroll from the bag and scan it over. He walked back to the table with his eyes glued to the page —seemed to pause for a moment to glance up at Effie before placing the paper flat in front of her.

The swirling calligraphy of Kelestina's scribes shaped a simple list of names. *Kendy Baris, Min Baris, Kai Bowker, Raji Caspar, Yara Dyfid...*

She glanced up from the parchment. "It's a list of the Volturnian Dragoons."

"It's a list of every Elementalist on Volturnus, actually." Muldoon reclaimed his seat. "It includes a few fliers retired from the corps and others with unique manifestations." He leaned over the page and tapped one name toward the bottom of the list—*Bolorus Withers.* "As I understand it, this man is stormsighted?"

Effie nodded. "Looks like I'm not the only one doing my homework."

Muldoon leaned back in his seat and drummed his fingers on the table-top. "I could use your counsel on a matter of import to our host."

"Kelestina needs *my* help?"

Muldoon nodded once. "In a manner of speaking. You know these Elementalists better than anyone at court. Even your Lord Governor seems unusually disinterested in the Gifts of his plebiscite."

Effie snorted. "Maybe he'd care more if they had fetlocks and an ivory mane."

"You might be onto something." Muldoon's easy laughter caught Effie off guard. He shook his head at her, smiling with both rows of immaculate teeth. Day by day, her Patrician tutor grew increasingly casual with her. She didn't hate it.

When the laughter subsided, he returned to the parchment. "I was wondering if you might provide your expert opinion—identify those fliers considered the most powerful in the Gift."

"That's easy." Effie pushed the paper away. "Vanna's the strongest Elementalist by leagues. Kendy's a distant second."

"Let's set the officers aside for the purposes of this exercise." Muldoon nudged the parchment back in front of her. "Who's next in the pecking order?"

Effie flashed her tutor a quizzical look, then returned to the list. So many Gifted on Volturnus...

She could ignore all the gliders. Half the corps lacked the strength to windshape. They got by harnessing whatever the weather granted them. Of the junior windshapers, she knew Kendy valued Dray, but according to Vanna that had more to do with their personal history than any uncommon facility with the Gift. Maya had been in the corps for decades —as had Deanna and Hal—but experience did not equal strength.

She lingered on Flynn's name. The former Wing Commander had been retired from the corps by force, but in her youth she'd been one of the few windshapers approaching Vanna's class.

Kai's name leapt suddenly from the page. He was windshaping within weeks of manifesting, and she knew Kendy and Vanna thought highly of his potential. His father had been Wing Commander before Flynn, so he came from sturdy stock. He no doubt deserved to be ranked among the strongest Elementalists, but his abandonment of her still chafed. It was petty, but Effie couldn't bring herself to elevate him in the eyes of Muldoon.

Effie finally settled on three names that stood out by reputation and her own gut sense: "Senna Ryot, Flynn Maier, and Kale Elon."

"Why those three?" Muldoon asked.

"Senna and Kale are the most dependable fliers in the corps. They're both at the top of the list for every mission over open sky. Vanna once described Kale's Gift as a bottomless well. To hear her tell it, he can keep himself aloft for days on end without tiring. And Senna—she manifested young. Made the corps before she even turned sixteen. She's the fastest in the air—faster even than Vanna.

"Flynn should be obvious," she added. "She used to be Wing Commander before she retired."

Muldoon took the list back and read it again. "You're certain, then?" Effie nodded. He produced a fountain pen from his jacket pocket and made three quick notations on the list, then furled up the parchment scroll and tapped it on the table before returning it to his bag.

"That will be all today."

Effie glanced at the timepiece ticking on the study desk—only half-past Fourth Bell. "It's early."

"I'm granting you a temporary stay." Muldoon's wry smile softened the edges of his almond eyes. "Unless you'd prefer another recitation on the social dynamics among the Patricians and the hereditary peerage?"

15

KAI

It took the dragoons several days to get back to Volturnus. They boarded Dama Sigyn's flagship and saw the Aeolian survivors back to their village. At Halle's request, the Volturnian wing stuck around to see everyone safely resettled while she notified the families of the deceased.

Afterward, Kendy insisted on escorting Taros' wing back to Avernus. The loss of Hal weighed on everyone—Kendy most of all. Their gregarious commander grew uncharacteristically contemplative after leaving the skerry. He seemed almost taciturn at times—and occasionally on edge. Kai witnessed him blow up at a group of fliers who snuck off to the Avernian tavern the evening before they were set to fly home. He wasn't eager to spark a similar reprimand, so he minded his instructions and gave the commander his space.

It was approaching midday when Kai's feet finally touched Volturnian ground. More than a week had passed since they left.

"Kai."

Kai snapped to attention and tapped out a stiff salute at the sound of his commander's voice, silently praying to the Jokai he hadn't unwittingly broken some regulation of the corps.

Kendy didn't seem to clock his nervousness. "I need a word with Vanna," he said. "But first I have to find Oona. Someone needs to tell her she's a widow, and I suppose that someone is me. Would you track down the lieutenant and see her to the barracks?"

"Aye, Commander."

Kai first checked the Strait cottage but found it empty. He went to Rindra's clinic next, but Vanna wasn't there, either. He was on the verge of giving up, when he caught a glimpse of a purple bob poking over two stacked cords of wood on the path down from the cutters' shed.

Kai waved until she noticed him. She dropped her burden, sighing audibly with relief. They ran to each other and fell into a comfortable embrace. Kai was pleased to see she'd shed her bandages

"Jokai fend," Vanna said. "What took you so long?"

Kai shook his head. Where did he even start? Better to leave it to the commander. "It was a complicated mission. Kendy wants to see you at the barracks. I'm sure he'll bring you up to speed."

They dropped Vanna's firewood on the stoop in front of her cottage and followed the cobblestone path out to the dragoon barracks at the edge of town.

"Kendy's not the only one with news to report," Vanna teased, brushing an errant lock of purple bangs from her face.

"Oh, yeah?" Kai glanced over, caught her playful grin. "Can I get a preview?"

"Effie's back." Vanna picked up her pace, pulling ahead along the path.

Kai's legs ground to a dumbfounded stop. "What?"

Vanna turned back as she reached the barracks. "She's staying up at Governor Ansel's manse for the foreseeable future. I'm sure she'd love to hear from you."

He heard the words she was saying, but they didn't make sense. Were they talking about the same Effie Strait?

Kai and Effie used to be inseparable, but she'd been distant with him ever since his Gift manifested. He'd been so consumed with his training in those early days; he had so much catching up to do. He thought Effie of all people would understand. When he did finally reach out to her, she rebuffed him.

For the longest time, her rejection ate at him. On her sixteenth name-day, he'd written her a heartfelt card on expensive stationery, apologizing for his absence and inviting her back into his life. Weeks later he learned that she'd spurned him yet again, left his card unopened and his sentiments unread. That had been the final straw.

Kai had loved Effie for as long as he could remember, but the gap that opened between them when he came into his power had only grown with each passing day. There were times when he felt a prickling of longing for the connection they once shared. He still remembered the taste of her lips —an innocent kiss that seemed to belong to another life—but the painful yearning that memory once instilled had lost much of its edge. With the news that she was back on Volturnus, Kai realized just how much his feelings for her had cooled.

Effie had made herself a stranger to him, and in her absence his gaze had wandered. Her sister had emerged to occupy the space in his heart that Effie had so pointedly abandoned. When Effie disappeared into Kelestina's carriage after the Ascension, he hardly registered the loss. As far as Kai was concerned, he'd already lost Effie—long ago—and he didn't have the strength to mourn her twice.

Kai shook himself back to the present and followed Vanna inside the barracks. Kendy was already waiting for them, returned from making the widow call to Oona. He looked like he'd aged a decade in the brief hours since their return, beset by new wrinkles around his eyes, cheekbones protruding from his strong jaw.

Maya, Dray, Senna, and Kale were also in attendance. Kai felt terribly out of place as he watched Vanna take her seat among the other senior dragoons. He tried to slip back out the door, but Kendy's voice pursued him.

"You can stay, if you want, Bowker," the commander said. "No secrets in the corps."

Kai nodded sheepishly, then crept over to take his seat at the far end of the command table.

Kendy recounted the mission for Vanna's benefit. Kai watched Vanna tearfully receive the news of Hal's demise. Dray offered her a cloth to dry her eyes, which she accepted, pausing only briefly before returning to her commander's report. Kai felt the urge to hold her, but he didn't dare upset the decorum of a meeting he already felt ill-equipped to attend. He was still so new to the corps.

As Kendy launched into a description of the Leviathan pirate who attacked the Aeolian zeppelin, Kai saw a twitch in Vanna's expression. She didn't react with any of the shock that Kai had expected. Vanna had lost both her parents to the last Leviathan pirate to terrorize the Zephyri skies. She had as much cause as anyone to fear a repeat of the Butcher's brutal reign.

"Our host has already called in the Armada," Kendy said. "The new Governor of Aeolus has a military bearing. She commands an armored airship and seems committed to the defense of the isles."

"I suppose that's a relief..." Vanna said.

Kendy nodded. "It's more firepower than we had when the Butcher arrived, but it's only one ship, and Aeolus is far away. I want to double our patrols and expand the perimeter. From this day forward, we cover the skies west to the lees of Avernus and north to the Frostwind Cayes."

Senna and Kale froze in their seats. Dray made a low whistle, and Maya's eyebrows crept up her brow.

"That's a lot of sky," Dray said.

The other dragoons made noises of agreement.

Maya had a more practical question: "What's Commander Taros going to think about Volturnian dragoons patrolling Avernian airspace?"

"I don't care what Taros thinks," Kendy said. "This is no time to be territorial. I don't want any surprises. First sign of trouble, we send word west to Governor Sigyn and north to Aquilon. I won't let this pirate catch Volturnus off guard. I'm breaking the corps into drafts of six. Every flier at this table will be responsible for leading a patrol." He waved dismissively in Kai's direction. "Except for Bowker, of course. Additionally, I'm elevating Philia, Jaffe, and Kadir to the active corps."

Kendy's eyes probed Vanna for objections, but to Kai's surprise she kept her mouth shut. "What about your thing?" he prompted, still locked on his lieutenant.

The question startled Vanna. She glanced around the table, lingering briefly on Kai before returning to the commander. "Shouldn't we discuss this in private?"

Kendy's voice came back clipped. "Your week is up. Either you've reached a resolution, or I'm taking the matter up to Ansel. I see no further need for discretion."

Vanna glared at the commander. Whatever he was asking for, she couldn't well deny him. Not now that everyone at the table's interest was piqued.

"I found him," she said.

"Found who?" Kale asked.

"Bael," Vanna said.

Dray, Senna, and Kale all reacted with the same shock and recognition. Only Maya looked as confused as Kai felt.

"The rabble-rouser we dislodged from Aeolus last year," Vanna explained. "He turned up on Volturnus during the Ascension. I found him camped near one of the abandoned landings to the south."

Kai saw Dray balling his meaty fists, while the rest of the dragoons leaned in with interest.

"Was he alone?" Kendy asked.

Vanna nodded. "He was marooned here waiting for a ride from his faction—this Gulliver Ring. I don't think he had any further designs on Volturnus."

"You don't *think*?" Senna pressed.

"I saw him off the island myself. He won't be back to trouble us, and if he does return, you have my blessing to sound the alarms."

Some of the tension seemed to leave Kendy's shoulders at this report. He released a deep breath like he'd been holding it for days. "That's that, then. I don't like the idea of Volturnus being used as a pirate waystation, but if you're certain he's gone?" His eyes narrowed on Vanna.

Kai thought he saw a moment's hesitation before Vanna nodded again. "I told you. I saw it myself."

"Then we'll consider this matter closed. The Jokai know, we've got enough to worry about with this Bone Adder stalking our skies." Kendy stood up from the table. The other dragoons followed his lead, with Kai scrambling last to his feet. "Everyone get some rest. First patrol starts at dusk."

Kai lingered at the back of the barracks while the more senior dragoons filed out. He watched Vanna engage Kendy in a private exchange. Vanna flexed her right arm for the commander, demonstrating her return to flexibility. Kendy accepted her performance and waved her away.

As they parted, Kai caught her by the sleeve. "Sounds like you've been keeping busy," he joked. "Hunting pirates with a busted wing?"

Vanna's lip quirked revealing her one twisted tooth. "And you've had your first taste of open sky. I'm sorry I didn't get to witness the maiden voyage."

"Plenty more to come with these double patrols."

Snorting, Vanna turned again to leave, but she paused in the barracks door, caught him staring. "You got anywhere to be?" she asked.

Kai shrugged. "Just planning to grab mess at the bunkhouse. Maybe try to get some sleep."

Vanna tapped one finger against her chin, eyes scanning him up and down. "You wouldn't want to eat with me, instead? The cottage has felt extra empty lately."

"Yes! I mean—that sounds nice."

Her green eyes sparkled with amusement. "Come on."

Vanna's cottage had always been a second home to Kai. He'd sat in this very chair through countless meals and cups of tea, joined card games that lasted long into the night. It had always been the three of them—Effie, Vanna, and Kai—but now he and Vanna were alone. The intimacy made the familiar space feel foreign and new.

Kai always ate quickly when he was nervous. He slurped down his second bowl of stew as Vanna left the table to set a kettle over the wood-burning stove. They'd cautiously avoided the topic of Effie throughout the meal, lingering instead on Kai's impressions of his first mission over open sky. Vanna seemed tickled by his zeal—vicariously thrilled by his fledgling enthusiasm for the mercurial winds. Kai grew gradually concerned that she might be patronizing him.

"It all starts to become second nature after a while," he said, performing what he hoped sounded like veteran indifference. "I honestly feel like I've been doing this my whole life."

"Is that right?" Vanna returned to the table with two mugs of tea. "Not for me. Every time I touch the open sky it's like it's my first time again."

Kai brought his mug quickly to his lips and burned his mouth in the process. Vanna laughed at the hot beverage dribbling down his chin and offered him a towel.

"So..." Kai prepared to broach the forbidden topic. "Has Effie been by much since she returned?"

"Only once," Vanna said. "I'm worried about her. I don't trust those Patricians as far as I can gust them."

"You think they'd hurt her? She's a Gifted Pilot."

Vanna's expression darkened as her eyes drifted down to her tea. "Oh,

I'm sure they wouldn't do anything to jeopardize her *value*, but there's more than one way to hurt someone."

Whatever Kai and Effie's relationship had become, the thought of anyone taking advantage of her made his insides run cold. Kai wasn't sure what he could do to protect her from the Patricians, but he was confident he'd figure it out. "We won't let that happen," he said.

Vanna looked up at him. It might have been the tea, but he thought he saw new lines of color blooming on her cheeks.

"It's late," she said. "You should go back to the bunkhouse and get some rest. Kendy seems serious about these new patrols."

Kai nodded slowly, careful not to break their shared gaze. "I could do that..."

Vanna chewed her lower lip between her teeth, still staring as she mindlessly stirred her tea. Kai's heart began to beat inside his throat. He drifted closer, started rising from his seat.

This was it.

When her gaze didn't falter, he thought she might ask him to stay, but the moment passed. She stood up from the table, breaking the spell, and led him to the door.

"Thank you for keeping me company," Vanna said. "I'm not used to being alone. Effie's back but she isn't *back*, you know?"

"I'll be here any time you'll have me," Kai said.

Vanna's smile was melancholy. She patted his chest and kissed him on the cheek—a sisterly peck. "It's good to have family around again."

Kai slumped against the cottage door as soon as Vanna closed it behind him.

Family.

It was the worst thing she could have possibly said.

16

MULDOON

Ansel surprised Muldoon with an invitation to attend a meeting with the island's Wing Commander. The governor no doubt hoped that outnumbering Commander Baris might intimidate the man and thus ease the delivery of an unwelcome writ. Muldoon was little more than a Patrician prop in this ploy. He knew when he was being used, but curiosity won the day.

It wasn't a bad plan, after all.

Muldoon had become increasingly convinced that Ansel was indeed a congenital imbecile, but even imbeciles tended to pass through the world by virtue of a certain low cunning.

He stood upright at Ansel's shoulder, casually adjusting his cravat as the governor peered across his desk at the uniformed dragoon. There was a severity to the commander's expression that well concealed the underlying exhaustion—only too obvious to Muldoon's practiced eye. He didn't know this Kendy Baris well enough to guess how he might react to the new conscription order, but a brittle spirit tended to push people one of two directions: pliancy or obstinance. Either way, Muldoon expected an entertaining evening.

Ansel threaded his fingers atop the office desk, displaying his ostentatious set of rings. "I appreciate the prompt response to my summons, Commander. Can I offer you a drink?"

Commander Baris shook his head. "No thank you, Sire. I'm due to fly patrol in a few hours, and I'd rather keep my wits."

Ansel accepted his refusal and dismissed the butler lingering at the back of the office with a wave.

"I assume you want to hear the report from our findings in the western isles?" Commander Baris asked.

"Eh?" Ansel's block head shifted like a boulder.

"The missing zeppelin from Aeolus…"

"Ah, right." Ansel waved the commander's assumption away. "Aquilon has already informed us of the attack. This Leviathan is not a concern at present."

The commander looked struck. "Not a *concern*?"

"Our host is aware of the issue, and it's being handled. I summoned you here to discuss a different matter." Ansel lifted his hand, and Muldoon pressed Kelestina's writ into his outstretched palm. The governor cut the ribbon binding the parchment scroll with a silver letter-opener and handed the missive across the desk to Commander Baris. The short message bore Kelestina's broken-serpent seal.

Baris glanced apprehensively at the two Patricians. Muldoon watched his eyes as they drifted down to the scroll. New wrinkles arrived to crease this young man's brow as he moved slowly over each line of text.

The commander lowered the writ and looked straight at Ansel. "Our host is conscripting Senna, Kale, and Flynn?"

Ansel nodded curtly. "They are to report to the manse this upcoming Moonday before Seventh Bell. From here, they'll be delivered to Aquilon, where they'll receive their assignment directly from Her Lightness."

The commander's expression tightened as he read the missive again, grip creasing the parchment as he lost the battle to restrain himself. "This is all very unusual, Sire. Where will they be sent?"

"Their final destination is for Her Lightness Kelestina to decide. Your job is to ensure compliance with the terms of this writ."

Commander Baris lowered the paper again, frown lines framing his strong chin. "This is a bad time to lose dragoons. Senna and Kale are two of the strongest fliers in the corps. I rely on them both to lead drafts on patrol."

"Our host will see to the defense of the isles," Ansel said.

"Like she defended the Aeolians?"

Ansel grunted at the challenge, but Commander Baris' temper had broken through, and he didn't appear likely to back down.

They'd arrived at a delicate crossroads.

Muldoon cleared his throat, drawing the attention of the smoldering dragoon. "If I may interject—Commander Baris has recently borne witness to a terrible tragedy. We can certainly understand why tempers might be running a little hot. It's also important to remember, however, that the Aeolians rebelled against our host, ousting their Patrician lord and protector. Had I remained at my post, this all could have been avoided. The rebel elements on the western isle bear much of the blame for their exposure."

This reversal unbalanced the commander. With no easy response at hand, his flinty eyes narrowed on Muldoon before drifting back to Ansel. "Senna is betrothed," he said. "And Flynn's on the wrong side of fifty. I don't think this order will be well-received."

Ansel puffed out his barrel chest like the brainless peacock he was. "I remind you, Commander, that we are all *guests* of the Crystal Throne. It is not for us to question the judgment of Her Lightness."

Muldoon saw Commander Baris' temper returning to simmer. He cut in to save Ansel from himself. "It is a high honor that Kelestina confers upon these Elementalists. They will be separated from their loved ones for a time, but with their ample Gifts, all three of these conscripts may someday be elevated to the Patrician class. If Miss Ryot's betrothed remains dedicated, there is no reason they can't reunite. If not, the Lord Governor is empowered to see their betrothal annulled."

"Yes." Ansel's side-eye warned Muldoon off any further interruptions. "You will inform the conscripts, Commander."

It wasn't a question, but Commander Baris nodded his acquiescence all the same.

Ansel's quiet butler returned to escort Commander Baris out of the manse. As soon as the office door closed behind them, Ansel hoisted his solid girth from his desk and walked over to a bar cart to pour himself a snifter of orange brandy. He didn't offer one to Muldoon.

"*Elevated to Patrician*, he says." Ansel sniffed his liquor and took a deep drink. "That is rich."

Muldoon couldn't tell if he meant the brandy or his own specious sentiments. "Anything's possible," he said, unfolding from his stately pose and stepping out from behind the desk.

Ansel's brandy sloshed as he waved the snifter at Muldoon. "This is your fault, you know."

Amused by the accusation, Muldoon allowed a slight smirk. "How do you figure?"

"All your talk up at Aquilon about *obligations* to the Armada." Ansel ventured a dainty sip, then drained his entire snifter in one boorish gulp. "That's where they're headed, I'd wager. A quick stop at Mol Hara or Klock Base, then a one-way ticket to the front lines."

"Oh, I sincerely doubt my goading had anything to do with it." Muldoon stroked the thin strip of beard along his chin. "We've simply reached a new phase of the occupation in this land. Her Lightness has been patient in her cultivation of these Zephyri Gifts. The time for harvest was bound to arrive sooner or later."

Ansel shook his block head as he turned back to the bar cart to pour himself another heavy snifter. "A harvest is well and good, but if Her Lightness eats her seed crop, she risks inciting another rebellion."

"Is your plebiscite so undisciplined? I thought you valued *decorum* on Volturnus."

Ansel bristled at his own words thrown back at him. His fingers tightened around his glass. "Speaking of *decorum*, how are your lessons with Miss Strait proceeding?"

"Exceedingly well, I'm pleased to report." Despite his best efforts to maintain an inscrutable facade, Muldoon felt a tight smile working its way across his lips. "You were right about the younger Strait girl—so unlike the elder. She's quick-witted and quite agreeable. I find myself enjoying our time together."

Ansel's grimace dripped with delicious resentment. "And here I thought you considered the assignment beneath your station. You lacked the *temperament* for tutoring—isn't that what you said?"

Muldoon shrugged. "It seems I contain multitudes, unbeknownst even to me."

Muldoon thought he could hear the governor's teeth popping as he ground his jaw at his drink. "Get out of my office now, Muldoon."

"By your leave, Sire." Muldoon performed a sweeping bow, hoping to conceal his wild grin.

17

EFFIE

Ina arrived at Effie's room on the morning of her next dreaded civics lesson. She came with a message from Muldoon.

"You're to report to the windward port this morning."

"The port?" Effie rubbed her eyes. She was groggy from the late night deciphering a dry treatise on the hereditary peerage.

"Yes. And he recommends sensible attire." Ina deposited a bundle of canvas pants and a thick blouse on Effie's bed before proceeding over to her closet and unearthing a brown woolen overcoat. She hung the overcoat from a bedpost and began meticulously brushing out the lapels.

Effie hoisted herself out of bed and tucked her feet into a pair of waiting slippers. As the young maid bent over to inspect a loose button on the overcoat, Effie noticed a ring of bruises around her collar.

"*Jokai fend*, Ina. What happened to you?"

Ina fumbled with the collar of her livery to conceal the bruise. "It's nothing. Sire Muldoon expects you promptly at the port—"

"Ina..." Effie crept toward her, but Ina withdrew, averting her eyes. "I know we were never close," Effie ventured, "but that doesn't mean—"

"Stop it, Effie!" Ina snapped. Her formal mask vanished in an instant, and Effie caught a fleeting glimpse of the self-assured young woman she knew from her previous life—the pretty knitter's daughter who had her pick of all the young dragoons and reveled in that power.

Ina huffed, then returned to brushing out Effie's coat in an obvious state of agitation.

Effie proceeded with caution. "If someone's hurting you..."

The pace of Ina's brushing quickened.

"If you need *help*—"

Ina threw the garment brush down, her sudden rage forcing Effie onto her back foot. "What would you know about it, hmm? We're not all well-kept Patrician pets like you. The rest of us serve at the pleasure of Governor Ansel." Ina's breast heaved inside her tight-fitting livery.

"It's him, isn't it?" Effie guessed. "Sire Ansel."

"I said *stop*." Tears began to well in Ina's eyes. She shook her head, rolling those wet eyes to the ceiling. "You don't know what it's like working here. Working for *him*."

"You're right," Effie said. "I don't know what it's like to be a conscript. But I do know Celestial law. No one has the right to lay hands on you—no matter their class."

"Celestial law?" Ina sniffed, shaking her head again as she brushed away tears. "You don't get it."

"I could talk to Sire Muldoon," Effie said. "He could intervene."

"No!" Ina nearly shouted it. "You'll only make things worse." Drying her eyes, she deposited Effie's overcoat on the bed next to her outfit and made for the door. "See that you aren't late for your appointment at the port. You won't be the one who's punished if you are."

Effie worried over the encounter the entire walk out to the port. She didn't want to get Ina in trouble, but nor could she erase the image of those angry bruises from her mind. There had to be something she could do.

When she arrived at the landing, she found a team of burly port workers rolling a kite-ship onto the northern launch. It was a grim day for flying. A stiff north wind whipped the ends of Effie's overcoat, and a low ceiling of dense, gray clouds compressed the sky, threatening rain.

Muldoon waved to her from the edge of the launch, his own long overcoat buttoned to the knee, collar flipped up to guard his neck against the chill.

Despite the ominous weather, Effie felt a trill of anticipation as she stepped into the thin shadow thrown by the kite-ship's singular masthead.

"Punctual as ever," Muldoon beamed.

Effie visored her eyes with one hand and gathered her windswept hair with the other. "No fealty charts today? I'm disappointed."

"Fear not. We'll be back to business as usual in the study tomorrow."

Not even Muldoon's careful grooming kept the north winds at bay. His auburn hair scattered across his eyes, and Effie found this rare chink in his Patrician armor strangely endearing. She stared at Muldoon until the sound of one of the port workers stoking the kite-ship's steam engine startled her from her trance. The chugging sound of steam cylinders filled the air. Tendrils of vapor began to creep from the aircraft's exhaust pipes as two stern propellers blurred into motion. "So, where are we going?" she asked over the din.

"Today's lesson is practical. I'll explain more on the way." Muldoon extended his arm to the starboard ladder. "After you."

The kite-ship's hold was well outfitted by comparison to the merchant crafts that typically sailed the archipelago. A dozen cushioned couches set with leather restraints ringed the cabin, broken only by a small larder casket with a brass handle. Effie strapped herself into one of the stern couches facing the cockpit, and Muldoon claimed the couch beside her, tightening the restraints around his chest and waist. Effie watched him, imitating each step as she went through the motions.

She was still fiddling with the restraints across her chest when the kite-ship lifted off from the launch. Her stomach dropped as the craft entered a brief freefall, righting only once its propellers reached the point of compensation. A pair of square sails dropped from the mast, and the kite-ship quickly gained altitude, accelerating through its shallow ascent. Effie gripped the armrests of her couch until her knuckles whitened. She felt Muldoon's hand arrive to cover her own and looked up.

"First time on a steamboat?" he asked without judgment.

"First time on any kite-ship," Effie admitted.

He patted her hand reassuringly. "The ride can be a little turbulent, but I promise you, they're quite safe."

Effie glanced at the receding shoreline through a starboard porthole and swallowed.

They soon reached their transit altitude and leveled off. Effie heard clockwork mechanisms set inside the cabin walls clicking into motion, deploying the keel and rudder from recessed compartments along the dorsal hull. Before beginning her studies in aeronautical engineering, the workings of a steamcraft like this one would have been a hopeless mystery to her. Now, she could almost picture the hidden engine powering the propellers and the interlocking matrix of gears communicating the pilot's commands to the ship's rudder and sails.

Effie swayed with the motion of the kite-ship as they banked starboard, pursuing a northbound route against the headwinds. The steady chop of turbulence continued to jostle her in her couch, even after they reached their constant speed.

"You planning to tell me where we're going or is it a surprise?" Effie asked.

Muldoon smoothed back his windswept hair. "We're en route to the Frostwind Cayes."

That was a great deal farther than Effie had expected.

Effie now knew the skies around the archipelago as well as any merchant shipman—and likely better than most dragoons. The Frostwinds were a small collection of barren islands northwest of Aquilon, at the navigator's edge of Zephyri airspace. The hostile cayes didn't support any permanent habitation, but their gentle topography did offer emergency landings for larger craft—safe harbors for ships blown off course by deadly northern storms.

"What's out there?" Effie asked.

Muldoon shook his head, glancing out his own adjacent porthole. "I'm afraid that's all I know. Our host will meet us there to provide additional context."

"Kelestina's coming?" Effie would have fallen out of her couch if not for the restraints.

Muldoon offered another reassuring pat on the hand. "Don't be nervous."

That was easy for him to say.

The crossing took the better half of the day. The north winds sharpened as they left the bracing influence of Volturnus and Aquilon. Intermittent gusts battered the kite-ship's sales and rattled the cabin. When their craft finally banked into a wide turn and began its descent, Muldoon drew Effie's attention to one of the starboard portholes.

The rocky shore of the leeward caye cut across the western sky. Beyond its jagged lip, an empty plain, flattened by constant north winds, stretched out to the horizon. Two massive airships had already converged on the

Frostwind. The larger of the two made landfall, turf-docked at the center of the island's flat expanse and propped up on emergency braces. The ship was more massive than a rock freighter—its hull a patchwork quilt of mismatched plating all soldered and bolted in place. Effie saw the iron mouths of cannons poking out from gunholes and two large harpoons mounted on the forecastle and stern. An iron crane jutted from the bowsprit. From its end, a barbed hook twisted in the chaotic winds on a short span of metal cable tied to a winch.

The second craft seemed almost genteel by comparison—a sleek blue shuttle shaped like a knife. Neither sails nor propellers disrupted its aerodynamic shape. It hovered offshore by the grace of some unknown force, the milky white of its ventral hull bobbing gently up and down.

Effie clocked a tightening around Muldoon's almond eyes as he surveyed the caye. "What is it?" she asked.

"I think I know why we're here..." His eyes narrowed on the armored airship with the gleaming hook.

"That bad?"

He probably intended his tight smile to reassure her, but Effie knew him well enough by now to see the anxiety hidden behind it. "What aren't you telling me?" she asked.

He turned back to the porthole as the kite-ship continued along its path of descent. "I believe our host may have need of your Gift."

They landed just beyond the rocky moraine at the island's edge. Effie disembarked behind Muldoon and followed him up to an assembly taking place beneath the armored airship's pointy bow. Kelestina stood out from a distance, shoulders draped with a fur coat of unblemished white. The quartzite crown of her head caught what little sunlight breached the ceiling of clouds. A dozen of her servants surrounded her in their strange blue livery—an entourage of dark-haired young men armed with brass-handled rapiers. Dagda stood at Kelestina's shoulder, her hands clasped at her waist, head piled with the same stack of immovable braids Effie remembered from her brief stay at Aquilon Palace.

The Aquilonian party received an animated report from an older man wearing a long red coat over a boiled leather cuirass. That overcoat was scored with burns and claw-mark wounds—some fresh, others stitched back together along unsightly seams. His face was darker even than Dagda's, cheeks cratered with pockmarks, brow disfigured by a long scar that disappeared beneath the brim of his three-cornered hat. Effie saw the hilts of at least four different daggers and swords sticking out from his beltline, as well as the handle of a flintlock pistol holstered at his opposite hip.

As she and Muldoon joined the assembly, Effie's eyes drifted to the crane overhead and the heavy hook dangling from its tip. Unlike the cannons, the hook looked more like fishing tackle than a weapon of war.

Kelestina held up one long-fingered hand, pausing this captain's report to acknowledge the new arrivals. Effie felt a cautioning tug on the back of her sleeve as Muldoon stepped in front of her to perform a deferential bow. "Your Lightness—we humbly apologize for any delay. We met with unfavorable winds out of Volturnus."

Kelestina waved this apology away. "You're right on time, Sire." A hungry gleam flashed across her green eyes as they found Effie. She extended her arms, summoning her forth.

Effie performed her best approximation of Muldoon's bow, while her tutor hovered protectively behind her, radiating unease.

"Miss Strait." Kelestina's chiming voice pierced the howling winds. "Sire Muldoon reports impressive progress with your studies. This pleases us."

"I have a good teacher, Lightness."

Kelestina's lips pressed together. She carefully picked across each of her teardrop nails with her thumb, before extending her arm to indicate the grizzled captain standing opposite. "Allow me to introduce Sire Meseret of Ib, Captain of the *Gravel Lizard*."

Effie's eyes widened as she scanned the heavily armed captain anew. He looked more like a pirate than a Patrician. When he smirked at her, she realized that one of his eyes didn't move with its pair. It looked like an orb of painted glass—a lifeless ornament staring sightlessly in one fixed direction. A leather patch would have been less unsettling.

"This is her, aye?" Meseret tipped his three-cornered hat to Kelestina. "The guppy Pilot?" His accent reminded Effie of Dadga's, though much thicker and less refined.

"Miss Strait is as Gifted a Pilot as we've identified in a century of searching," Kelestina confirmed.

Meseret's good eye probed Effie with skepticism. He shrugged. "She better be. Else she'll be chum, *nah sa sa*."

Captain Meseret's ship suddenly groaned, reverberating with a sound like the beating of some great war drum. The entire vessel shook from the force of it, and Effie reflexively braced, expecting it to topple off its thin supports.

Meseret snapped at a small group of crewmen gathered behind him and barked a few sharp commands. *"Busque a-ta pront pront! Hake pezca por le cunya. Pront!"*

The crewmen scrambled back inside the belly of the ship.

Meseret turned back to Kelestina's entourage, clucking with his tongue between his teeth. "Never seen such an ill-tempered hammerhead. Nearly knocked us from the sky with its thrashing—gave us all the Long Drop. Might need to renegotiate my fee, *sabi*?"

Dagda stepped forward, scowling. "Guard yourself, Sire. You will show respect. *Jeuno kay luze, sa? Adelant enamorada!*"

"Bah!" Meseret shooed the majordomo away. *"Aye cunya se la cunya."*

Dagda looked like she might explode, but Kelestina held her back. "We will see Sire Meseret properly compensated for his troubles—*if* he manages to complete the delivery."

Effie felt increasingly confused. She glanced back at Muldoon, but his expression had only grown more troubled. With Kelestina engaged watching Dagda and Meseret spar back and forth, she whispered to her tutor. "What language are they speaking?"

"Iberico," he said, still carefully watching the cryptic exchange playing out before them. "Old language—kin to the Skaldic tongue."

"Do you understand it?" Effie asked.

He shook his head. "Maybe one word in ten."

If that one word in ten was enough to set Muldoon this on edge, Effie didn't want to know the other nine.

The parties finally reached an accord, and Kelestina turned back to Effie. "Captain Meseret is one of the finest Anglers serving the Crystal Throne. He sails the skies of Ciel, procuring wild Leviathan to be bonded to our Gifted Pilots. He's come into possession of a hammerhead nymph destined for Aquilon, but the good Captain's crew seems *incapable* of completing their delivery."

"Aye, cunya," Meseret muttered. "Pup won't take the collar. Tore up every shipman who tried to place it, *sa*? Opened my First Mate groin to gullet. He's lying in his cabin now, all sewn up with gut-string like a *munyeca* doll. Useless."

Muldoon stepped forward to interject himself into the discussion. "I must object, Your Lightness. Effie is too valuable for such a risk."

"Miss Strait is Gifted, is she not?" Kelestina met Muldoon, her porcelain brow flawless despite the tightening of her emerald eyes.

Muldoon swallowed. "Yes, Lightness."

"She held an entire pod of dauphine in thrall before our very eyes, did she not?"

"Yes, Lightness."

Kelestina reached up to caress Muldoon's clean-shaven cheek. She patted him like a pet. "Then it should be no problem for her to approach a singular Leviathan nymph." Her eyes settled once again on Effie. "Isn't that right?"

What could she possibly say to that?

Effie followed Kelestina and Meseret up a corroded iron gangplank and into the gallery of the *Gravel Lizard*. She was grateful to have Muldoon's bolstering presence close at hand, but even that began to seem insufficient as the Patrician Angler led them down a dark ladder to a thick iron door guarding a massive armored containment tank that consumed a healthy share of the airship's bloated hold.

Clang. Clang.

The tank shook as the feral Leviathan within threw itself against the walls of its cage. Kelestina bent her crystalline head to peer inside the tank through a circular porthole.

Effie felt Muldoon's hand on the small of her back. "Do you hear it?" he asked.

"I think we all hear it," Effie grumbled.

"That's not what I mean. Do you *hear* it?"

Effie understood him the first time, but she didn't hear anything besides the beating of her own heart. She closed her eyes and attempted to focus on her breathing, bracing against the subtle pressure of Muldoon's hand on her back.

The ambient sounds of the airship's hold became distant, then melted away. A light prickled in the back of Effie's mind—like the opening of a third, internal eye. Her consciousness quested outward, grazing the mind of the captured hammerhead, but the connection seemed somehow more tenuous than the one she experienced with the dauphine. On Ascension Day, Effie had been aided by the dram of Nectar she'd stolen from the

Green Maw. She still didn't know how much of her success she could attribute to her own innate abilities or the arcane tincture's Gift-sharpening report.

The dauphine's connection flooded her mind, their thoughts as clear as spoken word. She communicated back to them as easily as speaking across a dinner table. From the hammerhead, she had to strain just to glean the barest wisp of intelligence—a fleeting whiff of inchoate thoughts and feelings that seemed to retreat from her every attempt to grasp them.

She felt it the moment the captured Leviathan noticed her trespass. A blast of wild desperation and irate fear induced a sharp pain behind her eyes. Effie must have winced, because she heard Muldoon's voice breaching her trance. "What is it? Do you feel something?"

Connection broken, Effie opened her eyes and shook her head. "It's terrified," she said. "*Jokai fend*, what have they done to this creature?"

Muldoon offered no comforting words to blunt his grave expression.

"Come, child." Kelestina summoned Effie to the armored door. She glanced back at Muldoon, but he coaxed her onward. A member of Meseret's crew handed the Celestial a strange device that looked like a bronze tiara too wide for any human brow. Its band was set with an ingot of jet and lined on the opposite side with needle spokes.

Kelestina held the ornament up to Effie. "The collar induces torpor in the Leviathan to facilitate safe transport. You will use your Gift to succeed where Sire Meseret's crew has failed. Calm the creature and affix the collar atop its brow so the *Gravel Lizard* may safely return to the skies."

Effie accepted the strange device from her host. It was lighter than she expected and warm around the setting. She gently probed the needle spokes along the inner band and nearly pricked the pad of her finger.

"It won't hurt the Leviathan, will it?" she asked.

The emerald light in Kelestina's eyes dimmed. "I assure you, it's quite *humane*."

Effie swallowed and stepped up to the cloudy porthole in the armored door.

Kelestina described the hammerhead as a "nymph," but even at this juvenile stage, it approached the size of a mature dauphine. Its dorsal skin was as black as the collar's jet—its belly the rich blue of a midnight lagoon, flecked with glittering motes like fixed stars across a blanket of firmament. It circled its cramped cage, pacing, pumping four pectoral wings and spitting gouts of air from its jet-pipe tail. The largest of its six dorsal fins clipped the container's ceiling as it bent its cartilaginous back and slammed its cephalofoil against the bulkhead wall, again shaking the hold with a *clang*.

Effie felt another painful spark of terror behind her eyes as the hammerhead's consciousness slipped in through her Gift.

Meseret produced another clucking sound, flicking his tongue against his teeth. "Nasty son of a bitch. I almost pity the poor *rigalo* who bonds him."

Without any further deliberation, Meseret depressed a metal handle on the tank. The heavy door squealed on its hinges as the Angler pulled it open. Effie felt the hands of two crewmen swarm over her, shoving her aggressively inside the tank.

"Wait!" She tried to run back to safety, but the armored door slammed shut in her face. Heads crowded on the other side of the murky porthole to watch, with Kelestina's quartzite rack gleaming from the center.

Breath quickening, Effie turned to the wild Leviathan, the collar dangling from one trembling hand.

Startled by the disturbance, the hammerhead stopped pacing. It hovered in a tight coil at the back of the tank, yellow eyes pointed at Effie from opposite sides of its flat cephalofoil.

Jokai fend... It seemed even bigger now that she was standing inside its tank.

She sensed the creature's apprehension—its unsteady balance between instincts: fight or flee. Effie tried to project her own sense of forced calm, hoping she might be able to prevent it from tipping toward the former.

I'm sorry for the way you've been treated, she sent. *I won't hurt you.*

She felt a stirring through their fuzzy connection, a ripple of latent trauma underpinning the more acute sense of fear. Still grasping the collar in one hand, Effie ventured forward—one step, then another.

She tried to focus on the Leviathan's light flickering in the back of her consciousness—more like a windswept candle than the burning sun of the alpha dauphine. She guarded that flame with an imagined palm, breathed gentle air to give it life.

Why? The question passed through their link with sudden clarity. *Why? Why? Why?*

Effie took another step. *Why what?*

The hammerhead ruffled its black wings. *Why are you doing this to me? I want my mother. I want to see the sky.*

The creature's infant longing nearly broke her. *I want that, too,* Effie sent.

A new pain seared through the bond like a white-hot brand. The Leviathan thrashed its head like the blade of an ax. *Then why are you carrying that chain!* Its sudden anger erupted in her mind as the hammerhead shot out from its coil like a broken spring.

Every instinct in Effie's body screamed to take cover, but a deeper part of her knew what would happen if she showed any fear. She met the charging Leviathan with an admonishing stare and shouted through the bond, *Enough!*

The hammerhead's charge crashed into an invisible wall. The creature stalled in mid-air, its cephalofoil hovering just inches from Effie's face. Slowly, it opened its jaws, revealing rows upon rows of serrated teeth. Those teeth, Effie knew, could tear her to ribbons faster than anyone outside the tank could save her—if they'd even attempt it.

Without breaking eye contact, Effie lowered the collar to the ground and showed the Leviathan her empty hands. The creature bent its head, keening.

I don't want to see you chained, Effie said. *And I'm sorry you were taken from your mother. I lost my mother, too. I know what it is to be frightened and alone.*

A quivering sensation crossed the bond—akin to weeping. Effie reached out a tentative hand and placed it on the hammerhead's cephalofoil. She felt the creature's massive weight leaning against her. *You will see the open sky again, but you have to stop fighting.* She bent over and picked up the collar. *This collar won't harm you. It will help you sleep—keep you from hurting yourself until you can be returned to the sky.*

She sensed the creature's hesitation. *I would like to sleep.*

May I place the collar? Effie asked.

In response, the hammerhead reduced its altitude until the blue skin of its belly grazed the floor of the tank. Effie still sensed its trepidation. She sent soothing notes through the bond as she lowered the collar atop its brow. *When you wake up, you'll see the sky again. I promise.*

The hammerhead cooed.

The collar's tines sank into the Leviathan's flesh on contact. The hammerhead's entire body went rigid with spasms. Effie felt a short blast of terror and betrayal surging through the bond, then its eyes became vacant. Its body stilled, bobbing gently on the stagnant air. The jet ingot in the collar's setting turned blood red, and the bond vanished from Effie's mind as the hammerhead entered floating torpor.

Effie sensed bodies rushing into the tank around her. Whether they belonged to Meseret's sunburnt crew or Kelestina's entourage, she couldn't say. Her vision tunneled around the insensate Leviathan floating guileless before her. The hammerhead reminded her of a sacrificial yak awaiting the climax of Vernal Fete, legs folded beneath its weight, tendons cut.

She felt soft hands guiding her away, back through the armored door and into the *Gravel Lizard*'s vaulted hold. Muldoon awaited her, face as white as Sire Ansel's ivory mares. Effie tried to reach him, but Kelestina's porcelain body intercepted her. Her green eyes burned hungrily as she pulled Effie into a glass embrace.

"Oh, well done, child." The sharp points of Kelestina's nails carved paths through Effie's long hair as the Celestial stroked the back of her head. "Well done."

18

EFFIE

They flew back to Volturnus in silence. When the kite-ship landed at port, it was already dark.

Muldoon sat rigid in his couch—even after the gangplank deployed, and the pilot invited them to disembark.

"I'm sorry," he said as Effie began to undo her restraints. "If I had known—"

"It wouldn't have mattered," Effie said. "You wouldn't have been able to deny Kelestina."

Muldoon continued staring vacantly at the bulkhead wall. "I could have prepared you."

"It's done. No use crying over *what ifs*." She lifted herself out of her couch and walked to the gangplank, but Muldoon remained in his couch. She had little patience for this remorseful performance. He hadn't been the one inside the tank with that nymph. He hadn't been the one to place the collar. "Are you going to escort me back to the manse, or am I on my own again?"

That seemed to shake him from his catatonia. He undid his restraints and followed her out of the cabin. By the time they reached the grounds of Sire Ansel's manse, Muldoon had regained some of his color.

"I apologize," he said as they walked shoulder-to-shoulder down the flagstone path.

"You already said that." Effie was still processing her own role in bringing the frightened hammerhead to heel, and she hadn't the space for Muldoon's self-pity.

"This time I'm apologizing for my own behavior. It was unbecoming."

"It wasn't helpful," Effie agreed.

She felt his hand on her shoulder, turning her to face him on the stoop of Ansel's manse. "I've shown better poise facing down legions of Toranese hoplites," he insisted.

"Maybe you're out of practice."

"It's not that..." Muldoon attempted to smooth his auburn hair, but it bounced right back out of place, hanging unbound to his chin. "I'm...fond of you."

The sincerity of the admission stunned Effie to silence.

"Our host has grand plans for you," Muldoon said. "I knew those plans would place you in danger—I just didn't realize how soon. I could not bear to see you harmed."

Effie felt herself softening at this unexpected confessional. The "practical lesson" on the caye haunted her, and she blamed Muldoon in part—even though she knew that wasn't fair. "Teach me, then," she said. "Teach me about the Leviathan."

"I—" Muldoon's voice caught in his throat, but when she goaded him with her eyes, he nodded. "I'll see what I can do."

"It's late," Effie said. "I'm tired."

"I'm suspending your syllabus tonight. We'll dedicate tomorrow's lesson to review."

A gift. She wasn't sure if she deserved it. "No recitation on the dead kings of Toran?"

"I think the kings of Toran can wait. They're dead, after all." Muldoon's smile possessed an uncharacteristic warmth that disarmed Effie yet again.

Freed from her reading obligations, Effie decided to seize the opportunity to walk down to the village and visit Vanna. She'd intended to call on the cottage more often, but she'd been so consumed by her studies that she never quite made the time. Weeks had passed since she first informed Vanna of her unlikely return. Another visit was long overdue.

She expected to find Vanna sitting alone over a bowl of reheated stew, but her sister had company. Kai occupied Effie's old chair, elbows propped on the table as he entertained Vanna with animated conversation. Vanna laughed along with the story, eyes marking Kai with unusual heat. They were so focused on each other that they didn't even notice Effie's arrival until she was nearly upon them.

"Hello, there."

Startled, Vanna jerked up in her seat. Kai scrambled his arms, unsure what to do with his hands. They both looked like they had stolen something.

"Effie," Vanna said. "This is a pleasant surprise."

Kai gawked at Effie, lines of color blooming on his cheeks. "I'd heard you were back," he stammered.

"Sire Muldoon granted me a night off from my studies." Effie's eyes narrowed with suspicion. "I thought I'd seize the opening to pay my sister a visit. I didn't realize she already had company."

"You're just in time—if you'd like to join us?" Vanna didn't wait for a response before quickly leaving the table to fetch another bowl and fill it from the cookpot. "Kai and I just finished our shift on patrol. We were too late for mess at the bunkhouse, so I invited him over."

The explanation seemed as unnecessary as it was forced. Effie watched the back of Vanna's head then shifted to Kai, now spooning stew into his mouth with extreme dedication. Effie found she didn't have the energy to sleuth out the source of the awkwardness. After the day she'd had, she just wanted to enjoy an uncomplicated meal with her sister. If Kai wanted to join them, so be it.

"You can eat with whoever you want, Vanna—both of you. It makes me...glad to see you two keeping each other company. Jokai know, I've been a ghost."

Vanna returned to the table and deposited the bowl in front of a third chair. "You mean that?" she asked.

"Of course." Effie smiled pleasantly and took her seat. "Even Kai's company beats brooding alone over reheated stew."

Kai dropped his spoon into his bowl, and Vanna's laughter broke the tension. Effie prodded Kai in the shoulder, kneading him until a tight smile worked its way onto his expression. She could almost see the many months of change and conflict evaporating from the room as the three of them fell back into old patterns.

It wouldn't have been possible before the Ascension. So overcome with envy for Kai and Vanna's Gifts, Effie could barely bring herself to look at either one of them. Now that she'd proven herself a Pilot in truth, it all seemed so inconsequential. She'd found her own path to the skies of Ciel. She could hardly begrudge Kai and Vanna their own tiny piece of them.

Effie discovered she wasn't the only one who had been changed by the tumultuous year. Kai had been elevated early to the active corps. He now possessed the body of a dedicated flier, arms thick with new muscle, and chest filled out to a man's physique. He looked nearly as solid as Kendy—and a head taller, at least. His earnest exuberance as he described his first mission over open sky rekindled Effie's long-dormant affection for her oldest friend. Kai had always worn his emotions on his sleeve, and it seemed no amount of training and experience would stamp that out of him.

In Vanna, the change was more subtle. Her sister seemed uncommonly subdued, as if she held the weight of some grievous burden that she could not—or would not—share. At several points during the conversation, Effie caught her sister drifting, staring off into some personal abyss.

"Reading every *night*?" Kai was appalled by Effie's description of her course of study. "*Balls of the deep*, how can you bear it?"

The curse jarred Vanna from one of her distracted trances. She slapped Kai's hand in reprimand. "You're in the presence of ladies!"

"It isn't so bad," Effie said. "I'm learning a lot. The world beyond the archipelago is a fascinating and troubled place."

When she described the tower of books Muldoon delivered on their first day, Kai nearly fell out of his seat.

"How have things been with Sire Muldoon?" Vanna asked. The question had clearly been eating at her. She'd just been waiting for her moment to wedge it in.

Effie smiled wistfully. "He treats me quite well. I don't know—he's a Patrician. He can be stiff and a bit condescending, but he means well. He's fond of me."

"*Fond* of you?" Vanna's brow wrinkled in disbelief. "I wouldn't have thought that creature capable of fondness."

"He's not who you think he is," Effie said. "He asked me to apologize to you on his behalf. I think he's ashamed of the way he spoke to you on Aeolus."

"He should be," Vanna said.

"Can you manage a little grace? He wasn't in his right mind. You should give him another chance."

"If you say so." Vanna still looked skeptical, but she'd run out of pithy retorts. "I am glad to hear he isn't mistreating you."

"Hardly!" Effie sniffed. "He protects me."

"Protects you from what?" Kai asked.

"Everyone else."

Kai snorted. "Sounds like someone's carrying a bit of a torch."

He might have meant it in jest, but Effie detected a bitter edge sharpening the joke. He couldn't possibly be jealous? She watched him stabbing at his empty bowl with his spoon, working his strong jaw back and forth.

"He is very gallant..." Effie teased.

Vanna slapped her arm. "*Jokai fend*, Effie. Don't even kid."

"Handsome, too," Effie added. "But he's too old for me."

She batted her eyes playfully at Kai's look of guarded relief, but he didn't return the flirtation. He tapped his spoon against his empty bowl, then stacked it on top of the other two and deposited them in the wash basin. "I should go see Senna," he said. "Raji said she's not doing well."

"What's wrong with Senna?" Effie checked Vanna, but her sister's expression had gone blank again. "Is she hurt?"

"I assumed you'd already know," Kai said, still scraping the leavings from their bowls. "All the time you spend up at the governor's manse—I thought you'd have been the first one to *know*."

"Stop it, Kai," Vanna said.

"Know *what*?" Effie demanded.

Kai whipped around from the basin and crossed his arms in front of his chest. "Kelestina's conscripted Flynn, Senna, and Kale. They're supposed to report to Sire Ansel in three days to be shipped off."

"What?" Effie checked Vanna for a correction, but her sister returned only silence.

Flynn, Senna, and Kale... It was too precise a list to be a coincidence.

Kai met Effie's look of confusion with a scowl. "Imagine how surprised we were."

"Do you have any insight into this?" Vanna asked. "Any idea where they'll be sent?"

Effie shook her head. "They could be sent anywhere in the sky under the influence of the Crystal Throne." That clearly wasn't the answer Vanna wanted to hear. "It's a high honor though," Effie quickly appended. "Gifted conscripts won't be treated like the governor's staff. They'll enjoy elevated status."

"Elevated status?" Kai said it with disgust. "I'm sure that will come as a great comfort to Senna's betrothed."

Effie expected Vanna to rise to her defense again, but her sister seemed lost in another one of her melancholy episodes. "I wouldn't expect you to understand," Effie said. She hadn't intended to sound so condescending, but so much time rubbing elbows with the Patricians had magnetized her voice. "If our host has a need for Elementalists, then it is our duty to answer the call. The conscripts will be well provided for—whatever higher purpose awaits them."

"You sound like one of *them*," Kai said. "Thank you for dinner, Vanna. I'll see you tomorrow at dusk for our next patrol?"

Vanna nodded absentmindedly, still lost in her own thoughts.

"Nice to see you again, Eff." Kai stalked out of the cottage and slammed the door behind him.

How quickly things had turned. Their pleasant dinner suddenly seemed like a cheap facade, a layer of foundation painted over all the scars time had wrought into their lives.

"I have to go, too," Vanna said, shaking herself back to the present. "Flynn asked to see me."

"Is she upset about the conscription, too?" Effie asked.

"Taking it better than the other two." Vanna stood up from the table. "I think she's happy to have a purpose again. It's been hard for her since the forced retirement."

That was something, at least.

"Will you be staying the night?" Vanna asked. "I've kept your room as you left it."

Part of Effie wanted to say yes. The familiar space would have been a welcome comfort after her encounter with the hammerhead and news of the conscription order, in which she'd played an unwitting role.

"I think I'd better go back to the manse," she said.

Vanna took the rejection in stride. "Stay as long as you like." She grabbed an old oil cloak on her way out the door. "Take care of yourself, Eff."

Alone again.

Effie *would* take care of herself. She'd be ready bright and early in Sire Ansel's study.

She had questions for Muldoon.

19

VANNA

Vanna found the door to Flynn's small cottage ajar. She called once for permission before letting herself inside. The sound of muffled voices led her down a splintering wooden staircase, into a dim root cellar at the back of the house.

Kendy and Ava had already arrived. They gathered within the glowing orb cast by a single oil lamp. The former commander and her successor stood over an iron bin of dried beans, while the old apothecary sat on a wooden stool hunched over a gnarled walking stick. To what end Flynn had convened this unlikely party, Vanna couldn't say, but she owed the retired officer enough not to question her summons. Vanna had Flynn to thank for much of her skill in the sky. When Vanna first manifested, Kendy had been the Draft Lieutenant in charge of training cadets, but Vanna quickly outstripped him. She entered the active corps after less than a year of training, full of raw, unmolded talent. It was Flynn's practiced hand more than any other that pressed her into the shape of a true dragoon.

And now she was leaving.

Flynn may have retired from the active corps, but Vanna liked knowing she still had access to her knowledge and experience. Losing her to Kelestina's conscription felt like having one of her wings clipped—and at an unusually dangerous time. She knew Kendy didn't see it the same way.

Flynn's mere existence sent him spiraling with insecurity. He chafed every time Vanna solicited her input. She guessed he'd be happy to get rid of her.

Flynn summoned Vanna over to the side of the bin, where she held the wide stance and stern posture of an officer addressing her draft. She might be aged, but she still exuded command.

Kendy met Flynn's severity with forced indifference. "What are we doing here, Flynn?" Not for the first time, Vanna wished he could muster a bit more maturity.

Ava's shrill voice crept out from the corner where she sat. "You sure the boy's ready for this? He seems brittle."

Kendy didn't deign to acknowledge the comment, but Vanna felt his tension emanating off him in waves.

"He'll have to be," Flynn said. "I'm leaving the island, and at my age, it'll probably be for good."

"Don't say that," Vanna said. "You'll be back. I've just been with my sister. She's convinced you'll be well treated. Afforded status, even."

Ava cackled in her corner, and Vanna thought she heard the old apothecary mutter something like "honest lies."

"How are you feeling about everything?" Vanna asked Flynn. "Sincerely."

"Sincerely?" Flynn flipped her long gray braid over her shoulder. "Looking forward to it. I'm wasting away here without the corps. Old Bolo keeps me busy working on the storm wall, but that's no life for a flier. If our host has a better use for my Gift, she's welcome to it. It's the fledglings I'm worried about."

"I hear Senna's put out," Vanna said. "What about Kale?"

"He doesn't know what to make of it," Kendy said. "Still in shock, I think."

Flynn nodded. "I'll keep an eye on 'em. I promise you that."

Ava loudly cleared her throat. "Can we get down to business? The shop needs tending, and one of my dutiful apprentices is trapped at home with two sick whelps."

Flynn nodded stiffly then bent to the iron bin. "Give me a hand with this."

Kendy helped her shift the heavy cache of dried beans across the cellar floor, revealing the outlines of a moldering wooden hatch. Curious, Vanna knelt to the secret compartment and brushed a thick layer of dust from its face. Without a handle, she didn't see any obvious way to open it.

Flynn saw her trying to work out the contraption and waved her off. "It's rigged with a pressure lock. Neat little trick. Your mother's design, Vanna."

"My mother?"

A nostalgic smile dimpled Flynn's leather cheeks. "Vera Strait always had a knack for design. Damn shame she went so young. Damn shame."

Vanna had only been four years old when the Butcher's attack claimed her parents' lives. Her mother had been an Elementalist and a dragoon, but that was only *what* she did and not *who* she was. Of Vera Strait the woman, Vanna remembered little and knew even less.

Flynn pointed at four small pinholes in the corners of the hatch. "Weave an equal stream of pressure through each valve."

Kendy stepped forward to answer the call, but Flynn pushed him back with a stiff arm. "Let Vanna do it."

He could hardly argue now that her dead mother had been invoked, but he did grumble through his deference. Out of the corner of her eye, Vanna saw Ava leaning over her cane, milky eye gleaming in the lamplight. Vanna glanced up at Flynn, then tapped into her Gift, shaping four tiny vortices of wind. She slipped each vortex into one of the pinholes precisely, and the hatch popped open on its hinge.

Flynn rewarded her with a satisfied nod. "Takes most folks a couple tries to get the trick of it."

Kendy was already peering into the secret sub-basement, but it was too dark to see anything within. Flynn picked up the oil lamp by the handle and dangled it over the open hatch.

The light revealed an array of wooden crates lining the secret chamber, and within each crate Vanna saw rows of glass vials—each one filled with an effervescent purple dram. The tincture fluoresced upon contact with the lamplight.

Vanna's eyes grew as wide as ostrich eggs. "Jokai fend..."

It was Nectar. Dozens of doses—enough to juice the entire dragoon corps several times over.

She heard the creak of a wicker chair, followed by Ava's feet scuffling across the floor. "Pretty, ain't she?" The old apothecary poked Vanna in the ribs with her stick.

"What the hell is this?" Kendy asked.

Ava swatted him with her cane. "A Jokai-damned present, that's what. Generations in the making. Where's your gratitude, boy?"

Flynn stood pridefully over the trove. "This cache has been passed down from wing commander to wing commander," she explained. "Surely, you understand the need for secrecy. If our host were to discover we were hoarding Nectar like this... I think we all know how that would go over."

Kendy shook his head, still gazing down into the priceless cache. When he looked up, he jabbed an accusatory finger at Flynn. "You should have told me about this the minute you retired."

"Telling you about it now," Flynn said.

"It's been over a year!"

"Put your feathers down, boy," Ava squawked. "I didn't think you were ready to carry this burden. Still don't, but our situation is what it is."

"The Volturnian Dragoons always kept a reserve for dire times," Flynn said. "When the Celestials arrived, the need for secrecy around the cache became more acute. Today, I pass this sacred responsibility off to you—both of you. Don't go dipping into it without good cause. Ava can only pinch a few drams from every harvest without triggering Governor Ansel's censors. You burn through your reserves, and it'll take years to replenish."

Flynn withdrew the lamp and summoned a gust, slamming the hatch back in place. Vanna helped her slide the bin of beans back over the hiding place.

"I'll have to move it," Kendy said. "I'm not comfortable leaving this treasure in an empty house."

"No, you won't," Flynn slapped one hand on his broad shoulder. "I'm leaving the cottage to you. The governor's lister already has the paperwork. Wing Commander shouldn't be living in the bunkhouse like a raw cadet."

Kendy rocked back on his heels, stunned to silence by the generous gift. "I—I don't know what to say."

Flynn winked at him, and it was more warmth than Vanna thought the old commander had ever shown her successor.

As Flynn and Kendy made peace, Vanna felt one of Ava's whiskers tickling her ear. "You'll keep the boy in line," she rasped. "See that he doesn't squander our efforts."

Vanna nodded, even though she wasn't sure how much of a guardrail she'd be able to provide. For most dragoons—especially those who were weaker in the Gift—the Nectar's allure would be difficult to resist.

20

EFFIE

Effie stared daggers at Muldoon as he lectured through a dry review of their last physics lesson.

"...lift is generated by the motion of fluid around an object. The pressure differential applies an upward force perpendicular to the direction of flow. I'm going to provide you the specifications of a hypothetical object—an aircraft—and I'd like you to come to the slate and use the equations from your text to calculate the velocity necessary to generate the requisite lift."

He turned from his slate board to hand her his wedge of chalk. She didn't rise from her seat to take it from him.

"What is it?" he asked.

Effie blew a lock of hair from her face, so he'd be certain to see her eyes narrow to slits.

Muldoon withdrew. "That's an awfully wrathful expression for fluid dynamics..."

"I hope you didn't need an equation to work *that* out," Effie said.

Muldoon set his chalk down. "Something's wrong."

Effie gently applauded, patting four fingers against an open palm.

"Care to enlighten me?"

"I don't like being used."

"I'm sorry?" Muldoon's shapely eyebrows pinched together. She was increasingly certain he plucked them to keep their form.

"I had dinner with my sister the other night."

"Oh? That sounds...nice?"

"Not really," Effie said. "She seemed a little put out by a new conscription order down from Aquilon. Flynn, Senna, and Kale—I believe it was? A familiar list of names."

Muldoon nervously licked his lips. "About that—it was always my intention to—"

"To tell me I was marking Volturnians for conscription?" Effie slammed her hands flat on the table. "Was it your intention to tell me *before* they vanished on an airship or after?"

Muldoon loosened his collar with a finger. She hadn't expected to induce so much discomfort by confronting her tutor, but she was happy to find she had the power to do so. He sat at the study table opposite her, as he was wont to do when he needed to goad her back to pliancy. "I am sorry you feel used. It was not my intention to deceive."

"And yet you managed it quite well. *Who are the strongest Elementalists, excepting only the officers.*" Effie scoffed. "What a fool I am—to hear such a question and find it innocent."

Muldoon tilted his head. "It was a bit credulous, if I'm being frank."

"You lied to me!" Effie shouted.

Muldoon raised his hands to calm her. "I didn't exactly *lie*. If I'm guilty of anything here, it's a deceptive omission."

"Three Volturnians are getting shipped off the island because of me! Do you know how that makes me feel? This conscription order rips them away from friends and family—Senna's due to *wed* this spring!"

"Which is exactly why I didn't tell you," Muldoon said. "I wanted your unvarnished assessment of their Gifts. I didn't want personal considerations to influence your selections."

"I wouldn't have *made* any selections," Effie said.

"More's the reason!" When her anger didn't cool, Muldoon sighed. "I apologize for misleading you, but you shouldn't blame yourself for the conscription. Kelestina made her decision. She would have found the Elementalists she needed—one way or another."

Effie glowered at her tutor. He made a fair point, but it didn't take any of the sting out of the deception. "What will become of them?" she asked. "We've never received a conscription order like this before."

Muldoon shook his head. "I cannot say—"

"Cannot or will not? What happened to the *sacred relationship between tutor and pupil*?"

Muldoon snorted at that. He tapped one finger against the tabletop. "It's not uncommon for a Celestial host to conscript the Gifted from her plebiscite."

"It's uncommon on Volturnus."

Muldoon tipped his head. "That may be about to change. The Crystal Throne has many uses for the Gifted. I'm telling you the truth when I say that I don't know the mind of Her Lightness, but I can tell you what's happened in the past—in other lands." Effie coaxed him to continue with her eyes. "The new conscripts are often taken to an Armada base and subjected to a brief training. Nothing that compares to our course of study. A more abbreviated preparation for their insertion into Celestial society. Considering their talents, I suspect they'll be attached to an Armada fleet as auxiliaries."

"She's sending them to war?" It was worse than Effie imagined.

"In a sense," Muldoon said. "But they won't be holding spears in the vanguard, if that's your concern. They'll be well protected. Their Gifts are too valuable to squander."

"They're people, Muldoon. *People* are too valuable to squander."

"As you say..." He sounded hesitant. "They will be well treated. You understand the kyriarchy now. They won't be mere household conscripts. Should they prove themselves in the Armada, they may even be elevated to the Patrician class."

It was much the same rationalization she'd provided to Vanna and Kai. Hearing it parroted back to her only confirmed how hollow it sounded.

"I should warn you," Muldoon said. Effie's eyes warned him in return, but he forged on all the same. "I do not expect these conscriptions will be the last. I would appreciate your advice when decisions need to be made."

"I don't like the sound of that," Effie said.

"You asked for honesty."

She had. Effie chewed the bitter news as she stared at her tutor blankly. She still guessed he was hiding something, but she wasn't sure how to draw it out. "I'll look at your lists," she finally said. "But next time you put one in front of me, I'm going to ask what it's for."

Today's lecture might have been intended for review, but she'd learned a new lesson, after all.

"I'd expect nothing less." Muldoon fingered his wedge of chalk again but placed it back down on the table. "I have something for you," he said. "Perhaps you'll accept it as a peace offering?"

Effie raised one eyebrow. "Depends what it is."

Muldoon led her back to his chamber in the west wing of Ansel's manse. He was acting awfully coy. That made Effie nervous, but as ever, curiosity got the better of her. It was her first time inside her tutor's private room. She paused in the doorway, scanning the odd decorations adorning the walls: strange maps and sky charts, each one mounted in an expensive wooden frame. Muldoon immediately began sorting through a stack of books beside the bed, while Effie perused a painted triptych of the Doric Sky hanging over his writing desk.

"Quite the interesting collection you've gathered." She moved across the wall until she landed in front of a bizarre map describing a singular island adrift in an unmarked sky. The map had a different character from its cousins along the walls—painted fancifully with sketches of odd beasts but missing useful information like a positional matrix or key. The aspect of a parchment scroll had been drawn across the top, filled with Skaldic runes she couldn't read.

"What's this one?" she asked.

Muldoon's head popped up over his bed. "Oh." Was that embarrassment she sensed? "A whimsical curio—nothing more."

Effie squinted, studying the strange island depicted on the map. "Where is this island supposed to be?"

"If I could answer that question, I wouldn't be marooned on Volturnus —ah!" He found the tome he was looking for and joined her in front of the hanging map.

"Not much of a map," Effie said.

"No," Muldoon agreed. "It's not really a map at all. It's some long-dead Skald's artistic rendering of the Lost Continent—the Island of Mu."

"Mu?" Effie returned to studying the picture with newfound interest.

Muldoon scanned the painting beside her, holding the book at his side.

"The Lost Continent is a holy island in the Skaldic faith—a *promised* land of sorts. It's said to be the destiny of the Hundred Frozen Souls to conquer its hidden shores."

"The Celestials are...looking for an island?"

Muldoon smiled patiently. "The island is symbolic. An avatar of conquest. To 'discover the Lost Continent' is a euphemism for bringing all Eight Skies of Ciel beneath the Crystal Throne. It is a land that exists only in the mind—a place to reunite the Hundred Frozen Souls from their millennial diaspora. There are some, however, who take the myth more literally—our host among them."

"Kelestina thinks this island actually exists?"

Muldoon hesitated before answering. "As I understand it, our host is rather orthodox in her beliefs."

Effie traced the outline of Mu's jagged shore with her eyes. She found that she preferred Kelestina's literal interpretation of the myth. A Lost Continent waiting to be discovered held more romance than a symbol of conquest.

"Enough religion," Muldoon said, holding up the book for Effie's appraisal. "I ordered this volume down from the library of Aquilon just for you."

Effie barely glanced at the leather-bound tome. "The last thing I need is another book."

"I think you'll change your mind once you see what it is." He drew her attention to the title, etched in golden calligraphy.

Leviathan of the Doric and Ionic Skies.

Effie accepted the book and began to flip through its pages. The heavy tome had been printed on sturdier stock than her other textbooks. As she thumbed through, she encountered page after page of full-color sketches— each one depicting a different exotic Leviathan in flight. Anatomical diagrams followed the color portraits, as well as maps representing known habitats and paths of migration.

"Well?" Muldoon eagerly awaited her approval. Effie wanted to hold onto her anger from earlier, but his enthusiasm proved hard to resist.

"It's incredible," she said.

A wave of relief washed over her tutor. "It's one of a kind!" he said. "A hand-drawn field guide. You said you wanted to learn more about the

Leviathan. The subject falls outside the Six Academic Graces, but I see no harm in slaking your curiosity—as long as it doesn't interfere with your syllabus."

Effie closed the book, clutching its cover against her chest. "Thank you for this."

Muldoon beamed. "You're very welcome."

21

KAI

By tradition, the junior fliers held the tips of the formation on patrol. That placed Kai in Lya's draft stream, staring jealously at Raji, who occupied the first position on Vanna's wing.

On this night, their patrol group drew the northway. Vanna drove a hard pace against the headwinds, pushing their formation V northwest to the edge of the Frostwind Cayes, then due east to the windward face of Aquilon. Once they finished casing the northern isle, they would sweep the leeward shore of Volturnus on their return flight to the village. If they were lucky, they'd be back at the bunkhouse in time for morning mess.

Kai had become more practiced at preserving his Gift. The double patrols necessitated it. Even so, his muscles burned, and his grasp on the winds became increasingly clumsy as Vanna guided their formation toward Aquilon's distant shore.

Raji had taught him the trick of applying wax to his cheeks to prevent windburn—another necessity with the north winds screaming in his face. The pivot eastward brought some relief, but the respite proved fleeting. A thin line of icy rain crossed their path just off the shore of the northern isle, layering new misery atop the exhaustion of patrol.

Kai realized he'd been spoiled by the adventure of his first mission over open sky. Service in the corps rarely involved the excitement of a missing zeppelin and a daring rescue of injured civilians. Even the threat of a lurking Leviathan pirate wasn't enough to get his blood up these days. He hoped they did find something. Flying into the jaws of a plumed serpent had to be better than this frigid monotony.

They didn't encounter anything.

The northern skies were as barren as the windswept plains of the Frostwind Cayes. A few merchant kite-ships hailed them from the transit lines out of Avernus, but beyond those innocuous aircraft, they encountered nothing more nefarious than freezing rain.

While he suffered inside his soaking flight suit, Kai imagined Effie curled up next to one of Ansel's hearths with servants tending the fire and kneading the tension from her shoulders. In his mind's eye, she twirled a strand of that long, violet hair around a finger, eating figs from a silver tray as she made moon eyes at Sire Muldoon.

Against all reason, she'd wormed her way back into his thoughts—ever since that dinner together at Vanna's cottage. The more he resisted, the more she insisted upon herself. That meal had been simultaneously strange and familiar. Almost comfortable—until he went and ruined it with his flapping mouth. It wasn't Effie's fault that Senna and Kale were gone. He knew that, even as he accused her of complicity. Then again, his anger didn't have anything to do with Senna or Kale—not really. He'd succumbed to long-simmering bitterness over the way she'd treated him since he joined the dragoons. At least when she was mad at him, he knew that she still cared. Envy and resentment, he understood. This Patrician indifference cut him deeper.

The rain picked up and changed directions, blasting westward into Kai's face. Visibility diminished as sheets of rainfall reflected back the light of their alchemical headlamps. Kai caught the air-sign to put down from Lya and followed her into a brisk descent.

They landed on the windward shore of Aquilon, and Vanna directed them to a grove of palm trees for cover. Clinging to the canopy for shelter, Kai huddled shoulder-to-shoulder with his draft, their faces ghoulish in the converging torchlight. He'd never set foot on the northern island before, though he'd seen its forbidding shoreline several times from the sky on patrol. Somewhere in the greater darkness beyond the grove, Kelestina's crystal palace lurked, its spired walls concealed behind sheets of falling rain.

The ground squelched as Kadir fell back on his haunches. Jaffe looked just as exhausted, but she wasn't about to let the wet grass soak through her suit liner. She leaned against Kadir's shoulder to catch her breath. Kai felt Lya shiver beside him. The headwinds had disheveled her braid, and her long pink hair now clung soaking to her flight suit. He watched her bend to wring it out. Nayla looked ready to murder someone.

Vanna surveyed her haggard draft, tapping one finger against her belt. "We wait here for the rain to pass. It's just a squall line. It shouldn't last."

Raji rubbed his hands together, then produced a tin flask from inside his flight suit and took a sip.

"Hey now." Lya flipped her hair back and snatched the flask from his lips to claim a sip for herself.

Vanna watched them with her tongue between her teeth. "What the hell is that?" she asked.

Lya blinked back tears as she handed the flask back to Raji. "Uhhh, water."

Vanna shook her head. "Give me that." Raji presented the flask to his lieutenant with a hangdog expression. Vanna sniffed its contents then, to Kai's surprise, took her own sip before tossing it back to Raji. When she exhaled, Kai tasted Raji's "water" on her breath.

"This is a shit assignment," Nayla said.

Raji took another swig from his flask.

"Am I wrong?" Nayla's eyes probed each of them. "We never see anything up this way, and the skies north of Aquilon are always foul."

"You'd rather fly into the jaws of this Bone Adder?" Lya asked.

"*Balls of the deep!*" Nayla ruffled her short brown locks with frustration, spraying them all with rainwater. "If we're the first ones to spot a Leviathan pirate over Aquilon, something's gone very wrong."

Kadir voiced his agreement from his muddy seat. "What's our tithe pay for anyway?"

"Careful, fledgling." Raji waved his flask at the new flier before taking another swig. "This island's the wrong place for that kind of talk." His eyes drifted up to the fronds hanging overhead. "The trees have ears on Aquilon."

That sounded like a ridiculous notion to Kai, but it was enough to frighten Kadir to silence. At least he came by his treason honestly. Kadir's father managed one of the ports outside the village. He'd grown up hearing his fair share of griping over the Celestial tithe.

"I'd like to hear what our esteemed Draft Lieutenant thinks of all this," Lya said.

Vanna looped her thumbs through her belt and glared at her fliers. "I agree with Kendy." Kai caught Nayla rolling her eyes. "We can't depend on Kelestina to keep us safe. We may be *guests* of the Crystal Throne, but these are still *our* islands. *Our* skies. The dragoons kept them safe before the Celestials arrived, and we'll be the ones keeping them safe long after they're gone."

Raji grimaced. "The trees!" he moaned.

The rain passed just as Vanna predicted, and the dragoons stepped out into the remnant drizzle. Both moons appeared through the retreating clouds, phases balanced so that Yeena's yellow wax matched Yanna's orange wane. The silhouette of Kelestina's palace revealed itself in their combined light, a rambling outline of towers, gatehouses, and crenelated walls. Kai squinted through the bracket described by two soaring spires where he saw a distant shadow perched over the northern sky, growing by inches as it processed along the firmament.

"Vanna..." he called out. "*Lieutenant!*"

Vanna finished patching a rent in Jaffe's flight suit and gusted over to his side. "What is it?"

He pointed at the shadow approaching from the horizon.

Vanna's chapped lips pressed together until they turned from pink to white.

"What does that look like to you?" Kai asked.

Instead of answering, she signaled the draft to assemble and led them into flight along the edge of the island, keeping distance between her dragoons and the palace's outer wall. Kai knew they were forbidden to disturb the sanctity of Kelestina's airspace, but those boundaries had always been poorly defined. More than ever, he wished that his status didn't place him at the back of the V. He was convinced that if he only flew at Vanna's wing, the proximity would be enough for him to glean some of her guarded intent.

As they banked north, Vanna passed back the air-sign to claim altitude. Kai tapped his flagging Gift to keep pace at Lya's heel, climbing until he flew level with the spiral peaks of the palace towers.

Vanna signaled for her draft to enter a holding pattern. She yielded the formation's point to Nayla, then shot off into the distance.

The draft continued to circle as they awaited their lieutenant's return. With each revolution, Kai caught a better glimpse of the object looming in the Aquilonian sky. It didn't look like a Leviathan—and that realization brought as much disappointment as relief. It was some kind of aircraft, though—something vast and armored—larger even than Governor Sigyn's *Jormunghast*. It had the rough shape of a zeppelin. The craft drew to a halt over Kelestina's palace, hovering a few feet from the nearest spire.

When Vanna returned from her survey, she flashed the sign to form up and led them streaking back down the Aquilonian shoreline and across the narrow gap to Volturnus' northern tip. As soon as the ends of the formation crossed the strait, she took them down in sight of the trolley station.

"What was it?" The question on the tips of all their tongues first burst from Raji's liquor-loosened lips.

Vanna's eyes seemed very distant as she picked the edge of her snaggle-tooth with her thumb. "An airship," she said. "Biggest one I've ever seen. Powered by steam and lumite lifts."

"You make any colors?" Lya asked. She knew all the right questions in a situation like this one. With Senna gone, she was next in line to become Kendy's favorite scout.

Vanna nodded, still deep in thought. "The Armada Serpent on one flank. The other banner, I didn't recognize—looked like a black owl with a branch in its mouth over a red- and gold-checkered field."

Kai added his blank stare to all the rest of them. "What does it mean?" he asked.

"Who cares?" Raji said. "If it's an Armada ship, it's no business of ours. It's not a pirate. That's all that matters."

"I have to go back to the village," Vanna said.

"But we aren't finished with our patrol!" Kai winced as Nayla punched him in the arm.

"It's easy air the rest of the way," Vanna said. "Stay within sight of the leeward shore until you reach the Green Maw, then circle home."

"You expect us to pick up your slack?" Nayla shot back.

"I do," Vanna said. "That's an order, and I'm leaving you in command, so see that's carried out."

"*Balls of the deep.*" Nayla shook her frazzled head, but tapped out a salute over her patches.

She began coaxing the other dragoons to gather themselves up and assemble for the final leg of the flight. Kai broke away to follow Vanna.

"Hey!" When she didn't turn, he seized her by the ruffles of her flight suit. "Where are you going?"

Vanna tugged herself free and waved him off. "Don't worry about me."

"I *am* worried about you! You've been acting weird for weeks. Losing track of conversations and staring off into the abyss. It's not like you to abandon your draft."

"That's enough, Kai." It was her tone that struck him more than the dismissal. She spoke to him like a nuisance little brother—the very impression he'd worked desperately to wipe away. Every time he and Vanna moved closer to becoming something more, a moment like this one reasserted the old boundaries of their relationship with too much ease. These Strait women seemed determined to frustrate him all the way to the lunatic colony on Lonely Spur. It must be something in their blood.

"I'm not abandoning the draft," she said. "You are. Go assemble under Nayla. That's an order."

Scowling, he tapped out a bitter salute. "Aye, Lieutenant."

Kai wanted to glance back—to see if his obstinance landed even a glancing blow—but before he gave in to the impulse, he felt the winds of Volturnus retreating behind him—Vanna gusting away on her abundant Gift.

22

VANNA

Kai's reprimand stung more than it should have. It might have been a routine patrol, but Vanna *had* abandoned her draft—no matter how she rationalized it.

She wasn't even sure why it felt so urgent. She wasn't sure why she made *any* of her decisions lately. Letting Bael slip through her fingers outside the pub. Lying to Kendy and the other dragoons. *Jokai fend*, there'd been a moment when she'd almost let Kai *kiss* her. Whether it was instinct or impulse that led, it was becoming increasingly difficult to say, and maybe that was a distinction without a difference. Neither motivation held up well to scrutiny.

The sight of that Armada juggernaut dropping anchor over Aquilon filled her with a kind of dread that defied easy description. She almost wished it had been a pirate Leviathan, instead. Vanna's whole world had been inverted. The Celestials were their allies—their *hosts*. When Maug the Butcher came down on Devil Ray to terrorize their shores, it had been the Armada that repelled him.

And yet...

In so few words, Bael had successfully seeded her mind with doubt. It *didn't* make sense that another Leviathan pirate would arrive just to attack a zeppelin transport. The purpose of that attack wasn't plunder. Retribution—now that seemed the finer fit.

Vanna needed answers. She didn't know what she would do once she found them, but these days she so rarely planned more than one step ahead. Only one man on Volturnus possessed the insight she needed.

A man who wasn't supposed to be there.

She soared south across the Volturnian jungle, now aided by the north wind that had harried her ascent. To elude any idle farmhands who might be watching the sky, she extinguished her alchemical headlamp and put down next to one of the farm roads that ran through the orchards. She only had a few hours before dawn stripped away the last of her cover. Checking over both shoulders, she set off toward the island's southern tip and the forbidden jungle that grew there.

The tree line of the Green Maw sprouted from the horizon, an impenetrable black shadow, guarded by stalking predators and ancient taboo. Even from the jungle's edge, the moonlight gave her nothing. Vanna knew what had to be done; still she hesitated, so deeply ingrained was the cultural taboo. Only Ava and her apprentices had cultivated some immunity to this superstition.

And Effie.

Ava said Effie broke the taboo—that she was the most recent Volturnian to enter the Maw, which suggested she had come here alone. Her sister's fortunes hardly seemed soured by the Jokai's ire. If Effie could return from the Green Maw unscathed, then so could Vanna.

With one last bracing breath of the open air, Vanna peeled back a curtain of fronds and hanging moss. The Green Maw swallowed her.

The jungle's denizens welcomed and warned her with their chittering calls. She fumbled her way through a thick layer of brush, stumbling over a rotten log that clipped her toes as she blindly tried to clear its impasse. Once she regained her feet, she illuminated her headlamp. Her torch flickered, on the verge of exhausting its alchemical fuel. She'd nearly drained it on the long patrol. She could only hope it would last long enough to find Bael's camp. Finding her way back was a problem for later.

Bael had been hiding in the Maw for weeks—since Effie's Ascension, at least, and potentially much longer. No matter how careful he'd been, there should be signs for Vanna to follow, but the jungle's armor grew thick, frustrating her progress. She used the dagger at her belt to cut through a wall of thorns and more hanging moss, until she crashed into a thick spider web that sent her spitting and flailing. She stumbled through the final feet of brush and into a relative clearing. By the grace of her failing torch, she picked up the edge of a cart path that wound deeper into the jungle, summoning an uncharacteristic prayer to her lips.

Whoever maintained this trail did a consistent job of it. Vanna's pace quickened, every step drawing her deeper inside the forbidden Maw. The jungle watched her passage with a thousand unseen eyes, and those weren't the only eyes that marked her.

Vanna realized she was being followed.

Her strength in the Gift offered many advantages. She spoke the language of the winds like her native tongue, and the winds accepted her authority without resistance. They honored her like a regent—whispered secrets that no other Elementalist had the skill to hear. Through her Gift, she sensed every footfall trailing her down the path, noting each aberrant current stirred up in her wake.

Keen to preserve her advantage, Vanna kept walking with her headlamp turned up the trail. Cautiously, she began to slow, permitting her stalker to gain on her. As soon as he drew within range, she grasped the handle of her dagger and the reins of her Gift, summoning a forceful gust behind her. She heard a yelp of surprise as she ensnared her stalker in a skein of wind solid as an angler's net. She whipped around with her dagger drawn just as the winds slammed her captive at her feet.

Vanna thrust the blade of her dagger across his neck then immediately withdrew.

"Kai?"

Kai's head bobbed from side to side. Groaning, he flipped his sandy hair away from his unfocused eyes. Vanna met his first attempt to hoist himself up with a blast of wind that planted him flat on his back.

She loomed over him, fuming. "What the hell do you think you're doing?"

He shielded himself from her torchlight with an arm. "Can you point that thing away?"

"I almost cut your throat!" Vanna let him struggle with his blindness another second before granting him his vision.

He sat upright, clutching his ribs with another pained groan. "You did enough damage without it." His eyes leapt to the side of the path, chasing the sound of some snarling predator.

"What the hell are you doing here, Kai?"

"What the hell am I doing here?" His jaw dropped.

"I won't ask again."

"I followed you—to make sure you were okay!"

She brandished her dagger as if she might really strike him. "You think I need your protection?"

"I don't know! The way you've been acting—" He shook his head. "What in creation are you doing in the Green Maw in the middle of the night? This jungle's cursed."

"Stupid fledgling..." Vanna shook her head, exasperated. She sheathed her dagger before she did something she'd regret and perched her hands on her hips. "Get up off the ground." She offered her hand and hoisted Kai back to his feet. "Go back to the village," she said as he dusted himself off. "Forget what you saw here."

His slackjawed expression seemed caught between outrage and despair. "I can't just leave you here."

"You can and you will," she shot back.

"Is that an order?" He sounded so petulant. To think, she'd nearly welcomed this child into her bed.

"It is," she said.

"I'm not going anywhere until you tell me what you're doing out here!"

A shriek in the distance and a rustling overhead interrupted the argument.

"What was that?" Fear banished all the obstinance from Kai's voice. He drew up beside her.

Vanna cast her torchlight up to the canopy—caught a lemur's striped tail scampering across a gnarled branch. She turned back, intending to shame Kai into compliance, but a louder rustling drew her attention back to the canopy. The winds shouted their warning too late. A pair of giant wings descended from the treetops. Her torchlight flashed on the end of a sharp beak cutting toward her, and Vanna drew upon her Gift, raising enough wind to shield them both.

The beak scythed through her currents, the leading edge of a hulking Avian that landed on the path in front of them. The creature's muscular legs bent as it folded up its wings.

An eight-foot hawk unsheathed a greatsword as tall as Kai and lunged, beak snapping over the edge of its blade. Vanna stumbled backward until she bumped into Kai. She fired a blast of wind to parry the Avian, but the hawk cut effortlessly through her gust until the point of its sword came level with the tip of Vanna's nose.

Vanna raised her hands in surrender, and the Avian slowly lowered its blade. As soon as it did, Kai threw himself in front of Vanna with his arms outstretched like the brazen idiot he was.

"I won't let you hurt her!" he shouted.

The Avian tilted its feathered head and ruffled its wings. It marked both of them with one yellow eye before returning its greatsword to the scabbard on its back.

Vanna recognized that eye.

"Sparrowhawk," she said. Not "it"; "he".

The Avian snapped his beak. "You're late." The screeching character of his voice startled Kai, but Vanna was prepared for it.

She pushed Kai out of the way to face Bael's flying soldier. "I need to talk to Bael," Vanna said. "Will you take me to your camp?"

Sparrowhawk's head thrust forward with a pigeon jerk. "It's not far. He's been waiting."

"Vanna..." Kai's voice trembled in her ear. "What's going on here?"

Jokai fend, Kai. "Go back to the village," she said.

"How can you expect me to leave you with—with *that*!"

"His name's Sparrowhawk," she said. "And he's no danger." She looked back up at the eight-foot hawk with the six-foot sword. "Right?"

"Bael would not see you harmed," Sparrowhawk squawked. "But the spare cannot leave."

"That's not going to work," Vanna countered.

Sparrowhawk snapped his beak. "He's seen too much. Bael will need to examine him."

Vanna glanced over her shoulder at Kai, who seemed content to keep quiet while events were moving in his favor. The reckless fool had found an unlikely ally in Sparrowhawk. He had no idea what he'd just blundered into. As much as she didn't want Kai to be tainted by her contact with Bael, she needed to meet with the Toranese pirate more than she needed to keep his hands clean.

With one warning glance over her shoulder at Kai, Vanna acquiesced. "Fine."

Sparrowhawk led them deeper into the jungle before diverting off the cart path. His broad profile carved a trail for the two dragoons to follow through another span of untamed jungle. Vanna picked up the scent of fire and cooking meat long before they reached a second clearing. Bael had made his bivouac in an auspicious pocket of jungle capped by unbroken canopy and guarded by tallow trunks that grew so thick they obscured the light from his campfire.

Beyond the tree line, a trellis of strange fetishes molded from fur and jungle debris ringed the camp. These charms dangled from tallow branches on fibrous rope. Vanna parted two of these bangles and found the Kenshan waiting patiently on the stump of a felled tree. He watched the skinned carcass of a rabbit as it sizzled on a makeshift spit over a low fire. Sparrowhawk broke off to inspect a set of fetishes as Bael rose from the fireside in greeting.

"Lieutenant. You made it." His eyes marked Kai. "And you brought a friend."

Vanna clung to a vain hope that Kai would have the good sense to keep silent, but of course he did not. "You're that pirate!" he blurted out. "The one from Aeolus."

Bael's thin mustache cast odd shadows across his face in the flickering light thrown by the fire. Ignoring Kai's outburst, he addressed Vanna instead. "Can we count on the boy's discretion?"

"Not generally," Vanna grumbled. She was certain Kai missed her irritated side-eye. "But he'll listen to me, and he knows how to follow orders—present circumstances notwithstanding."

The jab wounded Kai back to obedience, and Vanna was grateful for it. She didn't want to find out what happened if Bael decided that he couldn't be trusted.

"Good enough for me," Bael said.

Sparrowhawk squawked from the edge of the bivouac. "Did you touch this one?" He cupped one of the dangling fetishes in a three-fingered hand as he pointed his beak at Bael with an accusatory jab.

"Why would I touch one of your disgusting pellets?" Bael shot back.

Sparrowhawk snapped his beak. "This one needs to be repaired. The leylines are all broken."

"And somehow we've survived," Bael said.

Sparrowhawk's yellow eyes jumped to the treetops. "These wards are the only thing holding this jungle's restless spirits at bay."

Bael waved him off. "Do what you want, you superstitious bird."

With a sharp squawk, Sparrowhawk returned to tending his charms.

Bael's almond eyes shifted back to Vanna and Kai. He extended one arm in invitation, indicating a log around the campfire. "Please—step into my office. The accommodations aren't a match for the governor's manse on Aeolus, but we've got firewood and a fresh rabbit on the spit."

Vanna accepted the invitation without taking her eyes off Bael. Mercifully, Kai maintained his silence as he followed her lead.

"So," Bael said as he lowered himself back onto his stump. "What brings you out to my neck of the jungle? I'm not quite conceited enough to think it's just the allure of my convivial company."

Flametongues leapt to lick the rabbit's blackening flesh. Vanna stared through the fire at Bael. "I saw something on patrol tonight—over Aquilon."

"Vanna, don't—" She felt Kai's hand on her arm.

"Would you keep your Jokai-damned mouth shut for once?" She swatted him away and turned her attention back to Bael. "I don't know if it's anything, but in the context of everything else that's been happening around the archipelago, it feels significant."

"Everything else?" Bael stroked his goatee. "You mean Whitefang's attack?"

"I mean the conscriptions," Vanna said.

Bael released his chin and leaned in until the firelight reached his blue braids. "What conscriptions?"

"Dragoons," Vanna said. It might have been a trick of the firelight, but Bael's hazel eyes seemed to flicker. The unsettling flash reminded her of a hunter sighting prey, but Vanna shook the feeling away. "Kelestina issued a Writ of Conscription for three of the strongest Elementalists on Volturnus. They've already reported to Governor Ansel and been transferred up to Aquilon."

The predatory glint vanished as Bael sat back on his stump. Again, he stroked his goatee. "That *is* interesting."

"You once told me the Celestials coveted our Gifts," Vanna said.

As her voice trailed off, the Kenshan sat motionless, daring—or perhaps *inviting*—her to take the final leap of her own volition.

"Is that what's happening?" Vanna asked. "Has the time come for Kelestina to reap her harvest?"

Bael let the fire crackle between them for painful seconds before answering her question with another. "This ship over Aquilon—describe it to me."

Vanna shook her head, gathering every detail she could recall from her brief survey of the airship. "Big," she said. "Massive. At least 1,000 feet long. Body enclosed with no exterior deck. Powered by steam pistons and lumite lifts."

"Carvel hull or tapered cylinder?" he asked.

"Tapered cylinder, I guess—like a rolled cigar."

Bael nodded thoughtfully. "Sounds like an aero-marine transport. You catch the colors by any chance?"

"The Armada Serpent on one side." Vanna's throat felt suddenly dry. Her voice grew hoarse. "The other one looked like an owl with a branch in its beak—black over a red- and gold-checkered field."

A low cooing sound warbled in the back of Sparrowhawk's Avian throat. He'd drifted back toward the campfire after finishing his work with the damaged fetish.

"That's the banner of the Eostrix Legion," Bael explained. "They currently serve under Admiral Siprichor in Toran."

"What does that mean?" Vanna asked.

Bael stood up and threw another log on the fire, sending a stream of ashes billowing up toward the stifling canopy. "It means your instincts are good, Lieutenant. The transport and the conscripts are connected. Kelestina's sending your kin to stand on the front lines in Toran."

"The front lines..." The news should have been a greater shock, but Vanna realized she'd only come to Bael to hear him confirm what she already knew in her gut. Flynn, Senna, and Kale had been conscripted into the Armada. They'd be sent to a foreign land—to fight and die in somebody else's war.

A change in the winds blew a pillar of smoke in Kai's face, and he shifted on the log, drawing closer to Vanna. "Why would the Armada go to so much trouble for three dragoons?" he asked.

Vanna had been ready to shut him up again, but it was a reasonable question, so she let it stand.

"I can only speculate." Bael tapped a finger against his leg. "Our alliance with the Red-Tail Clan has turned the tides of war against Siprichor's legions. We can't match the Armada ship-for-ship, but small fliers are difficult for an unwieldy destroyer to repel. A flock of Avian warriors can sink an airship. You Elementalists would provide an appealing countermeasure against the Red-Tails."

Vanna looked over at Sparrowhawk's rigid profile in the firelight. She tried to imagine three dragoons flying into battle against a flock of his peers brandishing six-foot greatswords. It didn't end well for the dragoons.

"The occupation in the Zephyrs has reached a new phase," Bael said. "These conscriptions won't be the last. If you want to save your archipelago, the time to act is now."

"What if you're wrong?" Kai asked.

"I hope I am—for both our people's sake." Bael tossed another log on the fire and sat back on his stump. He turned the spit so the rabbit would cook more evenly. To Vanna, it all seemed very rehearsed.

"You sound like you've been preparing for this," Vanna ventured.

Bael and Sparrowhawk shared a meaningful glance as the Kenshan continued turning the spit. "It's all part of a pattern," he said, still watching his Avian companion.

Sparrowhawk snapped his beak. "Tell them," he squawked.

"Tell us what?" Kai demanded.

Bael released the handle of the makeshift spit and took a long sip from a gourd of water. "A story." He answered Kai's question, but his almond eyes settled on Vanna. "I think it's time I told you a story about Kensha."

23

EFFIE

Leviathan of the Doric and Ionic Skies proved a tempting distraction. Each night, Effie drifted further from her syllabus, drawn to the vibrant portraits of exotic creatures and the colorful descriptions of their habitats, many of which extended beyond the edges of her most expansive maps.

She read about the dauphine and their seasonal migration that took them only briefly to the Moonflow of Volturnus. The rest of the year, their pod processed in a wide ellipse across the eastern sky—to the peaks of the Caliban Range where they roosted to mate. The portrait of a hammerhead faithfully reproduced the creature she'd met in Sire Meseret's hold. According to the field guide, they schooled in three locations clustered in the frigid northern skies—300 leagues from the Zephyr Archipelago. The Celestial Armada prized this species for their violent demeanor and crushing bite. As she pushed deeper into the guide, she discovered even stranger breeds—eight-flippered chelenoid tortoises that lived for 1,000 years; the starwhals of Beospora, with lance-like tusks capable of piercing armored aircraft; and the terrifying tohili of Vangulmark—plumed serpents that grew to 500 feet in length.

On the eve of her next dreaded history lecture, Effie discovered a stunning creature at the back of the field guide. She was supposed to be reading a dry treatise on the Umari Civil War. The label "Sleipnir the Doric Titan (*mythic*)" loomed over a portrait that recalled a distant dream—a six-legged horse with feathered hooves and broad white wings. An eternal flame burned along the back of the creature's neck in place of a mane, and its eyes smoldered like activated charcoal.

No known habitat accompanied the portrait, and its entry was comparatively brief:

> *The mythical Titan of the Doric sky is said to grow up to 1,000 feet from nose to tail and is capable of claiming altitudes in excess of 20,000 feet above the meridian. The Sleipnir is rumored to maintain a small scope of habitation around the jungle island Bennu. Many expeditions to discover the elusive island have been attempted without success. In light of the Crystal Throne's extensive surveys of the Doric Sky, it's unlikely that such an island exists. The Sleipnir may, in fact, be extinct—if it ever existed.*

> *The Annals of Solaris contain no credible first-hand accounts of the Sleipnir. Artistic liberties have been taken in the production of this fanciful portrait, a composite produced from multiple impressions of dubious character.*

Effie turned back to the color portrait. Most of her Leviathan dreams faded quickly upon contact with the waking world, but this one persisted with the fidelity of conscious memory. As she looked at the image in her field guide, she could almost feel its rough white hide between her fingers— smell the ozone and charcoal of its burning mane. She knew the creature's name before she read it, though the title was new to her: the Titan of the Doric Sky.

A mythical creature from an island that didn't exist.

The next morning, Effie made an earnest effort to focus on Muldoon's history lesson, but her mind kept drifting to the Sleipnir and its uncanny presence in her dreamscape. Her distraction didn't pass unnoticed.

Muldoon caught her unfocused gaze and paused his lecture to snap his chalk against the slate board, jarring her back to attention.

"Something on your mind?" He sounded irritated.

"Sorry." Effie shook herself back to the present. "You were saying something about...Toran, I want to say?" Her playful smile didn't penetrate Muldoon's ill temper.

"Perhaps you'd like to recount the notable battles of the Umari Civil War from your readings?"

"I..." Effie hadn't finished the readings and had been too distracted by the field guide to retain what little she did get through. "I think I'd rather hear your expert take on the matter." She batted her eyes at her tutor, but Muldoon still wasn't biting.

"If you aren't going to complete the readings, then there's little reason for us to be here."

"I'm sorry!" Effie put on her best pout, but she was quickly burning through all the charms in her arsenal. "I just can't put down that field guide you gave me. Can't we have a lecture on the Leviathan instead?"

Muldoon set down his chalk and flexed his fingers, forcing patience. "You won't be tested on *Leviathan of the Doric and Ionic Skies*."

"But isn't that more relevant if I'm to become a Pilot in the Armada?" she protested. "These Toranese wars are all history! This can't possibly be relevant."

Effie expected a gentle reprimand or else a witty retort, but no such argument was forthcoming from her tutor. Muldoon's fingers tensed around his chalk, then his shoulders slumped as he turned away from her. Effie quickly shut her mouth.

"I'm sorry you don't consider the Umari Civil War worthy of your time or consideration." He sounded almost bitter. Muldoon usually met her playful defiance with good humor, but this time her disinterest seemed to wound him.

Effie bit down hard on her lower lip. She'd let herself become too familiar with Muldoon—let his fondness for her go to her head. No matter how much they'd grown to enjoy each other's company, their relationship was still student to pupil. In this study, they conducted the business of their host. She'd do well to remember that.

Effie uncrossed her legs beneath the table and hung her head. "I'm sorry. I'll make up the reading."

Muldoon accepted her apology with a silent nod before slowly lifting his chalk back to the slate board. His posture still looked deflated as he quietly returned to making notes. Effie pushed the Sleipnir from her mind and tried to focus on the lesson scrawled across the slate. As she scanned the relevant dates of the Umari Civil War, understanding dawned on her—and with it, a renewed sense of shame.

Muldoon had a very good reason for taking her disinterest to heart. This lesson was personal.

"You lived through this war," Effie said.

Muldoon stopped pecking with his chalk. He hung motionless over the slate board for a long moment before nodding with his back to the room.

"I'm sorry," Effie repeated.

"So you've said." He still didn't look at her.

"This *is* important." She reached out a hand until he turned, inviting him to join her at the table. "If only to better understand your life."

Her contrition seemed to kindle his spirits some. He accepted her invitation and claimed the seat opposite her at the study table.

Effie glanced back to the outline on the slate. He would have been very young, but this conflict must have touched his life in innumerable ways. "It's your origin story," she said. "This war—it's how the Celestials came to be involved in Umar. How you joined the Patrician class."

"I suppose you could say that." Muldoon fingered his goatee thoughtfully. "The story of Umar is a microcosm of the greater saga of the Crystal Throne. If you understand how the Celestials rose to power in southern Toran, then you may begin to understand the larger mission of the Crystal Throne and its virtue. But this isn't about me." He shook his head. "This is about you. Your place in a story that is still being written."

Muldoon's almond eyes drifted. Effie leaned in until she once again became the object of his gaze. "Maybe if you recounted it for me—in your own words. Your lived experience."

"My experience?" He eyed her skeptically.

"I think that would bring more life to the topic than any historian's rote account," Effie insisted.

Muldoon tapped one finger atop the table, eyes narrowing as he did. Effie thought he was on the verge of sending her back to her room and her books, until he sighed. "Very well. For the sake of your studies, mind."

Effie imbued her nod with more enthusiasm than she truly felt, but Muldoon took it for honesty.

"A story, then. A story about Umar."

24

VANNA & EFFIE

Bael:

Before the Shards darkened our shores, Toran was a land of culture and prosperity—the very pinnacle of civilization in the Doric Sky. It will be difficult for you to conceive of our country's scale—a million souls spread across twenty city-states, each as vast as all your Zephyri settlements combined. And Kensha—ah, Kensha—Bhardic jewel of Hellicon. Kensha was the diamond set at the apex of Toran's crown. A land of commerce and poetry; of science and philosophy; of wealth and equity in uncommon accord. In that Golden Age before the occupation, Kensha was ruled by an elected council of Merchant Mavens and Popular Tribunes. The city-state's position on the eastern tip of the Hellicon Peninsula brought lucrative trade, and the council saw the city's abundant wealth distributed among its citizens so that no Kenshan would live in poverty or squalor. The distributions allowed the great minds of that halcyon time to dedicate their lives to contemplation and innovation. Our people have never been as fecund with Gifts as you Zephyri. Those few Pugilists and Mentalists that did manifest enjoyed no elevated status or royal birthright. By tradition, Kensha's Gifted committed their lives to service, prosecuting the interests of our great society with humility and deference.

I don't mean to sound pollyannaish. The old times weren't without their share of trials. Petty squabbles between the city-states were common enough. A few even came to blows. The cities argued over resources and trade routes. Blood was shed from time to time, but nothing on the scale visited by the Shards. Our greater foes were always without. You have to understand, the western skies are more crowded than the east. Great civilizations grow on top of one another, creating points of friction where they intersect. Deep sky pirates harried our trading vessels out of port, and raiders from the neighboring Isles of Vangulmark made seasonal landfall to pillage our settlements and steal our harvest.

For generations, we treated these threats as mere annoyances. Our land enjoyed such abundant wealth—if we lost a portion of our harvest to the Vangish, then that was simply the price of our prosperity. That all changed with the ascension of Jarl Cithric, a charismatic Reaver-King who united the Isles of Vangulmark under his banner.

Cithric came to Toran looking for conquest. His horde landed at the lees of Hellicon and made their intentions clear with a brutal sack of Aoknassus, a neighboring city-state to Kensha. Cithric's army razed the city and put thousands of civilians to the sword.

Shockwaves from the attack reverberated across the continent. From the shoals of Kensha to the plains of Rydia—from the Steppes of Umar to Odenta-of-the-Inland-Sky—the Toranese peoples braced for war. Jarl Cithric sent embassies to each of the remaining city-states. His message was a simple one: pay tribute to the Jarl and acknowledge his regency or be destroyed. *The Kenshan Council attempted to muster a collaborative resistance, but Toran was 200 years removed from any land war of scale. The walled cities of the Inland Skies retreated behind their fixed defenses. The Rydians, who had not breathed the soot of Aoknassus, petitioned for compliance with the Jarl's demands. The Great Umafex of the southern steppe returned our emissaries' heads in a box. That left the remnant cities of Hellicon alone and exposed— the next targets in Cithric's crosshairs.*

With no standing army between us, resistance seemed futile. The meager alliance met at Eulus to plan for war, but every option presented seemed doomed to fail. In this dire hour, His Lightness Admiral Siprichor arrived on Toranese shores, a shadowcat in a savior's cloak...

∾

Muldoon:

Before the Celestial Court brought their civilizing influence to the west, Toran was a sorry land plagued by seasonal raids from the Agnar and the Vangish, as well a near-constant series of internecine conflicts between greedy city-states who coveted their neighbors' wealth. No city suffered under the privations of this dark time worse than Umar. My people toiled under the thousand-year reign of a brutal despot, the Great Umafex, an unworthy Vitalist Gifted with an unnaturally long life.*

As you likely read, the Umafex resented and feared his fellow Gifted. By decree, any Umari citizen who manifested a Gift would be banished to the desert or else enslaved, forced to serve at the despot's capricious whims. Umari society became stratified—not by merit, but by loyalty. Those sycophants willing to subjugate their peers and enforce the despot's code gained status in the Court of Umar, while the greater portion of the peasantry was left to suffer in want.

When the Celestial Armada first arrived in Toran, the Umafex rebuffed their early invitations to treat. He feared this new power burgeoning on distant Hellicon and, coward that he was, turned inward. By his decree, Umar became even more isolated from the rest of Toran—a hermit city in a forbidding land. So isolated, Umar could no longer absorb the seasonal raids carried out by the Agnar Tribes on its western border, and so the Umafex elected to gain their favor by making gifts of his own citizens as slaves. This one decision proved to be his downfall, for it set the city down a path that even its traumatized citizens could not endure.

A grassroots resistance against the Umafex grew up around the desert camps of the banished. These brave rebels congregated at the village Irudal on the northern steppe. Together, they began to plot the downfall of the Great Umafex who had suppressed their Gifts and turned their sons and daughters into currency. My mother was one of the leaders of this resistance. This was before I was born, mind. She numbered herself among the Gifted, a true healer of some local renown. She dedicated herself to saving the resistance warriors who sacrificed life and limb protecting the rebel fort at Irudal.

But the resistance forces were too few, and the Agnar Tribes had grown accustomed to their Umari slaves. The plains people answered the Umafex's call and rode in great numbers against Irudal. The resistance held their ground for months against successive waves of Agnar raiders, but each attack weakened their defenses until defeat seemed imminent. That's when a Patrician embassy from His Lightness Admiral Siprichor arrived to show us the path out of perdition...

~

Bael:

THE SHARDS THRIVE in environments of fear. The threat of Jarl Cithric's Vangish army forced all of Hellicon to face their mortality—our fragility as a people. We could not stand alone against the hardened raiders of Vangulmark. Our leaders would have agreed to anything. And so they did.

In exchange for Siprichor's help dislodging the Vangish from Hellicon, three city-states agreed to become vassals of the Crystal Throne. Siprichor promised a light hand—a few Patrician governors to exercise authority over the ruling councils and a nominal tithe paid to support the Armada's continued protection. In addition to the Armada's support, Siprichor promised greater access to new trade routes throughout the Doric Sky. To the ears of our Merchant Mavens and Provincial Tribunes, it must've sounded like a rich exchange. That's the thing about deals that sound too good to be true. They usually are.

Armada warships descended on Hellicon, bombarding Cithric's position in Aoknassus and sinking his reaver ships offshore. They dislodged the invaders by season's end, sent every raider limping back to Vangulmark. Admiral Siprichor celebrated a great Triumph, a ceremonial march through the cities of Hellicon, with days of festival following in his wake. His weeks-long celebration ended in Kensha, and that is where he remained.

Decades of salutary neglect followed the great defeat of Jarl Cithric. The merchants grumbled over the tithe, which increased by increments with each passing year, but overall the mood in Kensha remained sanguine. A Patrician Triumvirate from Siprichor's court usurped the ruling functions of our council, but in those early days they handled our customs and mores with care. The Shards solidified their position in Hellicon and began making overtures deeper into Toran—to the city-states of Rydia and the Inland Sky. Many cities opened their doors to their Patrician emissaries. Others were not so trusting.

A Rydian Warlord, Calynda of Kyokyu, became the face of resistance to

Celestial expansion in the north. Siprichor responded with a wide-reaching conscription targeting his guests in Hellicon—particularly the Kenshans. The Gifted were collected from their homes and transported to Siprichor's consulate on the Island of Brundis. The Giftless were impressed by the thousands, handed spears and sent to fight their Toranese kin.

Calynda proved a capable commander and a powerful foe. Her army decimated the conscripts of Hellicon, forcing Siprichor to retreat back to his strongholds and lick his wounds. In defeat, the Shard Admiral revealed his true colors, and the people of Kensha found them hideous. He doubled the tithe —conscripted soldiers from the plebiscite at an unsustainable rate. With so many citizens entering the Armada, our fields lay fallow, our great industries untended, left to rust and rot. The situation quickly became untenable, and the old council of Merchant Mavens and Provincial Tribunes reconvened to solve it. The council rightly determined that Celestial rule presented a greater threat to the city's enduring prosperity than any Vangish invasion. They voted to expel the Patrician Triumvirate and discontinue Kensha's vassalage to the Crystal Throne.

Siprichor accepted the council's decision and moved his Hellicon Court to neighboring Svartra. My people hoped they had closed the book on this chapter of fealty to the Shards. What a vain hope it was...

∾

Muldoon:

BY THE TIME the Patrician emissaries reached Umar, Admiral Siprichor's attempts to civilize Toran had reached an inflexion point in the north. After spending Celestial blood defending Hellicon from a powerful Vangish Jarl, the ungracious Kenshans turned on their saviors, casting their hosts from Hellicon's fertile shores. Admiral Siprichor had not been prepared for such duplicity, but neither had he given up on the Toranese cause. Instead of fighting the Kenshans, he hoped to establish a new stronghold for the Crystal Throne in the south. In exchange for fealty, he promised to rid us of the Great Umafex and every last vestige of his despicable reign.

The Admiral's greater force was tied down fighting a guerrilla war against the savage Rydians, and our battered resistance couldn't muster an army great enough to take Umar on its own. Fortunately, the Jokai blessed

Siprichor with a sharp strategic mind. With the aid of a single gunship, he turned fire—not on the Umafex himself—but on the Agnar riders performing his butcher's work along the steppe of Irudal. The Agnikai's army buckled under aerial assault, and His Lightness descended on the routed force in person to make an entreaty. He persuaded the Agnar to change sides, and so turned the Umafex's greatest weapon against him.

With aerial support from the Armada, the Agnar breached Umar's walls and rode up to the palace of the Umafex, delivering the despot in chains to the leaders of the resistance. Siprichor carried the deposed God-King up to his flagship. With my mother and her cohort standing witness, His Lightness rendered judgment. For all the generations of suffering he imposed on his people, the Long Drop seemed the only fitting end. And so, the Great Umafex's Gift became his curse. If there is justice in the Jokai's design, he still lives to this day, suffering through unending terror on his hurtling path through the eternal sky.

The Celestials rebuilt Umar in their image, for the Agnar had not been gentle in their sack. They constructed infirmaries and schools, restored the Gifted to a place of prominence within the city's new hierarchy. My mother and the other Gifted leaders of the resistance were raised to the Patrician class, branded by Siprichor himself. They formed the strong lattice of a new ruling council enforcing the just code of the Crystal Throne. His Lightness ushered in a new Golden Age for the people of Umar—one that endures to this day.

I was born in the First Year of our Host, the Gifted son of a Patrician mother and a warrior father who fell months before in defense of Irudal. Without Admiral Siprichor's intervention, my life might have been snuffed out in the womb—another unnamed casualty of the Great Umafex and his unworthy designs. Instead, I grew up at court, raised in the collegiate tradition of the Crystal Throne. At the age of ten, I earned my brand, and by sixteen I was made a magistrate of Admiral Siprichor's Court.

Much of Toran continues its selfish resistance, but Umar remembers the horror of life before the rule of law—before Siprichor and the stabilizing force of his Armada. We are the true zealots of the Toranese plebiscite, and we will not abandon our host until he liberates the rest of Toran from the petty despots who cling to their sorry reigns.

~

Bael:

THE SAME YEAR we banished the Shards from Kensha, the Vangish raids resumed. This time, we were better prepared. We'd gleaned much about the art of war from the occupying Armada. We fought the denizens of Vangulmark to a stalemate but soon found ourselves beset by another foe. Deep sky pirates descended from the east, harrying our ports and attacking merchant ships carrying the matériel of war. Our ruling council made entreaties to the other cities of Hellicon, but their Patrician masters denied our requests for aid. It wasn't until the Great Captain Olyscent of Kensha defeated a Leviathan pirate in aerial combat that we learned the depths of the Shards' duplicity.

Captain Olyscent returned to Kensha with the captured Pirate Lord Grimblade and revealed the serpent mark branded behind his ear. Yes. Grimblade was an agent of the Crystal Throne—a Patrician bonded to Siprichor's Court. We later learned that another Celestial Host had completed his own conquest of Vangulmark. The reavers stalking our coasts had been similarly impressed into the service of the Crystal Throne. This realization cast decades of Toranese history in a more sinister light.

Captain Olyscent presented Grimblade's head to our neighbors, with the Patrician cattlemark behind his ear preserved. Rather than a savior, Siprichor revealed himself to be the architect of our suffering. The Shards' fell intent could no longer be denied. Our leaders returned to the Rock of Eulus to sign a new treaty—a pact of mutual defense creating the Hellicon League. In one glorious Night of Liberation, the people of Hellicon rose up against their Patrician oppressors. Those who resisted died on the swords of the very people they'd deceived for so long. What few agents of the Crystal Throne escaped the slaughter, returned in shambles to their host decamped in Rydia. Hellicon was free, but the war had just begun—a war we are still fighting to this day.

It's all part of a sordid pattern. You see its outlines beginning to form right here on Volturnus. The Shards engineer a threat and offer protection. Your people join the plebiscite and enter a period of benign rule. As soon as the Crystal Throne's authority stabilizes, the demands on the plebiscite become more odious by increments.

The Shards are a parasite. They leech away your wealth, then your Gifts —then your lives. We let our host's roots sink too deep into the soil of Toran.

There's still time for Volturnus to avoid this fate, but if the conscriptions have begun, then that time is running short.

MULDOON'S EYES became glassy as he reached the end of his tale. They sat in silence for a time as Effie processed all she had heard.

She'd grown up under the even-handed justice of the Celestial Code. It was hard to imagine life under a brutal despot like the Great Umafex. If the Crystal Throne's expansion brought civility to such a long-suffering people, then that was a virtuous mission, indeed. When she daydreamed of Piloting Leviathan around the Eight Skies of Ciel, she served no higher end than her own curiosity and sense of adventure. Exploration was a goal in and of itself, and no higher calling had ever occurred to her.

"Thank you," Effie said.

Muldoon accepted her thanks with a weak smile. What had it taken for him to recall such a trying tale? Too much, perhaps. More than she had any right to ask.

"If my Gift can help turn the tides of this war..." Effie ventured. Muldoon perked up. "Then that seems a worthy calling."

Muldoon nodded, cupping his hand over his wedge of chalk left unattended atop the table. "In that case... I'll hear no more whining about the importance of your history lessons."

DAWN BREACHED THE STEADY CANOPY, dappling the jungle bivouac with anemic light. Kai sat still as the log beneath them in shared silence. Vanna's throat had become dry over the course of Bael's story. She indicated the gourd of water next to Bael, and he handed it to her across the flame. The water replenished her reserves, but her head still swam with implications for Volturnus.

She might have taken it all for another pirate ploy—and a dangerous one, at that—laced with venom from the serpent's tongue. She almost wished that simple explanation served. It would be so much easier if she believed Bael false, but she did not.

Bael's story fit too neatly inside the outlines of her life to be summarily dismissed. With every movement of his tale, senseless, unconnected events arranged themselves into an unsettling constellation. How much of her *own* history had been a lie—a plot orchestrated by Kelestina and the agents of the Crystal Throne?

"I know it's a lot to process," Bael said.

"Devil Ray's attack..." Vanna almost couldn't bring herself to say it out loud, as if giving voice to her suspicions might somehow make them true. "Was it all...designed?" She felt Kai stiffen beside her.

Bael scratched his chin. "That, I can't say. This Butcher is a creature of the eastern skies. We have no experience with him or his Leviathan in Kensha." That should have settled Vanna more than it did. "But Bone Adder—this latest aggression from Captain Whitefang—it has the stink of the Shards and their games."

Vanna nodded. She glanced over at Kai and was grateful that he looked too stunned to interject. "What can we do?" she asked.

Bael and Sparrowhawk shared another meaningful look. The Avian clicked his beak and squawked, goading the Kenshan on. "The Gulliver Ring can't fight a war for you," Bael said. "But there are more effective ways to dislodge the Shards—to make the occupation untenable."

"What can we do?" Vanna repeated.

"We'll need information. Names of conscripts. Numbers of armed retainers and notes on their deployment throughout the archipelago. I'll need you to mark any Armada ships you find on patrol and report on their size and affiliation, track their passages in and out of the Aquilonian skies."

"I can do that," Vanna said. She'd been expecting him to ask her to fight, but spying seemed an easier bridge to cross without sounding any alarms. "What do we get in exchange?"

"We have friends in the area I can reach out to for support. No one closer than Grenport, but that will have to be close enough." Bael picked up a piece of parchment from the ground next to his stump, rolled it up and tucked it inside a wooden tube, which he sealed with a glob of wax, melting it shut over the fire. He handed the message to Sparrowhawk. "Get this to Klaeda," he instructed. "She's been sniffing around our neck of the sky for some time. I have a feeling she might find some alignment with our present goals."

"I'm not a carrier pigeon," Sparrowhawk grumbled.

Bael poked him with the end of the tube. "You gonna take down a Leviathan on your own?"

Sparrowhawk's warble rang with discontent, but the scroll disappeared inside one massive brown claw without further argument.

"What about the conscripts?" Vanna asked. "The Elementalists."

"I'm afraid your friends are out of reach—for now." When Bael saw Vanna begin to withdraw, he added, "But there may be something we can do for the next batch—once the writs are issued. Our people might be able to secret them away before they're due to report—get them to safety."

Vanna nodded—more to herself. She felt herself drawn deeper inside Bael's conspiracy with every breath, trapped in a sucking vortex that even her ample Gift could not resist.

"It won't be easy—what I am asking," Bael said. "Standing against the Shards comes with substantial risk. If you want to walk away from this campfire and back to your old life as a guest of the Crystal Throne, I won't harbor any ill will. But if you accept our help, there won't be any turning back. I'll put my life on the line to help you save your people, and I expect the same dedication in return—" Bael's eyes jumped to Kai, "—from both of you."

"He's not part of this," Vanna snapped. Kai rose to protest, but she pushed him back down on the log. "He's going to forget everything he heard here and do his best to stay out of my way."

She stared Kai into submission and held that stare until she was certain the last fires of resistance fizzled to ash. It was one thing to compromise herself in collusion with Bael. She wouldn't drag Kai along with her. When her eyes returned to Bael, the Kenshan was standing.

"Very well." He extended his arm. "I'll have your oath, and I offer mine in return."

Vanna looked at his outstretched hand—read this man's struggle in every white scar hatching his palm.

She accepted that hand, marking another predatory glint in his almond eyes as she shook. This time, she didn't have the firelight for a scapegoat.

"Welcome to the resistance, Lieutenant."

With that handshake, everything changed.

25

KAI

The terrifying Avian—Sparrowhawk, apparently—escorted them back to the jungle's edge, then took off, presumably in pursuit of this Klaeda to deliver Bael's scroll.

Kai could think of nothing useful to say, and so he kept quiet, watching Vanna all the way back up the path to Volturnus. She looked deep in thought, but hardly reticent. If anything, a steely determination had possessed her, and that troubled him far more than the hesitation he hoped to find. None of it felt right.

When he watched her accept that pirate's hand across the fire, his heart sank into his stomach. In one brief gesture, she made herself complicit in gross treason against the Crystal Throne—against their *host!* And to what end? The dragoon conscriptions sat poorly with everyone on Volturnus, but they hardly warranted an open rebellion against the very people who'd kept them safe all these years. Oh, he'd listened to the same story that penetrated Vanna, but he wasn't half as credulous. The word of a pirate was worth less than yak dung, and these words in particular—so carefully baited to lure them in—begged for heavy skepticism.

And Vanna expected him to just forget? To put it out of his mind? How was he supposed to carry on with his daily life while she worked in the shadows to undermine their host? How could he follow her on patrol without questioning which details she catalogued to bring back to Bael?

And what if she stumbled? He knew how Kelestina dealt with pirates. She couldn't expect him to stand by and watch her throw away her life for a treacherous outlander.

They flew around the southern coast of the island to avoid any uncomfortable questions from the farmhands beginning their days. When they put down outside the village walls, they heard Second Bell ringing out from the campanile. In an hour, they were both expected to report to the barracks and debrief Kendy from their patrol. What new lies did Vanna plan to weave to keep the commander off their scent?

"I'm going to wash up before drills," Vanna said. She scanned him up and down, and Kai became aware of his unkempt hair—not to mention the mud and jungle debris that marred his flight suit. "You should do the same." She began to walk off.

"That's all you have to say to me?"

Vanna came to a stop and turned around to face him with her hands on her hips. She checked over both shoulders but found nobody lurking. "What else do you need to hear from me? I said my piece back at the campsite. I won't involve you in this. Forget everything you saw and heard."

"Forget everything..." Weakened by exhaustion and stress, Kai couldn't keep his frustration from boiling over. He pulled his hair with both hands and gnashed his teeth. "*Balls of the deep*—how am I supposed to carry on when I know you're in danger? He's a *pirate*, Vanna! You're walking into a trap. I can't believe you don't see it! I won't stand by and watch him destroy you."

"Keep your voice down!" She checked over her shoulders again and breathed a heavy sigh. "I've made my decision. You don't have to agree with it, but you do have to respect it."

"Well, you don't get to make mine!" he shot back. "And I don't respect it. I think you've lost your damn mind."

She marched back up to him and pressed a finger against his chest. "How would you feel if you got one of those letters of conscription, huh? How would you feel if someone you loved was ripped away from you, sent to fight and die in a distant land? How would you feel if it had been your family on that zeppelin, burned out of existence in some amoral game of control?"

Kai's expression tightened. It wasn't so hard to imagine. Someone he loved *had* been ripped away from him, but it wasn't Kelestina doing the ripping.

Vanna misinterpreted his silence for submission. "I expect your discretion, Kai. We won't speak of this again."

Kai may have been forbidden to speak of Bael, but erasing the evening's treason from his mind proved an impossible task. Bael's words and Vanna's handshake pursued him throughout the day, distracting him from drills to the extent that he had difficulty holding formation in the sky. Vanna seemed entirely unshaken. She looked as proficient in the sky as ever. He'd have never guessed that she spent a sleepless night in the jungle plotting to overthrow their Celestial host.

His mind wandered as he watched her assembling a draft of cadets across the landing, and his sparring partner seized the advantage to blast him off his feet. He landed painfully, cracking his head against a protruding stone. Nayla gusted over to help him up with a look of concern.

"You're not at the top of your game today," she said unhelpfully.

Kai rubbed the egg already forming on the back of his head as he let her drag him to his feet. "Just tired from last night," he answered honestly.

Nayla assumed he meant the patrol. "Why don't you go back to the bunkhouse and get some rest before you hurt yourself. I'll tell the commander you're not feeling well."

Kai's first instinct was to argue, but he couldn't deny that he'd benefit from a little time to himself, so he took Nayla's out and gusted back toward the village.

Sleep seemed like a fool's quest at this point. If he had any hope of finding some peace and putting Bael and Vanna out of his mind, it was at the bottom of a tankard of Janus' gut-rot ale.

At midday, the tavern was sparsely populated—just a smattering of regulars clustered around the bar and a lone table of craftsmen who performed the bulk of their duties overnight. Among them, Kai's uncle Kellen nursed a tankard and a half-eaten turkey leg cooked on the bone. Kellen's eyes followed Kai to an empty table. Kai prayed his uncle would continue to let him be.

The Jokai granted those prayers, and as the hours wore on, Kai was left to chew over the impossible position that Vanna had put him in. He wouldn't rat her out—that was for certain—but nor could he simply stand by while she put herself at this pirate's disposal. If he could only *help* her somehow. A pleasant notion, except she didn't want his help—had forbidden it, in fact. This Bael had thrown a new wedge between them, and that was the last thing their relationship needed. History and rank and the Jokai-damned ghost of Effie already presented enough obstacles to drive him mad. He feared for Vanna, but it was the squandered potential of their relationship he mourned. It wasn't fair.

As Janus deposited a third tankard in front of him and bussed the empty vessels, Kai's frustration began to melt into a drunken puddle of malaise. Kellen's companions dwindled away and, at last, the soft-spoken baker made his way over to his troubled nephew.

"Mind if I take a seat?"

Kai acquiesced with a wave of his hand. Among other things, the ale had stripped him of all his fight. Kellen watched him take a long sip from his fourth serving with parental concern.

"I know that look," Kellen said.

"What look?" Kai's words slurred, but Kellen didn't judge him for it.

His uncle's smile exuded warmth, but it was also sad. "The look of a man suffering a woman's scorn."

Kai took another long sip and lowered his tankard to the table. How easily his uncle had sniffed him out. He knew Kai as well as anyone on Volturnus. Kellen never married—never had any children—but after Kai's father, Imani, fell to the Butcher, Kellen had taken Kai in and raised him as his own. He was more of a father than an uncle—the closest thing to a parent Kai had really known. He'd been so young when Imani died.

Kellen took Kai's silence for the confirmation it was. "This wouldn't have anything to do with a purple-haired lieutenant, would it?"

The precision of this assumption made Kai's arm slip, and he nearly face-planted into his tankard of ale. His moan sounded pathetic, even to his own ears. "Am I that obvious?"

"Obvious enough to someone who knows you." Kellen shook his head and clapped a hand on his shoulder. He wasn't a dragoon or an Elementalist, but all those years kneading dough over a hot kiln had imbued his uncle with strength of a different character. "To be honest, I used to think it was the younger one you had an eye for."

"Effie's moved on to better things," Kai grumbled.

"You too, it seems." Kai shot him an irritated glance, and Kellen pumped his hands, begging patience. "It makes sense. Vanna's grown into a fine woman. Effie has her charms, but she always seemed a bit high on herself—even as a kid. Can't say I ever cared for the way she treated you—like some sidekick who was lucky to stand in her shadow."

Kai turned his face back down to his drink. Kellen's sentiments came from a kind place, but his appraisal stung. Is that really all he'd been to Effie? A supporting character in the story of her life? It had felt that way sometimes, but there'd been love between them, too—love that felt honest and real. If that had all been artifice, then he was the greatest fool on Volturnus.

"Can't say you don't come by it honest," Kellen said. "The Dryas women have always had this effect on Bowker men."

Kai surfaced from the drunken fog. "The who?"

"That's their mother's maiden name," Kellen explained. "Vera Dryas, before she married that cocky flyboy, Errol Strait. Vera and I grew up together—a lot like you and Effie. She was the only woman I ever loved, and she loved me—I think—as much as any kid can be in love. Always thought we'd end up together, but then Vera's Gift manifested and mine didn't. She threw herself into her training, and I was content to give her some space. She'd taken the first steps down a road I couldn't follow, and I guess I assumed she'd come back to bring me along when she was ready." Kellen laughed at his own naïveté. "Let's just say that never happened. Vera caught Errol's eye early on, and that fast-talking flier gusted his way inside her flight suit quicker than a crescent roll takes to rise. I know I shouldn't speak ill of our fallen heroes, but it's the truth! Falling in the Butcher's war don't erase a man's poor character. Effie's got more than a stroke of her father in her, come to think of it, but Vanna's her mother's daughter through and through. Vera forgot about me, but I never forgot about her."

"I had no idea." Kai set his drink aside and leaned in, listening to his uncle's story with rapt attention.

"Don't talk about it much. It's not a pleasant memory. Still hurts, even after all this time and with her and Errol both moved on to the Otherworld."

"Is that why you never married?" Kai wouldn't have asked it if not for the ale loosening his lips.

Kellen sat back in his chair. "I had other prospects, mind. Plenty of 'em. It just never seemed fair. I couldn't marry someone else until I stopped loving her. Never stopped, so I never wed. That's that. The only peace I ever found was over the kiln. That's why I opened the bakery."

Kai considered these new layers revealed inside a man he'd known his entire life. Seeing them so raw and exposed only deepened his malaise. "That's a sad story," he said. "And now I'm doomed to repeat it."

"You aren't listening." Kellen slapped his palm on the table. "Like all our stories, mine's a cautionary tale. You're an Elementalist just like Vanna. You don't have to deal with the same obstacles that came between me and Vera. And even if you did, waiting around for a Dryas woman to come begging is a coward's slow surrender. Do you love this girl?"

"I think so... Yes."

"Then stop drowning yourself in Janus' pisswater and go be with her. Stand by her side and don't look back. Don't leave her until she tells you it's not to be. Have you even asked her what *she* wants?"

Kai hadn't, but the thought of making such a brazen overture filled him with dread. How could he carry on if she rebuffed him? Every drill, each long patrol would only humiliate him anew. "I appreciate you, Uncle Kellen, but I think I need some time alone."

Kellen submitted and skulked back to his table.

Kai didn't finish his fourth tankard. He stared absently at the amber draft and the crackling hearth beyond as the evening's dark blanket descended over Volturnus. Lonely hours passed, until one of Janus' serving girls approached the table after finishing her shift. Kai recognized the girl— Teia Laurens, one of the knitter's daughters. Her sister Ina used to watch the dragoons at drills before Sire Ansel conscripted her to his household staff. Teia flipped her long brown hair to catch his attention and grasped the hem of her knee-length skirt.

"Your uncle asked me to check in on you."

"My uncle should mind his own business," Kai grumbled.

"He thought you could use some company."

Kai sighed as he looked up at her apple-cheeked smile. She seemed to glow in the firelight. Teia was pretty—all the Laurens girls were—and Kai could certainly use some company.

Just not hers.

His polite refusal didn't phase her. Teia trotted off to another table as Kai gathered himself up from his seat and left the tavern. He crossed the village on a determined path for Vanna's cottage and knocked as soon as he reached the stoop. If he gave himself any time to reconsider, he knew his resolve would crumble.

He heard a scuffling sound as Vanna removed the bar from her door—saw the look of surprise when she appeared in the frame, hair still wet from bathing. A linen nightgown trailed from the straps on her shoulders to the knobs of her knees, hanging from her bust and concealing all the lean curves beneath.

Her expression turned quizzical, and Kai seized the moment before that question devolved to impatience.

"I can't forget what I saw, Vanna. I can't just put it out of my mind. If you're in trouble, then that's the *only* thing on my mind."

"Kai—"

"I'm not finished. I don't trust Bael, but I do trust *you*. If you think this is what's best for Volturnus, then I want to help. You don't have to do this alone. Let me help you carry this burden."

He expected protest, but his words struck her silent. He watched her lips beginning to part, grasping for some trite rebuttal. Before she found it, he stepped up onto the stoop and pressed his own lips between them.

There was a moment when Kai feared she might pull away. He felt her whole body tense through the point of contact between their lips, but she did not withdraw. He leaned in, gently prying her lips apart, tasting her with his tongue. Her body responded, drawing him deeper inside herself, grasping him by the head, and filling him with urgent heat.

It was so unlike the kiss he shared with Effie. Vanna's kiss carried desperation and force, where her sister's had been tentative and coy. She took control of the moment, guiding him step-by-step, just as he had guided her on the dancing round during Vernal Fete—the moment he realized he loved her. He continued to chase her even as he felt her hands working down to his chest, prying them apart as she disentangled their tongues.

She looked at him with a concerned wrinkle crooked at the center of her brow. Without a word, she turned back, retreating from the doorway.

Kai fell back on his heels as he watched her drifting away.

What had he done wrong? Only everything. He'd been too eager—too forceful with his lips, too questing with his tongue.

When he looked up, he saw a snaggletoothed smile perched over a naked shoulder where the strap of Vanna's nightgown had slipped down.

"Are you coming inside, or what?"

Kai nearly stumbled flat on his face in his haste to answer the summons. He hardly paused to slam the door behind him.

26

EFFIE

The seasons changed, and Volturnus changed with them—more than Effie could ever recall. She continued to pay infrequent visits to her sister, but Kendy's paranoia kept the whole corps running double patrols. More often than not, Effie found their family cottage empty, and when Vanna *was* home, she always seemed exhausted and strung out. Kai was often lurking. Effie grew accustomed to his frosty regard, and though she frequently attempted to penetrate it, he'd thrown up walls that seemed tempered against her ample charms.

Effie listened to them both complain about the extended patrols. They'd seen no further trouble from this Leviathan pirate who attacked the Aeolian zeppelin, and every passing day made that tragedy seem more of an unfortunate outlier than an ominous portend of trials to come. Raji and Prestor stepped into the senior roles vacated by Senna and Kale, and still Kendy pushed Vanna to elevate her cadets to the active corps before she judged them ready. Her sister used to have more stomach for the fight, but in a troubling change of habit, she'd been yielding to Kendy's demands. Her focus seemed to have shifted elsewhere, though Effie couldn't fathom where that might be.

Just as Muldoon had warned, another round of conscriptions came down from Aquilon in the spring. He put the same list of names in front of Effie, and this time he made his intentions clear.

"Five Elementalists," Muldoon said.

"So many... that can't be right."

"It is the number our host requires."

A requirement wasn't a request.

Muldoon had been honest with her, which was all she had asked. So, she picked. This time, Effie allowed her own preferences to inform her choices. She granted clemency to Maya and Nadeen, who each had a family and children to raise. She spared the rest of Kendy's patrol leaders as well, even though they accounted for the strongest fliers. Again, she lingered over Kai. Even considering his sour disposition of late, she couldn't bring herself to send him away. Part of her still hoped they'd find their way back to each other—even though that hope seemed increasingly vain.

After much consideration, she marked five names and passed the list back to Muldoon. Lya, Jin, Nayla, Whatley and Bors.

Muldoon's eyes drifted upward as he read the names. "You're certain these are the strongest?"

"I'm certain they are the best selections to serve our host," Effie said. It wasn't a lie, but nor was it the truth.

Effie contented herself with the knowledge that she'd bent her small power to serve Volturnus—to shield those who most needed shielding. Even so, she knew how the conscription order was likely to be received, and so she avoided the village for a time after its issue. To distract herself, she descended deeper into her books.

After months of readings and lectures, Effie finally felt in command of her studies. No subject had bested her, and the deeper she sank into the Six Academic Graces, the more she discovered an unlikely well of power in the knowledge they cultivated within her. The tower of textbooks that had seemed so intimidating at the outset began to dwindle. Each tome fell to her voracious mind as fast as Muldoon could replenish them with new requests from the library of Aquilon.

Muldoon's oral examinations began soon after the spring equinox. The academic ritual followed a strict pattern. Effie stood in front of the slate with a wedge of chalk, forbidden to sit for the duration of the exam. In a reversal of their typical roles, Muldoon sat in a heavy, high-backed chair dragged to the center of the room. He faced her with legs crossed, issuing questions in rapid succession. Some of these exams focused on one specific Academic Grace. Others ranged from topic to topic in an obvious attempt to unbalance her. At first, the impromptu format flustered her, but she grew accustomed to the pressure. She became more confident speaking off the cuff, as well, but never quite got the hang of solving timed equations on the slate.

The first week of the Berry Moon, an oppressive wave of heat and humidity descended on Volturnus. Even with all the windows open, Ansel's study sweltered. Effie wore the thinnest linen top she owned and an airy skirt that barely grazed the tops of her knees. It barely made a difference. Even half naked, the simple act of sitting was enough to make her sweat. She became so uncomfortable that she considered lopping off her violet tresses but opted instead to tie them up in a messy bun that at least kept them off the back of her clammy neck. In the midst of this stifling milieu, Muldoon sprung one of his exams on her without warning.

She stood before him in the study, acutely aware of the sweat beading on her brow and moistening her palm around the wedge of chalk. By some unjust sorcery, her tutor seemed immune to the heat, his only concession to the weather, abandoning the thick overcoat and cravat he typically wore over his long-sleeved tunic.

Effie made her displeasure known. "How are you not sweltering?"

"You forget, I grew up in the desert." Muldoon tried to conceal his thin smile, but not really. The bastard was enjoying this. "This weather would be considered brisk in Umar."

"You're an evil man," Effie said.

"I'd attempt to defend myself, but I'm afraid today's exam is unlikely to bolster my case. Are you prepared?"

Sighing, Effie flashed the shallowest of curtsies to commence the exam.

It would be another multi-subject test, and Effie was actually grateful for the variety. If Muldoon had asked her to peck out solutions to algebraic equations for hours over the slate, she would have passed out. He asked her to recite the last two centuries of Odentine Kings and to name the forest tribes of Walder. She drew a map of the Vangulmark Islands from memory and reproduced the seasonal wind vectors around the Bolkan Straits. She faithfully recounted the plot of a Skaldic Saga about a mythic war between the Jokai, then quickly pivoted to explain the inner workings of a twelve-cylinder steam engine. When asked for a catalog of the Armada's western legions, she recalled the first four from memory and then drew a blank.

Muldoon prompted her with a picture: a black owl banner with an aspen branch in its mouth.

"The Eostrix Legion!" Effie said. "Two steam destroyers and five lumite strike ships. Five-hundred aero-marines stationed at... Brundis?" Muldoon nodded. "Two-thousand infantry legionnaires and another 1,000 auxiliaries. Currently deployed to Toran under Admiral Siprichor."

"*His Lightness* Admiral Siprichor," Muldoon corrected. "Let's keep it formal during these exams. Better to form the habit now. What about the senior officers?"

Effie searched her patchwork memory from those distant civics lessons. Months had passed since they last covered military organization. It seemed a cruel inclusion in the exam.

"Commodore Adal of the flagship *Thunder Mare*. Captain Loryssa of the destroyer *Heartsquall*. General Broon of the Fifth Legion." She paused then shook her head. "That's all I've got."

Muldoon crossed his arms and let her dangle, tapping one finger against his elbow in time with his bobbing foot. At last, he dipped his head. "That's enough, I suppose, though I'd prefer you retained the names of the strike ship captains and the legates serving under General Broon."

How many foreign names did he expect her to keep in her head? Effie felt the urge to roll her eyes, but she knew better than to break the decorum of the exam. Muldoon permitted her much latitude in the familiar way they addressed each other, but he'd been clear that he wanted her to treat these exams as if she stood before their host.

The civics question brought an end to their exam, and Muldoon assigned her a passing grade to her great relief. She began packing up her supplies in a leather satchel that he'd gifted her on her seventeenth name-day. When she finished, he was standing next to her holding a scroll wrapped in gold leaf.

"What is it?" she asked.

"It's for you," Muldoon said. "It's a crime to open a message intended for another guest."

Effie eyed her tutor warily as she accepted the scroll and cut the gold-leaf binding with her nail. She'd become much more practiced at reading the decadent calligraphy produced by the Aquilonian scribes. Even so, she read the brief message three times before looking up at Muldoon, who eagerly awaited her appraisal.

"It's an invitation," she said. "To Her Lightness' Solstice Ball at Aquilon."

"I assumed as much. I received my own invitation from the same courier—as did Ansel."

Effie looked blankly at the Celestial Seal pressed into the bottom of the page.

"You don't seem excited," Muldoon observed.

"What tipped you off?" Terrified and anxious seemed the more appropriate response. Effie read the invitation again, sure it must be some kind of mistake.

"You know how highly Her Lightness thinks of you," Muldoon said. "It shouldn't come as a shock that she wants to include you in the social functions of her court. This," he flicked the parchment in her hand, "is quite a privilege. You'll be among Patrician magistrates and other honored guests from across Kelestina's fiefdom and beyond. There will be other Celestials in attendance, as well. I'd expect His Lightness Hallidrax of Vangulmark and Her Lightness Minerviana of Takomar to attend, at the very least. They're both close allies of our host and her sect."

That didn't make Effie feel any more at ease. One Celestial was quite enough to turn her bowels to jelly.

Muldoon guided the invitation away from her face and placed an affectionate hand on her bare arm. He kindly ignored the dampness that greeted him. "You don't have to be nervous. I'll do my best to prepare you for what to expect so you aren't blindsided by the customs of court. Also..." his eyes drifted down to the parchment. He pointed to one line near the bottom. "You are permitted to bring an escort—any partner of your choosing. He'll be a lucky man, if you don't mind my saying so."

Effie swallowed. That notion brought some mild relief. At least she wouldn't have to face Kelestina's court alone.

But who could she possibly subject to this?

27

MULDOON

Muldoon and Ansel shared a kite-ship out to the lees of Avernus, where Dama Sigyn's *Jormunghast* lay in wait. Ansel pried open one of the porthole windows and loosened his suit collar to fend against the heat. The governor was always so obvious in his discomfort. It amused Muldoon to no end.

"Do you know what this is about?" Muldoon asked.

"Nothing good," Ansel grunted. He produced a handkerchief from his coat pocket and patted his moist brow. "The plebiscite's up in arms over these latest conscriptions. The tradesmen started clipping their tithes, and the censors are meeting increased resistance putting the laborers to work. Ruffians assaulted one of my levies—left him bloodied and bruised in an alley outside a public house. Volturnus isn't known for such disobedience."

Ill tidings. This was just how the troubles started on Aeolus. Muldoon caught a whiff of this kindling discontent from Effie, but he'd been foolish enough to hope the treasonous rumblings were limited to the dragoons, who bore the brunt of the conscriptions. Perhaps he could use her access to the plebiscite to ease the tensions. Her sister occupied a place of high esteem in the village. If Effie could convince Vanna to cool the Volturnian tempers, that would go a long way toward maintaining the peace. He still hadn't decided if he was inclined to do that favor for Ansel, however.

The waiting airship's three masts cast long shadows in the evening's dying light. Muldoon counted the open barrels of her cannon line fixed ominously on the Volturnian shore. A troubling thought occurred to him. "You don't think Her Lightness means to send a message?"

Ansel stared out the open porthole, likely counting the same row of artillery. "Let's hope not."

The *Jormunghast*'s top deck was large enough for their kite-ship to land amidships. A unit of uniformed aero-marines greeted Muldoon and Ansel with military salutes and led them into the quarterdeck and down a short ladder to the captain's cabin. Kelestina and Sigyn awaited their arrival, seated next to each other at a small table bolted to the cabin's deck. Sigyn was unattended, but Kelestina's proud majordomo lurked at her shoulder, eyeing the Patrician cohort with a flat expression and an upturned nose. The Celestial form always seemed out of place in the cramped confines of an airship. The vaulted ceilings and sweeping corridors of a crystal palace better suited Kelestina's glass profile and the sharp ends of her quartzite head.

Muldoon and Ansel both performed the obligatory bow then waited for the invitation to sit, which Kelestina granted with an extended arm.

"Please, Sires. Join us."

Muldoon matched Ansel's rigid posture at the edge of his seat. As had become her custom, Dama Sigyn made herself the odd one out, slouching over one armrest and tapping the hilt of her seax with imminent threat. She shouldn't have been permitted to bear arms in such proximity to Her Lightness, but Kelestina had a habit of making strange allowances for these breaches in decorum.

"You boys look nervous," Sigyn said.

Muldoon cringed. He'd never get used to that sibilant voice. "You mistake nerves for curiosity, Dama."

"That right?" Sigyn's lip curled, revealing a flash of canine fang.

"Allow me to satisfy your curiosity," Kelestina cut in. Her green eyes fastened on Ansel. "I've convened this cohort to discuss a troubling intercession undertaken on your behalf by the honorable Governor of Aeolus."

"On my behalf?" Ansel nearly choked on his tongue.

Kelestina tipped her narrow chin. "What news of the latest conscripts?"

"They're due to report to the manse tomorrow, Lightness," Ansel said. "With your permission, we granted them extra time to set their affairs in order. I assure you, they'll be transferred to Aquilon on schedule."

Kelestina and Sigyn shared a meaningful look. Muldoon knew that he was missing something, and he didn't like the feeling.

"What if I were to tell you the conscripts' request for an extension proved a cunning feint?" Kelestina asked.

Ansel glanced from Kelestina to Sigyn and back again. "Lightness?"

"It was a delay tactic!" Sigyn screeched. "Your tricky plebeians were buying time to make an escape."

Ansel seemed confused. "That can't—it isn't possible. My censors collect daily manifests from every port of call on Volturnus. They would have flagged any problems."

A sound like clinking glass as Kelestina picked one of her teardrop nails with her thumb. "It seems we've found a gap in your oversight, Governor. This troubles us."

"Lightness—I assure you—"

Just shut your dissembling mouth for once, Ansel.

Kelestina raised a hand to shut it for him. "If you'll accompany us to the brig, you'll see what I mean."

Muldoon followed the retinue into the bowels of the *Jormunghast*. As they descended through the busy tween deck to the hold, Kelestina kept Ansel by her side, and Sigyn drifted to the back to draw Muldoon's attention.

"Your landlord is quickly losing favor with our host," she hissed in his ear. "Might be an opportunity for an ambitious, well-positioned Patrician."

The frizzy ends of her white-blonde hair tickled Muldoon's cheek, inducing a shiver. "I'm quite content with my current assignment, truth be told."

"For now, maybe." Sigyn withdrew, but not far enough for Muldoon's taste. "The Pilot won't need a tutor forever."

When they reached the brig, they found two plebeian prisoners huddled in the corner of a cramped cell. Neither looked particularly well handled. The girl had a long gash across her scalp, and dried blood matted one side of her short, brown hair. The boy looked small by comparison, though it might have been the way he sat in a crumpled ball clutching his midsection. He looked up, tracking the sound of their party's arrival. One of his eyes was swollen shut, mottled with black and purple bruising. The other one flared with terror. Muldoon saw their host's porcelain visage reflected in his dilated pupil.

Muldoon's mood quickly darkened. Since his own term of incarceration, he no longer had the stomach to see prisoners treated roughly. No matter what they'd done, these Volturnians no longer posed any threat, and any needless cruelty seemed unbecoming. Not that he expected better from Sigyn. The Vangish weren't known for gentility.

Kelestina cast her emerald gaze over the prisoners like animals in a menagerie. "Nayla Keist and Jin Trake." Their names rang like a gong in Kelestina's Celestial timbre.

The prisoners drew together. Nayla put a protective arm around Jin.

"These are two of the Elementalists included in my recent Writ of Conscription, no?" Kelestina asked.

"Yes, Lightness," Ansel stuttered.

Kelestina's nose wrinkled with disgust. "Dama Sigyn intercepted them on a Tamarind sprite-ship transiting the archipelago with unusual haste. Had the Governor of Aeolus failed to intervene, they might already be well on their way to Cailex or Imhuacan—beyond the Crystal Throne's reach."

Ansel's discomfort turned to anger as he stepped up to the wooden bars of the cell to inspect the prisoners. "Is this true?" he demanded. When no response was forthcoming, he raised his voice. "Answer your governor!"

Nayla tightened her grip on Jin and scowled up at the blocky head looming over them. "Jokai damn you." She spat and, for her sake, Muldoon was glad her sputum never reached the edge of her cage. "We won't be fodder for your Armada to throw against foreign enemies across the sky. The dragoons of Volturnus don't recognize these illegal conscriptions. Our lives are our own."

Ansel grasped the bars of the cell. "You insolent little bitch—"

The curse froze on his lips at a gentle touch from Kelestina—a glancing gesture, the tips of her teardrop nails dragging along his back. "Instead of berating your plebeians, perhaps you should be thanking Dama Sigyn for her timely intervention."

Kelestina waited until Ansel realized she meant her suggestion literally. "*Err*, of course, Lightness." He turned to acknowledge Sigyn with a shallow bow. "Many thanks for your intervention, Dama."

Sigyn flipped her white-blonde hair dismissively. "Any time, Governor."

"If I may," Muldoon ventured into the conversation. "These prisoners represent but two of the five Elementalists submitted for conscription. What of the other three?"

"What indeed." Kelestina's lips pressed white across her pale blue face. "Either the remaining conscripts will report to Governor Ansel on the morrow as planned," her eyes narrowed on Ansel, voice sharpening to match her nails, "or else they slipped through your bumbling fingers and have escaped beyond our reach."

Muldoon cast his gaze back over the prisoners. The boy trembled in his companion's arms, too terrified to even countenance the discussion taking place just beyond the bars of his cage. The girl on the other hand—Nayla— she seemed to have enough fight in her for both of them. She lifted her chin to meet his eyes on an even plane, defiance and loathing burning within.

"What will become of them?" Muldoon asked.

"They'll be shipped to Klock Base as planned—as prisoners rather than honored guests. The Armada is expecting a quota, and our court is in no position to defer these obligations. What troubles me more is the conscripts' uncanny knowledge of their destination."

That fact had struck Muldoon as well, but he didn't dare give it voice.

"Your household has a leak, Governor." Sigyn seemed to enjoy making the accusation, but Kelestina wasn't so amused.

"It didn't come from me!" Ansel insisted.

"Oh, I'm sure the failure wasn't intentional," Sigyn said. "You haven't got the spine for subterfuge. But how many Volturnians serve on your staff, hmm? How many household conscripts have you taken into your bed? Pillow talk has been the downfall of greater men than you, Ansel."

Ansel puffed out his barrel chest. "I resent the insinuation!"

"Enough." Kelestina's voice chimed the assembly back to order. "Sigyn is right. You *will* be more discreet in the handling of your staff. Moreover, you will discover the elements on Volturnus working to help these Elementalists evade conscription. They couldn't have staged this escape attempt without foreign aid. The archipelago does not engage in regular intercourse with Tamarind Island. Have we made ourselves clear?"

Ansel hung his head in defeat. "Yes, Lightness. Any rebel faction operating on Volturnus will be brought to justice."

"Swiftly, Ansel."

"Of course, Lightness."

Muldoon badly wanted to accept Sigyn's accusation at face value, but an alternate explanation worried him as he followed Sigyn and Kelestina back above deck. Effie knew much and more about the conscription orders

—including their likely destinations. She also spent time with her sister and some of the other dragoons. He didn't suspect her of any intentional treason—nothing like that—but if she'd let information slip to Vanna...

Muldoon had failed to impress upon her the need for discretion around the conscriptions. If Effie was indeed the source of this leak, the fault lay with him as much as with her.

Dagda pulled him aside just as he was about to board the kite-ship behind Ansel. "Her Lightness would like a word in private."

"Of course."

The majordomo led him to Kelestina, who stood at the edge of the airship with her long fingers wrapped around the taffrail.

"You requested a word, Lightness?"

Kelestina stared off into the darkness, in the direction of Volturnus' distant shore. "Yes, Sire. I'd hoped to inquire about the progress of Miss Strait's studies?"

Muldoon breathed a quiet sigh of relief. "Miss Strait is performing quite admirably, I'm pleased to report. Her pace of study increases with every passing week. Within the year, I daresay she'd be well-furnished for a preliminary assessment at the Collegium."

"That is welcome news." Kelestina's pointy shoulders seemed to relax, shifting beneath the gemstone fabric of her gown. The Celestials maintained such an inscrutable facade. Sometimes he wondered if their inhuman souls were frozen in truth. Rare were the opportunities to read their inner lives, and yet this subtle gesture revealed much. His host seemed rife with tension—exhausted by the need to maintain the perception of rigid control. "It's proving more challenging than I imagined to keep her existence a secret of the court," she offered.

Muldoon sensed a rare window opening into the mind of his host. He dared not peer inside it too eagerly, lest she slam it shut. "Lightness?"

"The Elementalist conscriptions have kept the Armada at bay," Kelestina said. "But Master Vinson's work has encountered a delay. I need more time—before Miss Strait can be elevated to her purpose."

"I'm sorry, Lightness—what purpose?"

Kelestina's eyes flashed in his direction. "Come now, Muldoon. You're an intelligent man raised in a Celestial court of high esteem. Don't tell me you haven't worked out the aims of our sect."

"I—" *Tread carefully now.* "I...might have arrived at some suspicions."

Kelestina's voice took on a numinous, almost Skaldic cast. "Conquest will not unite the Hundred Frozen Souls. If we are to see the Lost Shores of Mu in our lifetimes, then we must cross the mountains of Toran and unlock the Locrian Sky."

The Locrian Sky... Muldoon had always thought Kelestina too parochial, but he misjudged her by an order of magnitude. Her ambitions reached beyond the most distant horizon on the face of Ciel.

"Skald Caelig spoke of the Titan's Lair," Muldoon said. "I assume he wasn't speaking figuratively."

Kelestina tipped her head. Moonlight danced in waves across the jagged tips of her quartzite crown. "The Titan of the Doric Sky remains at large. Our best hope for crossing the mountain peaks rests on the back of the Sleipnir."

Esoteric indeed. It was just as Muldoon assumed. Kelestina believed the Lost Continent a literal promised land. Was it such a shock to discover she pursued a mythic Leviathan, as well?

"This Myinese cartographer—Master Vinson—you believe he can find Bennu?"

"I do." Her voice rang with impatience, but not a note of doubt. "And when he does, we will have a pressing need for a very Gifted Pilot."

28

VANNA

Vanna's back complained against the cramped confines of a merchant lighter's steerage compartment. Bael looked even more uncomfortable, his greater stature compressed between lumpy sacks of millet grain. She endured this indignity for his sake—and to keep her name off the censors' list. Their covert work to save the conscripts had started drawing greater scrutiny from Ansel's agents, and she wasn't eager to explain why her name appeared on a manifest bound for Avernus the same night three Elementalists disappeared.

Thankfully, the crossing to the neighboring isle only took a few hours. If she had to spend any longer in steerage, she was likely to emerge as crooked and ornery as Ava.

Bael had been true to his word. In exchange for Vanna's information, he'd wrangled safe passage for Nayla and Jin, who both balked at their Writs of Conscription. Vanna had tried to coax Lya and Whatley into the same decision, but they didn't catch her subtle cues. Bors was a lost cause. He actually seemed excited to receive the conscription order.

Over the long months of their collusion, Vanna learned just how far the tendrils of Bael's Gulliver Ring threaded throughout the Doric Sky. For Nayla and Jin's protection, Vanna only knew that they were destined for a distant island called Tamarind—a land that hosted countless neutral cities where a fugitive Volturnian could easily disappear. Someday, once they'd rid themselves of the Shards, she'd find the lost sons and daughters of Volturnus and bring them home. This, she swore.

The merchant ship put down on the island's north end—at one of two freight ports servicing the quarry. A scheduled delivery of grain destined for the miners' larder provided adequate cover. Entering through the New Village was out of the question. As an officer in the corps, Vanna was well known throughout the isles. The risk that they'd be spotted by another dragoon in the village was too high. Through clandestine channels known only to him, Bael got word to his co-conspirators and set up a rendezvous at one of the mining camps near the island's windward shore. Volturnus wasn't the only island inundated with unwanted conscriptions.

They waited for the merchant crew to finish unloading their cargo onto oxcarts alongside the local longshoremen. Once the Avernian crew was out of sight, the pilot delivered three sharp taps against the bulkhead wall to indicate the coast was clear. Bael slipped him a pouch of coppers for the transit and an extra silver to buy his silence. The pilot agreed to wait at the quarry until dawn for their return, but no later.

"We appreciate it," Bael said.

The merchant pilot shrugged him off, weighing his purse approvingly. "You're paying for it. The miners are better company than the villagers, anyway."

Vanna found that difficult to believe, but she wasn't in any position to dispute it.

They crossed Avernus in the shadow of the Lumite Mountains, keeping their distance from the camp circles that dotted the northern plains. Between Vanna's notoriety and Bael's foreign cast, they stuck out like a pair of emus in a chicken coop. With so many agents of Aquilon sniffing around for subterfuge, the fewer eyes that marked their passage, the better.

Bael's gaze kept drifting toward the mountain peaks carving dim silhouettes in the moonlight overhead as they crossed the island.

"Something on your mind?" Vanna pried.

"This is an old mountain range," Bael said. He traced the line of flat peaks with an outstretched finger. "You can tell from their profile. Younger mountains are sharper."

"Okay." Vanna hadn't been expecting a geology lesson.

"Old ranges like this one are treasure troves of lumite ore. The island needs time to push the material up from its bowels and through its crust. The richest veins accumulate over time."

That made sense, she supposed. "The quarry's big business on Avernus."

Bael tapped the patch of blue beard on his chin as they continued walking. "The Shards are always hungry for lumite," he said after a long silence. "Their shipyards need a steady supply to build strike ships."

Vanna thought she saw where this was going. She'd spent enough time with Bael to get a sense for how his mind worked. The man was a saboteur through and through. Everywhere he looked, he saw new opportunities for disruption.

"The Ring's been working hard to keep the Shards' greedy hands off the rich quarries in North Tamarind. If we could cut off their supply on Avernus..."

Vanna intervened before his wheels got to spinning. "How you gonna manage that without hurting the Avernians?"

"Tricky needle to thread," Bael agreed. "But sometimes a little short-term pain is worth it for a greater cause."

Vanna didn't like the sound of it, but she knew Bael's idle musings when she heard them, so she didn't waste her energy arguing. "Why don't we keep our focus on the task at hand. We've got three Avernian Elementalists to vanish."

They continued walking for the better part of an hour before they sighted the bonfire at the center of the outermost mining camp. Vanna made out several figures moving around a distant ring of yurts. The crowd made her nervous.

"You trust these miners to keep their mouths shut?" she asked.

Bael's shrug wasn't particularly reassuring. "As much as I trust any guest of the Crystal Throne." Vanna assumed that included her. "Don't get jumpy on me, now. I've been in contact with this crew since my time on Aeolus. Their shift leader isn't exactly a rebel at heart, but she's got no love for the Shards, and she's grown accustomed to my generous patronage."

Of course. It always came down to coin. At first, Vanna had been surprised just how much of Bael's support was bought and paid for. She'd watched him toss around heavy purses like they were bags of sawdust. She couldn't begin to fathom where he came by such abundance, and she didn't really want to know.

They walked right up to the fire burning in the rusted remains of a tin barrel. Bael hailed a heavyset woman with short gray hair and skin burnt to leather. She sat in the campsite's only chair, flanked by two younger laborers who seemed content enough on the ground. One of them prodded a dented cookpot dangling over the fire with a charred stick. The female laborer in the proper seat moved a bulge of tobacco from one side of her lip to the other with her tongue. She launched a wad of black sputum into the fire as she clocked Vanna and Bael's approach. Vanna tried to hide her revulsion, but the way the woman sneered at her told her she'd done a poor job of it.

Bael tipped his braided head to the miner. "Been a minute, Gar."

"Six months, two weeks, and a day." Gar's voice ground out of her like gravel pulled from the quarry. "But who's counting?"

Bael cast his gaze around the cluster of yurts. "Our friends make it out on time?"

"They're here," Gar said. "Before we bring 'em out, I'll be counting our gratuity."

Bael pulled a second purse from his satchel and tossed it across the fire into Gar's waiting lap. Its contents landed with a wealthy *clink*.

Gar shook the pouch to hear the sound again, then dumped the coins on the ground to count them in the firelight. Vanna's eyes widened as she took in the pile of silver bars mixed with a few golden shekels clipped at their center with tiny holes. This was a heavy purse, even for him—a Shard's ransom in truth. She raised her eyebrows in his direction, and he shrugged back at her.

"Price of doing business."

Gar picked up one of the shekels and bit it. Apparently satisfied, she scooped the horde back into the purse and jabbed one of the younger laborers in the arm. "Go fetch 'em."

The laborer disappeared into one of the yurts without question and returned trailing three women of an age with Vanna—and two small children, one boy and one girl. The children looked like siblings, with the same moon-faced glow and coarse, sandy hair. Vanna glanced over at Bael as the group crept tentatively toward the fire, caught a tightening around his almond eyes.

Two of the women wore dragoon flight suits with the South Wind of Avernus sewn over the breast. The third wore a simple linen shirt and canvas pants, matching the laborers' attire. The two children gathered close to her, one clinging to each leg.

"This is Lotti, Samana, and Tova," Gar said.

"Tayna," one of the dragoons corrected.

"Doesn't matter," Gar said, spitting another black wad into the fire.

Vanna watched from a distance as Bael circled the fire to inspect these Avernians who were hoping to escape conscription. He crouched, bringing himself eye-to-eye with the two young children clinging to their mother's leg. "And who might you be?"

The boy hid his face in the canvas of his mother's pants, but the girl answered the question. "I'm Lee. I'm six."

"Nearly a woman grown!" Bael patted Lee on the head.

"My son's name is Cade," the mother—Lotti—said. "He's shy."

Bael looked at Lee again then straightened to his full height. He fingered his goatee as he considered Lotti and her brood. "Only arranged passage for three," he said.

Lotti pulled her children closer as the dragoon named Samana jumped in to save her. "They're only children. They don't take up much space."

"Space isn't the only concern." Bael was still watching Lotti. "More passengers means more risk—especially wains."

"You can't expect Lotti to leave her kids behind!" Samana said. "Their father died in a mining accident last year. They'll be sent to the longhouse."

Bael glanced at Gar for confirmation, but she was too busy sorting her new wealth to notice. He turned back to the group of Avernians with his knuckles on his hips. His gaze settled on Lotti. "I can guess what these two are good for, but you seem like a bit of a mystery box. What's your Gift, then?"

Lotti's thin lips trembled. "I—I silence the winds."

Even by the dim light of the fire, Vanna read the surprise on Bael's face.

"I speak to them like an Elementalist," Lotti explained. "But I can't summon them. I can only...*banish* them."

Curiosity piqued, Vanna drifted closer.

"Truly?" Bael's eyebrows arched, and Lotti shrunk away, still clutching her kids.

"There's no other Elementalist like her in the archipelago," Samana said. "She can still the currents for leagues around—shaped or otherwise. I've seen her drop an entire dragoon wing from the sky."

Vanna knew that she was gawking, but she couldn't help it. She almost couldn't *believe* it. Very few Gifts frightened Vanna, but the power this Avernian claimed—this soft-spoken *mother*—its devastating potential chilled her.

"Negation..." Bael muttered to himself. "Let me speak with my companion. Just a moment."

"Do you believe her?" Vanna asked as soon as Bael led her out of earshot of the mining camp.

"Negation is a rare Gift," he mused. "But it isn't unheard of." He glanced back over his shoulder at the Avernians awaiting judgment. "I don't have any reason to think she's lying."

"No wonder the Shards want her," Vanna said. "If they could weaponize her Gift... They could neutralize any advantage held by the dragoons."

"Or a flock of Red-Tail Avians," Bael said, then his voice became dark. "The whelps are an unfortunate wrinkle."

Vanna shook her head. "You can't expect a mother to abandon her children."

"Not willingly, no."

Vanna looked at him flatly. "You can't be serious."

Bael pulled a timepiece out of his shirt pocket and checked the hour. "Our smuggler will be here before Witching. If he refuses to take the wains, there's not much I can do to persuade him."

Vanna pointed at Gar, still ogling her riches by the firelight. "Your coin seems pretty convincing."

"This op's already running over budget," he grumbled.

Vanna poked him in the chest with a stiff finger. "What good are we to the archipelago if we can't even save a few Avernians from conscription?"

Bael raised his hands in surrender. "All right, all right. You've made your point. I'll see if I can haggle passage for the wains. But you need to steel yourself. I can't allow the Shards to get their hands on an Elemental negationist."

"Steel myself against what?"

Bael's jawline hardened. "Miss Lotti is getting on that smuggler's ship. One way or another."

Vanna liked the sound of that even less than Bael's daydreams about disrupting the Avernian quarry.

The smuggler arrived just ahead of schedule—a silent sprite-ship powered solely by lumite lifts. The inconspicuous vessel lent itself well to illegal commerce. Vanna waited with the Avernian fugitives while Bael went up to negotiate.

"I won't leave my children," Lotti said. Her fear had hardened into a kind of brittle defiance.

Vanna never knew what to say at times like these. "If you stay on Avernus, Governor Aeryon's agents will come for you. They'll take you away from your children and you may never see them again." She heard the little boy whimpering softly into his mother's canvas pants.

Tayna scowled at her. "Where's your Jokai-damned heart?"

Left it somewhere in the Green Maw, I think. "It's the truth," Vanna said. "Heart's got nothing to do with it." She saw Bael's silhouette gesticulating animatedly as he haggled with the smuggler. "Bael will do everything he can to get your kids on that ship. Trust him."

Lotti knelt to her crying son and stroked the back of his sandy head, quietly hushing.

Samana sidled up next to Vanna. "Trust's a scarce commodity these days."

Vanna had no argument, there.

Bael returned with a grave expression, and Vanna's heart sank into her stomach. He looked at each of the Avernians.

"He'll take the wains," he finally said.

All three of the Avernians breathed an audible sigh, and Vanna found herself sharing in their relief. Lotti kissed each of her children, overcome to the brink of tears.

Bael nodded up the way to the smuggler's landing. "Go load up before he changes his mind. Do as you're told, and don't ask any questions." As the Avernians scrambled to comply, he grabbed Samana by the arm. "You're going to have to work for your passage. Lucky for you, the captain lost one of his deck hands to scurvy and left him at Grenport. Think you can handle that task?"

Samana nodded once then followed the other fugitives to the landing.

Vanna and Bael stood side-by-side, watching until the Avernians vanished inside the smuggler's ship.

"Thank you," Vanna said.

Bael waved her thanks away. "Saving them serves us both. The Gifted are human resources to the Shards. Every Elementalist we deny them weakens their hold. We'll bleed 'em to death by a thousand cuts like this one.

"Even if it takes a lifetime."

29

KAI

Kai followed his draft into a sudden landing on the windward shore of Aquilon. Dray flashed the sign to put down before leading his patrol group into a sharp descent.

Everyone in the patrol group knew the reason for the unplanned pitstop and quickly circled to discuss. Dray looked as haggard as Kai had ever seen him, face darkened by stubble, eyes glassy and drooping. This was supposed to be Vanna's patrol. The Commander called Dray up at the last minute to replace her.

Kai lied for Vanna—told Kendy she'd taken ill and wasn't fit to fly. He even put in an order for a flux tonic with the apothecaries to add a layer of depth to her cover. It wasn't the first time he'd lied for her, and it wouldn't be the last. Vanna's excuses always frustrated Kendy, but this time Kai sensed a fresh dash of suspicion, as well. They couldn't keep this up forever.

Kai's romantic relationship with Vanna continued to blossom, but she only opened the door to her collusion with Bael halfway. He knew that she'd be gone for the night and half the next day, but she hadn't shared where she was going nor what she was doing when she got there. He hated how she kept him in the dark, but his blindness did make it easier to lie for her.

"I've never seen so many ships over Aquilon," Kadir said.

"Big ships, too," Nadeen added. "No idea what those galleons are hauling, but I'm willing to guess it isn't turnips."

Dray exhaled and wiped the sweat from his brow. Without the cool winds whipping past them at altitude, they were subject to the heat and humidity that settled over the islands and remained for the season. "Not our business if the Armada's congregating around Kelestina's palace. We're not patrolling for Celestial aero-marines."

Kai sensed the draft leader's reluctance to extend the patrol. If Dray had his way, they'd burn a straight line back to Volturnus and his waiting bed. Kai hated to deny him that comfort, but the unusual traffic around Aquilon was exactly the kind of detail Vanna instructed him to collect. If he was going to bring back anything useful, he needed to get a closer look, and his eagerness to please her overrode every competing concern.

"We're already here," Kai said. "It wouldn't hurt to run one flyby—circle the palace and get a better view. The Commander will want a more thorough report than we're prepared to give him."

"Kendy doesn't care about the Armada," Dray complained.

"The kid's right," Nadeen said. "One flyby will only cost us an hour or so." She visored her eyes and glanced up at the dark shadows converging on the northern horizon. By the wan light of the moons, they looked like thunderheads gathering—an uncanny sight, for the night was otherwise cloudless and clear.

Too tired to argue, Dray produced a hoarse growl. "Fine. One flyby. Then we cut a straight path for Volturnus by the lees. On my mark."

Dray kept their formation wide of the palace airspace. They counted four heavy airships docking over Aquilon—and a dozen hidden lighters grounded at port. Kai marked the make of each airship and its colors, soaking up what information his brain could hold. He recorded these details in a litany that he repeated to himself over and over on the long flight back to Volturnus Village.

Dray disbanded the draft as soon as they landed, but Kai didn't follow Kadir back to the bunkhouse. He needed to disgorge himself to Vanna before crucial details began to slip away.

"Where are you going?" Kadir asked. "Aren't you beat?"

"Sleeping out tonight," Kai said.

The young flier pumped his eyebrows suggestively. "Staying with your mystery woman again?"

"Mind your business."

"Whatever." Kadir swatted away his denials. "We're onto you Bowker. Your bunk's empty more nights than it's filled. You can't keep your girl a secret forever. She got a husband or something?"

Kai left the nosey fledgling standing on the landing with his assumptions. He and Vanna had been plenty discreet, but it was hard to keep your whereabouts a secret when you slept in a bunkhouse with fifteen other dragoons.

He found Vanna's cottage open, so he let himself inside. She hadn't returned yet from whatever mischief she was about. Thanks to Bael's distractions, Vanna had let her home fall into mild disrepair. A patina of dust coated every surface, and the wash basin was piled high with encrusted dishes. With time to kill, he decided to make himself useful and grabbed the underutilized broom from the kitchen closet.

He practiced his litany as he swept the foyer and the kitchen, ticking off each ship he'd marked around Aquilon and every banner he could remember. A few of the foreign banners had already become scrambled in his mind, but whatever he retained would have to be good enough. He washed the tower of dirty dishes and scoured an iron skillet that was starting to smell. Once finished, he wrung out the washrag and wiped down the kitchen table. Second Bell rang from the campanile as he worked, then Third. It was nearing midday when the cottage door finally swung open and Vanna hauled herself inside.

She'd been gone all night, and Kai doubted she spent any of that time asleep. Even so, she looked strangely bright-eyed and energized. Only her violet hair was out of place. She'd let it grow out and now wore it swept to the side over one shoulder. With longer hair and plain clothes, she looked more like Effie than ever before. The resemblance excited Kai more than it should have, bringing with it a kindling of shame.

Vanna smiled when she saw him waiting over her kitchen table. She stretched up on her toes to plant a routine kiss on his lips as she passed on her way to the basin. Even the quotidian peck was enough to ignite Kai's young desire. He considered carrying her over his shoulder into the bedroom right then and there—or else laying her out across the table he'd just cleaned and tearing off her tunic with his teeth. When had he become so ardent? They had more important things to discuss. His memory from the patrol wasn't getting any sharper over time, and a bout of lovemaking was certain to wipe the slate clean.

Vanna filled a cup with pure water from a pitcher on the counter and slumped into one of the chairs around the kitchen table. They'd grown comfortable in shared silence, progressed beyond greetings and small talk. Kai rinsed out the rag in his hands and hung it to dry over the basin. Vanna quietly sipped from her cup.

"How was patrol?" Vanna finally asked.

"Eventful," Kai said, turning back to the table but keeping his feet. "But not half as eventful as your night, I'm guessing."

Vanna took another small sip of her water. "You can guess all you want."

"Sure am curious what you were up to."

"Better you don't know," Vanna said.

"How about where you've been?"

"Same answer." She flashed a seductive smile crafted to disarm him. As usual, it worked as intended.

"It's getting harder to cover for you," Kai said, at last taking a seat opposite Vanna. "I think Kendy's getting suspicious."

"You let me deal with Kendy." Vanna kicked her legs up on Effie's empty seat and crossed her ankles.

"But you're not the one who has to deal with him. I am." Kai tried to sound stern, but he couldn't quite manage it—not while his eyes probed every curve of her long legs stretched out inside those form-tailored pants.

"Are you mad at me?" She batted her green eyes. She hadn't quite mastered the subtlety of the gesture the way Effie had, but even the clumsy flirtation was enough to send Kai reeling.

"I'm annoyed," he said, his obvious hunger undermining the sentiment.

She reached over with one toe and prodded his knee, his inner thigh, the outskirts of his groin... "Don't be annoyed," she goaded. Kai grabbed her foot and held it by the arch. He began kneading it with his strong palms. She moaned. "That feels good."

"I wish you'd tell me more about what you're doing with Bael." He kept kneading as she slid down the back of her chair. "I want to help you."

"You are helping," she said. "A little higher—toward the ball." Kai stopped kneading. She shook her foot in his hands, almost whining, "Don't tease me!"

"Don't you want to hear what I saw on patrol over Aquilon?"

Vanna withdrew her leg and sat up, the massage forgotten. "More ships?"

Kai nodded. "A lot of 'em."

Vanna leapt from her seat and disappeared into her room. She came back seconds later brandishing a sheaf of parchment, a black pen, and a pot of ink.

"Where'd you get that?" Kai asked, eyeing the expensive supplies.

"Gift from Bael." She dipped the tip of her pen into the inkpot. "I can't keep sneaking out to the Green Maw every time I need to get a message back to him. We've got a system now."

"A system?" This affair was becoming more cloak and dagger with every passing week.

"A hiding place where I leave messages for Sparrowhawk to deliver."

"Isn't that risky?"

"Less risky than sneaking past all the nosey farmhands." She blotted her pen's silver tip then placed it against the paper. "What did you see?"

Kai sighed and began delivering his report. "Four heavy airships docking at the spireport."

"Four?" Vanna's eyes leapt up from the page.

Kai nodded. "And twelve more lighters parked inside the outer walls."

"*Jokai fend...*" Vanna took down notes as he spoke. "You get their colors?"

"Celestial Seal on three of the airships. Armada Serpent on the fourth. I got a good look at the regional banners on the three Celestial galleons: An ax and sword over a cobalt field; a red horsehead over white-striped-with-gold; and three gold lances in a vertical row over a green- and gray-checkered field."

"Hold on," Vanna paused him until her writing caught up with his report. "What about the Armada ship? Did you catch its banner?"

Kai shook his head. "I never got a good look at it."

"Think, Kai."

Now he *was* getting annoyed. "I don't know—looked like some kind of bear maybe?"

"What colors?"

"I said I don't remember!"

Vanna stopped writing and looked up at him, softening. "I'm sorry. You did well." She tapped the parchment with the dry end of her pen. "Bael will want to know about this."

Kai looked at her skeptically. "Why does he care if the Celestials are gathering at Aquilon?" Vanna's hesitation only sharpened his irritation. "Come on, Vanna. Give me something here. I'm tired of feeling like your unwitting spy."

She reached over with her toe again and prodded his inner thigh. "Oh, you're plenty witting," she said.

"Be serious." He swatted her away, though it took every ounce of his willpower to do so.

She acquiesced. "Fine. Bael doesn't tell me everything, but when the Shards move resources out to the Zephyrs, it opens up opportunities for his ring elsewhere in the Doric Sky. The banners you saw—they belong to other consulates. The axe-and-sword is the crest of Vangulmark. The horse-head is Brundis. The three lances... I'm not sure. Maybe Takomar?"

Kai shook his head. "Those names don't mean anything to me."

"They're other islands. Other hosts. Those airships you're describing sound like Shard flagships. If the Celestials are on Aquilon in person, it means they aren't minding the shop at home. Bael has operatives on all those islands. He'll try to get word out that the rooster's left the coop."

So, he was helping Bael stir up trouble across the Doric Sky. Fantastic. "How does this help the archipelago?"

For the first time, agitation flashed across Vanna's face. "It's an exchange, Kai. I give Bael information, and he helps me protect the islands from Kelestina and her conscriptions."

"Is that where you were last night?" Kai probed. "Saving conscripts?"

Vanna set down her quill and crossed her arms. "I'm not sure I care for your tone."

"I'm not sure I care for you running around the archipelago undermining Kelestina's writs."

Rolling her eyes, Vanna got up from the table to refill her cup. "This is why I don't want you inside our operation."

"I'm already inside it, Vanna—you're just forcing me to help you blind and half deaf."

He'd pushed her too far, and he immediately regretted it. When she turned around to glare at him, all the flirtation had vanished from her cast. She looked at him like her idiot little brother again, and he knew what came next.

"I need to get some sleep."

"Don't be like that—"

"I'm not *being* any way. I'm taking the next two night patrols to make up for my absences."

Kai heard the implication loud and clear. He'd been dismissed. He wished he could roll back the clock on this entire interaction, but begging wasn't likely to move the needle in his favor. Nothing less erotic than a pleading lover.

"Fine." Kai gathered himself up from the table and moved for the door. "I'm not giving up on you so easily," he added. "I only pray that you'll let me inside before this whole conspiracy crumbles beneath your feet. I'm not going to let anything happen to you, Vanna, and it'll be a lot easier to save you if I know what the hell is going on."

Vanna scoffed.

Kai slammed the cottage door on his way out and wound his way back toward the bunkhouse. He had the next two patrols off, but he was expected to report for evening drills at Fifth Bell. Hardly enough time to make a proper dent in his exhaustion, but some sleep was better than no sleep, he supposed.

He stopped by the Command Room to see who else was around, and what a mistake that turned out to be.

He found Effie occupying Kendy's seat at the head of the command table—holding court with Maya, Dray, Raji, and a handful of junior dragoons. She glowed like the gemstone in the top setting of a queen's diadem, dressed in an immaculate mint sundress hemmed with thread-of-gold, shoulders and knees exposed to the room. She looked every inch the young Patrician Dama, with her long hair pressed into a permanent wave and appealing purple accents applied to her eyelashes and cheeks. He watched her olive breasts heaving in the low bust of her sundress as she laughed along to one of Dray's clumsy jokes.

Raja caught Kai edging back toward the door, and waved him over to join them. "Bowker! Look who it is. Volturnus' prodigal daughter returns."

Effie's vibrant eyes flashed playfully as she probed him. "Kai! Just the man I was looking for." Her mellifluous voice rang discordant in his ears.

She'd affected some semblance of the Patrician accent she'd immersed herself in these many months—just a touch, but enough to pollute the familiar sound of her.

Reluctantly, Kai took a seat next to Maya, keeping as much distance as possible between him and Effie.

"Effie was just telling us about a Leviathan she tamed on the Frostwind Cayes." Raji sounded as lovestruck as he was impressed. "What did you call it?"

"A hammerhead," Effie said. "Just a nymph, but he'd already torn through half an Angler's crew before I got there to set things right."

"Incredible," Dray said.

Effie's painted eyes settled on Kai at the end of the table, and he suddenly felt like toothless prey in a predator's sights. "Would you all grant us the room? I need to speak with Kai about a personal matter. It relates to our host."

Unable to decline now that Kelestina had been invoked, the dragoons filed out of the Command Room as if they'd received an order directly from Kendy's lips. Raji dragged his gaze along Effie as he passed. He paused just behind her and licked his lips before crudely pumping his eyebrows in Kai's direction.

Jokai fend… What fresh hell?

Effie clearly expected Kai to close the gap between them once the room had emptied. Instead, he placed his feet flat on the floor and flopped his arms onto the table. He wasn't going anywhere.

Effie smiled at him with sealed lips. Only her eyes belied any confusion at his reluctant behavior. "I've been invited to our host's Solstice Ball at Aquilon," she finally said.

Kai snorted. "How nice for you."

"It is. It's a high honor, I'm told. There will be guests in attendance from across the Doric Sky. Patricians. Other Celestials."

"Sounds stuffy," Kai said.

Effie laughed playfully. "I was a bit intimidated when I first heard about it, as well, but I'm starting to get excited. I'm permitted to bring a guest… An escort."

Oh no. Kai's mouth felt suddenly dry.

Effie's nerves began to break her Patrician mask, and through the cracks Kai saw hints of the girl he'd known and loved for so long. That glimpse worked to melt the walls of ice he'd erected around his dormant feelings, but the slight thaw only revealed to Kai just how much those feelings had cooled through their long confinement. He still yearned for Effie in a strange, dim way, but the space he held for her in his heart had been claimed by another.

"I'd like you to be my escort," Effie said. "Would you accompany me to the Solstice Ball?"

"Effie…"

"You don't have to worry about your attire. I'll have a proper suit commissioned from Sire Ansel's personal tailor."

"It's not that—"

"And I can prepare you for what to expect. We'll be together the entire time. You only have to follow my lead. It will be a night unlike any other. You'll get to rub elbows with our host's entire court!"

She wasn't listening.

"Why would I want to do that?" Kai's words struck the playful smile from Effie's face. "I can't just run off with you to wine and dine at Aquilon Palace! Kendy will never permit it. I have patrols to run—and drills. We're already undermanned from these damn conscriptions."

"Oh, come off it!" Effie's shapely eyebrows pinched inward. "Surely this is more important. I think an invitation from Her Lightness supersedes your little patrols."

"Our *little patrols*?" Kai scowled across the table. "Is this a joke to you?"

Color began to rise in Effie's cheeks to match her make-up. "It is a joke," she shot back. "How many times have I had to listen to you and Vanna complain about these overwrought patrols? *Counting skygulls*, I think you called it."

Kai sat up straighter in his seat. "We're protecting Volturnus."

"You're not protecting *anything*," Effie said. "Kelestina protects Volturnus. But if it makes you feel important to flap your wings in laps around the island, then good for you, I guess."

Kai pushed away from the table, chair screeching angrily across the floorboards. "You don't just *sound* like one of them. You've become one of them. The transformation is complete." He stood up and performed a mocking bow. "I decline your invitation, Miss Strait. I hope you enjoy a lavish evening while we mere plebeians *fly laps* and *count skygulls* on our fingers and toes."

Kai left Effie gawking and stormed out. As soon as he stepped outside, he punched the wall of the barracks—so hard his knuckles cracked and bled.

Damn it to all Nine Hells! Why was it still so easy for her to get under his skin?

The Strait girls wouldn't be content just to see him consigned to the lunatic colony on Lonely Spur. They must have conspired to kill him, and they were both determined to make it hurt.

30

EFFIE

Tears burned in Effie's eyes as she fled the village. For once, she actually yearned for the isolation of Ansel's manse.

She thought she was past this.

She hated how deeply and easily Kai's words still wounded her. Each time he made her cry, she swore it would be the last, and yet he'd managed to make her a liar to herself once again—another injury piled atop all the rest.

She shouldn't have provoked him. Belittling his service was beneath her—*unbecoming of her station*, as Muldoon would say. She hadn't even meant it, but it seemed the only bare defense she could muster against the embarrassment of rejection. Kai hadn't made any effort to hide his displeasure at the invitation. He looked positively *repulsed* by the prospect of escorting her to Kelestina's Solstice Ball. Was she truly such a hag?

Effie caught Sire Ansel's attention as she stormed past him on her way through the manse. He paused from delivering instructions to his butler to mark her passage. "Miss Strait?"

"Not now, Governor." It was poor form to rebuff the governor in front of his staff, but she felt far too fragile to receive him.

When she at last reached the safety of her room, she found Ina there performing her afternoon service—turning down the bed and laying out a nightgown fresh from the laundry.

"I'm sorry, Effie." Ina's cheeks reddened as she tucked into one of her obsequious bows. "I didn't expect you back so soon. I can come back with your dinner."

At least she hadn't called her "Miss Strait."

"It's no matter." Effie's voice cracked as she walked to her desk to hide her shame behind a stack of books. She heard Ina place the nightgown over the bedspread. Tentative footsteps approached, and Effie turned her face down to a shuttered text.

Ina ventured closer. "...Is something the matter?"

"It's nothing important." Fresh tears burned in Effie's eyes at the earnest sound of her servant's concern. She turned her head, but sensed Ina lingering.

"If there's something you'd like to talk about—the staff is required to keep the confidences of the household and its guests."

Effie sniffed and wiped her eyes. When Ina did not withdraw, she looked up at her. "It's nothing really—a stupid *boy*."

"Ah." Ina's tight-lipped smile carried no judgment. "I think I may know a thing or two about that. I don't have the benefit of your schooling, but stupid boys are an area of expertise—or, at least, they used to be."

It was more words than Ina had spoken to Effie in all the months she'd lived up at the manse. Effie had never been one to share her troubles—particularly when they were personal—but the rare breach in Ina's staff decorum drew her out of her shell.

"I doubt you ever had to deal with this kind of problem," Effie sniffed. "What boy would reject you?"

Ina sat back on Effie's bed and folded her hands across her aproned lap. "Stupid ones," she said. "And Volturnus is lousy with them."

Effie laughed through her tears. "How do you handle it?"

"I pity them," Ina said. Her coy smile didn't belong on the face of a beaten conscript. It reminded Effie too much of the pretty girl who made a trade of flouncing for the drilling dragoons. "In my experience, a rejection has less to do with a girl's inadequacy and more to do with the boy's insecurity and foolishness." Ina stood up and guided Effie's face gently to the looking glass over her desk. "Look at yourself. Even with your eye make-up running, you'd outshine half the Damas of a Celestial court. Boys are so fragile. Whoever this fool is, I'm sure the thought of standing in your shadow was too intimidating for his tiny ego to bear."

Effie dabbed the corners of her eyes as she stared at her reflection. "How do I make myself—I don't know—*less* intimidating."

"Why would you want to do that?" In the reflection, Effie saw Ina scowl. "Effie Strait doesn't have the time for a little boy too insecure to stand at her side. Effie Strait needs a proper *man*."

A proper man. Effie sniffed again and wiped the last of her tears from her painted cheeks. She glanced over her shoulder at Ina. "Any idea where I can find one of those?"

"I'll certainly let you know when I meet one."

They shared a cathartic laugh as Ina drew back toward the bed.

"Am I interrupting something?" Muldoon had sidled up to Effie's open doorway. He was dressed in his typical Patrician finery and held a long black garment bag over one shoulder from its metal hook.

"Apologies, Sire." Ina restored her empty servant cast and performed a deep bow.

"No apologies are called for," Effie quickly added. "Ina was helping me with a personal problem."

Muldoon's eyes probed the bowing handmaid then moved back to Effie. "I assume you reached a satisfactory resolution?"

"As much as that's ever possible where matters of the heart are concerned." Effie waved to Ina. "Thank you, Ina. You're dismissed."

Muldoon continued inspecting Effie with that quizzical stare as Ina scuttled past him into the hall. "I have something for you," he finally said. "I hope you won't think it's too forward."

Curious now, Effie welcomed him into her chamber. Muldoon seemed almost giddy as he hung the garment bag from her bedpost and unlatched the front. He peeled back the black fabric, revealing the most elegant Avernian gown that Effie had ever seen. Waves of lavender silk poured down from the single strap, twisting in braids around the bust and overlapping at the waist where the fabric dropped into a tight princess silhouette. A band of gold ran around the waist, accented with crushed emeralds woven into a layer of gauze.

Effie drew up from her seat to inspect the lavish gift. She ran her fingers along the soft fabric of the silhouette—true silk, unadulterated by lesser fibers. It was the most expensive dress she'd ever held—excepting only the diamond gown from Kelestina's palace—but this one excited her more for its familiar Avernian form. Still holding the gown between her fingers, she looked up at Muldoon, standing stiffly, awaiting her appraisal.

"This is for me?"

He nodded. "It's customary for guests at a Celestial ball to present wearing their local attire. I have it on good authority that the Avernian dressmakers are the envy of the Zephyr Isles, and this was the finest model they could produce. I had to guess at your measurements, but I like to think I have a keen eye for such things."

Effie couldn't stop running her fingers over the expensive fabric. The gemstone augmentations were ground so fine as to be smooth to the touch.

"I thought the color a nice match for your hair," Muldoon continued, his excitement obvious and endearing. "And the stones a pleasing complement to your striking eyes. We can instruct the governor's tailor to craft your escort an appropriate match. A violet cravat would suffice. A colored doublet might be too loud, but perhaps an emerald brocade..." He thumbed his strip of goatee, considering.

At the mention of her escort, Effie felt another gorge forming in her throat. Her eyes began to burn, renewing the threat of tears.

Muldoon's giddy expression fell away. "It's too much. I knew it would be too forward. I'm sorry, Effie. I can have it returned. You should wear whatever you're comfortable in. I only wanted you to have a gown befitting your station."

"It isn't that." Effie choked on her words, tears again falling freely. "It's beautiful—and too kind. I love it."

Muldoon looked confused again. "Then what is it?"

"I don't *have* an escort," Effie moaned. At last, she released the gown. "I'm afraid I'll be attending unaccompanied."

Muldoon's shoulders relaxed as he watched her pawing at her tears. He silently produced a handkerchief from his overcoat. She accepted it with a sniff and tried to hide her face. A startled intake of breath as she felt his finger gently guiding her back to him by the chin.

"Come now." He bent his head to her, probing with his soft, almond eyes. "You needn't hide yourself from me. We're well beyond that."

"I shouldn't be crying," Effie croaked. "I feel so foolish."

"No, you shouldn't," Muldoon said. "But you are hardly a fool. Tears rarely bow to logic, in my experience. Truth be told, I'm not surprised you're having difficulty procuring an escort from the plebiscite."

Effie sniffed and patted her nose with the handkerchief. "Am I so repulsive?"

"I think you know you're not," Muldoon said. "You've simply elevated yourself above your peers. They see you as a near-Patrician now. What common boy of Volturnus could bear to stand in your light?"

"Ina said much the same thing."

"Ina?"

"My handmaid."

"Ah." Muldoon drew back an inch, and Effie pursued him with her eyes. The way he considered her from a distance reminded her of their first introduction in Kelestina's palace. This time, she knew him well enough to read the bashfulness bubbling beneath the surface of his Patrician poise. He rubbed his goatee. "I think I may have a solution—a proposal really, if you would entertain it?"

Effie blinked up at him. She felt her tears beginning to ebb, restoring some of her composure.

"I wonder..." Muldoon took a deep breath. He seemed to be girding himself. "I wonder if you might consider me as an acceptable escort—in the absence of an alternative? I haven't made the time for many social calls since arriving on Volturnus, and I find myself bereft of relationships to call upon. I'd consider it a great honor if you'd allow me to attend the Solstice Ball at your side."

The solicitation surprised Effie to silence, which her tutor misinterpreted for reticence.

"Please don't misconstrue my intentions," he stammered. "We'll both be arriving by the same coach, and I know we enjoy each other's company —at least, I suspect—"

"Stop," Effie said.

Muldoon paled. "I'm sorry, Effie—I shouldn't have—"

"I would love to have you as my escort." Effie bowed to him. "You honor me."

Color restored, Muldoon seemed to grow a foot in an instant. His entire bearing brightened at her acceptance. They looked into each other's eyes for a long time without speaking.

She saw this neat young Patrician anew, recognized his foreign features as handsome and exotic—noticed his rich attire, always tailored to perfect form. She couldn't have found someone more unlike Kai anywhere in the

Eight Skies of Ciel. He was sharp where Kai was blunt; soft where Kai was hard; lean in all the places Kai had thickened; so refined where Kai was hopelessly coarse. Effie could almost taste the flavor of their student-teacher relationship changing as they stared at each other.

She didn't mind it at all.

31

VANNA

Vanna leaned against her washbasin, nervously watching the door to the cottage. Bael sat at her kitchen table, looking over her scribbled notes from Kai's scouting report.

He shouldn't be here.

He'd arrived at her cottage door in the middle of the night—a flagrant breach of the protocol they'd established to keep them both safe. Like any small village, Volturnus was lousy with busybodies. The last thing they needed was a mysterious caller providing fodder for gossip around Janus' hearth. Fortunately for both of them, nobody ever visited Vanna besides Kai—and occasionally Effie.

Wouldn't that be an unfortunate twist?

Vanna tapped her elbow impatiently while Bael continued to read. "You're certain nobody saw you?"

"As certain as one can be," Bael muttered, eyes still scanning the parchment.

Vanna slammed her hands down on the table in front of him, glowering at the top of his braided head. "You'll have to do better than that. If Ansel's agents connect us—"

"Peace, Vanna." He finally looked up. "I'm reasonably adept at remaining unseen. You might say it's a core competency of mine. Trust." He tapped the parchment with a finger. "This is very interesting."

"Something you can use?"

He nodded gravely. "Kelestina must be hosting some kind of summit. Three Celestial flagships and an Armada galleon?" He made a clucking sound with his tongue. "I know some people who will find this very interesting, indeed."

"You know who's on those ships?" Vanna pried.

"At least two more Shards," Bael said. "By the designs, I'm guessing Hallidrax of Vangulmark and Minerviana of Takomar. An interesting cadre; no friends to Admiral Siprichor." He glanced back down at the parchment and shook his head. "I don't see any colors for the galleon…"

"My scout didn't catch them."

"That's an unfortunate oversight." Bael sounded annoyed. He chewed his lower lip, quickly bouncing one foot beneath the table. "Not even a glimpse?"

Vanna rolled her eyes. "He said it might have looked like a bear."

"Not a bear," Bael said. "A sun badger. That's the banner of the Fifth Umari Legion. If their officers are over Aquilon, then they're a month away from Toran. That represents a major opportunity for the Hellicon League to press their advantage."

Toran again. Bael had a one-track mind. Vanna let her impatience seep into her voice. "What does it mean for *Volturnus*?"

"Probably nothing," Bael said absently.

"*Nothing*?"

Bael looked up from the page at her. "The Shards love their formal events. Given the crowd, I'm guessing this summit is social in nature. I don't think this impacts Kelestina's plans for Volturnus one way or another."

Vanna exhaled and took a seat at the table. "That's a good thing, I guess."

"This is a *very* good thing." Bael rolled up her parchment notes and tucked them inside his cloak.

"What are you doing here, Bael? We're not supposed to make contact inside the village."

"Extenuating circumstances."

Vanna leaned back in her chair and crossed her arms. "What kind of extenuating circumstances?"

"The unfortunate kind." Bael drummed his fingers on the tabletop as

Vanna waited for him to elaborate. "The Volturnian conscripts we exfil-trated never made it to Tamarind."

"What?" Vanna's heart stopped beating in her chest. "You told me your smugglers were reliable."

"They usually are." Bael shrugged.

"Then what the hell happened?"

"Sparrowhawk says the new Governor of Aeolus is keeping a close eye on all the sky routes west out of the archipelago. She's got a heavy gunship at her disposal. It's possible she intercepted our man."

Vanna felt a sharpness in her chest—like an Avian's taloned claw tight-ening around her ribs. If she'd sent Nayla and Jin to their deaths, she'd never forgive herself. She'd never forgive Bael, either. "What will happen to them?"

"Hard to say." Bael curled one end of his thin mustache around a finger. "I doubt they'll be harmed, if that's what you're worried about—though the condition of their transport is likely to be less than comfortable. The Shards wanted them for the Armada. That's where they're headed—even if it's in chains."

"This wasn't supposed to happen!" Vanna realized she'd balled up the fabric of her flight suit in angry fists and quickly released the tension.

"Casualty of war, I'm afraid." If Bael didn't stop twirling his mustache, Vanna was going to gust across the table and rip it off his face. "There are no guarantees in this game we play. We save who we can and move on after injury. If you dwell on every minor setback, you'll never stay ahead of the ax."

"This isn't a minor setback, and it isn't a game—not to me! Not to Volturnus!"

"Wait." Bael raised his palms to absorb her outrage. "There's more."

Jokai save us...

"Sparrowhawk made contact with our friend," Bael said. "She had an interesting story to tell. It seems Bone Adder's been lurking in the Lees of Nevis, raiding merchant vessels and living fat."

"The Lees of Nevis?"

"Six independent islands surface west of Grenport," Bael explained. "They're lightly policed and well-positioned near the richer trade routes. Popular pirate ports, for obvious reasons. According to our friend, Captain

Whitefang's taken a peculiar interest in lumite freighters hauling Avernian ore."

"That doesn't make any sense," Vanna said. "Why would a pirate working for the Shards hit Avernian freighters? That ore belongs to the Crystal Throne."

"Why, indeed." Bael passed one hand thoughtfully over his phalanx of braids. "I haven't untangled it yet, but Sparrowhawk says Nevis has gone quiet. After months of lucrative pillaging, it seems like Captain Whitefang has moved on."

Vanna pointed an accusatory finger across the table at Bael. "Maybe you're wrong about this Whitefang. Maybe he isn't working for the Shards. Maybe he's just a pirate, after all."

"Could be." Bael tilted his head, considering, then shook it. "But it doesn't smell right. The Shards are up to something, and Bone Adder's at the center of it. My instincts tell me this is the first phrase of a larger composition."

Vanna jumped at the sound of her cottage door slamming open. Bael eyed her warily, then turned to glance over his shoulder. Kai stormed inside like he owned the place in an obvious state of pique. He looked like he'd just come from drills, sandy hair windswept, flight suit spattered with mud. He made it five steps inside the cottage before he noticed Bael seated at the table with Vanna.

"You!" His feet ground to a halt in the entrance to the kitchen.

Bael waved genially. "Been a minute, kid."

Ignoring the greeting, Kai's eyes shot to Vanna. "What's he doing here? Are you mad?"

"Don't you knock anymore?" Vanna wasn't in the mood for his hot temper.

"Haven't knocked in months," he shot back. "You never seemed to care before."

"Well, now she's got company," Bael said. "Care to join us?" He glanced over at Vanna for approval, but Kai didn't wait for a second invitation. He brazenly claimed the seat between them and planted his elbows on the table.

"Well?" Kai prompted, looking from one to the other. "Did you tell him?"

Vanna closed her eyes and massaged her temples with the pads of two fingers on each hand. Her permanent state of exhaustion had graced her with an unrelenting headache that throbbed behind her eyes.

"You're the scout, aren't you?" Bael made the connection out loud, ever quick to assemble the pieces of any puzzle laid out before him. "Well done, kid. Gonna save a lot of lives with the information you gathered."

Kai sat up straighter in his seat and puffed out his chest. How easy it was to fluff him up with a little commendation. Vanna had only grown increasingly convinced she'd made the right decision keeping him out of Bael's operation officially, though he kept finding ways to force himself deeper inside.

"I think I know what all those ships are doing up at Aquilon," Kai said, still riding the wave of Bael's approval.

Vanna stopped rubbing her temples and looked at him.

"Care to enlighten us?" Bael prompted.

"Kelestina's hosting a Solstice Ball," Kai said. "There will be other Celestials and Patrician lords in attendance from across the Doric Sky."

"How do you know this?" Vanna asked.

He deflated, then—lines of color blossoming on his cheeks.

"Kai..." Vanna prodded.

"Effie," he said, glancing up at her sheepishly. "She...invited me to be her escort."

Vanna closed her lips, expression frozen as she watched him.

"I turned her down, obviously," he quickly added.

"Well, that was stupid," Bael said. "Just think of all the information you could have gathered from *inside* a Celestial ball! And you just pissed that opportunity away?" Bael's eyebrows bent inward as he chastised Kai. It was the closest thing to anger Vanna had ever heard from the Kenshan.

Kai raised his voice in sputtering defense. "I don't *want* to go to a ball at Aquilon! Not with anyone—but especially not with her."

"You damned infant." Bael pressed a palm across his face, shaking his head.

Kai stared at Vanna for support, but she wasn't in a giving mood. "He's right," she said. "You should have considered the opportunity. You could have at least talked to me before throwing it away."

Her answer cut him much deeper than Bael's disappointment. He tried hard to hide it, but she saw the wound plainly in his glassy eyes. "That's your response." It wasn't a question. "After all we've been through together —I thought you of *all* people—"

"Enough, Kai." She needed to stop him before he said something to humiliate her in front of Bael.

Kai huffed and slumped back in his seat, staring at Vanna like a kicked puppy.

"Maybe we can weave something of value from this misstep," Bael said. "Sabotage only gets you so far, and it's starting to feel like the trade winds are turning against us."

Vanna didn't like the sound of that. Any time Bael spoke in metaphor, it presaged some dire appeal.

"We can't risk smuggling anymore conscripts out of the archipelago— not with the Governor of Aeolus and her airship on high alert. It's time to raise the stakes—move toward liberating your islands in truth."

Is that all?

"I thought you said you and Sparrowhawk couldn't fight a war for us?" Vanna pressed.

Bael bent his head to her, still stroking his beard. "And so we can't. At least, not alone. Our friend hovering out around Nevis is willing to help us. She'll bring some much-needed muscle to our cause."

"What kind of muscle?" Kai asked.

"A Leviathan." Bael let that pronouncement sink in, weighing the silence it elicited. "A heavy one, too. Hekuba Klaeda's no freedom fighter, but as luck would have it, she's got her own ax to grind with Aquilon. She can counter Governor Sigyn's gunship and go tooth-to-claw with Bone Adder if it comes down to it. If we set the stage for her, she'll hit Aquilon and decapitate the beast."

Another Leviathan pirate. *Jokai fend,* what had she gotten the Zephyrs into? Vanna's head swam with fiery images of Leviathan locked in aerial combat over Volturnus. They'd ventured far beyond the realm of subterfuge and into all-out war. Decapitate the beast? What Bael suggested —it was nothing short of armed rebellion against the Crystal Throne.

She glanced over at Kai, but he'd become fixated on Bael, his strong jawline set and unreadable. "Won't Kelestina bring in the Armada at the first sign of trouble?" he asked.

Bael spent an eternity considering the question. "It's possible," he finally admitted. "But if we act quickly to shatter her hold, there's a good chance the Shards will cut their losses in the Zephyrs and move on. Kelestina and her sect —they're out of favor with the military elite, and the Armada's got every eye they can spare in the Doric Sky turned toward Toran. We have a window."

"You really think the Celestials would just *give up* the whole archipelago?" Kai's skepticism mirrored Vanna's, while Bael's nod exuded confidence she didn't share.

"You have to become ungovernable," Bael said. "Pull up the provincial governors—root and stem. If we do that, Klaeda will take care of Aquilon. The Crystal Palace shatters, and Kelestina gets the Long Drop. With their feudal host expended, the Crystal Throne won't throw anymore good after bad."

Vanna counted her own heartbeats as she chewed over the possibilities. She'd begun this course to save her people from military conscription, but even as she took her first seditious steps arm-in-arm with this Kenshan saboteur, she knew what the ultimate goal would be—what it *needed* to be. They couldn't operate in the shadows forever. Volturnus was too small, its skies too crowded with watchful eyes. Whether it was Kendy or Ansel or Kelestina herself—someone was bound to unearth her treachery. Time wasn't on their side.

Liberation was the only happy ending for Vanna and Volturnus. Every other path led to discovery and execution.

"This rebellion," Vanna said. "What would it look like?"

"Only one way to do it right." Bael slammed the edge of one hand against an open palm. "A coordinated strike. Sleeper soldiers on every island rise up against their governors in a simultaneous attack. Depose the governors, eliminate their agents, and let our friend on the Leviathan deal with Aquilon."

"How do you expect us to manage that?" Vanna shook her head. "We're only two people and an Avian."

Bael glanced around the kitchen table. "I see three in this very room."

"Kai isn't part of this." This was the point when Vanna typically objected, but the words no longer held any power or any truth.

"Who put you in charge of my life?" Kai's chair slid across the floor as he jumped to his feet. Vanna watched the lines of his muscular arms tense as he extended one calloused hand to Bael. "I want to join the resistance."

Bael eyed Kai's open hand hungrily. Vanna knew what he saw—over six feet of seasoned flier, braided with lean muscle and cursed with the vulnerability of youth. Bael saw nothing of the shy boy who used to scamper around the village after Effie, nor the gangly adolescent impatiently awaiting his Gift. Bael didn't know him for the eager lover that Vanna had accepted into her bed—and how could he? As Kai stood in her kitchen—pledging his life to a foreign pirate out of obstinance and misplaced hurt—Bael saw only one thing.

An asset.

Bael accepted Kai's hand, and Vanna watched them shake. "You know the terms," Bael said. "I'll give my life for you, and I expect nothing less in return."

"So be it," Kai said. When the deal was done, he turned to Vanna, projecting his victory. Whatever he was hoping to receive in return, Vanna's flat affect denied him. Suddenly awkward on his feet, he sank anticlimactically back to his seat.

"Three, then." Vanna surrendered. "Hardly an army."

"We will need more," Bael agreed. "I have a few contacts around the islands that will help. You've met some of my people on Avernus. We've made inroads on Nimbion and in the Spurs, as well. On Aeolus, I've got an open channel to Commander Halle."

"You've been busy," Vanna grumbled. Bael revealed the depth of his support to reassure her, but it only unsettled her more.

Bael actually had the gall to wink at her. "Can't expect a man of my talents to sit on his thumbs."

"I thought Halle banished you," Vanna said.

"Aye. You didn't leave her with much of a choice. But who do you think helped me get set up on Volturnus?"

Vanna hissed. "That sneaky bitch."

Bael wagged his finger at her. "Don't be so quick to judge. That sneaky bitch commands sympathetic fliers. They've already sacked a governor's manse once. They'll be ready to strike at Sigyn when the time is right. But Volturnus is the crown jewel. Governor Ansel commands the largest staff, and he's got enough conscripts to turn his manse into a fortress. You'll need to find like-minded compatriots and turn them to the cause. Your sister..." Bael began tapping his foot beneath the table again and stroking his bearded chin. "She must be in pretty deep to receive an invitation to Kelestina's ball..."

Vanna couldn't deny it. Effie had immersed herself in the culture of the Shards. Each time Vanna saw her, she felt her sister drifting further away. Kelestina may have returned Effie to Volturnus, but she'd never felt more out of reach.

"Can she be turned?" Bael asked, and as he looked at her, Vanna felt those sharp eyes attempting to pry inside her head.

Kai snorted before Vanna could answer. "You'd have better luck soliciting Kelestina herself."

"That's not fair," Vanna scolded. "Effie's misguided. She can't see through all the gifts and status the Shards have lavished upon her. I know her heart, though. If she saw all the harm Kelestina was doing to Volturnus—if she had even an inkling that the pirate attacks had been *orchestrated* by the Crystal Throne—she'd give it all up to save her people."

Kai rolled his eyes, but he didn't contradict her. Bael seemed to be weighing both of their responses as he thought. "It would be a great boon to our cause to have an ally inside Kelestina's court. I'm working another angle on Nimbion, but it's always good to have a backup plan. If an opportunity presents itself to make the dangle to your sister, do it. But tread carefully. Exposure risks everything."

Vanna nodded.

"Even if Vanna gets Effie to see the light, she's no soldier," Kai said.

Bael clapped a hand on his shoulder. "That's where you come in, kid. It's time to recruit."

"How is he supposed to do that?" Vanna liked this plan less and less the more she heard, but she couldn't see her way out of it. Bael had dragged her in too deep.

"The same way I found you!" Bael grinned. "Approach the villagers. Anyone you think might be amenable—friends and family fed up with the Shards, sick of their writs and their tithes. Plant the seeds of doubt and bring them to the jungle.

"I'll take care of the rest."

32

MULDOON

Another Moonday arrived. For Ansel's final feast before the Solstice Ball, the Governor of Avernus made an unexpected call. Aeryon kept the conversation casual throughout the meal, but Muldoon sensed a more serious purpose boiling beneath the surface of his courtly manner.

Effie attended the feast in pristine form, her spirits restored, wit as sharp as ever. Selfishly, Muldoon attributed the revitalization to his offer to serve as her escort. The prospect—and her ebullient acceptance—had improved his own mood, as well. For the first time, he looked forward to an event at Aquilon with eagerness instead of dread.

The greater transformation in Effie had happened gradually, but Aeryon's arrival offered Muldoon the opportunity to see his pupil through fresh eyes. At the table, she presented the perfect image of a young collegiate well on her way down the gilded path to the Patrician brand. She found subtle ways to demonstrate the fruits of her schooling in conversation and entertained Aeryon with playful banter and gentle ribbing at Muldoon and Ansel's expense. By the time the servants delivered the dessert course, she had Aeryon eating from the palm of her hand.

Muldoon brimmed with pride. He let Effie lead, smiling as he watched her. Whoever this fool boy was who had upset her, he'd done a great service for Muldoon. Everyone at the table reveled in her performance—except for

Ansel, of course. The ill-tempered governor chewed his food in dower silence as the conversation played out before him.

How foolish Muldoon had been to resist this appointment, and how lucky that Kelestina insisted on seeing it through. These last few months playing tutor had been his happiest since leaving Toran. He'd gained as much from Effie as he'd given in return, and he now saw clearly the wisdom of Dama Lilyn's advice. In time, Effie would become his ladder back to status. Watching her effortlessly control a formal dinner opposite three Patrician lords, anyone could see her potential. With her Gifts and ample charms, she'd rise high in the Celestial Court.

She wouldn't be his student forever, but that didn't mean their association needed to end. Every magistrate of the Crystal Throne needed courtiers they could trust, and who better to call upon than the man who'd befriended her and molded her to proper form. In time, she'd become his patron...and perhaps more.

At the end of the meal, Effie bid farewell with a delicate curtsey. She thanked Aeryon for the conversation and rewarded him with a gentle peck on the cheek. One hand lingered on his chest as she took her leave. It was all very well performed from Muldoon's vantage, though he felt an unwelcome pang of jealousy as her lips touched Aeryon's cheek. He noted the way Aeryon's eyes pursued her through the dining room door.

The Patricians retired to Ansel's sitting room, where his butler served a bitter digestif before granting their privacy. They each settled into padded leather armchairs, though Ansel's chair stood the highest and possessed the wealthiest trim. The way the man clung to every superficial indicator of status only revealed to Muldoon how small he truly was.

Aeryon swirled his drink in his glass. "I must say, Muldoon—I'm quite taken with your student. You've performed an impressive transmutation. Hard to believe she's the same disheveled plebeian we plucked off that dauphine."

Muldoon grinned behind his glass. "It would be disingenuous to take so much credit. Miss Strait is a model student. She's grown much this past year."

"Truly." Aeryon sipped his drink. "Not too hard on the eyes, either. Does she have any suitors?"

"Not to my knowledge," Muldoon said. "Though, she's not likely to find a worthy match among the plebiscite."

"Too true," Aeryon agreed.

Ansel shifted in his high-backed chair. "How is the girl supposed to find a match when Muldoon here keeps her all to himself?"

"Is that right?" Aeryon's gray eyebrows drifted up his head. "Are you grooming your young pupil? Not that I'd blame you."

Muldoon set down his glass and uncrossed his legs. "Nothing so insidious. Our relationship is strictly professional." He met Ansel's scoff with an irritated side-eye. "There's only room for one lecherous Patrician on Volturnus."

"Deny it all you want," Ansel grunted. "I see the way you look at her—the way you've poisoned her mind against the competition. That girl was practically falling over herself to earn my favor before *you* arrived. Now, she won't even look at me."

Aeryon shook his spiky head as he laughed and took another sip from his drink. "You two sound like hounds grappling over a shank of meat."

Muldoon smiled acidly. "As the governor readily admits—it isn't much of a grappling match."

Ansel snorted and drained his digestif. He left his armchair to refill from a glass decanter before returning to his seat.

"Has she found an escort to the ball?" Aeryon asked.

"She has." Muldoon cradled his glass in one hand, watching Ansel slowly untangle the implication. When he did, the governor's hooded eyes began to twitch, square jaw shifting back and forth as he ground his teeth.

"A dog, indeed!" Aeryon laughed again, though Muldoon picked up a trickle of disappointment. "I thought you said your relationship was *strictly professional*?"

"And so it is." Muldoon shrugged. "I consider Miss Strait's presentation at Aquilon an extension of my duties as her guardian and tutor."

"I've heard enough about the girl," Ansel growled. "You had something to discuss with us, Governor?"

"Yes." Aeryon took another dainty sip of digestif then set down his glass and steepled his fingers over his lap. "I'm afraid I've encountered a bit of a predicament on Avernus, and I could use some advice—from *both* of you." Ansel propped his arms casually on the armrests of his plush chair, but Muldoon saw no reason to feign disinterest. He leaned in to receive the governor's request. "My agents have uncovered evidence of sabotage on the island. For the first time in the course of my stewardship, the quarry will miss its quota. More concerning, we've lost Gifted conscripts. The censors watch our ports of entry night and day, but these fugitives have found other paths off the island. I am shamed to admit it, but my oversight is leaking. I believe you encountered a similar issue on Volturnus?"

"The Volturnian fugitives were apprehended in the attempt," Ansel quickly answered.

Aeryon craned his neck in Ansel's direction. "Apprehended by Governor Sigyn, as I understand it?"

Ansel allowed the qualification with a tilt of his block head.

"Alas," Aeryon said. "We were not so fortunate. Her Lightness is displeased."

Ansel drummed his fingers along the rim of his glass. "*How* displeased?"

Aeryon's voice became very low. "I am told a disciplinary action is forthcoming. Her Lightness intends to bring military force to Avernus— martial law in the village and at the ports. She plans to *commandeer* the quarry."

Muldoon felt a slight tremor in his hand as he lowered his glass to an adjacent table. The tension in Ansel had little to do with empathy and everything to do with his own self-interest. Volturnus had its own unresolved issues. If Kelestina was willing to bring the jagged hand of the Crystal Throne down on Avernus, there was nothing stopping her from doing the same on his island.

"You mentioned sabotage," Muldoon ventured. "Do you suspect foreign influence?"

Aeryon turned up his hands. "How else are these back-sky plebeians evading my agents? *Someone* is helping them escape the archipelago. Someone with a network and considerable means. You dealt with something similar on Aeolus, did you not, Sire?"

Muldoon nodded gravely. "The Bluethorn. He infiltrated the Aeolian dragoons."

"Not this again," Ansel groaned.

Ignoring him, Aeryon turned to Muldoon. "Does this latest sabotage not bear the stink of the Gulliver Ring?"

"It does," Muldoon agreed. "But that serpent-tongued bastard hasn't resurfaced since his banishment from Aeolus."

Aeryon tapped his finger on his glass. "In your experience, are the Gullivari so easily dislodged?"

They are not, but Muldoon didn't have to confirm what all three of them already knew. "If Kelestina suspects the Gullivari, then she's taking appropriate action. The Bluethorn and his saboteurs can't raise an army. The only way to counter them is to come down with overwhelming force. The Bluethorn grows in shadow. We must deny him his habitat with the blinding light of the Crystal Throne."

Aeryon finished his drink. "I was afraid you were going to say that."

"When will it happen?" Muldoon asked.

"While we're all off-island during the Solstice Ball. Gives the rest of us plausible deniability."

"How will your plebeians respond?" Ansel asked.

Aeryon shook his head. "Not well. Which is why I'm seeking your advice." His eyes landed on Muldoon. "How can I avoid your fate, Sire? How can I quench the embers of rebellion before they ignite a conflagration?"

Muldoon bristled, suddenly uncomfortable on the edge of his leather chair. The indignity visited upon his noble person by that Toranese pirate still stung him—even after so much time. The pettiest part of him wanted to leave Aeryon to his fate, but the governor had come to him in good faith. It wouldn't do to meet the man's humility with defiance.

Muldoon grasped the armrests of his chair, leaning in. "You need to act now to neutralize any potential nexus of provincial power. If the Bluethorn is indeed operating on Avernus, he'll seize on the plebiscite's discontent and turn their hearts to his cause. He likes to work his mischief through folk heroes—your dragoons, perhaps?"

Aeryon nodded thoughtfully. "Yes...and maybe the shift leaders at the quarry. Those senior laborers, however uncouth, do command respect."

"Take them out of the game," Muldoon said. "Neuter the threat before it matures."

"Much to think on..." Aeryon tapped the rim of his empty glass then pushed it aside. "I thank you both for your counsel—and for your hospitality, Governor. We Patrician servants of Her Lightness must stand united in these trying times. It may be my island in the crosshairs now, but the Zephyrs are all interconnected. I sincerely hope we'll find time to speak at the Solstice Ball. As it stands, we're all likely to return from Aquilon to a new state of play.

"I wouldn't expect Volturnus to escape disruption."

33

EFFIE

The night of the Solstice Ball arrived with a break in the brutal heat that held the archipelago in its grasp for so many weeks. A squall blew in from the lees of Avernus, shelling Volturnus with sheets of rain and nut-sized hail. It struck fast and hard, leaving placid skies and cooler temperatures in its wake.

Effie's lessons concluded early that day, and she returned to her bed chamber to find three handmaids waiting to prepare her for the ball. She submitted to their ministrations without argument, and two of the servants went to work on her make-up and her hair. Beside her closet, Ina ironed her dress and brushed her shoes. Effie thought herself more than capable of managing her own grooming, but the servants insisted on their doting, and she ultimately relented.

The first maid curled her long violet hair into a gentle wave, then bound it up in a complicated chignon knot that hung to the nape of her neck. A second, tighter braid encircled the crown of her head, while two curls dangled from her bangs, asymmetrically framing her face. The second maid painted a thin layer of olive foundation across her face, then sketched her cheekbones with six shades of contour and applied a dark mascara that extended her lashes top and bottom. She coated her fingernails and toenails with three layers of gloss, then capped their points with thin emerald bands, a perfect match for the gems set inside the waist of her Avernian gown.

Ina helped Effie latch the back of her dress. Effie shifted uncomfortably as the girl pulled and prodded at the fabric, inserting dozens of pins to tighten the garment around her bust and waist, preserving the narrow silhouette's intentional form. All told, the preparations took over three hours. The sun had nearly set by the time they were done. Effie saw Ina standing over her shoulder in the mirror as they appraised the finished work. An undeniable current of longing seasoned the young maid's satisfaction at a job well done.

The reflection staring back at Effie belonged to a different woman. Through aesthetic alchemy, Ansel's maids had transformed her into a Patrician Dama in truth. The only thing missing was the brand. If she worried her plebeian class would make her seem out of place at the Aquilonian ball, the costume, at least, offered cover.

"*Jokai bless*, Effie." Ina beamed at her. "You'll outshine Kelestina herself."

"Let's hope not." Effie rolled her painted eyes, but a small smile lingered on her lips.

"Sire Muldoon's a lucky *man*." Effie didn't miss Ina's emphasis.

"Ah-hem." One of the older maids stepped forward.

In the reflection, Effie saw her holding a velvet jewel case. She turned to her, curious, and placed one hand over the lid of the box. "What's this?"

"A gift from Governor Ansel," the maid said.

That was unexpected. Effie accepted the box and gently opened the lid. Inside, she found a layered choker of braided silver chains. Diamonds set throughout the necklace captured motes of light. A polished, round opal sat at its center.

"Whoa." Ina's dewy eyes grew wide and round, reflecting the diamonds' light.

Effie shared her astonishment. It must have cost a fortune. Why would Ansel do this? She'd hardly spoken to him in months, and when she did, she wasn't exactly cordial. "I can't accept this," she said, placing the necklace back in its box.

"Don't be ridiculous," Ina said, snatching the velvet jewel case from her hand. "The governor will be insulted if you refuse." She took the choker back out of its case and latched it around Effie's neck. The piece fit snugly around her throat, but it wasn't uncomfortable.

Effie inspected herself anew in the looking glass.

"You already looked like a Dama," Ina said. "Now, you look like a queen."

Effie dismissed the other two maids and permitted Ina to escort her from the manse and out to the yard where a carriage drawn by four Aquilonian hippocampi had arrived to transport them to the northern isle. Muldoon awaited her reveal outside the carriage. He always dressed well, but he'd still found a way to elevate himself for the occasion.

He wore a dark brown Umari kurta with silver piping that extended beyond his knees, every thread tapered to complement his slender form. A dizzying fractal brocade patterned the exotic garment, as did a long line of dainty opal buttons binding the suit along a single diagonal seam. The kurta allowed only glimpses of his cream hosen, as well a straight-cuffed undershirt fastened with links. He'd foregone his typical folded ponytail, auburn hair straightened and trimmed so that it hung in curtains to his chin. A simple ring of wooden beads encircled the crown of his head.

Ina made a great performance of presenting Effie to her escort, and Effie could only hope her copious layers of make-up concealed her blushing cheeks. Muldoon examined her from head to toe, eyes glowing with admiration. His lips parted as he lingered on her breasts, propped up by underwire threaded through her slip so they crested over the gown's inviting bust. Effie adjusted the single strap across her shoulder, inching her bust line upward to claim as much modesty as the gown would permit. At last, Muldoon found her eyes.

"You look stunning."

"Stop it," Effie said, sure her natural blush had now begun to bleed through.

"It's the truth."

Effie rolled her eyes. "It only took three hours and six doting hands to make it so."

"Ansel's staff deserves a pay raise," Muldoon quipped.

Effie pointed her toes together. "I'd say you clean up well yourself, but I can't think of a time when you haven't been clean."

They both looked at each other, spellbound, the pressure building toward that first moment of contact, neither one ready to breach the bare inches of landscaped ground that separated them. One of the hippocampi trumpeted a spritely whinny and whipped its floating tail, breaking the spell.

Muldoon bowed to her and presented his arm. "Our carriage awaits."

His extended elbow drew her toward him. She threaded her bare arm through his brocade and allowed herself to be led, grasping his offered hand as she mounted the steps inside the coach. His Patrician fingers felt even softer than her own lathered hands. She noticed the way the emerald tips of her nails matched his square cufflinks—no doubt by design.

A blast of florid perfume wafting from Ansel's escort assaulted her as soon as she entered the coach. The governor and his escort sat together on the bench facing the driver. For the occasion, Ansel donned a ruffled shirt beneath a burgundy overcoat with gaudy gold buttons and pearl horse-head pins fastened atop each lapel. His thick helmet of salt-and-pepper hair gleamed, slicked back and held by the generous application of wax. Effie didn't recognize his partner—a buxom honey blonde with voluminous hair that crashed in waves across her shoulders to the ledge of her heaving breasts. Her wide hips made a solid match for Ansel's girth, curves barely contained by the lines of her tight red dress. A long slit down the side of her silhouette exposed one bare thigh to the coach as she sat on Ansel's arm with her plump legs crossed. She turned up her pointy nose when she caught Effie gawking at the gold necklaces and rings crowding her fingers and throat.

Muldoon claimed the seat beside Effie on the opposite bench, and his attention immediately shifted to Ansel. The way the two men glowered at each other—Effie got the sense that she and her voluptuous counterpart had become the objects of some unspoken competition between them. Ansel's haughty expression slowly soured, and Muldoon's chest reciprocally swelled, suggesting he had won.

Effie knew she should feel objectified, but the attention only buttressed her confidence. She tucked back her shoulders and crossed her legs, mirroring Ansel's escort, and placed her hands atop her knees.

"This is Lady Estreya, just arrived from Brundis," Ansel said. "She's a cousin to the Archduke of Beringia and an old friend."

Effie read the subtext as clearly as if it had been printed on a parchment leaflet. If Ansel's escort couldn't compete on presentation, then status would have to do. The woman's face didn't move an inch through her introduction.

A younger Effie Strait might have been intimidated, but her lessons had inoculated her against this manner of bullying. Provincial nobility held no formal status in the Celestial kyriarchy. This cousin to the Archduke of Beringea was as good as a plebeian in the eyes of the Crystal Throne.

"A pleasure to see you again, My Lady." Muldoon tipped his head, the smug smile still dancing across his lips.

Effie realized it was her turn to speak. Feeling mischievous, she opted to forego the empty platitudes. "You've traveled quite a distance to accompany our Lord Governor, My Lady," Effie said. "He must be very special to you."

Estreya's pointy nose wrinkled as she sniffed. "The occasion is special enough. One doesn't balk at the opportunity to attend a Celestial ball." If Ansel had taken any insult, he didn't let it show. Quite the contrary, he seemed pointedly disinterested in his escort beyond any penumbral esteem she might cast his way.

Estreya narrowed her eyes on Effie. Cracks formed in the mauve lacquer painted over the noblewoman's eyelids as she stared. "Sire Muldoon, I already know," Estreya said. "But who might you be?"

"This is Miss Effie Strait of Volturnus," Muldoon cut in.

"*Miss?*" Estreya's necklaces jingled as she drew her head back. "This pretty young thing is a plebeian?"

Ansel shifted uncomfortably on his bench, pulling his overcoat's wide lapels.

"She is," Muldoon acknowledged. "And an honored guest of Her Lightness Kelestina's court."

Effie met the woman's judgment with passivity—a demure smile and a bat of her eyes. Estreya peered at her like some kind of confounding puzzle. Once she gave up on divining the solution, she and Ansel turned from each other to gaze out opposite windows of the coach. Effie and Muldoon seized the opportunity to share an amused look.

They sat in tense silence until the hippocampi pulled their carriage onto the trolley to Aquilon. Estreya reached between her breasts and produced a small crystal vial shaped like a dagger. Ansel's upper lip curled as he watched her shake the thin, white liquid within before unscrewing the cap between two fingers.

"What?" Estreya noticed the eyes of the carriage upon her and stuck her nose defiantly in the air. "You can't expect me to enter the ball without a little lubricant." She took a small sip from the vial, quirked her lips, then ventured another. "Beringean Moonshine," she explained, even though no one had asked. "Shortest path to the stars." She smiled slyly as she offered the drink to the coach.

Muldoon declined with a grimace, but Ansel reached over and plucked the vial from her outstretched hand.

"It wouldn't be courtly of me to fall behind my escort," he said, taking a long sip. His eyes bugged from his square head as soon as the white spirit reached his throat. He choked it down with vocal effort, coughing into his sleeve as he removed the vial from his lips.

The astringent scent of the Beringean Moonshine, carried by Ansel's breath, cut straight through Estreya's perfume. Once he recovered, Ansel passed the vial back to Estreya. She laughed mockingly at his weak response and took another leisurely sip before returning the drink to the secure location between her breasts.

Their carriage landed on the southern tip of Aquilon amid a busy congregation of arriving kite-ships, carriages, and lighters. Effie learned from Muldoon that the more distant attendees had been drifting in over several days, so the landing craft must have belonged to local courtiers. Beyond the Patrician governors and a few wealthy merchants, Effie couldn't fathom who else might have received the invitation to attend.

She left the carriage on Muldoon's arm and followed a loose throng of well-dressed guests up the marble walkway to Aquilon Palace. The entering masses condensed inside the foreyard. They passed through a line of Doves wearing blue livery tapered to the Avian form. The white birds stood still as statues in their receiving line, red-rimmed eyes staring off at fixed points in the distance. One snapped its beak as Effie passed, startling her.

"Friend of yours?" Muldoon asked.

She playfully swatted his chest as they entered the palace vestibule. The Volturnian party came to a stop just behind a band of middle-aged men in matching green doublets, escorted by a complement of black-gowned women too young for them by decades.

Effie drew up on her toes to whisper in Muldoon's ear. "Nice of them to bring their daughters."

He smirked. "No one marries a Grenish Merchant Maven for his good looks and charm."

A brigade of Kelestina's watchful guards stood sentinel at the door to the ballroom in black dress uniforms with gold-buckled belts. They held serrated pikes over their shoulders, marking each entrant as a balding servant checked them in.

Muldoon noticed Effie warily eyeing the long row of armed men. "You won't see any armed guards inside the ballroom," he assured her. "Kills the mood. But Kelestina's soldiery is always close at hand."

As their party reached the entryway, Ansel boxed out Muldoon to lead Estreya first by the hand. They gave their names and stations and disappeared beyond the vaulted doorway.

Muldoon sighed. "If we're lucky, that will be the last we'll have to see of those two tonight."

Effie could only pray to the Jokai time would prove him right. Muldoon led her up to the servant marking the guest list with a feathered quill. "Miss Effie Strait of Volturnus," Muldoon said. "Accompanied by Sire Muldoon of Umar."

The servant gave them each a cursory glance, checked their names off his list, then waved them inside. "Enjoy the festivities—Sire, Miss."

Effie began to curtsey but felt a tug on her arm as Muldoon ushered her through the door.

"We don't pay obeisance to servants," he chided.

Effie frowned. "Just trying to be polite."

"There's a fine line between courteous and provincial. Let's try and stay on the right side of it tonight, shall we?"

They crossed a short hall, still walking arm-in-arm. Two liveried servants opened a banded door at their approach. The world beyond the palace vanished as they crossed the threshold. Kelestina's ballroom was a vast cathedral, crowned by three domed rotundas at the apex of a 100-foot ceiling. Stained glass murals watched from a ring of lancet windows encircling the event, their reverent images glowing with endemic light. Hundreds of guests moved about the chamber, their competing conversations blurring together in one gregarious din.

A background of string music seasoned the noisome chatter. Effie sourced the pleasant sound to a sextet of well-dressed musicians performing beneath a resonator in one corner of the room. Alchemical lanterns hovered overhead, suspended in mid-air on lumite trays. Their tidy fires burned in metallic shades of silver, green, and blue. Effie stopped to crane her neck, gawking at the accents.

Muldoon permitted her a moment to take it in, before ushering her along with another tug on the arm. The ballroom hosted no central table —no dining space set for a sit-down meal. The whole event seemed designed to keep the party fluid, driving guests from point to point and forcing them to mingle. Drinks and decoratively plated food sprang up from buffet tables positioned at intervals around the room. Cliques began to form around the myriad glass standing tables that freckled the event, but even these ephemeral gatherings traded bodies back and forth at a steady clip. She saw guests in similar garb gravitating toward each other, bearing cups of wine and colorful liqueur, small plates stacked high with exotic food.

"I'll say one thing for our host," Muldoon said. "She certainly knows how to dress up an affair."

As they pushed deeper into the ballroom, Effie stared at a table surrounded by dark-skinned foreign nobility wearing strange white robes with striped stoles draped over their shoulders. They all wore the same square hat crowded with gold and enamel pins.

She felt Muldoon's finger beneath her chin, gently guiding her mouth closed. "Iban sultans," he said, tracking her gaze. "Would you like an introduction?"

"Maybe later," Effie said.

Muldoon smiled warmly and patted her hand. "Why don't we start with a drink."

He directed her toward the nearest buffet table, but a group of young men already furnished with wine glasses intercepted them on the way. A straw-haired man at the cadre's leading edge hailed Muldoon with a wide-mouthed grin. The glassy cast to his almond eyes and the rosy color along his cheeks suggested the glass of wine in his hand wasn't his first.

"Can it be?" The man's voice carried the Patrician lilt. "Sire Muldoon of Umar! I'd heard the Admiral shipped you out east, and here you are."

To Effie's practiced eye, Muldoon's return smile seemed forced. "Sire Nymicus of Odenta. It has been too long."

"Years!" Nymicus clarified. "And it's *Imperator* Nymicus now—of Takomar." He paused from his greeting to sip his wine. When he finished, his eyes flashed on Effie, walking hungrily up and down her figure. "Who is this lovely creature? I'm certain I've not had the pleasure. I've an eidetic memory for the great beauties of the Doric Sky."

Effie felt those almond eyes prying at the seams of her dress, searching for a path inside. She adjusted the strap of her gown and drew closer to Muldoon.

"This is—" Muldoon started.

"Effie Strait," Effie interrupted. "Of Volturnus." She bent one knee in a shallow curtsey.

"You don't say." The Patrician's expression struck with equal parts amusement and interest. He prodded Muldoon with his elbow, still marking Effie with his eyes. "If I'd known they grew their plebeians so fine on the Zephyr Isles, I'd have found cause to visit much sooner." He shook his head with a forced chuckle and took another sip from his glass, draining it.

Effie felt Muldoon's grip on her arm tightening protectively. "Sire Nymicus hails from Toran, as well," Muldoon explained. "We spent time together in His Lightness Admiral Siprichor's court." He turned his head to Nymicus. "But it seems you've moved on to bigger things."

"Aye, onward and upward, as they say. Stagnation is the death of honor at court—for all the good it's done me." He tried to take another sip of wine and scowled at his empty glass.

Muldoon's eyebrows drifted toward the beaded circlet set upon his brow. "Trouble in Takomar?"

"Not on the island proper," Nymicus said. He leaned in, guarding his face with a white-gloved hand, though he continued speaking at inebriated volume. "Between us three, Her Lightness Minerviana has more expansive imperial designs. Her eyes are too big for her stomach, if you ask me. With the Armada still overcommitted in Toran, she hasn't the muscle to make a proper push into Borja."

"Borja?" Muldoon invited the Patrician to continue running his mouth.

"Aye," Nymicus confirmed. "If a fouler land floats across the Doric Sky, I've not seen it. Frigid, mountainous, and wracked by civil war. And whose business do you think it is to tame it?"

Effie recalled the name from a distant geography reading—a large island near the center of the Doric Sky. Neutral in the conflict with Toran and self-sorted into three warring states. The Crystal Throne had a general reluctance to venture into any provincial civil war, Umar notwithstanding.

"Sounds like you've got your work cut out for you," Muldoon said.

"Bah." Nymicus tried to drink from his empty glass again then shook it in frustration. "It appears I'm in need of refurbishment. Do find me later so we can continue catching up. I wouldn't mind a turn with your conscript once the dancing commences, either." He winked at Muldoon then led his silent cohort away.

As soon as he was gone, Effie withdrew her arm from Muldoon's and propped her fists on the waistband of her gown. "Conscript?"

"Ignore him," Muldoon said, rolling his eyes. "Nymicus has always been an insufferable peacock. He hardly lasted a year at Admiral Siprichor's court before His Lightness seized the first opportunity to transfer him out to Minerviana. He can be a cunning magistrate I suppose, but he has a well-earned reputation for cowardice."

Effie squinted at Muldoon, cautiously slipping back inside his arm as they continued on their way to the buffet table. "Is it a common practice for the Celestials to trade their Patricians like gaming chits?" she asked.

"I suppose," Muldoon said. "When there's some gain in the exchange... or when they find a Patrician particularly odious."

Effie snorted as she laughed and bashfully covered her face with a hand.

The light music emanating from the string sextet swelled as they crossed the ballroom. When they finally reached the buffet, Effie caught her first glimpse of Kelestina. Her Celestial host stood on a raised platform at the back of the ballroom behind a velvet rope. Two other Celestials joined her, one in a matching gemstone gown and another in a gold two-piece suit without any visible buttons or seams. The male Celestial's quartzite rack sprouted wide about his head, granting him the imposing aspect of some majestic antlered beast. Twelve black-suited armsmen without any arms surrounded the platform, while Dagda guarded its lone entrance, approving and rejecting guests attempting to call.

The two visiting Celestials interacted graciously with those guests permitted access, but Kelestina loomed above them all, watching her event unfold with quiet appraisal. Effie stared at her host surveying the ballroom until Muldoon returned from the buffet table and pressed a glass of effervescent golden wine into her empty hand.

"You're unusually quiet tonight," he said.

"You would have preferred I dazzle Sire Nymicus with my wit?" Effie tasted the drink he'd handed her and found its dry bouquet to her liking. "He was having a hard enough time keeping his tongue in his mouth as is."

Muldoon chuckled. "Fair enough." He swirled his cherry liqueur then stuck his nose in the glass to take in its aroma before venturing a sip. "I just want you to enjoy yourself," he said.

"The night's still young." Effie glanced down the line of guests congregating beside the buffet table. A group of older women in black and green dresses, their hair in matching gray buns, hovered over an ice tray of raw shellfish, braying at each other between eager slurps. She didn't recognize the emblem embroidered in thread-of-gold over their busts. She turned to Muldoon to ask him about it, but he'd drifted several feet away, staring off at some object of interest in the distance.

She sidled up to him, tracking his line of sight to a standing table across the ballroom ringed by stern military types wearing short-cropped haircuts and formal parade dress. The table pressed a void inside the revelry. The soldiers kept to themselves, watching the other guests with blank expressions—engaging with exactly none of them. One decorated officer stood out, his uniformed chest laden with ribbons and medals. Golden accents in the shape of serpents coiled atop his bright red epaulettes.

"Not exactly the life of the party over there," Effie said as she took another sip from her drink.

Muldoon's response came back distant. "I don't think they came for the catering—or the company."

Effie lowered her wine glass from her lips. "Something I should know?"

Muldoon's gaze continued to drift. "Would you excuse me for a moment, Effie." It wasn't really a question.

"You're abandoning me already?"

"I'll only be a moment. I'll find you." He was already walking away.

Effie watched the back of his auburn head receding across the ballroom floor. "As you will, Sire!" she called after him. "But don't be surprised if you find me draped over Sire Nymicus' arm!"

He didn't hear her—or else chose to ignore her. Effie scoffed, even though no one was paying enough attention to see it. Suddenly without an escort, she surveyed the party bubbling around her. Elegant bodies vacillated between conversation and consumption. The whole ballroom seemed to throb as the guests collectively descended deeper into their cups.

Sighing, Effie finished her drink and drifted back toward the buffet table. As she reached for a second glass of sparkling gold, she spotted the last thing she expected to find there: a familiar face.

Imerigo Vinson loitered beside a tray of ribs, alone and looking just as misplaced as Effie felt. His bland black jacket poorly fit his slender adolescent build. He wore the coat unbuttoned, exposing every line of his ruffled cream shirt and silver cravat. Effie watched him carefully select a rack of ribs from the tray and place it on his plate—a bold choice, given his attire.

She edged around the table, closing on the boy as he licked the sticky sauce from his fingers. He didn't notice until she was nearly upon him.

"Master Vinson!" Effie's greeting froze him mid-bite. "What a pleasure to find you amid this rabble."

Imerigo's limp brown hair quivered as he removed the rib from his mouth. She sensed him struggling to peel through all the layers of polish concealing her identity. "Dama?" he guessed. "I'm sorry—err—have we met?"

"*Miss*," she corrected, performing an exaggerated frown. "I guess I didn't leave much of an impression."

"That's not it!" he stammered. "You're very memorable. I mean to say —you're quite beautiful—err—elegant, is what I mean—what I *meant*. To say. I'm sure I would have remembered—" He cut himself off with a *gulp*.

Effie laughed, demurely covering her lips with four fingers. The sound of her laughter jogged his memory, and his face lit up with recognition.

"Effie Strait!" he said. "Of Volturnus!"

Effie performed her deepest curtsey of the night, thankful Muldoon wasn't here to reprimand her. "At your service."

His jaw fell open as he stared at her, unblinking. "You look..."

"Overdone?" she provided.

"That's not how I would put it." His wide eyes never left her face. Such innocent admiration—a stark contrast with Nymicus' lascivious ogling. It went a long way toward sanding the edges from Effie's prickly mood.

To reward him, Effie edged closer and took him by the arm, casting her gaze around the room before leaning in conspiratorially. "Quite the party. We seem to be the odd ones out."

"You don't look out-of-place at all," Imerigo said. "I can't imagine you arrived unattended."

"I didn't arrive that way," Effie conceded. "And yet, here I am. My escort has more important places to be."

Imerigo's arm tightened around her own. "Is he a blind man or a fool?"

Effie's honest laughter tumbled out of her. "I didn't realize you were such a charmer." Imerigo tried to hide his blushing face. "Perhaps you would accompany me in the interim? I thought we might take in some of the amusements provided by our host."

"Of course!" His blush returned. "I mean to say—that sounds nice."

Smiling still, Effie took the plate of ribs from his hand and left it on the edge of the buffet table before dragging him off to explore the rest of the ball.

Beyond the forest of standing tables and congregating guests, an array of attractions awaited on the periphery of the event. Only a few of the guests had begun to avail themselves of Kelestina's amusements, but as the party wore on, more and more began to gravitate over from their drinks and plates of food, seeking other pleasures. Effie and Imerigo walked through a gallery of oil paintings, landscapes of distant islands and portraits of stately Celestials—even a few prurient nudes. The artist left little to the imagination, rendering plump bodies in such agonizing detail that Effie felt compelled to avert her eyes. She felt a tug as Imerigo lingered on a wide painting of a heavy-breasted woman, thighs spread, exposing her florid sex as small furry creatures slathered her with mud.

"Her Lightness certainly has provocative tastes," Effie observed.

Imerigo nodded, eyes dragging across the final row of nudes as she ushered him onward. They followed a trail of floating lanterns around the edge of the ball, stopping briefly to watch a jester juggle ten torches at once and a pair of contortionists rolling around a padded circle, bodies twisted into inconceivable knots. One of the contortionists walked to the edge of the mat on his hands, back bent so that his neck and torso threaded through his legs. Imerigo applauded excitedly, but the sight of him made Effie a bit queasy.

They finally reached a short line of guests awaiting their turn to sit for a commissioned portraitist working on demand with charcoal and easel.

"You have to let him draw you!" Imerigo said, eagerly tugging her by the hand toward the back of the queue.

Effie resisted. "I don't know..."

"Come on!" Imerigo looked aghast. "Have you seen yourself? It would be a crime not to have this moment preserved."

Effie stuck her tongue in her cheek and pursed her lips, but his enthusiasm was too much to overcome. She grudgingly acquiesced.

The portraitist worked quickly, Effie's nerves stirring as the line before her shrank. When at last her turn arrived, Imerigo shrank away to watch the artist over his shoulder, while Effie took her place in the model's chair.

"Very fine." The artist nodded at his canvas approvingly. "Very fine, indeed." He peeked around his easel. "Don't slouch, now. Back arched and shoulders tucked. *Deliver* the bust. Shift your legs to the side—a quarter turn." He bracketed his hands, miming the movement he desired from her. "Head turned toward me. Good. Excellent. Now, lower your chin—just an inch. Eyes up."

Effie did as she was told, though the position felt completely awkward. "Who sits like this?" she asked.

"No talking," the portraitist instructed. "And do try to remain still."

Easy for you to say.

Imerigo beamed at her frozen pose all throughout the portrait. After what seemed like an eternity, the artist set down his charcoal with a satisfied nod and summoned her up from the model's chair to appraise the work.

"It's incredible," Imerigo said. "The likeness!"

Effie wasn't so sure. The artist captured the shape of her face—even suggested the lightness of her hair and eyes with delicate charcoal shading—but he'd been too generous with her curves, exaggerating her breasts and hips. He'd taken similar artistic license with her hair, adding layers and curls that didn't exist. Eager to draw the attention away from herself, she elbowed Imerigo in the ribs. "A lot better than your drawings."

He frowned at her. "I told you they're not drawings."

"I know, I know—you're a mapmaker."

"A cartographer," he corrected.

She tried to lead him away to discover the next attraction, but a pair of liveried servants materialized from the crowd to intercept them.

The first servant to reach them performed a stiff bow. "Master Vinson—your presence is requested in the keep."

"So soon?" Imerigo's shoulders slumped. "I was just beginning to enjoy myself." Effie shared his disappointment.

"Her Lightness insists that you prepare for the exhibition," the servant said.

Imerigo looked longingly at Effie. "I'm sorry, Effie."

Effie shrugged her bare shoulders. "It was fun while it lasted." There was no sense debating. A request from Kelestina was no request at all.

The servants led Imerigo away, and Effie once again found herself alone.

Imerigo's company provided a welcome distraction, but now she began to wonder what was taking Muldoon so long. Even more bodies crowded the ballroom than when he had left her. It was possible he was somewhere among them, actively searching her out. It did no good to make herself a moving target, so she planted herself at the edge of a loose conglomeration hovering around the resonator to watch the sextet perform.

The musicians moved seamlessly from one composition to the next, faces expressionless, graceful limbs sawing their instruments with horse-hair bows. They paused only to turn the pages of their sheet music and somehow managed each transition without breaking a phrase. Effie swayed with the song until she sensed the weight of another body drawing up behind her.

A man's body, she was certain—a man much larger than Muldoon. He continued pressing closer until she could smell his cedar cologne, at which point his intentions became clear. Effie turned to deliver this lurking stranger a sharp rebuke, but the stark image that greeted her stole the words off the tip of her tongue.

Her stalker stood over six feet tall, broad as a dragoon and wearing a long burgundy coat with gold piping and double-breasted buttons to match. Oiled ringlets of thick black hair dripped to his bearded chin, framing a face so thickly coated in make-up that he looked more like a mummer than a Patrician lord. The painted face made him look soft, reminding her of a wax figurine. Effie might have believed him a lifeless figure in truth—if not for the mischief alight in his powder blue eyes.

"Enjoying the music?" he asked. His rich baritone voice possessed none of the Patrician glamor.

Effie's eyebrows drew together, pinching the bridge of her nose. "It's a pleasant diversion."

His blue eyes moved to the sextet as he clasped his hands behind his back. "I never had an ear for Solarian Baroque." He squinted at one of the violinists. "Too stiff and repetitive. Hits me like a sleeping draft. Give me a proper drinking song or a shanty, instead. How do they expect anyone to dance to this drivel?" He drew back, cupping one white-gloved hand over his mouth to shout at the musicians, "Let's hear the *Cabin Boy's Rumpus*— or *Slap-cheeked Mae!*"

Effie jumped, aghast at the sudden breach in decorum. Some of the other guests in the audience shot distasteful looks in their direction, though none of them spoke up. The man laughed to himself.

Effie turned back to the musicians, hoping this cake-faced courtier would leave her be. He hadn't ogled her nor made any unwanted advances, but something felt off about him. His mere presence unsettled her.

She sensed him lingering at her back, felt his breath on the nape of her neck as he leaned forward. "Have we met somewhere before?" he asked.

"I'm certain we haven't," Effie answered too quickly.

"Certain? Truly?" She heard a crunching sound as he stroked his coarse black beard. "No...maybe not. I never forget a pretty face... Even still, I do sense a *connection*."

Effie stretched her neck and straightened her posture, trying to ignore him. The popping sound of his fingers snapping right next to her ear made her flinch.

"I know what it is." His chin drifted closer, voice whispering like an angry asp. "You're Kelestina's dirty little secret. The girl who doesn't exist."

34

MULDOON

Muldoon approached the general's table, locking eyes with his former commanding officer. Four stone-faced legates drew up beside him, closing ranks. The intimidating display amused Muldoon more than anything else. He and the Supreme Commander of the Fifth Legion went way back.

"General Broon." Muldoon set down his glass and folded his hands atop the standing table between them. He bowed his head respectfully. "Not the last person I expected to see tonight, but certainly somewhere near the bottom of the list." Broon's unusual status complicated their honorific relationship. Without a Gift, the general would never wear the brand, but his rank demanded some degree of deference.

Broon's clean-shaven upper lip twitched. He raised a hand to his legates. "At ease."

Each soldier took a cautious step away from their commander, blank, military stares undisturbed.

"*More* at ease," Broon clarified.

With that, the legates drifted away from the table, fanning out with their backs to the exchange. Muldoon realized he'd been surrounded.

"Looks like you've adapted well to your new commission," Broon observed.

Muldoon opened his hands to the general. "I'm an adaptable man. I am whatever the Crystal Throne needs me to be."

"You always were more comfortable in a kurta than a battle kit."

"I could say the same of you in reverse."

Broon sniffed, wide nose wrinkling as if he found the odor offensive. "If I had your Gift, I'd be standing with the van on the Rydian Planum."

"I did my time on those killing fields," Muldoon countered. "There's more than one way to serve the war effort."

"That's what you're doing here, is it?" Broon's sneer exposed his teeth, as yellow as the serpents of rank coiled atop his epaulettes. "Serving the war effort?"

Muldoon didn't rise to the bait. "What are *you* doing here, General?"

"I thought that would be obvious. It wouldn't do to have Admiral Siprichor's interests *unrepresented* at such a gala affair."

Over the general's shoulder, Muldoon saw a pair of drunken Vangish Patricians attempt to approach. The line of legates turned them away.

Muldoon smirked. Frosty reception notwithstanding, Broon *wanted* to have this conversation—expected it, even. "Are you suggesting Her Lightness Kelestina finds herself at odds with the Admiral's interests?" he fished.

Broon cast his gaze around the room. "She certainly didn't extend many invitations to the military elite."

The two men measured each other across the narrow glass table—sons of Umar cast from their desert home along divergent paths through the Celestial Court. Those paths had intersected once again.

"May we speak frankly?" Muldoon asked.

"I'm not certain we may," Broon said. "I wouldn't ask you to betray the confidences of your Celestial liege."

"Nor would I deign to breach them," Muldoon added.

Broon's jaw tightened as he glanced up at the blue and gold lanterns painting their table with alchemical light. Muldoon read the man's transparent thoughts. Kelestina's decorations converted enough lumite ore to outfit a lighter fleet. For a man like Broon, such decadent waste bordered on treason.

Broon's eyes returned to Muldoon. "The Admiral grows increasingly suspicious of Her Lightness' contrarian sect. He's exhausted of all the foot-dragging and dissembling coming from Aquilon—as am I."

Muldoon didn't have much standing to argue. He'd expressed a similar critique when he first arrived in the Zephyrs, but so much had changed since then. He frowned, feigning ignorance. "Are the latest conscripts not to your liking?"

Broon tapped one finger slowly atop the standing table. "The Elementalists are impressive," he allowed. "But it's too little too late. And I can't help but wonder if these Gifted conscripts aren't some ill-considered feint delivered to conceal a greater deceit."

Muldoon took a careful sip from his glass to wet his throat, which ran suddenly dry. Treading carefully, he licked his lips. "You suspect Her Lightness is withholding—*what*, exactly?"

Broon snorted. His square shoulders hadn't shifted once during the tense conversation. "Rumors travel faster than Leviathan wings across the expanse of the Doric Sky. We know your court is hiding a Pilot, Muldoon. I can't begin to fathom why such a valuable *military* asset is being withheld, but I intend to find out."

Muldoon swallowed with effort. The high collar of his kurta felt suddenly tight around his throat. "That is quite the accusation."

Broon arched one eyebrow. "Do you deny it?"

"I fear any confirmation or denial might be viewed as a breach of my oath to Her Lightness."

"Hmph." Broon withdrew his head. Muldoon's silence provided the only confirmation he required. "If you're granted an audience with Her Lightness this evening, do feel empowered to deliver my message."

"What message is that?"

"This isn't a social call." Broon's voice was all menace. "I'll be leaving Aquilon with her little secret in my flagship's hold. My instincts tell me Her Lightness keeps her contraband close at hand."

Muldoon could only hope his disciplined expression did not betray his racing heart. *Effie. Of course, it was Effie.* What else would draw Broon from his soldiers on the front lines?

"I will deliver that message faithfully—if I am, indeed, granted the honor of an audience before the night is through." He tipped another shallow bow to the general, suddenly eager to escape the conversation he'd initiated. "I fear I've left my escort too long to her own devices. Do try to enjoy yourself, General. It's a party, after all."

Muldoon didn't exhale until he'd breached the line of legates guarding the discussion at a careful distance. How quickly the situation had devolved from suspicious to grave. General Broon didn't just come to Aquilon to serve as Siprichor's eyes and ears.

Months ago, he would have welcomed Broon to the archipelago as a savior—blessed the Jokai for sending an emissary to counter Kelestina's sedition. He would have worked in the shadows to help Siprichor achieve his aims.

But Muldoon's heart had changed as quickly as the Volturnian weather. Now, that very same prospect terrified him—and not just for the fondness burgeoning into something more ardent. If Broon succeeded in exfiltrating Effie, Muldoon would be cut off from his most valuable asset—his most promising path back to prestige. With no higher purpose at Kelestina's court, he'd be consigned back to his ambiguous place without a magistracy, and this time—he was certain—he'd be left there to rot.

Effie...

He should never have left her side.

Muldoon walked with speed, trying and failing to appear casual. He first checked the buffet table where he'd left Effie but found nothing besides a quartet of Myinese elders nattering like hens around an icy tray of raw clams. He cursed quietly under his breath. Of course, she had moved on. He hadn't instructed her otherwise.

He searched the adjacent tables for any sign of her; found nothing. Pulse quickening, he began to thread his way methodically through the crowd, turning away all the pleasant greetings that assaulted him from every side. He reached the edge of the ballroom where a pair of contortionists in black body suits strutted around a circular mat, bending their androgyn shapes into grotesque positions. Governor Maribel of the Spurs watched the performance with morbid fascination, and Muldoon quickly turned the other direction to avoid a time-sucking interaction. So focused on the task at hand, he didn't catch the clumsy body barreling toward him until it was too late.

He pivoted straight into the bumbling path of Lady Estreya, inebriated to the point of stumbling. The force of her nearly bowled him over. She yelped as she tumbled cackling to the floor, blonde locks flopping across her face and heaving bust. Muldoon clenched his jaw, patting the lines of his kurta and adjusting the beaded crown jostled out of place.

"*Jokai fend*, woman." He glared angrily at Estreya, who was chuckling like a crazed sparrow in a pool of fabric and hair.

She looked up at him, face swollen and flushed from overindulgence. "Sire Muldoon!" she cooed. "Better watch where you're going. This trolley's off the tracks!" She flipped her voluminous hair back, cackling all along. "Don't just stand there looking forlorn!" she scolded. "Help a lady up!"

Seething, conscious of all the guests now watching them with scornful amusement, Muldoon extended one hand and hoisted the heavy noblewoman to her feet. She howled as he lifted her, stumbling forward into Muldoon's unwitting arms and draping her own around his shoulders.

Repulsed, Muldoon leaned as far back as her grip permitted, but she pursued, breathing Beringean Moonshine down his throat. "If you wanted to sample the wares, Sire, you only needed to ask." Estreya batted her drooping eyes an inch from his face.

Muldoon's cheeks warmed with mixed humiliation and rage. He quickly extricated himself from Estreya's slovenly grasp. Over her shoulder, he caught sight of Sire Ansel elbowing his way through the crowd as he stumbled after his rogue escort.

"There you are, M'lady!"

Jokai fend—the boor was slurring as badly as she was. His bloated face matched Estreya's. What a pair they made.

Eager to return to the task of locating Effie, Muldoon deposited Estreya back in Ansel's care. "Do try to keep a tighter grip on your escort," he grumbled.

Ansel waved this suggestion away. "Estreya has a mind of her own, Muldoon."

Estreya flashed an evil grin, lip tint staining her off-white teeth. "Hardly my fault if the good governor can't keep pace."

Rolling his eyes, Muldoon attempted to slink away. "I'll leave you two to your game of chase."

He saw Ansel lasso Estreya with one grasping arm around her waist. "You won't slither away that easily!" Ansel barked at her. "Lighten up, Muldoon! It's a party! Act like it!"

Estreya cackled on his arm, playfully fighting his hold.

Imbeciles. Cursing his misfortune, Muldoon continued probing the sea of guests from the ballroom's periphery. The crowd had thickened over time. He could hardly see through the mass of frenetic bodies from one end of the room to the other. All told, he lost a sobering hour in his search for

Effie, before he bumped into Dama Lilyn standing near a charcoal portraitist at his work.

"Sire!" She greeted him with a pleasant wave, trilling her gloved fingers. "Enjoying the festivities?"

"Of course," he answered, well aware that he didn't appear to be enjoying much at all. "Except I seem to have misplaced my escort. You haven't seen Miss Strait around, have you?"

"You accompanied your charge?" A knowing smirk worked its way across her face. "I'm glad to hear my advice didn't fall upon deaf ears."

"Yes." Lilyn's advice had proven apt, but Muldoon didn't have the patience for the governor's gloating just now. "Have you seen her?"

"It just so happens I have." She pointed to the portraitist fussing over his charcoal pens. "She sat for a portrait not long ago. I believe she found the company of Master Vinson."

"The cartographer?" What were the chances? Vinson wasn't the worst companion she could have chosen. At least she didn't find herself accosted by Nymicus—or worse, a clandestine agent of General Broon.

"That's the one," Lilyn said. "She couldn't have gotten far."

"Thank you, Dama."

"Of course." Lilyn swirled her glass of sherry. "Happy to be of service. I'm always rooting for you, Muldoon."

Whatever that meant. Muldoon hadn't the time to speculate. He continued working his way around the trail of amusements encircling the ballroom floor. He passed the contortionists for a second time, then a small gallery of oil paintings. The music wafting from the string sextet swelled as he neared the resonator.

And there she was.

Her violet chignon bun hailed him like a beacon. He breathed a great sigh, but the relief was short-lived. If she had in fact found the company of Imerigo Vinson, the boy was no longer at her side. In his place, stood a hulking black-haired guest in a sailor's burgundy overcoat. He stood too close to her—well beyond the bounds of propriety. Muldoon didn't know the man's name, and he looked just out-of-place enough to be an agent of General Broon.

The mystery man continued hectoring Effie as Muldoon approached, and from Effie's stiff body language she didn't seem to be enjoying his overtures. "Miss Strait!" he called, quickly crossing to her. Effie perked up at the sound of her name, and he deftly inserted himself between them.

"Sire!" Effie squeaked.

Emboldened by her obvious relief, he slipped his arm around her waist and pulled her toward him protectively. "I've been looking all over for you."

"Took you long enough," Effie grumbled in his ear.

"My sincerest apologies for the delay." Muldoon tipped his head, turning to the black-haired assailant.

The man who had been accosting her propped his fists on his hips, probing him with sharp blue eyes. "This is your escort, then?" His baritone voice rang with amusement.

"Yes." Effie stuck her chin in the air and drew closer to Muldoon. "This is Sire Muldoon of Umar. And this is...I'm sorry—I don't think I caught your name."

"I didn't give it." The man hadn't moved, but his mere presence filled the space. He loomed over Muldoon, emphasizing the difference in size and height. His head shifted to Effie as he pointed to Muldoon with his thumb. "A bit effete for a woman of your caliber."

The brazen insult caught Muldoon flat-footed. Courtly discourse was rife with insults, but custom demanded these witticisms be delivered with greater subtlety and panache. So struck, he fumbled the retort.

Fortunately, Effie jumped to his defense. "I'll be the judge of how well an escort suits my caliber—Sire, is it?"

The man rubbed his beard, still smirking at the two of them. "No accounting for taste, I suppose. I'll leave you two to each other's company. It's been a *distinct* pleasure—at least for me. I suspect we'll see each other soon." Without confirming his status, he sauntered off.

Muldoon watched his burgundy overcoat receding into the crowd, and with it Effie's tension slowly released.

"Who was that rude man?" Effie asked.

Muldoon shook his head, still staring at the wake the man had carved through the crowd. "I don't believe I've had the pleasure of a formal introduction."

"Is he with the Armada?" Effie guessed.

Muldoon swallowed. "That man's not Armada—at least not formally."

Effie's voice became very quiet. Her whispering breath tickled Muldoon's ear. "He knows who I am. Or, rather, he knows *what* I am."

The confirmation flushed his veins with ice. Muldoon closed his eyes for several heartbeats. His ears began to ring, drowning out the sextet as he stood there, silent and still.

"Is this going to be a problem?" Effie whispered.

He didn't want to frighten her, but she needed to be on her guard. "It's probably best if you stay by my side for the duration of the ball. No wandering."

"I'm not the one who left," Effie hissed back.

He conceded the point with a tilt of his head. "I'll try to be more dutiful. Come."

Muldoon led Effie back toward the buffet table, standing intentionally in sight of Kelestina's roped dais and the unarmed sentinels surrounding her. He selected another drink to calm his nerves and watched Effie help herself to a second flute of sparkling gold. General Broon still hovered around the same table with his legates, joylessly staring through the party carrying on around him. Muldoon kept waiting for the black-haired man to materialize and whisper his discovery in the general's ear, but it never came to pass.

"You look like you've seen a haint," Effie said, returning to his side. "Liqueur not sitting well?"

Muldoon realized he was chewing his thumbnail and removed the digit from his mouth. "Court politics," he said, hoping the vague explanation might reassure her.

The light string music dressing the event diminished to a pause, leaving the white sound of noisome chatter to claim first position in the ambient din. A gap formed in the crowd around the white marble of the ballroom dancing floor. Kelestina's majordomo left her post at the gate of the dais to address the crowd.

A few distinct, inebriated voices rose above the dying chatter. Muldoon was certain he picked out Estreya's chaotic chortle among them. Once even those uninhibited voices subsided, Dadga addressed the room.

"Welcome, honored guests, to the Fifteenth Annual Solstice Ball. On behalf of our Celestial host, Her Lightness Kelestina of Aquilon, we hope that you are enjoying the refreshments and sundry diversions provided for your amusement. At this time, we humbly invite the Court of Aquilon to the floor to commence the promenade."

A few interested murmurs bubbled up from the surrounding gaggle.

Guests began drifting toward the ballroom floor, forming a wall of spectators at its edge. The music returned at greater volume than before, and with a more rhythmic character.

Sire Aeryon and his escort became the first invited courtiers to breach the crowd and begin dancing. Dama Lilyn and her husband soon followed, trailed by Dama Maribel and a fit, young Nimbion who looked to have been plucked from her plebiscite.

"Aren't *you* a member of Her Lightness' court?" Effie's voice jarred Muldoon back to attention.

He flashed her a weak smile. "As you say."

"Well?" Effie coaxed him with her eyes. "Aren't you going to ask me to dance?"

The last thing he wanted to do was make a spectacle of Effie before the entire ball, but he could hardly turn her down without dealing insult. And there was always the chance that his absence would offer a more dangerous clue than his performance. "It would seem that I'm obliged to do so." He turned one hand to her. "Would you do me the honor?"

Smiling brightly, Effie took his hand and allowed herself to be led through the thronging spectators and onto the ballroom floor. As soon as they reached the marble tiles, Muldoon pivoted to face Effie. He placed one hand at the small of her back and led her into a simple box step, moving sharply to each staccato note of melody struck by the violin.

Only four other couples shared the floor. Muldoon made use of the negative space, sweeping Effie through wide figure-eights and spotting her eyes as they circled the ballroom. To his delight, she followed his steps faithfully and with equal grace. Keenly aware of her breasts propped between them by the underwire of her corset, he drew her closer and pressed his cheek against her own to keep himself from staring.

"You're quite light on your feet," he complimented.

"These court dances aren't half as complicated as a Volturnian contra," Effie said.

"Shall we truss it up?"

"By your lead, Sire."

The sextet picked up the tempo, and Muldoon swept Effie into a Toranese Waltz. He watched her brow furrow with concentration, determined not to see herself bested by the dance. He built trust with his sure-footed leadership, and over time Effie found her rhythm, cheeks reddening with a pleasant flush, shoulders relaxing in Muldoon's capable embrace. He spun her once and then twice. She yelped with playful shock as he dipped her so low that her hair brushed the floor. He let her hang there for a full meter of music before lifting her off her feet and back into the steps of the waltz. Through it all, Effie's green eyes burned with a kindling passion. He dared not stare into them too long, lest he lose what remained of his flagging composure.

Effie's lips banished any remnant glamor cast by her inviting bust. They were full and bright with violet tint, parted ever-so-slightly, offering hints of the teeth and tongue that lay within. Her breath tasted of cardamom and golden wine, and it was all Muldoon could do to keep himself from venturing an ill-considered sip. Effie seemed to sense the erotic tension building between them, as all women did. She pressed her lips together, eyes alight with youthful seduction.

It wasn't appropriate. He was her tutor, after all, and she a project—an investment against future rewards...

In that moment, he would have thrown it all away for a single kiss.

She broke the spell by seizing the lead, pirouetting through a triplet turn, maintaining their connection through a single bridge of arms. The respite didn't last. She folded her slim body back into his arms, and the glamour returned even more entrancing than before.

Muldoon might have succumbed to his desires in that moment—if not for the general's threat occupying some space in his Patrician mind, anchoring him to higher purpose. The imminent dissolution of whatever was building between them lurked just beyond the line of guests at the edge of the floor.

He wouldn't let that happen.

Muldoon had always been a pragmatist, singularly focused on the advancement of his career. His mother had fought and bled to give him this privileged chance at life in the Celestial Court. Whatever time he was given, he felt duty-bound to use it in service of his people. Never before in his long career had he allowed himself to become so hopelessly distracted.

It was not duty to his mother nor to Umar—nor even to Kelestina— that filled him with this urgent need to shield Effie. He assumed that responsibility selfishly. How fortunate that his own desires should align with the directives of his liege and host.

"Where are you?" Effie's voice tickled his ear. She had drawn her warm cheek back against his own.

"At your side, as ever," Muldoon replied.

"Maybe." They moved effortlessly through the complicated bridge of the Toranese Waltz. "You seemed far away."

Muldoon realized the ballroom floor had become more crowded in his mental absence. The other guests accepted the invitation to join Kelestina's court, and the marble tiles now thronged with black boots and pointy-toed shoes shifting to the rhythm of the string sextet. Still wary, Muldoon searched over Effie's shoulder for any sign of the general or his clandestine agents, but none of the dancers presented any obvious threat. He directed their waltz nearer to the edge of Kelestina's dais—felt a third hand pressing against his shoulder once he got there.

"Sire Muldoon." The thick Iban accent belonged to Dagda. He paused from his steps to find her dark face awaiting him.

Muldoon dropped his arm from Effie's waist as the two parted to receive this unwelcome interruption. The majordomo bowed her head piled high with ropey braids.

"Don't tell me you want to cut in?" Effie said.

Dagda rose from her bow to peer down her pointy nose at Effie before returning her attention to Muldoon. "Not as such. Her Lightness requests a word in her salon. I'm to escort you without delay."

Muldoon furrowed his brow, glancing up at the looming dais beyond its cordon of velvet ropes. All three Celestials had vanished from their perch, and the platform now lay fallow.

"Is Miss Strait invited to join us?" he asked.

"She is not." Dagda smiled acidly. "Right this way, Sire."

A moment of panic seized Muldoon, and he held his position at Effie's side. Dagda sensed his reluctance to follow and peered at him quizzically. He couldn't very well decline an invitation from Kelestina, but nor could he leave Effie unattended—not with the vultures circling.

"I'm afraid it would be *unwise* for me to abandon my escort at this time," Muldoon replied, praying Kelestina's majordomo would be savvy enough to read his implication.

"Miss Strait will be quite fine on her own," Dagda countered. "Isn't that right?"

Effie propped her hands on her hips with an exasperated huff. "I guess I'll have to be!"

"As you say," Dagda confirmed. "This audience is not expected to take long. The exhibition awaits at the top of the hour. Please. Come."

"Just one moment." Muldoon frantically searched for some sanctuary port amid the ball, somewhere he could safely store Effie until he returned. Nothing seemed sufficient. He caught a flash of blonde hair across the floor and cursed his predicament. It would have to do.

"Imperator!" He waved his hand until he drew Nymicus' attention and summoned him to their side. As soon as the man's eyes found Effie, he eagerly abandoned his partner to join them.

Effie pressed the heel of her foot down on Muldoon's toe, applying pressure on the cusp of pain. "What are you *doing?*" she hissed.

"I'm sorry," Muldoon whispered back. "It's for your protection." He extracted his foot to greet Nymicus. "Imperator—I'm afraid I've been called to attend our host. You wouldn't mind entertaining Miss Strait for a few moments while she awaits my return?"

"It would be my pleasure." Nymicus swept into a courtly bow with one arm folded behind his back. When he rose, he elbowed Muldoon in the ribs. "Fear not, Muldoon. I'll handle her gently."

Muldoon ground his teeth through the forced smile, cursing the gross necessity of this exchange. Nymicus met Effie's scowl with a lascivious grin and an extended hand. "If you would do me the privilege, Miss?"

Muldoon checked Dagda waiting impatiently at the edge of the ballroom floor. "I'm sorry," he whispered in Effie's ear. "Stay with Nymicus until I return and don't leave the floor. Try to remain in sight of Her Lightness' armsmen if you can."

Before Effie could reply, Nymicus seized her hand and began dragging her off. She turned back, glowering angrily as the two of them vanished into the dancing mass.

Jokai preserve my suffering soul. Muldoon turned his head to the vaulted ceiling, quickly collecting himself before he followed Dagda to Kelestina's salon.

35

VANNA

Kendy's runner came for Vanna after Seventh Bell.

She and Kai were due at Bael's bivouac in the Green Maw to present their recruits. She'd given so much of herself over the last year to the Kenshan's cause. She barely got by, shaving her other responsibilities at the edges. At last, she'd arrived at an intractable conflict. She could either furnish this runner with one more hollow excuse—send him sprinting back to Kendy with her predictable regrets—or she could answer her commander's summons and leave Bael twisting in the humid jungle wind.

In the end, it wasn't much of a conflict. The moral clarity that came with her decision felt like emerging from a dense fog into the bright light of summer. Duty called, and Lieutenant Vanna Strait would not ignore it.

Vanna fell in with a small group of flight-suited dragoons pouring out of the village and onto the path to the windward launch. The entire corps must have received Kendy's summons. The bunkhouse had already emptied. By the time Vanna's cohort claimed the landing, they were among the last to arrive.

Vanna saw Kai's head bobbing above the mass of junior dragoons gathered in tense conversation around the sparring ground. Missing was Kendy, but Vanna quickly spotted him standing at the island's edge flanked by Dray, Maya, Raji, and Prestor. She bypassed the gaggle and gusted herself up the landing to set down at her commander's right hand—where she belonged.

Corps leadership formed a line along the shore, staring off at the hazy silhouette of Avernus. Kendy spared Vanna the briefest glance before returning his focus to the horizon. "I wasn't sure you'd be joining us."

She deserved that. "I'm here," Vanna said. "*Why* am I here?"

Kendy slowly extended one arm, pointing west to where the solstice sun guttered just below the edge of the horizon. With both moons occluded, their line of sight shouldn't have extended as far as it did, but new light fended off the evening's perfect dark. An uneasy glow saturated the northern savannah of the neighboring island, refracted through the sky by a gauzy shroud of smoke. As Vanna squinted into the eerie glow, she heard a dull sound like a drumbeat that carried across the gulf.

Cannon fire.

Avernus burned. Kelestina and all her Patrician courtiers were cloistered safely away inside Aquilon Palace and in their absence, Avernus burned.

The image uncorked a traumatic well of memory, transporting Vanna back in time. Just like that, she was four years old again, standing at her mother's side watching Devil Ray's black wings sweep the horizon. That night revealed the first cracks in Vanna's foundation, the flaw that would ultimately bring her world down around her.

Back then, she could only watch—could only hide in the longhouse, covering Effie's tiny body while their parents flew to their eventual demise. She wasn't a girl anymore. This time, things would be different.

Vanna shook herself back to the present. Much had changed over the last fifteen years. She wouldn't be a bystander again. "The Governor's off Avernus," she said. "Kelestina's hosting a Solstice Ball. The islands are undefended."

Maya turned to Vanna, her face a mask of uncharacteristic horror. Maya was a mother as well as a dragoon and, in that moment, concern for her two small daughters controlled.

Dray punched one thick fist into his open palm. For the first time in Vanna's memory, the bastard sword at his back looked less like a burden and more like a boon. "We have to help them," Dray said. "Come down on Avernus with the full weight of the Volturnian Corps."

Raji shook his head, still locked on the burning shore. "We don't even know what's waiting out there."

"What does it matter?" Dray shot back. "We're under attack. Zephyri are suffering."

Vanna glanced past Kendy to Prestor, hollow-cheeked and beset by a thousand-yard stare. He was the last Volturnian dragoon to see any real combat, and the experience had changed him. He'd returned to Volturnus a thin shade of his former self, quieter and prone to melancholy bouts. Kendy still trusted him with leadership, but Vanna knew he carried the trauma of that Aeolian zeppelin—an extra weight to pull each time he took flight.

"We can't leave Volturnus unprotected," Maya said.

"The fighting's not *on* Volturnus," Dray countered.

"Not *yet*," Vanna pointed out. When Devil Ray attacked, the bloodshed on Aeolus and Avernus had only been a prelude, and this sudden strike felt so much the same.

"What'll it be, Commander?" Raji pressed for a decision.

Kendy ran his hands over the wide strip of black hair atop his head. "Dray's right," he said. "*And* Maya's right. We don't know what's out there, but it's our duty to find out." He came to a decision, nodding to himself. "The five of us fly for Avernus—help out in any way we can. The junior fliers stay home to protect Volturnus."

He bent his head to Vanna, blue eyes questing. It took her a minute to realize he sought her approval. "It's a good plan," she said.

Nodding again, he pivoted back toward the dragoons gathered on the sparring ground. "I'll lay out the plan for the corps."

"No," Vanna grabbed him by the sleeve of his flight suit. "You sketch out our assault path with leadership. I'll handle the corps."

This distribution of responsibilities made sense, so Kendy agreed to it, but Vanna had an ulterior motive.

She left the draft forming up around Kendy and gusted down amid the gaggle of junior dragoons. Nervous voices bubbled up around her, their anxious questions competing for air. Vanna stuck two fingers in her mouth and blew a sharp whistle, leaning on her Gift for extra volume. The piercing sound silenced the corps, drawing them around her.

Vanna described the situation on Avernus in what limited detail she had. She labeled Kendy's plan a "scouting mission" to assuage any percolating fear.

"The whole corps is on duty tonight," she said. "Deeana." A sturdy flier with two brown braids snapped to attention at the sound of her name. "You have command on Volturnus. Break the corps into drafts. Patrol the western shore in tight formation—no gaps—and leave four drafts at the village gates to guard the people."

"What about the homesteads?" The question came from Tanya Sutherland. Her family owned one of the orchards in the southern lees.

"We don't have enough bodies to cover that much territory," Vanna said. "If the drafts patrolling the coast do their jobs, the homesteads should have nothing to fear."

Judging by Tanya's darkening gaze, that answer wasn't good enough, but she withheld any further argument.

Vanna surveyed the corps once more. With no questions forthcoming, she covered the patches of her flight suit with one open palm. "Get to it then. On Deeana for your draft assignments."

Deeana tapped out a stoic salute as the junior fliers stuttered into motion, gravitating her way. *So few*, Vanna realized as the weight of the gaggle shifted away from her. The conscription orders had thinned their ranks. Kelestina claimed so many of their strongest fliers, and even those few souls Vanna managed to save were still lost to the corps. They'd be ground down to nothing if they permitted this madness to continue apace—a skeleton force incapable of protecting a single skerry, let alone an island the size of Volturnus.

Vanna caught Kai lingering at the back of the corps and stealthily drew him away.

"I want to go with you," he said.

She shook her head. "Not going to happen. Senior dragoons only."

His loamy eyes tightened. "I'm as strong a flier as Prestor—and better than Raji by far."

"Stop." Vanna didn't have time to do this dance with him. It wasn't the reason she pulled him aside. "You've got other business to manage tonight —or have you forgotten? I won't be able to make the meeting with Bael, but you still need to get those recruits out to the Green Maw by Witching."

Turmoil. His brow creased with lines belonging to a much older man. Vanna was asking him to abandon his draft on a night when Volturnus sorely needed its dragoons. If she had been anyone else, Kai would have denied her, but she wasn't anyone else. Duty be damned, he'd do anything she asked of him.

Kai shook his head. "We can push it back. I can get word to everyone—"

"We're not doing that. Avernus is burning, Kai. If this is the Shards again—playing their games..." she trailed off. "We need Bael more than ever."

Kai took a deep, halting breath and exhaled all the wind inside of him. He'd never bought into Bael's narrative—not entirely. It was the main reason Vanna hadn't wanted him involved. Bael needed true believers, and Kai was something else entirely. He hadn't pledged his service to the resistance for Bael's sake. If anything, he did it despite Bael. Vanna read his intentions as clearly as if they'd been staked to the crier's post in the village square. Clasping that Kenshan's hand had been an act of lovesick naïveté, an ill-conceived attempt to bind himself closer to *her*. How tragic that it worked exactly as he planned. Perhaps Vanna was the greater fool, after all.

For better or worse, Kai had forced the issue and made himself complicit. Tonight, she would have to lean on him.

"It doesn't feel right sneaking out there without you..." he said.

"You don't need me for this." Vanna clapped one hand on his shoulder, then lifted it to tenderly cup his cheek. Kai brightened at her touch, his soft brown eyes melting onto her. Such a simple gesture, but the rare public display had its intended effect. "You did most of the recruiting anyway," Vanna said. "I'm shit at this part, but you've actually brought people to the cause."

It was true. Vanna lacked the subtlety for the dangle, but Kai had successfully threaded Bael's tentacles throughout Volturnus, drawing in conspirators she wouldn't have even thought to approach.

"Bring our people to Bael," Vanna said.

Kai laid his larger hand over hers, gently threading their fingers. He drew her away from his cheek and kissed her knuckles before dropping her hand to tap out a salute. "Aye, Lieutenant. Just see that you come back to me."

Vanna rewarded him with a seductive smile. "I'll be back," she assured him. "And when I am, I'll expect to receive your report." She stretched up on her toes, lips glancing against the lobe of his ear. "You can wait for me in my bedroom."

Mutually girded by the promise of intimacy, Vanna and Kai diverged toward their respective trials.

Kendy led the draft across the gulf to Avernus in V-formation, with Vanna and Dray holding his wings. With only the senior fliers to account for, he drove a hard pace, drawing gusts beneath the ruffles of his flight suit.

They approached the neighboring island from a high enough altitude to survey the field. Fires burned along the foothills of the lumite mountains, their flickering light revealing the scars of a cannon enfilade. Flames licked the edge of the Avernian jungle, setting a western strip of canopy alight. A benevolent wind carried the pillars of smoke westward, and though this serendipitous quirk of the weather kept their flight path clear, it also occluded any view they might hope to gain of the distant shore. The attacker lurked somewhere beyond that opaque wall of ash and smoke, shrouded by the ejecta of their own assault.

Kendy flashed the air-sign to put down, and Vanna followed him into a sharp descent. A hot updraft slammed into their formation as soon as they crossed the jungle. Vanna leaned on her Gift to hold her trajectory as she sensed the other dragoons rattled out of formation. Each flier eventually battled their way to the ground outside the quarry where a chaotic scene awaited them.

Panicked miners swarmed the foothills, many in various states of undress. They looked like they'd been awakened by the surprise attack. Most ran for the packing center, seeking whatever meager cover its corrugated walls might afford. Others cried for help, indicating piles of the wounded. A woman's distant shriek pierced the night.

Raji landed awkwardly and turned an ankle, cursing. Vanna helped him to his feet before attending Kendy.

Her commander surveyed the scene with all the military poise she'd come to expect from him. In so short a time, he'd become one of the most experienced combat leaders in the history of the Volturnian Corps. The Zephyr Isles would need his leadership in the days to come.

"So much damage," Dray said. Firelight washed in from every side, underscoring his point.

"Only a heavy gunship could have dealt this kind of bombardment," Kendy said.

Vanna swallowed, pulling soot and ash down the back of her throat. "Why would they hit the Avernian quarry like this?"

Kendy shook his head. His steely eyes fell on a shirtless laborer running from a burning camp in the distance. He carried an injured friend in his arms. Kendy caught him by the arm as he attempted to pass them.

Pinprick burns freckled one side of the laborer's body, but he was in much better shape than the thin man he carried. An explosion had torn through one of his legs. The limb hung in place by threads of tendon and charred meat, exposing the blackened ends of broken bones in two places. The trauma hadn't killed him—his chest still rattled with shallow breaths—but he'd passed out from the pain.

The shirtless laborer looked like he was ready to lower his head and charge right through the line of Volturnian dragoons. "Peace," Kendy said, tightening his grip on the man's arm. "We're here to help. Dray—fly this wounded man back to the packing center and see him tended."

Dray came around to comply, but the laborer cradled his friend's body against his bare chest.

"I can get up there faster than you can," Dray said. "Every second counts."

The laborer's face curdled with indecision. Dray coaxed him with open hands and, reluctantly, he allowed the dragoon to relieve him of his burden. The laborer watched Dray sail off into the fire-lit sky with tears burning in his glassy eyes. Who had the unconscious man been to him? Vanna wondered.

"Tell us what happened here," Kendy said, voice steady, compassionate but stern.

The laborer's broad shoulders shook with a stuttering breath. "Came out of nowhere," he said. "We was sleeping with the rest of the third shift. Woke up to a sound like thunder. But the way the yurt shook—we knew it wasn't thunder. Thought the mountains might have come crashing down on us."

"Cannon," Vanna said, confirming what they all suspected.

The laborer's frightened eyes leapt to her with a mad gleam. "Weren't no cannon, Miss."

"What do you mean?" Kendy asked. "Did you see the attacking ship?"

"I don't know what I saw." The laborer was as tall as Kendy and as thick as Dray, but he was young, Vanna realized—of an age with Kai and

Effie. His report came in fragments. "So much smoke. I heard Sep screaming from the next yurt over. Had to get him out of there. Next shot came. Took out the rest of the camp. Blue fire falling from the skies. Burned up everything... Everything...

"Barely got a glimpse."

Kendy placed a firm hand on the man's arm—the one that wasn't pock-marked with fresh burns. "What did you see?" he asked, forcing the laborer to meet his gaze.

"Looked like *jaws*," the laborer answered with a shiver. "Looked like fangs. Looked like a head as wide as a hauler." Recovering his wits, the laborer shook Kendy off. "Need to get up to Sep. He doesn't like to be alone."

"Go on." Kendy dismissed him with a nod and the laborer lumbered off.

Maya drifted over. She'd listened to the young man's report from a distance while she guarded their flank. "A lot of chaos in the moments after an attack. The eyes play tricks."

Maya sounded more hopeful than convinced. She was right, but in this instance, Vanna wasn't so sure. From the set of Kendy's jawline, he didn't buy it either.

Kendy called the rest of the draft to assemble just as Dray returned from the packing center with a freshly haunted cast. He shook his head solemnly to the commander as he approached, his message plain—the laborer wasn't going to make it in time. Sep had died alone.

"We need to help the civilians," Kendy said. "Maya, Dray, Raji, and Prestor—fan out and find the survivors. Get everyone who can walk into the packing center and cover them from the air. If they can't walk, Dray will carry them. I haven't heard any incoming fire since we landed, but the enemy ship could still be out there reloading for a second assault. Keep your guard up."

The four of them tapped out matching salutes.

"What are you two doing?" Raji asked. He tried mightily to hide it, but Vanna saw the way he favored his right foot.

Kendy looked at Vanna, and she returned a stoic nod.

"We're going to the front," Kendy said.

36

MULDOON

Muldoon wasn't the only one summoned from the festivities to attend Kelestina in her private salon. By the time he arrived with Dagda, the rest of the court had already assembled, except for Sigyn, whom he realized he'd yet to encounter at the ball. In addition to the regular courtiers, the Celestials Hallidrax and Minerviana stood at Kelestina's side, a crystalline triumvirate presiding over the impromptu summit.

Minerviana looked so much the same as Kelestina. Muldoon would have had difficulty telling them apart if not for the subtle differences in the fuchsia shades of their gemstone gowns. Hallidrax, he'd never have mistaken. The Celestial host of Vangulmark struck a more imposing profile than either female with his wide rack of quartzite shards like branching arms extending from either side of his crown. It had been a long time since Muldoon last faced a full quorum. The Celestials were solitary creatures. Not since Siprichor's court had he seen so many of the Hundred Frozen Souls assembled in one place.

Muldoon passed Aeryon to stand at the side of Lilyn and Maribel. Ansel was the only one seated, trying mightily to hide his red-faced inebriation. Skald Caelig lurked near the line of Celestials, face concealed beneath the hood of his dark blue robe.

Small shelves supporting hundreds of crystal globes lined the walls of the inner sanctum. Many of the globes billowed with stormy contents, rendered opaque by the black nebulae trapped within; others remained clear as Stijian glass. The occluded samples squirmed, their contents straining against their confines—almost willful. Each time Muldoon attempted to peer directly into their unsettled geas, he was overcome by the urge to look away.

Kelestina bent her glass head to acknowledge Muldoon's arrival. "It seems we are all in attendance," she chimed.

Lilyn glanced around the salon. "If I'm not mistaken, we're still missing one, Lightness."

"Governor Sigyn is indisposed this evening." As she spoke, Kelestina's gaze drifted over Muldoon's shoulder, touching Aeryon still lingering at the back. "It's regrettable that she cannot attend the ball, but she's otherwise occupied prosecuting the business of this court."

Lilyn quietly accepted the vague explanation.

Kelestina extended her bare arms to each of her flanking kin. "I believe you are all acquainted with my cousins, His Lightness Hallidrax of Vangulmark and Her Lightness Minerviana of Takomar."

Muldoon followed each of his fellow courtiers into a deep, respectful bow that the Celestials received with faint disinterest.

Kelestina continued, "Rare are our opportunities to convene our sect beneath one roof. It seemed to us too fine an opportunity to forgo—especially as we approach a critical inflection point in our generational work. We appreciate your indulgence."

A cruel smile spread across Hallidrax's porcelain face, revealing the pointy tips of his cracked glass teeth. "We are all of us quite curious to hear of the progress you've made with this Gifted cartographer." The male Celestial's voice had the same sonorous character as Kelestina's, but if hers was the delicate chime of a dinner bell, his was the ringing of a town campanile.

"And this Pilot, as well." Minerviana stepped forward, adding her own husky alto to the proceedings. "We are very curious to meet her and test the character of her Gift. Your dispatches have been...*infrequent.*"

"By necessity," Kelestina said. "You will both have satisfaction in due time. First, I would have you share your progress with my court, so that my Patrician servants may see the outlines of our great work and come to understand their place in it as we move toward the final phase."

Hallidrax seized the floor without hesitation. "The Jarls of Vangulmark have all been brought to heel. We've withdrawn our support for the campaign in Toran, and their fleet now awaits the Titan's arrival. When we at last cross the Mountains of Toran and unlock the Locrian Sky, we will have an army of Vangish reavers at our backs."

Maribel stepped forward, clearing her mouth to speak. Hallidrax's entire quartzite rack shifted as he turned his glass expression to face her. "My eyes and ears return rumors of subterfuge on the Vangish Isles. Is it not true that the Gullivari continue to operate with Impunity on Jarvik and Kossaveen?"

Hallidrax's stark expression froze, red eyes burning with intrinsic heat. "The saboteurs work their mischief in Vangulmark," he admitted. "This is true. But their greater gambits have been neutralized. I expect to have their last stubborn embers stamped out by year's end." Maribel accepted his explanation with a nod, and Hallidrax glanced around the room, begging further challenge. Seeing none, he stepped back in line with Kelestina and Minerviana. "Besides. It is our understanding that even *these* distant isles have not been immune to the Gullivari's tampering."

Kelestina's white lips pressed flat across her face. "Our success draws unwanted attention, but we intend to put an end to it on this very night. Perhaps Governor Aeryon can speak to the difficulties on Avernus?"

Muldoon turned his body to see Aeryon standing rigid as a saber, alone. An unusual pallor washed out his complexion, and Muldoon suspected it had little to do with any overindulgence in the ball's largesse.

"We've encountered some interference—" Stymied by hoarseness, Aeryon covered his mouth with one fist and cleared his throat. "Some of our Gifted Elementalists recently escaped conscription, and we suspect Gullivari involvement. It is the judgment of Her Lightness that Avernus be placed under martial law and its lumite quarries seized until such a time that we can rid ourselves of the foreign saboteurs. As I understand it, Governor Sigyn is en route this very hour to prosecute these orders."

Kelestina nodded in confirmation of Aeryon's report. "A problem presented, and a problem solved." She pivoted to her cousin from Takomar. "What news of the excavation, Minerviana?"

Minerviana threaded her long fingers together in front of her gemstone gown. She made a point of locking eyes with each Patrician present before addressing the question. "Before I answer, let us not forget that it was our agents who first identified and procured the cartographer on the Isle of

Min, and our court who first divined the location of the Borjan ruins based on one of Master Vinson's maps."

"Didn't pirates drive your court from Myin?" Ansel's voice slurred from the pit of his armchair. "Or am I thinking of a different island?"

A white flash crossed Minerviana's face as she focused on the seated inebriate. "Who is this man, Kelestina?"

"Sire Ansel," she answered. "Patrician Governor of Volturnus."

Ansel's glassy eyes bounced between the two Celestials.

"He speaks boldly," Minerviana hissed.

"He does." Kelestina's pointed stare silenced Ansel's drunken muttering. "He is intoxicated. Ignore him."

Muldoon battled the smirk threatening to dance across his face.

"We're not here to discuss Myin," Kelestina said. "Borja is the present concern."

"We've only begun to make proper inroads," Minerviana submitted, her eyes still burning on Ansel in his seat. "The intractable civil war in the north is a complication, but I've granted imperium to a capable Patrician servant of my court, and he's already brought the southern city of Vanerin under the auspices of the Crystal Throne. Laborers conscripted from the nascent plebiscite have begun preparing the excavation."

Kelestina picked the teardrop nail of her forefinger with her thumb as she considered Minerviana's timeline. "Please proceed with all due haste, cousin. We're at a stalemate without Harriman's Crown."

Muldoon stared blankly at Kelestina. He almost thought he'd misheard her, but of course he did not. He'd heard many myths and fairy stories bandied about this court like granted fact. Bennu; Sleipnir; the Locrian Sky. Why not add the Crown of Harriman Drakma to the list? *Jokai fend*, she didn't just intend to discover the fabled Titan of the Doric Sky; she planned to yoke it with a puissant relic. Kelestina built her sect's entire project on a foundation of smoke and sand. Would nobody object to this madness?

It seemed that nobody would, for the discussion quickly moved on. "When do we get to meet this Pilot?" Mierviana asked. "I assume she's in attendance."

"She's here," Ansel grumbled. "She's been strutting the floor on Muldoon's arm like a nubile debutante."

Muldoon found himself decreasingly amused by his uninhibited colleague. Judging by the emerald slits of Kelestina's eyes, she shared the sentiment. Kelestina's attention snapped back to the Governor of Volturnus. "If you can't manage the proper decorum, Ansel, consider yourself dismissed."

A pregnant pause followed, and Muldoon thought Ansel might actually take his leave, but the governor instead shrank back into his armchair, sufficiently cowed—if only temporarily.

"Sire Muldoon." Kelestina extended one hand, summoning him. He glanced to either side and took a small step forward, allowing his host to present him like a prize mare. "This is the Patrician courtier I tasked with the girl's tutelage. Despite some early reticence, his performance in the role of guardian and tutor has exceeded my expectations."

As Hallidrax appraised him, Muldoon saw his own distorted image reflected in the broad rack of his quartzite crown. "Sire Muldoon...of Umar," the Celestial said.

Muldoon bowed. "I am pleased to have made an impression, Lightness."

Hallidrax turned to Kelestina. "You are aware that this one is a creature of our cousin Siprichor's court?"

"We are aware." Kelestina let the unspoken implication circulate the salon. "Sire Muldoon has remained loyal to his oath. He has earned my trust."

"Thank you for your confidence, Lightness." Muldoon's eyes flicked to Hallidrax, then back to Kelestina. "And in the spirit of that loyalty, I feel compelled to share a troubling discovery." Muldoon tucked one finger under the collar of his kurta, loosening the garment's hold on his throat. "You are aware that General Broon and a substantial entourage from the Fifth Legion are in attendance tonight?"

The crackling tension in Minerviana's jaw was about the closest thing to a violent reaction to ever grace the Celestial form. Hallidrax simply craned forward with interest, while Kelestina threaded her long fingers together, inscrutable as ever.

"General Broon's flagship arrived at Aquilon six days prior," Kelestina said. "We've hosted his entourage at the palace in a manner befitting his service and rank."

Muldoon nodded. He had assumed as much. Broon had no need to conceal his arrival. Kelestina couldn't very well turn away such a high-ranking emissary from the Admiral's court. It was probably the reason

Siprichor selected Broon for the mission to Aquilon in the first place, even though it drew one of his most valuable officers away from the war.

"I encountered the general at the ball, and we exchanged pleasantries," Muldoon said. "He furnished me with a message intended to reach you, Lightness. He knows that we've uncovered a Pilot with considerable strength in the Gift. He intends to abscond with her back to Toran—claims he won't be leaving Aquilon without this prize in hand."

Out of the corner of his eye, Muldoon saw Lilyn raise an open palm to her bust, clutching a gaudy necklace that dripped with jet and pearl.

"By what right?" Minerviana's outrage filled the salon. "Siprichor's upjumped plebeian lapdog has no standing to interfere in matters of this court."

"Begging your pardon, Lightness, but that's not entirely true," Lilyn said. "Gifted Pilot though she may be, Effie Strait remains a mere plebeian subject of the Crystal Throne. If His Lightness Admiral Siprichor has issued a writ for her conscription, his military authority exceeds any right of possession we might hope to exercise as the girl's feudal host."

Ah, Lilyn. Ever the pedant.

Minerviana scoffed, flipping the train of her gemstone gown, but she didn't argue.

Muldoon had already arrived at the same dire conclusion. Broon's threat carried enough teeth to claim its pound of flesh. They had little recourse to stand in his way.

Kelestina's eyes remained fixed on Muldoon. Her head rose in front of him, revealing a small twitch in the corners of her lips. She seemed almost amused by Broon's threat, and that was somehow more unsettling than the threat itself. Muldoon wasn't sure what reaction he'd been expecting from his guarded host, but it wasn't this.

Caelig had remained a silent voyeur up to this point, but now the hooded Skald brought his arched back forward to add his curdled voice to the fray. "Forgive my intrusion, Lightness, but we cannot allow Admiral Siprichor to squander all the time and energy we've invested by converting our great prize."

"It's no intrusion, Skald," Kelestina said. "This assembly values the priesthood's council in all matters of court."

Caelig chewed his withered lips, moistening his mouth. "The path before us is obvious. The Jokai do not deal in coincidence. We are blessed to host a holy quorum of the Hundred Frozen Souls on this very night. Let the Pilot stand for oration. See her branded before the thousand eyes of Aquilon Hall and so bonded to our court."

Muldoon's eyes jumped from the Skald to Kelestina. "Lightness?"

Kelestina tapped her smirking lips with one long finger. At last, Muldoon saw the choreographed performance for what it was. Muldoon braced himself as Kelestina delivered her scripted lines, "Sire, you yourself claim Miss Strait is well-equipped to pass muster before the proctors of Bol Haram."

"Sh-she is quite capable. Yes, Lightness. She's a quick study." Muldoon hated the babbling sounds coming out of him. Kelestina's trap had already sprung. Dissembling only dishonored him. He afforded himself one slow breath to gather his composure. "It's hardly been a year, Lightness. No initiate has been asked to stand for oration after such a short course of study."

"Desperate times, Sire," Kelestina countered. "Do you have an alternate suggestion?"

Muldoon didn't, and he knew he'd not find any other options forthcoming from his fellow Patricians gathered around the salon. This was Kelestina's gambit, issued forth from Skald Caelig's swollen tongue. It was too elegant to be anything else. Siprichor enjoyed many powers as Admiral of the Celestial Armada, but the power to compel service from a Patrician bonded to another Celestial's court was not among them. The broken serpent brand was the only thing that would place Effie beyond the admiral's reach.

Muldoon knew when he'd been beaten. "I do not, Lightness."

"Excellent." Kelestina clapped her hands together. "Then we will summon the girl to stand for oration as the exhibition's grand conclusion. My cousins will keep in mind the initiate's deficiencies in the administration of the rite?" Her eyes marked Hallidrax and Minerviana on her flanks.

"It would be unworthy of us to neuter the demands of a sacred exam," Hallidrax said. "I'm sure your Skald would quite agree."

Caelig straightened his back to address the visiting Celestial, but Kelestina intervened. "I only ask that you *consider* our position. The oration will proceed by the letter of the law. We must remain above reproach."

Hallidrax shifted his rack but ultimately withdrew without voicing further objection.

Kelestina raised her arms to embrace the gathering. "I see no reason for further disruption to the evening. Please return to the festivities with my blessings and my thanks. A new day is dawning over the Doric Sky. We can almost see its twinkling edges along that most distant horizon. By your faith and through our communal efforts, our path will be proven righteous. When we reunite the Hundred Frozen Souls, even cousin Siprichor will be forced to fall in line and follow our sect to the lost shores of sacred Mu."

37

VANNA

Vanna and Kendy took flight, driving west.

The smoke thickened the further they pushed, stinging Vanna's eyes and throat. The scene below grew more dire as they approached the windward shore. Flames crackled over the corpse of every campsite—yakcarts, yurts, and bodies fueling charnel conflagrations. Black scars remained where the fires of earlier attacks had guttered. From their vantage high above the aftermath, they saw fewer and fewer survivors scattering, more bodies and parts of bodies in their place. So many dead and wounded. Even if they managed to turn back the attack, the damage was done. The quarry would be crippled. Avernus could not sustain itself without the lumite trade. Many of her fortunate sons might well survive this night, but the island had been dealt a killing blow.

The smoke and ejecta thickened until they could hardly see more than a few feet ahead. Kendy and Vanna both extinguished their alchemical headlamps, which had become more of a hindrance than a help.

Kendy caught a mouthful of particulate that sent him coughing in a fit, banking out of formation. As soon as the cough subsided, he flashed the air-sign to put down. The skies of Avernus weren't fit for flight.

Vanna's feet touched down just a second after Kendy's. On their northern flank, the burning remains of three mining camps had joined together in a wall of punishing fire. The stench of it struck just as hard as the heat. Vanna covered her mouth with one arm, fending off the scent of burning brush and canvas, of open bowels and cooking meat. Kendy seemed to be struggling even more with the stifling atmosphere. He staggered through several steps, dizzy from lack of air, fighting to maintain his feet.

By instinct, Vanna drew upon her Gift. She shaped the winds around them, carefully setting each layer of a vortex and extending its influence as far around them as her power would permit. An air pocket formed, shaped winds siphoning the particulate away, clearing the air around them. Even the sickly stench abated, though it never left them entirely. It still clung to Vanna's hair and the porous fibers of her suit.

Kendy righted himself, bolstered by a clean, deep breath. His eyes found her, filled with reverence and an awestruck note of longing. "You really are the most Gifted Elementalist in the archipelago—maybe on the face of Ciel."

Vanna averted her gaze, her Gift still holding their bubble inviolate. Such praise from her commander would have humbled her under any other circumstance, but given her duplicitous behavior over the last year, her humility yielded to shame.

Eager to turn the discussion back to the mission, she pointed toward the windward shore. Through the haze, they saw the silhouettes of fliers circling in the distance. Vanna couldn't imagine how they withstood the smoke. The dragoons spotted them in return and fell quickly into formation along a sharp line of descent.

Six Avernian fliers landed inside the influence of Vanna's vortex. Vanna identified them by the South Wind patches proudly displayed on the breasts of their flight suits. Some kind of industrial mask made of layered cloth and mesh concealed their faces.

A thin woman leading the Avernian draft tugged down her mask, leaving a ring of soot around her mouth and nose.

"Kendahl." Kendy recognized the flier, though Vanna did not. The two dragoons closed with each other and clasped arms.

"Commander Baris." The Avernian's drawn voice crackled with grit. "We thought we might be on our own."

"We saw the fires from Volturnus," Kendy said. "Got here as fast as we could."

Kendahl took a swig from the canteen clipped to her belt and nodded.

She peered over Kendy's shoulder at Vanna waiting in the wings. "Not to sound ungrateful," she said. "But we could use more than two. You don't happen to have a spare army waiting back there, do you?"

Kendy wiped sweat from his brow and shook his head. "We brought six —the most experienced dragoons on Volturnus. The others are back by the quarry helping the survivors get to safety."

Kendahl cleared soot from the back of her throat with vocal effort and spat a black wad onto the ground. She wiped her mouth, returning to Kendy. "Won't be anywhere safe on Avernus if we can't fend off that Leviathan."

"The plumed serpent," Kendy supplied.

Kendahl stared at him gravely.

Bone Adder. Captain Whitefang must have tired of hitting all those freighters carrying Avernian ore. In the most brazen act of piracy to visit the isles since the Butcher's reign of terror, he'd come straight to the source.

Another one of Bael's dire warnings proved prescient.

"Blew in from the north," Kendahl said. "By the time the warning sirens went up, the beast was already on our shore. Looks like a nightmare. Narrow deck bolted all along its feathered back. White face like a bleached skull. The draft got real close—saw scores of pirate crewmen, all of 'em armed to the teeth."

"Heavy artillery?" Kendy asked.

"Sure," Kendahl said. "Not that they need it. The snake issues lightning from its jaws. Hits harder than any cannon fire and doesn't take time to reload."

"Jokai fend..." Kendy muttered.

Vanna finally drew up to her commander's side, earning an appraising glance up and down from the Avernian. "Where's Commander Taros?" she asked. "Did he engage the Leviathan?"

"Taros is gone," Kendahl said.

"What?" Kendy's sturdy body blanched with shock.

"Governor Aeryon's sentinels came for him a few days back," Kendahl explained. "Took him and Lieutenant Farino out of their beds in the middle of the night. Nobody's seen them since."

"*Balls of the deep,*" Kendy cursed.

Vanna cast her gaze up to the western sky. The smoke hung so thick that she couldn't even see the outlines of the looming mountains. The light of competing fires collected beneath the ceiling of particulate, ripples of orange, red, and white cascading down to the surface of Avernus. Amid the sound and fury—all the destruction Bone Adder had wrought—Vanna saw the Shards' design with maddening lucidity.

How long had Kelestina planned this?

She'd neutralized the island's dragoons. Compromised its industry. And now, with her Patrician magistrates hiding behind Aquilon's crystal walls, she delivered her punishment.

Bael had been right all along. Bone Adder was an instrument of the Crystal Throne.

"The Leviathan withdrew after it made its first pass over the quarry," Kendahl said. "I don't think it's finished."

"How many fliers do you have?" Kendy asked.

"You're looking at 'em. Started with ten. Four didn't survive the first attack—" Kendahl's voice caught, but she played it off with a forced cough as if the soot had been the culprit. "We made a run at the beast—went for the eyes, trying to cripple it. Creature's demon fast, and its hide's tougher than any bulkhead wall."

"That was very brave," Kendy said.

Vanna agreed.

"We're ready to regroup for another round," Kendahl said.

"Dragoons can't fight off a Leviathan," Vanna countered. "We know how this ends. You can't risk losing any more fliers. Avernus needs you."

One of the other Avernian fliers stepped forward and pulled off his mask, revealing a narrow face that drew to a cleft chin. "We're not going stand by and watch this monster destroy our island."

Kendahl raised her hand to silence him. "We've got one more card to play. Governor Aeryon fortified the windward shore after the Butcher's attack to protect the quarry from pirates. The first strike hit so quickly that the miners didn't have time to get to the artillery, but we've got a team in place now. If that Leviathan circles back, we'll give it a mouthful of lead."

"You've got cannons?" Kendy asked.

"A few," Kendahl said. "And ballistae. High-gauge."

"Ballistae take a long time to reload," Vanna said.

"Then we better make it count the first time," Kendahl shot back.

Vanna demurred, not wishing to argue.

Kendy chewed his lower lip. She knew he shared her skepticism. "Those ground defenses are intended to repel kite-ships and lighters. *Might* even be enough to make a heavy airship think twice. Leviathan are too fast—too agile. They can turn on a coin. The only way to engage one is from the air."

"Yes." Kendahl nodded stiffly.

Kendy arched one bushy eyebrow. "Yes, what?"

"We engage the slithering bastard from the air. The draft pens it in—holds it steady just long enough for our people on the ground to empty their cans."

It was madness. Six dragoons might be able to hector the beast—could maybe pick off a few sloppy crewmen exposed above deck—but any distraction they caused would be fleeting. Mere seconds. A vanishingly small window for their artillery on the ground.

"You'll all be killed," Vanna said.

Kendahl shrugged—so nonchalant. "The Jokai come for us all in the end."

All eight dragoons staggered, turning their eyes to the sky as a rasping hiss filled the air, injected from somewhere beyond the windward shore. The chilling sound overpowered even the roar of the surrounding flames. Vanna searched the unrelenting shroud, but the smoke yielded nothing.

"Time's up," Kendahl said, turning back to her draft. "We check in with the laborers manning the defenses, then we take to the sky." She pulled her mask back over her face as she directed her fliers into formation.

Kendy turned back to Vanna. She read his determination in every tightening line around his tired eyes, in the steady set of his square jaw. The Avernian dragoons had made their decision, and he couldn't let them fly alone. He wouldn't ask her to follow him, but he didn't need to.

Vanna dipped her head, then tapped out a salute to her commander—four fingers pressed over the bronze-wing patch of rank. She hadn't done much over the last year to deserve that patch, but on this night, she would honor it to the fullest extent.

Vanna had worn many costumes in the service of Bael's sabotage. Tonight, she shed all but one. She met this threat not as a spy or saboteur, but as an officer of the Volturnian Dragoons.

"We're coming with you," Kendy told Kendahl.

"Took your sweet time getting there," Kendahl griped, but Vanna heard the relief in her muffled voice. The Avernian flagged one of her adjacent fliers. The dragoon dug two more of the cloth masks from her pack and tossed them to Kendy. "Filter masks," Kendahl explained. "The quarrymen use them when they're in the pit. Keeps the ash and rock dust out of their lungs—for the most part, at least."

Kendy tied the simple piece of equipment around his head and helped Vanna do the same. The mesh was layered so thick inside the masks' cloth casing that Vanna struggled just to draw fresh breath through its barrier. It would be a hindrance in heavy combat, though she supposed the effort beat choking on soot and smoke.

When they were both situated, Kendahl raised her fist to the coordinated draft. "On my mark."

Another rasping hiss greeted their ascent—like the sound of a tempered blade quenched in water. Vanna still couldn't see more than a few feet ahead, but the filter mask did help her breathing.

Eight dragoons landed at the island's edge, where a small team of soiled quarrymen gathered in anticipation before a line of defensive artillery. Six ballistae and two cannons on wheeled carts held the shoreline, each unit armed with heavy ordinance and pointed west. Vanna recognized Gar among the Avernians tasked with manning the artillery. Once the dragoons all set down, Gar lingered on Vanna, though the squat shift leader had the good sense not to make any hay about it.

Kendahl directed the quarrymen to their stations, but they all waved away her instructions. These men had been trained on the quarry's ground defenses, and they likely knew their way around them better than any dragoon.

Vanna found Kendy inspecting one of the ballistae, his saber already drawn. At the sight of her commander's silver blade sliding out of its scabbard, Vanna fingered the hilt of her own sword and checked the short daggers clipped at her belt.

The hissing sound returned, growing quickly to a crescendo that vibrated the very ground on which they stood. Vanna saw Kendahl's silhouette waving further down the shoreline, heard her muffled shouts for *cover, cover, cover!*

Thunder.

A scaring blue beam split the clouds of smoke overhead, pouring onto the island to deliver its cleansing report. Vanna and Kendy were both thrown by the impact. Ears ringing, they huddled together on the ground, watching the Leviathan's lightning crawl across Avernus, drawing a black scar along the savannah and lighting new fires on every clutch of brush or canvas yurt it touched.

Desperate seconds passed before the lightning at last expended itself, vanishing just as suddenly as it had appeared. Vanna heard shouting voices in the silent aftermath, but she couldn't track them. Her eyes moved to the windward shore and in the narrow gap of sky cleared by the Leviathan's searing breath, she saw it.

Wreathed in the smoke of its own destruction, a serpent's head the size of a freighter's hull stretched its crushing jaws. Saber fangs slid from the pits of black gums, their tips gleaming venomous green. The Leviathan's eyes burned molten gold in their hooded sockets, and Vanna suppressed a scream. Fresh plumes of smoke and ejecta billowed around the horrific image, engulfing it from her sight.

"Missiles at the ready!" one of the laborers yelled.

Kendy was already standing with his saber in hand. He extended his other arm to Vanna and hoisted her to her feet. "Think you can hold that thing steady long enough for Avernus to take its shot?"

"I think we're about to find out," Vanna said. She saw the lean shadows of Avernian dragoons launching into flight further down the shore.

"We follow Kendahl's lead," Kendy said. "On my wing, Lieutenant."

"Aye, Commander."

Summoning gusts through their ample Gifts, the two Volturnians soared blindly into the burning haze.

Kendy carved an almost vertical path of ascent. Vanna's cheeks screamed with friction, smoke and ash whipping around her in turbulent streams. They continued their unbroken path, claiming altitude until they burst through the thickest plumes and into rarefied sky.

The winds carried them higher than the Leviathan's assault path. From their Avian's vantage, they saw the creature's serpentine body—a black shadow 200 feet long, snaking through plumes of suffocating gray. Bone Adder slithered across the open sky, cloaked in smoke, doubling back each time its arrow head approached the Avernian shoreline. Across the field of engagement, Kendahl's draft joined them at altitude, chevron formation rendered in miniature by the vast gulf of open sky between them.

Vanna pulled down her mask and drew up close enough to speak to Kendy. "It won't cross the island."

He nodded his closed fist by habit. "That pirate's cautious. He doesn't want to risk any return fire from ground defenses. Over open sky, the Leviathan has the advantage—especially with that hideous breath."

Vanna agreed with her commander's assessment. If Captain Whitefang feared incoming fire, then that meant Bone Adder was vulnerable. This madcap plan of Kendahl's just might work.

The writhing shadow of Bone Adder completed another revolution through the smoking skies below. Another clap of thunder struck beneath them. Plumes glowed skeletal blue with the light of the Leviathan's second report.

The fine hairs on the back of Vanna's neck prickled with frisson. After agonizing seconds, the lightning strike abated, and Kendahl's chevron entered a shallow dive. Kendy flashed an air-sign and led Vanna along a complementary path of assault. They plunged toward the retreating head of the serpentine shadow, preparing to hit the beast from either side—an attempt to pen it in—but Bone Adder didn't hold to its pattern. The Leviathan's tail curled up in a loose coil, its head snapping upward, knifing through the plumes at impossible speed to meet them at altitude.

Bone Adder burst into the rarefied air, jaws wide, catching both Vanna and Kendy in the crosshairs of its dripping fangs. Reacting by instinct, Vanna summoned a concussive gust between her and her commander, blowing them off in opposite directions in an uncontrolled spin. They skirted death on Leviathan fangs by mere inches, and though the wild tactic might have sunk a less powerful flier, both Vanna and Kendy managed to right themselves in midair.

Bone Adder's hissing taunt vibrated Vanna's skull. Carried by the sheer momentum of its attempted strike, the length of its plumed body slithered through the gap she had opened between her and Kendy.

Vanna saw the full extent of the iron deck bolted onto the serpent's back, clocked the jeering faces of Whitefang's crew gathered along the taff-rail. They waved sabers and axeheads, fired pistols wantonly into the open sky. In each rotten face—in every inch of plumage—Vanna saw the futility of their cause.

A hundred dragoons wouldn't be enough to hold that creature at bay —not for more than a heartbeat. Even she of such abundant Gift couldn't hope to stand against a creature so beautiful and terrible—the living chariot of a wrathful god.

Bone Adder's tale whipped past, and Vanna banked into a sharp turn, circling through the serpent's wake to join up with Kendy and Kendahl. She found them hovering in a tight huddle over open sky, with two Avernian fliers following a holding pattern on either flank.

"—can't give it another pass," Kendahl was saying.

"Barely escaped the first one," Kendy agreed.

Kendahl pointed at the Leviathan's sinuous body curling in the distance. The creature dove back inside its protective plume, circling around for another attack on the island. "We can't let it get off another shot. We need to make our stand now!"

"We come at it from both sides," Vanna shouted over the wind. "Hack at its eyes and gums—try to aim for the Pilot. Anything to slow it down."

Kendahl nodded her fist in agreement.

"The men on the ground won't have more than a second," Kendy shouted.

"It will have to be enough," Kendahl said.

Bone Adder's black shadow completed its turn, straightening along its deadly path back to shore. No time for further discussion. On Kendahl's mark, the eight dragoons dispersed into a spread formation. Vanna followed Kendy on the serpent's starboard flank, while the Avernians took the portside.

With sabers drawn, Vanna and Kendy dove toward the plumes on a direct collision course with the monstrous creature plumbing its smoky depths. Bone Adder's serpentine wakes scattered the particulate at this lower altitude. Through the clarified air, the Leviathan's cadaverous head shot toward them like a missile, slit nostrils issuing sparks, static crackling along its gum line. Vanna smelled ozone and ash and something like decay as the Leviathan opened its jaws to deliver the final strike.

In the black depths of the creature's throat, Vanna saw the spidery legs of blue lightning beginning to gather. She summoned gusts beneath the ruffles of her flight suit and juked out of the way, arcing for the golden jewel of the creature's eye, leading with the point of her sword.

Bone Adder slammed its jaws shut and swung its head like a cudgel, shifting Vanna's target just out of reach. Too late to adjust her trajectory, she crashed into the side of the Leviathan's white head. The impact blew all the air from her lungs and bound her insides in painful knots. She saw Bone Adder's thrashing head snapping at her feet, but the force of the impact ejected her beyond its reach. The Leviathan drew back, preparing to strike anew. It wouldn't miss a second time.

Vanna gritted her teeth and blinked back tears, pulling with every ounce of her Gift to correct her path and regain control. She caught herself on a bracing wall of wind, pushing vomit into the back of her throat. Shaking away the daze, she choked down her gorge. She expected to find Bone Adder's head striking toward her, but the snake had withdrawn, hectored by a different nuisance.

Kendy hadn't shared her fate. He circled Bone Adder's head with the Avernian dragoons, swarming like bullet wasps kicked to frenzy. The dragoons engaged the Leviathan in erratic turns, diving for its vulnerable eyes and mouth, blades flashing. Each blow glanced harmlessly off the creature's skull, but it didn't matter. They hadn't flown to slay the beast. They only needed to distract it.

From Vanna's position, she had a clear view of the Leviathan's deck. Atop the elevated fo'c'sle, a caped silhouette presided over the slaughter, his figure transected by the erect line of the bowsprit jutting forth like a narwhal's tusk. He raised a gleaming ivory blade overhead, a regent waving his deadly scepter.

Captain Whitefang. It had to be him.

Bone Adder's head sawed back and forth through the skies, but the swarming dragoons held their position. The fliers evaded each snap of thrashing jaws, and the creature's movements were starting to slow. Vanna gathered her strength and her wits, summoned winds to carry her back into the fray. As she accelerated, she saw one lean flier eject herself from the swarm, climbing high above the confrontation.

Kendahl.

The Avernian dragoon reached the apex of her climb, then darted for the fo'c'sle like a falling payload launched by a trebuchet. Arrows, bolts, and bullets assailed her from the deck of Bone Adder. Most of these missiles flew harmlessly by, but too many struck true. Kendahl's body jerked with each impact, but her flight path held. Sword outstretched, her body feathered with arrows, she struck at Whitefang's silhouette, and the Gifted pirate collapsed.

Vanna gasped, holding tight to the reins of her Gift as she continued gusting toward the action. Bone Adder loosed an anguished hiss, head writhing madly without its Pilot to guide it. Kendy and the other swarming dragoons withdrew, but the damage had been done. Bone Adder had stalled.

Vanna drew up next to Kendy to the sound of cannons fired from the shores of Avernus. The first ballista javelin sailed harmlessly off its mark, but the next two struck true, finding purchase on the Leviathan's plumed underbelly. Bone Adder's long body arched from the impact of a cannonball on its underside, throwing several bodies from its deck and into the unforgiving sky. A second cannonball struck under the serpent's jaw, slamming its fanged mouth shut and extinguishing the blast of lightning gathering in its gullet.

Bone Adder bucked. Vanna heard Kendy *whoop*, mistaking the creature's bracing paroxysm for death throes. The Leviathan rolled back into a wounded retreat, and Kendy raised the air-sign to form up, summoning Vanna to follow him in pursuit. She fell into formation on her commander's wing—saw Bone Adder regaining control, shaking off the jerks of paroxysm and correcting its starboard list. The cannonball left a cratered black scar under its jaw, but the creature seemed no less lethal for the injury. Ballista javelins fell away from its belly like a porcupine's discarded quills. The heavy missiles hit their mark, but their barbed spearheads hadn't pierced the Leviathan's armored plumes.

Bone Adder circled. By the time Kendy realized his mistake, it was too late.

Bone Adder struck out of its retreat, tail cracking like the end of a whip, bruised head lancing back to meet their formation. Atop the foc's'le set behind the Leviathan's head, Whitefang's silhouette reemerged, resurrected despite the heroism of Kendahl's assault. He held the Avernian dragoon's broken body overhead like a sack of grain, the fletched ends of arrows still jutting up from her punctured chest. Bone Adder continued to accelerate as Whitefang tossed Kendahl's body overboard, into the open sky.

Vanna could only hope the Avernian flier was already dead.

They wouldn't be far behind her. Vanna pulled down her mask and shouted at Kendy, but wind carried away every scrap of voice she threw after him. The Wing Commander raised his saber, pointed its tapered tip at one of the Leviathan's golden eyes, chambering this doomed assault. Vanna drew upon her Gift, slapping his ankles with grasping winds, attempting to pull him off this fool's course. Kendy rebuffed her.

Vanna had always been the stronger Elementalist by far, but in this moment Kendy's determination made him her match.

Only a few hundred feet separated Leviathan from dragoon, with Bone Adder closing fast. The Leviathan once again opened its jaws, exposing fangs and gums and the crackling discharge already gathering in its bottomless throat.

Please!

In the last fleeting moments before impact, Vanna summoned every scrap of her Gift. She threw the full weight of the sky at Kendy.

Her gust struck a wall of iron will. The repulsive force of Kendy's rebuttal cast her aside, cartwheeling through open sky and away from Bone Adder's yawning maw.

She righted herself just in time to see the blue lightning issue forth from the Leviathan's mouth. Kendy, flying mere feet from the creature's head, bore the brunt of it. The beam tore through his body, rendering him down to a glowing silhouette before casting his broken shell off into the sky—limbs, hair, and the burning shreds of his flight suit whipping like a ragdoll.

Vanna screamed as she gusted into a torrid descent. She hurtled toward her fallen commander, Gift bleeding into her anguish, spreading her cries throughout the Avernian sky. She tore through layers of smoke and ash, quickly overcoming the speed of his descent, bleary eyes fixed on a single point in the open sky. Her arms made contact with his limp body, Gift absorbing the impact. She wailed again at the way her fingers sank into his charred skin. She continued her dive, sobbing all the way to the ground.

She brought Kendy's body down on the Avernian shore just beyond the ineffective line of artillery that had imbued this mission with such false hope.

Blood of the Jokai—he'd been mutilated.

The dragoon's handsome face looked surprisingly serene, unblemished by Bone Adder's scourging breath—so unlike everything beneath. Half his flight suit had been burned away, and what remained of the flesh within bubbled, cracked, and bled. His right leg had almost no skin left. Vanna could see every twist of muscle and sinew, the white eyes of peeking bone. His broad chest stirred with a death rattle—

—except it wasn't a death rattle. His body kept moving—the steady rise and fall of shallow breathing.

"Jokai bless..."

Kendy lived. Despite all that damage, her commander still found the strength to draw breath.

She sensed the surviving Avernian dragoons landing around her, though none dared approach. Their arrival only served as a reminder that the primary threat remained. Captain Whitefang was unlikely to settle for a couple felled dragoons.

It seemed a cruel joke that her commander should survive a pointblank attack just to die moments later in an impersonal enfilade. Then again, the Jokai always did enjoy their petty ironies.

Bone Adder's hiss rolled back over the Avernian shore. Billowing shrouds of smoke parted, peeling back in plumes from the white outline of the Leviathan's head. Its smoldering eyes seemed to mark her and only her.

"I'll take this one," Vanna said, leaving Kendy's side. "It's my turn." She widened her stance, lean body shielding her commander.

The Avernian dragoons fell into formation at her side, forming a protective line around Kendy. The narrow-headed flier with the cleft chin lowered his mask again and nodded to her. "You bled for us, now we'll bleed for you. Zephyri stand together."

Bone Adder lowered its head, static crackling around the white seam of its jaw.

This must have been how her mother felt in her final moments, flying against an insurmountable threat no flier could survive. Part of Vanna always resented the waste; Vera's sacrifice only bought Volturnus time, and little of it.

What a child she'd been.

Her mother continued to teach her lessons—even from beyond the grave. Standing on that riven shore beneath Bone Adder's electric jaws, Vanna finally understood.

Time was the most precious resource on the face of Ciel—and if anything was truly worth dying for, that was it. Time for the Avernians huddled inside the thin walls of the packing center. Time for Bael to awaken the Zephyrs to Kelestina's treachery. Time for her dragoons. Time for Effie. Time for Kai.

For all that time, Vanna's life seemed an even trade.

Bone Adder's fangs slid once more from the pits of its gums, its throat gathering charge, tensing to deliver its electric report. Peace washed over Vanna. She closed her eyes and extended her arms, imagining flight, grasping her Gift so that it might speed her passage to the Otherworld.

Thunder.

At least it would be quick.

More thunder. The steady percussion of an enfilade.

Vanna lowered her arms and opened her eyes to see Bone Adder's head writhing in agony, its jaws shut, lightning quenched. Explosions erupted along the length of its sinuous body—a barrage of cannon fire delivered with unrelenting precision. The Leviathan's hissing call became strangled, expressing shock and pain instead of threat. It disappeared into the fog of gun smoke, and in its place another vessel emerged—the carvel hull of a heavy airship. The ship's cannons continued to fire, pursuing Bone Adder through its hasty retreat.

Vanna heard the Leviathan's cries receding over the distant skies as the airship descended toward Avernus. The hull split on hydraulic valves. A gangplank extended, groaning into place along the rocky shore. Aero-marines in Armada blues poured down from the airship's hold, commandeering the small collection of artillery and swarming across the island's battered plain. The ship's captain marched behind these vanguard troops, trailing an honor guard in parade ranks, flintlock rifles propped over their golden epaulettes. Wreathed in threads of smoke, her image dancing with heat shimmer, she looked like a warrior queen from antiquity—dauntless in blue-enameled mail and a chain-link skirt, the Armada Serpent boasting from her pauldrons.

"Dama Sigyn," one of the Avernians muttered. "*Bless the Jokai*—it's the Governor of Aeolus."

Vanna had only heard this woman described by Kai. *Unlike any Patrician on the Zephyr Isles,* he said. *A soldier first and a magistrate second.* Dama Sigyn spotted the bedraggled line of dragoons defending Kendy. She descended the gangplank in short order and walked straight to greet them.

Vanna raised her chin to her dubious savior. Sigyn's hair—so blonde it appeared almost white in the firelight—hung loose to her armored shoulders, the narrow ring of a circlet braid crowning her. She quickly surveyed the six fliers standing at attention.

Marking Vanna for their leader, she pressed a gauntleted palm over one pauldron and bowed her head. "We came as fast as we could." The governor's raspy voice reminded Vanna too much of Bone Adder's hiss, as did her slit nostrils, which flared as Sigyn rose from her shallow bow. She quirked one thin eyebrow, a white arch that pulled the rough sienna skin of her brow. "You flew against the tohil?"

"What else could we do?" Vanna said.

"Incredible," Sigyn muttered to herself, clicking her tongue. She craned up on her toes, glancing over Vanna's shoulder at Kendy's crumpled form. "He alive?" she asked.

"Barely," Vanna said. "Please help him."

Sigyn directed a trauma team to Kendy's side. They hoisted his scalded body onto a stretcher and marched him back up the gangplank and into the airship's hold. The governor took a step back, surveying the dragoons once more. "You Elementalists did a brave thing tonight. Governor Aeryon should have been here to protect you." She snapped at her honor guard. "Get these dragoons on the *Jormunghast* and see them tended."

At the command, aero-marines dispersed around Vanna's line, separating them, flanking each of them, guiding them toward the shore by either arm.

Vanna called back from the lip of the gangplank. "The survivors are hiding inside the packing center!"

Sigyn turned to her. "Don't worry, soldier. We'll take care of your people. The Armada's not going anywhere. Avernus is safe."

Safe, she says.

Vanna caught one last glimpse of the armored Patrician over her shoulder before the aero-marines dragged her inside the airship's hold.

Safe from whom?

38

EFFIE

If Muldoon ever found his way back to her, Effie was going to kill him. She wasn't sure how she would manage it, exactly—perhaps a pin from her dress pushed straight through his treasonous heart. No other punishment seemed an adequate match for the crime.

For what must have been the hundredth time, she slid Nymicus' grasping paw from her backside. He squeezed her opposite hand possessively and drew her toward him, fumbling the steps of their dance just to grind his hips against her. She felt his excitement brushing her midriff and nearly vomited into her mouth.

Effie extricated her hand from his and pushed against his chest, opening as much space between them as the crowded dance floor allowed. Her resistance only goaded him.

"So demure!" Nymicus licked his lips. He clearly loved the chase. The entire unpleasant experience had the tenor of a fencing match, with points earned for every groping touch. He seized her by the waist and jerked her body toward him, lips brushing against her cheek.

Effie clamped her own lips shut, craning her neck to avoid his questing kiss.

"Surely you aren't this difficult to master for Sire Muldoon." Again, Nymicus lurched forward, leading with his lips, but Effie pivoted quickly enough that he landed only a mouthful of violet hair. "Come now." Nymicus' voice strained with budding frustration. "A little modesty is all fun and games, but this is starting to feel personal."

Again, his fingers roamed the back of Effie's dress.

She'd had enough.

She pushed Nymicus so hard that he stumbled several steps away before regaining his balance. Regardless of Muldoon's warning, she wouldn't tolerate another second of Nymicus' attention. Nymicus glowered at her across the space she'd opened between them. He took one step forward, fixing to tame his obstinate prize, when a break in the music saved Effie from any further assault.

The dancers slowly fell out of step and began shuffling to the edges of the ballroom floor. With one glance back at Nymicus, still advancing, Effie slipped through a gap in the migrating crowd and continued sawing through tight seams until she was certain she'd lost him. She exited the ball-room floor near one of the standing tables, which she leaned against, breathing a sigh of relief. Contrary to her instructions, she'd left Nymicus' *guardianship* and couldn't see any of Kelestina's guards. Even so, she felt safer than she had been for the last hour at least.

She watched the rest of the crowd settling around the other tables until the ballroom floor finally emptied. The light string music that seasoned the cocktail hour never returned, but Kelestina's entourage did. The three Celestials reclaimed their dais behind the velvet ropes, attended by a dozen servants wearing Kelestina's blue livery coats. Six of those servants brought out purple-cushioned chairs with high wooden backs crowned by silver and gilt. All three chairs looked like thrones to Effie, though Kelestina's sat the highest.

Her host tilted her quartzite head, blue face an expressionless mask as she engaged in a whispered exchange with her majordomo.

"*Jokai bless*—there you are!"

For a terrifying moment, Effie feared Sire Nymicus had managed to track her down, but the Patrician accent belonged to Muldoon. Her fear quickly turned to fury.

She turned her head away, refusing to receive him even after he hurried across the ballroom to her side. Murder seemed unwise with so many noble witnesses in attendance, but she couldn't just let him off scot-free.

"I apologize for my absence," Muldoon huffed, out of breath. He glanced around, failing to clock her frosty reception. "Where's Imperator Nymicus?"

Effie ground her teeth. "Probably looking for another unwitting plebeian to molest."

Muldoon's head swung back to her. "He didn't...?"

She let the question's implication dangle between them. *Let him believe he'd consigned her to violation.* That was the least of what he deserved.

"Effie," Muldoon probed. "He didn't...*force* himself?"

Finally, Effie whipped around to face her absentee escort. She blew one of her purple curls from her face. "Not *successfully*," she hissed. "And not for lack of trying."

Muldoon's obvious relief irritated her. He didn't deserve it. "Please accept my apologies, Effie. If there had been any other way—"

"Any other way to *what*?" Effie knew she shouldn't raise her voice, but this whole night had been one indignity after another. She was over it. Her anger seemed to pain Muldoon, but she was all out of sympathy. He did look unusually pale... "What are you so afraid of?" she asked.

The apple in his throat bobbed as he swallowed spit. He glanced around the room, anxiously tugging at the collar of his kurta. His beaded crown sat crooked on his combed head. She couldn't remember the last time she'd seen him in such disarray. "I don't want you to panic." He stopped himself as quickly as he started, and Effie rolled her eyes. "I didn't want to frighten you!" he stammered. "Those men you saw me speaking to earlier. I have reason to believe they came here for—for you."

Effie became suddenly conscious of her heart beating against the bodice of her dress. "What do you mean, they came here for me?"

"They know that Kelestina discovered a Pilot among her plebiscite," Muldoon said. "They want to take you away from here." Effie rose up defensively, but Muldoon raised his palms to calm her. "Please, don't draw attention. Her Lightness has a plan. You needn't worry."

"*Don't worry?*" Effie's thin eyebrows knit together across her brow. "You just told me there's a unit of legionnaires here to *abduct* me."

"Please, keep your voice down." Muldoon glanced over both shoulders. "We won't let that happen, but it's going to require an unexpected change of plans."

Before Effie could push Muldoon to elaborate, Dagda's steady voice claimed attention from the center of the ballroom floor. Muldoon flashed her a cautioning look, and they both turned to receive the majordomo's address.

"Greetings again, honored guests of Aquilon. Please use this time to furnish yourselves with refreshments before the exhibition commences." She paused expectantly as a few shambolic guests shuttled between their standing tables and the assorted buffets. "We hope that the amusements of our humble court have been to your liking, but the greatest wonders are yet to come. I am but a humble servant of Aquilon, unmatched to the task of introducing such marvels. Therefore, I hereby yield the orchestration of ceremonies to our benevolent host, Her Lightness the Celestial Kelestina of Aquilon, Host of the Zephyr Isles."

As Dagda vacated the floor, Effie's eyes walked up the dais steps. Kelestina rose from her throne and cut a perfect line to the platform's edge, the fuchsia train of her gown flowing behind her like a puddle of liquid gem. Out of the corner of her eye, Effie saw Muldoon place one hand over his heart and bow his head in reverence. All around her, the gathered guests performed the same obeisance.

"Please rise, my honored guests." Kelestina's resonant voice echoed across the chamber, swirling to the vaulted rotundas capping the ballroom. When Effie looked up, her host stood anchored on the cusp of the platform's edge, long arms extended to embrace the assembly before her. "To honor this grand occasion, we have prepared a demonstration. A performance to celebrate the great works of our tireless court, endeavors undertaken in service of the Crystal Throne." Green eyes scanned the expectant guests. "From the meanest feudal serf to the Hundred Frozen Souls, we all have a crucial role to play in the perfection of our great society. It is our hope that the glimpses offered this night rekindle your zeal for this noble purpose. We must draw the skeins of civilization tight as we advance toward the future that was promised."

So raptured by Kelestina's speech, Effie felt the urge to applaud, but none of the other guests made a sound, and so she remained silent.

The floating lanterns dressing the ballroom slowly dimmed as Kelestina's eyes swept the crowd once more. She raised one arm, extending her long fingers in a fan. Her wrist snapped taught, and a wave of white light rolled across the glass wall behind her, eliciting gasps and awestruck noises from the floor.

The strange blue material of the palace began to quiver and shift, its once-perfect glass pane astir with disruption. Ripples coursed outward, breaking against the edges of the wall, turning the frosted glass transparent by increments.

The crowd fell suddenly silent. The wall behind the dais had become a vast window peering into an untold abyss. This hidden chamber seemed to stretch to infinity, a long, dim corridor floored by diamond-shaped tiles, its far end cloaked in lightless ink. Blue alchemical lights burned on the walls of the chamber at intervals, though these ornaments also vanished over distance, succumbing to the chamber's impossible depth. The transmutation was impressive enough, but judging by the crowd's anticipation, Effie assumed there was still more to see.

She didn't have to wait long for satisfaction.

A small figure emerged from the umbral shroud. It hovered halfway between the floor of the hidden chamber and its arched ceiling, shimmying forth with piscine grace. Not a figure at all, Effie soon realized, nor was it small. She covered her mouth to stifle a gasp. A flat cephalofoil came into relief, carving a serpentine path down the vaulted hall, black fins scything through the stagnant air.

Not a chamber, then; a tank—something akin to the cage built into Sire Meseret's hold, but far grander.

Effie heard murmurs of recognition from around the ballroom—a few delighted cheers and light applause as the Leviathan flashed the midnight starscape of its belly at the end of its approach. The creature bowed its body and tucked into a spinning turn, retreating back toward the tank's hidden depths.

This specimen was so much larger than the nymph Effie encountered on the Frostwind Caye that she first thought it a different individual altogether. The Leviathan completed its second revolution, nearly slamming its broad cephalofoil against the wall of its cage. The yellow eyes anchored at the sides of its flat head flashed with a familiar glint. More troubling, its black brow now bore a long, red scar—precisely where Effie had placed the collar.

Kelestina's voice returned to narrate the performance. "The Ordovishan hammerheads school in the frigid skies north of Takomar, just on the cusp of the Ugallu Storm's influence. A Patrician Angler apprehended this specimen at our court's direction and returned it to Aquilon intact. The breed possesses a violent nature. Very difficult to capture without the aid of a Gifted Pilot's bond. This specimen has been raised in captivity in our facility beneath the palace, where we trained it on an experimental protocol developed by the Solarian Skalds."

Kelestina's voice trailed off, and small doors opened in the sides of the tank. Armored figures entered, brandishing long lances, iron cables, and strange polearms capped with barbed hooks. These trainers looked like toy figurines through the ballroom portal, their minuscule aspect bestowing a new sense of scale on the scene inside the tank. By some arcane process, the portal through the ballroom wall contained an image many times larger than the ballroom itself. The hammerhead soared over the trainers' heads, a beast as long as an Armada galleon. At least twenty feet of open air separated its glittering belly from the trainers on the ground. Effie shook her head in wonder. Even Aquilon Palace, in all its grandeur, seemed incapable of containing a chamber so vast as this tank.

One of the lance-wielding trainers stuck its weapon in the air as the hammerhead passed. The lance's tip sparked on contact with one of the Leviathan's fins, and the creature froze in midair. Two more crackles erupted across its ventral flesh, and the creature began to rotate, turning its dorsal side to the ground.

The ballroom applauded this display of command, but Effie didn't join them. The performance troubled her, and her mood only darkened the longer it went on. Months ago, she had promised this creature it would be returned to the open sky. A lie in hindsight. Kelestina had kept it confined.

The trainers coaxed the hammerhead to flip right-side up again before deploying three glowing drones shaped like discuses. At a sudden crackle from one of the sparking lances, the hammerhead bent its great back like a bow and opened its jaws, revealing row upon row of serrated teeth. The creature launched into a precision attack, carving a sharp path with its cephalofoil and crushing each drone between its powerful jaws. The ballroom erupted with cheers as the hammerhead retreated back to the tank's occluded depths, its jet-pipe tail glowing with propulsive heat.

"It can take years for a Pilot to perfect their bond with a wild Leviathan," Kelestina said. "Much time is lost preparing a bonded pair for active deployment. This new training protocol will cut that time to zero. Once this hammerhead is matched with an Armada Pilot, the pair will be ready for deployment within days."

The audience rang with polite applause, but Effie didn't join them.

The hammerhead returned to the front of the tank, its winged flippers extended at its sides in display. At its nearest point of approach, its wide cephalofoil nearly covered the width of the portal wall.

Effie focused on one barred yellow eye, reaching out with her mind. She sensed the hammerhead's consciousness in the cognitive distance, but some sorcery of the tank or the portal or the palace itself held the creature just out of reach. She bit down on her cheek, pressing harder on her Gift. She could almost touch the creature's emotions, those few sensitive vibrations erupting from the surface of its mind.

The brief connection forced her back against the table with a sudden intake of breath.

The nymph had been so frightened when she'd encountered it in Sire Meseret's hold. It wasn't frightened anymore. This fresh spark of emotion felt more like blinding rage.

"Are you all right?" Muldoon asked.

"No," Effie answered.

The creature froze in its position, hovering just beyond the portal's boundary. The bars of its eyes dilated. A quartet of tiny trainers attempted to marshal the Leviathan back to compliance with lances and hooks, but the hammerhead ignored them.

Sensing that her exhibition was about to go awry, Kelestina carved a sigil in the air with one long-fingered hand. Effie caught a fleeting glimpse through the rippling portal: trainers frantically closing ranks beneath the hammerhead. The entire image vanished behind the opacity of the ballroom wall.

Kelestina's white lips pressed flat as she extended her arms, soliciting another round of applause from her guests. Effie sensed Muldoon attempting to catch her eye, but she remained fixated on her host and the undeniable cast of frustration hardening her porcelain features.

Kelestina only lowered her arms once the applause began to ebb. She sent Dagda scurrying off with a sharp gesture before introducing the exhibition's second act. "While all men may find a place in service of the Crystal Throne, our Gifted servants occupy a privileged class. The Annals of Solaris are filled with the deeds of Elementalists and Alchemists; Pugilists and Vitalists; Mentalists, Naturalists, and Occultists. But the skies of Ciel are rife with these common Gifts. Rare is the opportunity to cultivate a true

Erratic—a peerless scion of the Crystal Throne imbued with a solitary trade."

Dagda reappeared and, behind her, trailed Imerigo Vinson.

Effie's eyes tracked the boy puttering in Dagda's wake as Kelestina continued. "On the Isle of Myin, our sect recently discovered one such individual possessed of a Gift that will transform the great task of our vaunted civilization. We submit to you, the gathered guests of Aquilon, Master Imerigo Vinson of Myin, for a demonstration of his Erratic Gift."

Coaxed by Dagda, Imerigo walked tentatively to the foot of the dais. In his arms, he held a bundle of rolled scrolls bound with black ribbon—a collection of his illegible maps. The boy looked so small, ground down by the collective attention of the Solstice Ball. Effie thought she saw a tremor as he turned his head up to Kelestina, seeking approval. The Celestial pointed one sharp nail at the ballroom floor. "Show them," she directed.

Effie felt a stirring of protectiveness for the boy. Even after months practicing her oral performance in Ansel's study, she didn't envy his position.

Imerigo braced himself with one stuttering breath. He laid his bundle of canvas scrolls along the ground, then carefully selected one and undid the ribbon binding. His footfalls echoed in the ballroom's complete silence as he walked several steps onto the marble floor and knelt to the ground, clumsily unfurling the canvas. The map's edges curled, resisting his efforts to flatten them. Effie bristled at the cruel chuckles peppering him from the crowd. Undeterred by the mockery, Imerigo produced four small black stones from his pocket and placed one at each corner until the canvas lay perfectly flat.

Effie craned her neck to see the chaotic charcoal lines that she knew adorned the scroll, but her table stood too far back for her to gain a proper vantage. The entire ballroom seemed to draw up with her as Imerigo stepped back from his map and dropped his arms to his sides. He balled his fists and closed his eyes for the span of three deep breaths.

When he opened them, his brown eyes had turned white as the marble floor of Aquilon Palace. Light burned at the edges of his unbroken sclera, a match for the canvas now emanating the same ethereal glow.

No one was chuckling anymore.

Effie shared in the communal shock as black lines began to rise from the scroll. Charcoal markings flew through the air, expanding and rearranging themselves, pouring from the face of the canvas into the stagnant ballroom air. The pace of the exchange accelerated, adding detail and shading to the hovering design.

Clear images emerged from the chaotic dance of shape and shade—a shoreline's edge; a jagged ridge; jungle canopies and low-lying liquid pools. An entire sksyscape assembled itself in three dimensions, with topographic features reproduced to scale, settlements sketched out and labeled. Once the major formations settled, trade routes and wind vectors sprouted across the open sky.

Effie rubbed her eyes, but the impossible image remained, awaiting her.

In expanded form, the sky chart spanned at least 100 feet—the entire width of the ballroom floor: five major islands connected by lines of commerce and prevailing winds, their surfaces breaching within a few feet of the Prime Meridian. Smaller islands speckled the portrait at more eccentric altitudes—dozens of tiny skerries, barrier spits, and far-flung cayes.

Jokai fend, it's the Zephyr Archipelago!

Imerigo's map faithfully reproduced every detail of her native sky— every indentation of savannah; every mass of jungle; every trickle of river and speck of skerry. Effie's eyes traced the familiar shoreline of Volturnus, then the neighboring coast of Avernus and its northern mountain range. She marked the long line of Nimbion at the sky chart's eastern edge and distant Aeolus in the west. The Spurs held formation in the northwest quadrant of the map, surfacing at a greater altitude than any of the other permanently inhabited islands. Effie knew these details academically, but seeing them reproduced in this way granted new perspective. How easily an inattentive pilot could pass above or beneath her port of call.

Kelestina permitted her guests to ogle the sprawling sky chart before returning with her narration. "Perfect simulacrum," she said. "Master Vinson's Gift produces immaculate sky charts depicting lands known and unknown, from the most well-trafficked corners of the Doric Sky to fabled islands untouched by modern cartography. His Gift does not require that he set foot on the subject's shore to distill its essence from materials no more exotic than simple charcoal and canvas. All he requires is inspiration's elusive spark.

"Since the dawn of civilization, our most studied cartographers have grappled with the impossible problem of depth in their flat reproductions of Ciel. As you can see, no such spatial limitations plague Master Vinson's craft."

Imerigo's white-eyed trance continued for long minutes, his three-dimensional sky chart suspended for all the assembled guests to study. At Kelestina's signal, the light began to fade from his eyes. The sky chart disassembled itself. Charcoal lines collapsed, pouring back onto the face of the canvas until the cluttered air of the ballroom had emptied.

With a gasping breath, Imerigo's body went rigid, then slumped. He collected himself through a few deep breaths, then looked up sheepishly with only the mundane scroll before him.

Kelestina dismissed Imerigo to a round of enthusiastic applause, then turned back to conference with the other two Celestials seated upon the dais.

Effie felt a tug on her gown and turned to find Muldoon, a few shades paler than when he found her. Nervous sweat plastered loose strands of hair to his brow. Imerigo's performance had been spectacular, but a man like Muldoon had surely seen plenty of remarkable Gifts demonstrated in his time.

"What's wrong with you?" The question came out harsher than she intended. She was still annoyed with him for abandoning her, but fear of abduction had diminished her white-hot fury to a smoldering ember.

He dabbed his brow with a handkerchief and shook his head. Was he trembling? "I'm sorry, Effie.

"I'm sorry we didn't have more time to prepare."

39

EFFIE

Muldoon's voice cracked.

"What are you talking about?" He wasn't making any sense.

He went on without context, "Remember your decorum—and our practice exams. Mind your honorifics when you address the Celestial quorum. Give complete answers, but don't venture off into any unnecessary tangents."

"Are you drunk?"

"I only wish that were it." He looked just as brittle as he sounded.

"You're scaring me."

"May it please the ball." Kelestina's voice returned, drawing both of their attentions back to the dais. "It is the proud duty of the Hundred Frozen Souls to identify plebeian individuals possessed of remarkable Gift and character. We offer these special few the opportunity to elevate themselves to the Patrician class. Patricianage is a privilege always earned and never granted. Civil service and Gift are the necessary prerequisites to occupy the higher class, but neither is sufficient to wear the brand. We conduct the sacred Rite of Oration so that an initiate may test themselves before a holy quorum of the Hundred Frozen Souls. We are so blessed to host such a quorum at Aquilon Hall on this very night, and it is the judgment of our court that we should seize this opportunity to examine one such noble aspirant in attendance."

Effie slowly turned her head back to Muldoon. He stood frozen across the standing table, glassy eyes fixed on Kelestina.

"His Lightness Hallidrax of Vangulmark." Kelestina indicated the wide-racked Celestial to her right. "Her Lightness Minerviana of Takomar." she indicated the near-twin seated to her left. "These Frozen Souls will join me in the examination of our initiate, with Skald Caelig sanctifying the exchange."

Kelestina's emerald eyes found Effie across the ballroom. "The quorum calls Miss Effie Strait of Volturnus to stand for the Rite of Oration."

Effie sensed the curious murmurs swirling around her, but she never really heard them. Her ears were too full of rushing blood and the sound of her own heart furiously pumping. Her host had summoned her, but her feet felt rooted to the ballroom floor. Her vision tunneled around the image of Kelestina standing rigid on the dais' edge, one long arm extended. Teardrop nails challenged Effie like a line of spears.

She felt Muldoon thread his arm through hers. Still, she could not move. His tug became more insistent. "Come, Effie." His lips brushed her ear. "You can do this," he whispered. "I wouldn't have allowed it if I didn't think you were prepared."

It sounded like a lie, if a kind one. That kindness filled Effie with enough courage to take one step and then another.

Time slowed to a crawl. Effie's world shrank around her as Muldoon led her before the dais and the Celestials looming just beyond its velvet gate. Muldoon left Effie on her feet to kneel before Kelestina with his head bowed. "May it please the court. I, Sire Muldoon of Umar, Patrician guardian of Miss Effie Strait, humbly submit my pupil for the Rite of Oration. She has been schooled in the Six Academic Graces to the collegiate standards of Bol Haram. May you find her achievements meritorious, and may she long serve the Crystal Throne."

Kelestina nodded, then gestured for Muldoon to rise. Effie watched the gemstone silhouette of Kelestina's gown shimmer and swirl as she turned and walked back to claim her high seat between her Celestial peers. She felt Muldoon's touch—a bracing squeeze of her hand. Too brief, for as soon as she felt it, she sensed him drifting away.

Effie stood before three Celestials and one hooded Skald, with the noble guests of Aquilon Palace at her back. She was surrounded and profoundly alone.

A new sound like withering bark jarred Effie from her petrified trance. Her eyes darted around the dais until she found Skald Caelig, working his wrinkled lips beneath his hood. "The initiate will respond to three questions spanning three of the Academic Graces. The questions have not been revealed to the initiate beforehand and are known only to the Celestial quorum presiding over the sacred rite. The quorum demands completion and perfect accuracy from the initiate's oration. Anything less will result in failure, the termination of the initiate's course of study, and her return to the plebiscite. Does the initiate accept these terms?"

It took Effie the span of several breaths to realize the question had been addressed to her, and that the assembled Celestial hosts and guests of Aquilon were all waiting for a response.

"Yes...Holiness," she answered, nearly forgetting to append the honorific.

Satisfied, the Skald withdrew, yielding the dais back to the Celestial quorum lording over her from their harsh thrones.

Remembering her training, Effie girded herself with deep breaths—in through the nose and out through pursed lips. It worked to her benefit that she couldn't see the audience behind her, though she felt their pressure, like a gathering storm.

One chance.

That was all the rite afforded her. If she must fail, it wouldn't be for lack of poise.

A Leviathan and the Eight Skies of Ciel awaited her at the other end of this trial. She still suffered many deficits. She couldn't know what she hadn't learned. But she was Effie Strait—the girl who bargained with Jokai and breached the Ascension to impose her will on reality. If anyone could do this, it was her.

Slowly, her pulse began to recede from her ears. She fixed her posture, tucking back her shoulders and locking her knees beneath the purple fabric of her Avernian gown. She found Kelestina's eyes at the center of the dais— thought she caught a small smile dancing across her host's pressed lips.

"The court recognizes Her Lightness Kelestina of Aquilon," Caelig declared.

Kelestina gripped the armrests of her throne, leaning forward. "Miss Strait, from the Grace of Geography, please describe for this quorum the most fecund trade routes between Brundis and the Bolkan Lees, including their seasonal variations."

Effie breathed out. The question was a courtesy. Not half as complex as the geography questions hammered by Muldoon during their practice exams in Ansel's study. Her confidence built as she answered, "Three trade routes connect the northern ports of Brundis to the Bolkan Lees, with favorable prevailing winds in summer and spring. The Duke's Way is the most direct route, skirting the windward side of Goa Island on a clean geodesic path to the Port of Renshai on Isla Larga. The Middle Way passes antiwindward on the path to Isla Larga and windward on the return to Brundis. It's an easy path to navigate for any steam-powered craft, and navigable by wind-powered craft under favorable weather conditions. The Third Way runs contiguous with the northern section of the Path of Brass and requires steam power to navigate. It turns hyperbolically around the Beringean coast, sweeping east through the Straits of Longinus on its path to the interior Port of Hyleia. Tropical systems that gather in the Brundisian Lees render all but the Third Way impassable in autumn."

Kelestina's smile expanded as she nodded approvingly. "And how would an enterprising Brundisian merchant reach the exterior ports of Isla Larga in autumn?" she asked.

"By exercising patience, Lightness." The audience's laughter further bolstered Effie's growing confidence, but she didn't think it wise to end her answer on a quip. "But Brundisian merchants aren't known for their patience," she added. "So, I'd recommend following the Third Way and diverting along the Path of Brass through Hellicon and up to Isla Lacan. From inside the Bolkan Archipelago there are myriad paths out to Isla Larga, but this hypothetical merchant would have to accept the heavy duties attached."

Kelestina relaxed back into her throne, releasing her grip on the armrests and folding her long-fingered hands across her lap. "We judge the initiate's answer accurate and complete."

Effie settled into her element. *One down; two to go.*

"The court recognizes His Lightness Hallidrax of Vangulmark," Caelig announced.

This time, Effie nodded her thanks to the Skald before shifting to receive her question from the Celestial seated to Kelestina's right.

"It's an honor to finally meet you, Miss Strait." Hallidrax bent his head, and Effie caught her reflection in both wide antlers of his Celestial crown. "From the Grace of History, please recite for me the High Kings of Takomar prior to the Crystal Throne's stewardship."

Effie froze.

Takomar. Why did it have to be Takomar? She and Muldoon had spent months worrying over every detail of pre-colonial Toranese history and spared but one night's reading and the equivalent lecture for the Takomari.

Effie asked for clarification to buy time. "How far back would you like me to go, Lightness?"

"The extent of the Suyima Dynasty should be sufficient."

Jokai fend—the Suyima Kings ruled Takomar for 200 years. Effie began sorting through all those rote lists of dead kings she dreaded memorizing. She at least knew where to start.

"Suyima Jai the First founded the dynasty after emerging victorious from the Cousins War. He was succeeded by his son Suyima Ikami the First, Ikami the Conqueror, who tamed the barrier islands resisting dynastic rule. Suyima Ikami the First was succeeded by Suyima Jai the Second. Jai the Second begat Yoshino the Cruel, who was deposed by his nephew, Suyima Ikami the Second, Ikami the Wise. Ikami the Wise begat Suyima Jai the Third who begat Suyima Murikamo the First." Effie clenched her teeth, sure she'd forgotten something, but her hazy memories of that distant lecture offered nothing for her to latch onto, and so she forged on. "Suyima Murikamo the Second abdicated to Her Lightness the Celestial Minerviana, ushering in the First Year of Their Host."

Hallidrax's white lips turned down as he inched forward in his throne. "What of Suyima Jai the Fourth?"

Jai the Fourth? Effie searched her faded memory, but she had no recollection of a fourth Jai. Why did all these kings give their sons the same damned names? She tried to remember the details of Muldoon's lone lecture on the subject. Much of that lesson had lingered on the depravity of the Suyima kings and their barbaric traditions. She remembered grisly accounts of punitive torture and trial by combat, but at no point did he mention Suyima Jai the Fourth—

—Because there *was* no Suyima Jai the Fourth.

Effie cleared her throat to answer. "Suyima Jai, son of High King Suyima Murikamo the First, was his father's chosen successor. But he didn't live to see his formal coronation. A notorious wastrel, Suyima Jai the

Latter was accused of rape and incest by his sister Suyima Pree. His four brothers stormed the Palatine Fortress and deposed him. They saw him drawn and quartered for his crimes. Suyima Murikamo the Second's horse came away with the biggest chunk of Suyima Jai, and by tradition he assumed the throne."

Effie drew up with confidence. She knew she had the right of this one, but Hallidrax's enduring frown gave her pause. They stared at each other for long seconds before Minerviana's voice tolled from the corner of the dais.

"She's right, cousin. Suyima Jai the Latter never received his formal coronation."

Forced to accept this explanation, Hallidrax responded with a dismissive wave and sat back in his throne. "We judge the initiate's answer accurate *and* complete." To Effie's ears, he added this final assessment only grudgingly, but she'd take it all the same.

Two down.

Effie turned her attention preemptively to Minerviana, seated on the left side of the dais.

"The court recognizes Her Lightness Minerviana of Takomar," Caelig declared.

Counter to the regal poise of her cousins, Minerviana slouched in her throne. She drummed one set of long fingers against her armrest, tapping her lips thoughtfully with the other hand. "Miss Strait," she said. "From the Grace of Physics, please describe Alvestor's Paradox...*and* its solution."

Jokai fend.

Physics was one of Effie's greatest strengths. If it hadn't been, she might not have known that Alvestor's Paradox *had* no solution—at least none that she'd covered in her abbreviated course of study. That's what made it a paradox.

"Alvestor's Paradox," Effie repeated, answering as much of the question as she could. "From *Principium Aeronautica*, 'Why should it be that the islands of Ciel float at equilibrium, while a single stone carved from those islands will sink when dropped from its parent's shore?'"

"Very good," Minerviana complimented. "You perform lines as well as my parrot. The solution, then?"

Effie shook her head. "The paradox *has* no solution, Lightness."

"Oh?" Minerviana sat up from her slouch, looking around the ballroom, performing her mocking dismay. "I didn't realize we were all hurtling toward our deaths. I wish I'd set my affairs in order."

The polite cruelty of the audience's laughter filled Effie with indignation. She returned to her oration with a sharper edge to her voice. "I didn't say Alvestor's observation wasn't apt, Lightness, only that the paradox it implies evades simple resolution. What are the islands of Ciel if not collections of rock and sediment. No one denies these geoforms float at equilibrium in the aggregate, but nor can anyone deny the plainly obvious observation that discrete pieces of the geoform lose this property when separated from the whole."

"Is that your final answer?" Minerviana probed.

Effie bit back a frustrated retort. There was a time for obstinance, but harsh words wouldn't ingratiate her to the quorum. What did this Celestial want from her? So much of her studies boiled down to rote memorization, but memorizing facts and figures didn't equate to true knowledge. It was certainly possible Minerviana wanted her to fail—had designed the question to ruin her. Effie didn't pretend to understand the subtle politics of the Celestial Court. How was she supposed to respond to a question without an answer?

By inventing her own, she realized.

"I do have a theory," Effie offered. "Informed by the Gestalt School of Toranese Sophists." Minerviana's expression revealed nothing, but Effie forged on. "The autodidacts of Kensha describe the phenomenon of *emergence*, a process by which a collective entity manifests characteristics unknown to its constituent parts. A hand cannot possess its own will. Nor can a foot, a finger, or a nose. Will is therefore an emergent property of a whole person. It's my belief that the islands of Ciel demonstrate the same phenomenon. Their suspension in the skies of Ciel is an emergent characteristic of the aggregate, a property unknown to each individual stone."

So complete was the silence that greeted her response, that Effie could have heard the very stone at issue drop through open sky. Minerviana peered across the dais at each of her Celestial peers before returning to her slouch. "Very nice, Miss Strait. May this be the final time you endure that diminished address." She raised her voice. "We judge the initiate's answer accurate and complete."

The implication didn't immediately land for Effie. She expected some kind of applause or valediction to meet her success, but none was forth-coming. Was she expected to bow? To return to her table?

Hovering torches dimmed a second time, alchemical fires shrinking on their lumite lifts until the ballroom became cloaked in twilight. Effie was conscious of servants moving around her, liveried bodies flitting between the dais and the aisles at its side. She half-expected Muldoon to reappear on her arm, but there was only silence behind her—silence and the firm hands of two dark-skinned servants clasping her by the shoulders, pushing her up the stairs—toward the dais where Kelestina, Hallidrax, and Minerviana still sat.

Dagda's eyes marked her with heat as she crossed the velvet rope. Four of Kelestina's black-suited armsmen carried a heavy stone between them—an altar that they set on the dais between Effie and the Celestial thrones. The servants guiding her vanished back into the ballroom, while several more wheeled out a golden brazier already glowing with white flame. Ferocious heat thrown by the brazier burned Effie's cheek, threatening to melt her cosmetic mask.

"Kneel, child." Dagda's accented voice in her ear. When had the majordomo made her approach? Without a glance back, Effie complied, lowering her head until her curled bangs came to rest on the stone altar before her. Two long indentations dimpled the flat surface of the stone, and Effie realized it wasn't an altar at all but a mortar—the Anvil of Caste.

A long shadow fell across her bent form.

"Jokai bless this child in the eternal light of the Hundred Frozen Souls." Her host's voice sounded deeper than before—sonorous, like the great brass bell that hung from the campanile on Volturnus. Effie felt a finger under her chin, drawing her face up until she found Kelestina's eyes, two alchemical lanterns outshining all the paltry imitations decorating the ball. "Do you vow to honor and serve faithfully the divine will of the Crystal Throne?"

Acquiescence came to Effie's lips, summoned by the glamor of her host's voice. "Yes, Lightness."

"Do you forsake all prior allegiances and so devote yourself singularly to the toils of your class?"

Effie allowed herself a breath before answering. "Yes, Lightness."

"Do you vow to shepherd the plebiscite with justice and faithfulness to the Celestial Code?"

"Yes, Lightness."

Kelestina's white tongue passed over the pointy ends of her glass teeth. "And do you accept us as your liege and thereby pledge yourself to the mission of this court?"

Effie suppressed a shudder. How cold, the anvil beneath her head. How unrelenting, the weight of its stone. "Yes, Lightness."

It was done.

Four vows. Words with more power to alter a life than any spell or Skaldic cant.

Kelestina's emerald eyes receded, and Skald Caelig's hooded visage emerged to replace them. Kneeling before the Anvil of Caste, she saw the Skald's face emerge from his hood. His image glowed, flickering with light conferred by the molten tip of the branding iron clasped in his knobby hands.

Servants closed around her, pressing her body down over the stone anvil. They drew her arms through the depressions on either side, latching her in place.

Panic, then. Effie began to protest, and Skald Caelig placed a rod of bark between her teeth. Scabby hands collapsed her jaw, encouraging her to bite. The sensation of his brittle skin against her chin made her shiver.

The Skald's shadow withdrew. Waves of heat beat against the back of Effie's head, bleeding through her skin and into the hollow of her ear so that she could almost *hear* the branding iron's molten report. A smell like roasting pork at Vernal Fete filled every cavity in her skull.

That's when the pain came—sublime agony like she'd never felt—strong enough to set her screaming and thrashing against her restraints. Effie felt the bark rod drop from her mouth as she collapsed inside herself. Stark white oblivion crept in around the edges of her vision, crowding the quartzite beacon of Kelestina's looming head.

By the time it finally consumed her, nothing hurt.

EPILOGUE: KAI

Bael stood over the campfire with his arms crossed, surveying the fruits of Kai's labor with stern regard.

In the end, Kai had managed to turn five Volturnians to the cause. He almost had a sixth, but the thought of breaching the jungle's taboo had been enough to scare off Theo Hyatt. Kai could only hope the thatcher's boy would keep his mouth shut for everyone else's sake. The rest of the recruits followed him willingly into the Green Maw's forbidden depths. They all stood before Bael, stoic in their silence as they awaited the blue-haired saboteur's appraisal.

Hal's widow Oona had been the first to join up. She'd all but vanished from Volturnian life, lost in the pits of grief without her husband. The prospect of standing against Kelestina—whom Kai blamed for Hal's death—resurrected her spirit, imbuing her with fresh resolve. In the end, all she'd needed was a purpose. A barren widow might not seem like the most valuable resistance fighter, but Kai knew that Oona was as capable a swordsman as Hal had been. When it came time to storm Governor Ansel's manse, he'd be grateful to have her on his wing.

Nayla's twin sister Vayla came next. She never manifested her sister's Gift, but she was ornery as a wild boar and strong as a golden yak. She already blamed Kelestina for her sister's sudden conscription. All she needed from Kai was a nudge.

Micah Craglin, Senna's former betrothed, followed for similar reasons —and he brought his brother Uthar along for the ride. The Craglins came from one of the thinnest bloodlines on Volturnus. Neither one had a whiff of Elementalist Gift, but they were each sturdy and dependable, possessed of thick bodies hardened by long hours pounding stones for the storm wall.

Kai's final recruit was the most unlikely of the bunch. The dangle only came about thanks to Uncle Kellen's unwitting tip. Helga Brandt had run the busiest port on Volturnus since before Kai was born. To hear Uncle Kellen tell it, she made a habit of cursing the Celestials' tithe every time she got inside her cups. She was pushing sixty summers, short and surly—built like a rake. Kai didn't think she'd be much help in a melee, but having the port chief on their side opened other doors. No one on Volturnus was better positioned to help Bael evade Governor Ansel's agents as he moved men and contraband around the Zephyr Isles.

Kai proudly presented his haul. It wasn't an army by any means, but it would have to do.

"Where's Vanna?" Bael finally asked.

"Dragoon business," Kai said. "Trouble on Avernus. You're dealing with me tonight."

Bael plucked one end of his blue mustache. "So, these are your people? The loyal sons and daughters of Volturnus?" He walked down the line of recruits, surveying each one head-to-toe. He stopped in front of Uthar Craglin. "You're a big one. You tired of living as a guest on your sovereign land, son?"

"Yes, sir!" Uthar clicked his heels together and tapped out an imitation of a dragoon salute.

"Don't call me 'sir'," Bael said. "And don't ever salute me again." He continued down the line. "It's the Shards that demand obeisance. I'm just one man among peers. No hierarchy. No rank." He stopped again in front of Helga. "What's your name, Miss?"

Helga snorted and spat into the flame before answering, "Helga Brandt."

Bael nodded. "What service do you perform for your *host*, Helga Brandt?"

"Same damn service I performed before that greedy glass bitch dug in on Aquilon, and I don't do it for her. I do it for Volturnus and for my own damn self. I run the windward port outside the village. Every longshoreman and stevedore reports up to me. If the governor's censors want a manifest or a ledger, they gotta get it from me."

Bael turned slowly to Kai. He winked, pointing at Helga with his thumb. "That's a good one, kid."

Kai brimmed with the compliment.

Helga's permanent scowl followed Bael back around the campfire. He went to retrieve a large canvas bundle before returning to address the group. "Not sure how much the kid here already told you, but here's the rub. You want freedom from the Shards, you're gonna have to fight for it. I can help you plan and coordinate—give our mission the best chance of success—but in the end, it's going to come down to *you*. The deal's a simple one. I'll give my life for you and for Volturnus, and I expect the same in return."

No handshake consecrated the pledge this time, but Bael waited for verbal confirmation from each Volturnian. Once he got it, he unfurled the canvas bundle with a flourish, spreading its contents over the ground.

Kai crowded around with his recruits, staring at Bael's cache in the flickering light thrown by the fire. Uthar loosed a low whistle at his back.

Guns.

Bael bestowed a cache of artillery worthy of a pirate horde. Kai's eyes painted pistols and flintlock rifles, sail cutters and shoulder-mounted cannons. Grenados, as well, and plenty of them—fist-sized explosives armed with a trigger pin. It was more firepower than Volturnus had ever known.

"Go on, then," Bael coaxed. "Test out the wares."

Kai watched Uthar and Micah pick up a pair of flintlock rifles, reverently stroking their barrels and fingering the triggers. Helga helped Vayla hoist the shoulder cannon over her back, testing its weight. Kai bent to pick up a pistol in one hand and a grenade in the other. The pistol fit comfortably on the belt of his flight suit. He practiced drawing and holstering it. Only Oona lingered at the back.

Bael clocked her reluctance. "Nothing to your liking?"

"Prefer a sword," Oona said. "More personal." She shook her head, brown hair bound back in a kerchief, as she watched the other Volturnians playing with their guns. Her eyes drifted back to Bael. "It's not enough," she said.

The rest of the Volturnians lowered their weapons to turn toward her.

"Kelestina's got an army up at Aquilon," Oona continued. "We're just seven people. Governor Ansel's conscripts outnumber us four-to-one."

She had a point. Kai made the same one to Bael just a few weeks back. Guns were useless without more fingers to fire them.

"About that." Bael scratched his blue cornrows. "I took the liberty of calling in the cavalry."

At the cue, the jungle rustled with movement. Hanging branches parted, and Sparrowhawk stepped into the bivouac. The sight of his Avian body drove even bold Uthar Craglin back on his heels.

"It's okay," Kai reassured his people. "He's friendly."

But Sparrowhawk was only the procession's leading edge. Behind him, three more bodies entered the bivouac. First came a lean woman built to match the rapier sheathed at her hip; second, a heavy-set man bald as a newborn, strapped with nothing more violent than his melon-sized fists. They flanked a second woman who exuded such an air of command that she had to be their leader. She swaggered into the firelight between her compatriots, her mere presence shunting Bael to the side, demanding the attention of everybody present.

Here was a woman accustomed to making an impression. She tucked a lock of dirty blonde hair under the brim of a three-pointed hat and sprayed them with a jagged smile, its cruelty undercut by the glint of her alluring eyes.

"This is it?" She planted both fists on her hips. "Where's the girl?" she asked, turning her head to Bael. "This Elementalist I've heard so much about."

Bael shrugged. "She couldn't join us."

"That's a shame." The woman's lips turned down as she pivoted back to the Volturnians. Her two compatriots stood silently at her side. Those attractive eyes lingered on Kai, and her smile widened. "This one, at least, looks housebroken." She folded her arms and tapped her foot impatiently. "Well? Where's my introduction, snake?"

Bael absorbed the insult with a creased brow. Submitting to her demands, he extended one arm to the new arrivals. "Freedom fighters of Volturnus, meet the cavalry: Captain Hekuba Klaeda of the Leviathan Tortuga."

Captain Klaeda nodded approvingly. The swordsman flipped her red hair and smiled, while the thick-waisted sailor pounded one meaty fist into the palm of his other hand.

Pirates, all of them. Kai saw them plainly for what they were. He'd invited Leviathan pirates to the Zephyr Isles. What else had he expected from the likes of Bael? The Kenshan saboteur didn't seem like a man with many savory friends.

Kai sensed the other Volturnians drawing up behind him, closing ranks.

"Aw, no need to be frightened!" Captain Klaeda said, frighteningly. "We're on the same team, you and me. I got my own ax to grind with that Shard-faced slag squatting up at Aquilon. Let's all take a deep breath and tuck up our britches." She spat into the fire and winked.

"Don't worry, kiddos. Mommy's home."

ACKNOWLEDGMENTS

Independent publishing is an adventure of its own sort. Not quite as magical or harrowing as Effie's, but fraught in other ways. When I first withdrew *Ardent Wings on Jealous Skies* from consideration with traditional publishers and decided to forge out on my own with High Trestle Press, I could not have anticipated the scale of the response. I *suspected* Effie's story would resonate. I *believed* we'd find our readership. But I also tempered my expectations. The market is flooded with stories, and even excellent novels have a hard time staying afloat without substantial marketing and an evangelical fan base. I didn't have a substantial marketing budget, and a new series needs time to find its base. Fortunately, Effie spoke for herself, and readers like you responded. It's your support that made *Ardent Wings* an unexpected success. For that reason, I reserve this space to thank you, Dear Reader. It's an act of immense faith to follow a new author into a new world, and I'm truly humbled that so many of you have placed that faith in me. I promise to continue earning your time and attention by delivering Effie's story with speed and consistency.

In some sense, Book 1 functions as an extended prologue to the Tales of Ciel. *Ophiuchus Flinched* widens the aperture, offering a better glimpse of the story's scope and grand ambition. Book 3 will conclude the first arc of Effie's story, offering both a resolution to plots begun in *Ardent Wings* and an inflection point in the larger saga. I hope to see you on the next page.

Much more to come.

ABOUT THE AUTHOR

Z. Bennett Lorimer is the author of several SFF series and short stories, including the *Tales of Ciel* and *The Divine Heretic*. In 2019, he received the Iowa Home Voices Award for his short story "American Drone Pilot", first published in *The Superstition Review*. He is a graduate of the 2014 Clarion Science Fiction and Fantasy Writers Workshop at UC-San Diego, and he holds an MFA in creative writing from Iowa State University. He formerly worked as the managing editor of the international literary journal *Flyway: Journal of Writing and Environment*.

A Long Island native, he currently lives in Ames, Iowa, with his partner and children.

WANT TO SEE WHAT HAPPENS NEXT?

Scan the QR code to download your free preview of Book 3: *The Mark of Cain*.

And don't forget to sign up for the High Trestle Press newsletter by visiting www.hightrestlepress.com for weekly updates about upcoming books from Z. Bennett Lorimer.